Praise for
Playing by Heart

"Mary Flinn once again proves herself an astute student of the human heart in her newest novel, *Playing by Heart*. This stand-alone novel dives deep into themes of love, conflict, race, religion, sexual orientation, history, and survival. From discrimination to the coronavirus pandemic, readers will find themselves cheering on the characters as they struggle to overcome the problems facing them. Readers of Flinn's past novels will also enjoy once more sitting on AB's porch with Elle and friends and diving back into the world of those who once danced at Lumina, the magical pavilion that forever will sparkle in the reader's mind."

— **Tyler R. Tichelaar, PhD and award-winning author of**
When Teddy Came to Town

"In *Playing by Heart*, Mary Flinn furthers the story started in her novel *LUMINA*, allowing us to follow Sylvie and Kip into the next chapter of their lives. Once more, we are gathered with the others on AB's porch as they read her mother Sylvie's diary and letters, but this time COVID has descended, affecting even the smallest gatherings. When telling Sylvie's story, Flinn brings her world at Oberlin to life, from her desire to be a concert pianist to her own personal growth. Flinn masterfully weaves in accurate accounts of Wilmington's darker history, gracefully taking on sensitive subjects, like race relations and acceptance of others' religions or choices, as they impact Sylvie and her friends. Readers will get swept up in reliving the trying circumstances of the modern-day characters as well as the burgeoning evolution of Sylvie's life at the Conservatory, encouraging them to keep reading to see how both stories end."

— **Suzanne Goodwyn, author of** *Wrightsville Beach*

"Mary Flinn's latest novel is a walk on the beach with dear friends, shimmering like sunlight on the ocean from beginning to end. A blooming love story among 1920s characters introduced in Flinn's LUMINA is recounted through diary entries and letters shared by modern-day friends on a familiar front porch, at a time when social distancing is required. The naivety of young Sylvie slowly fades in her time away at college, where she discovers social injustice, prejudice, and the strength to face her own challenges and dreams. And her story provides clarity to our favorite badass Barbie, Elle, who has also had to face much the same in her life—each step on the beach bringing her closer to her own happy ending. A must read for any fan of North Carolina historical fiction."

— **Laura S. Wharton, award-winning author of** *The Pirate's Bastard*, *Leaving Lukens*, *In Julia's Garden*, **and others**

"Mary Flinn weaves our past and present history all through her new novel *Playing by Heart*. With parallel love stories set in Wilmington and Wrightsville Beach told a century apart in the 1920s through diaries and old letters, and through characters' lives during the 2020 pandemic, it makes a great beach read!"

— **Elaine Henson, beach historian and author of** *Carolina Beach, a Postcard History*

Playing By Heart

A Novel

To Aisling,
Enjoy the music!

♡
Mary Flinn

MARY FLINN

Address all inquiries to:
Mary Flinn
Fiction Worx
Mflinn56@gmail.com
www.TheOneNovel.com

Print ISBN: 978-0-9907197-9-3
eBook ISBN: 978-0-9977696-0-9

Editor and proofreader: Tyler R. Tichelaar, Superior Book Productions
Cover and Interior Layout: Fusion Creative Works, www.fusioncw.com
Author photo: Kamaron Goodrich, KamGoodrichPhotography.com

Printed in the United States of America

First Printing 2022

For additional copies, please visit: www.TheOneNovel.com

For all my music teachers

Acknowledgments

I would like to extend thanks to the kind people who lent their expertise for this book: John Foy who graduated from Oberlin College and is now Head Concert Piano Technician at Brevard Music Center; Ken Grossi, Oberlin College Archivist, for providing documents and answering my questions about campus life and curriculum in the late 1920s; Christina Larson, owner of Guilford Garden Center in Greensboro, North Carolina; Robin Davis, owner of Maxie B's Bakery in Greensboro; Greg Pray for U.S. Naval Academy advice; Dick Hyatt and Laura Wharton for sailing references. Special thanks to my editor, Tyler Tichelaar, PhD for his editing genius, and Shiloh Schroeder and her graphic design team at Fusion Creative Works for making a beautiful book. Thank you to Laura Wharton, Suzanne Goodwyn, and Elaine Henson for reading the manuscript and giving their testimonials. As always, I raise a glass to my husband Mike, this time around for checking tasks off the punch list in Greensboro, getting me to Wilmington for good, and being the dream of a quarantine partner I knew he would be. I've never doubted our match, and I'm thankful I said "yes" forty years ago! Finally, gratitude goes to all my music teachers for sharing their joy of music with me: Jean Breed, Lara Hoggard, Peggy Russell, Marta Force, Ron Hill, Richard Cox, David Pegg, and Lindsay Peters. In the best and worst of times, music has lifted me and carried me onward.

"And the people stayed home."

— Kitty O'Meara

CHAPTER ONE

Anne Borden Montgomery

It was Friday the thirteenth, and it certainly felt like it. The world had stopped. Attempting to avoid more of the day's bad news, Anne Borden handed the last of the boxes of old diaries and letters down from the attic to Bernard's waiting hands. It was unfortunate that it had taken an epidemic to drive her back into the attic to cull through her mother Sylvie's possessions. At the same time, the attic dive was a good stay-at-home activity and a cheerful diversion. On Wednesday, they had heard the World Health Organization declare that the novel coronavirus or COVID-19 was now a global pandemic. Due to their age and Bernard's compromised health, they would be staying at home.

Indefinitely.

Bernard's lymphoma and the treatments begun to save him started at summer's end. The treatments had grown from anxious weeks to months and then lasted through the holidays. Then it took the usual winter hibernation for him to recuperate fully, and for both of them to adjust to living together in her home at the improbable age of eighty. Without any of Bernard's relatives close enough to take care of him, it fell to Anne Borden to take charge. Having him move in with her was the easiest solution. Even though she'd had a mad crush on him in the 1950s, they were not presently romantically involved; however, Bernard needed her, and it seemed natural to accept the duties of caring for her old and dear friend.

As if Bernard's illness hadn't been enough, the coronavirus that began in late 2019 had blindsided the entire world. Today was warm for March in Wilmington, ironically Friday the thirteenth, and in just two months, the deadly virus had seeped like poison vapor from China to Italy, to South Korea, and then to the United States. Woefully unprepared for the monumental health crisis challenge, the US government was backpedaling to catch up with the effects the nation would soon be facing along with upheaval and uncertainty.

Social distancing, a new term meaning staying at least six feet from others, was recommended to keep the virus from spreading. Mitigation, they called it. Social gatherings were limited to fifty people or fewer. Handshaking and hugging were suddenly taboo. Handwashing was paramount, as well as not touching one's face. Daily routines and expectations were changing literally day by day and hour by hour. Elderly people and those with pre-existing conditions were the most susceptible to the disease and were advised to stay home, which explained the day's attic exploration.

The likes of this pandemic were so unfamiliar and unknown, not what anyone had expected in scope or the rapid advancement of infection. AB and Bernard were some of the few who recalled the alarming polio outbreaks in the 1940s and '50s, and then the AIDS crisis in the 1980s, but this pandemic seemed different even to them, more insidious. Having so much news at one's fingertips was unsettling and distracting. It was hard to know what was true and what was exaggeration. Who knew what to believe?

Churches were closing for services and gatherings. The ACC and NCAA basketball tournaments had been abruptly canceled. All sports events—golf tournaments in mid-swing, NBA championship games, and baseball practices were suddenly off. The annual Azalea Festival that drew thousands to Wilmington in April would probably be canceled, as well as every other festival, concert, and fundraiser. Even the fate of the upcoming summer Olympic Games in Tokyo was being discussed. Disney World was closed! It was as if a plug had been pulled on the whole country. And for Anne Borden, it was all too much to digest in just one day's worth of headlines. Both of her children had called to check in on her in a single day, which was truly remarkable. Who knew how long this thing would last?

Looking for a cheerful indoor diversion finally led AB to wonder what of her mother's things she had left uncovered in the attic. When Bernie's cancer had caused the postponement of her attic diving last summer, AB felt the discovery of Sylvie's manuscript at the time might be the only treasure she would ever find. But then she had decided to climb those steps today. In the past, AB might have thought cleaning out the attic and purging her possessions was tedious and tiring, even with the rewards that dangled, but today she was reenergized. What they had found today might well be the motherlode! And thanks to the pandemic, they had all the time in the world to dig in and relish their find.

"Well…do you think our young friends would care to hear more tales of your mother Sylvie and her gang?" Bernard asked, wiping his hands of the dust from the old boxes, and sneezing discreetly into his elbow.

"Bless you! Maybe they would. I'm sure it would be a nice diversion from talking about COVID-19. I hate to think that we'd have to distance ourselves from our young friends, but that just might be the case at our age…." She left *and your tenuous health* unsaid. "Anyway, Elle and Nate certainly seemed sad that the story about Lumina had come to an end last time we gathered on the porch. The dancing and the romance, it was all quite magical. That was just August…seems like so long ago, doesn't it, Bernie?"

"Yes. It really does."

"After Nate surprised Elle with that Valentine's Day trip to Italy, I can't imagine these diaries would hold much excitement for them in comparison, but what else are we all going to do since we have to hunker down together during this pandemic?" AB carried a large box to the dining table for a look. "Oof," she muttered, clapping dust off her hands, and rubbing her palms on her sore sacrum.

"Agreed," said Bernard, wiping dust off a diary with a rag. "I'm up for a distraction. Maybe they will be too."

AB gave him a slight wink. "Well, maybe not; they have moved in together after all. I imagine they are distracted enough quarantining with each other. Don't you think they might be tired of us old fogies anyway?"

"Maybe so, but I miss them. Planning their wedding and working full-time must keep them busy enough. I definitely don't miss those days—of working full-time, I mean," Bernard mused, looking into his own box on the table. "I never quite thought about it this way before, but I'm spoiled with the guilty luxury of being retired, when every day can be Saturday if you want it to be." His eyes crinkled at the corners even more when he smiled. "Still, it couldn't hurt to ask them over. We can sit at opposite ends of the porch and read to each other. That would be safe enough, six feet apart. I'll even wear my hearing aids!"

AB laughed. "You promise? I like that idea. Elle sure does have a lot on her plate with running her bakery. And Nate's TV show keeps him so busy! Let's see what's in here before we send up flares."

"Good idea. Looks like there will be quite a bit of organizing to do," Bernard said, examining his piles of letters and diaries on the table beside AB's growing stack, and glancing again at the blue dress hanging over the chair.

"Yes, Mother was quite meticulous in documenting her life."

"Did you keep diaries like this?" Bernard laughed at the piles of journals he was creating on the table, catching one before it slid onto the floor.

AB chuckled. "No! I wasn't much on writing. I didn't keep a diary after about the fifth grade. I did keep all my letters, the ones from important people, at least. But I didn't have piles of them like Mother did!" she replied, picking up a pack of old letters.

"Look how she tied pretty ribbons around the packs," he said, fingering a bundle of letters tied with a faded ivory ribbon. "I suppose that was fairly typical in those days?"

"Yes, it was."

"She was smart to save them."

"People who lived through the Great Depression never threw anything away, you know. Letters were their history. Imagine all the stories in these letters! Didn't Daphne keep the ones you wrote to her?" AB pried, trying to keep the emotion from her voice. AB's best friend Daphne had snagged Bernard from under her nose, and they'd been married for almost fifty years when Daphne died. The old scar still tugged at AB at times. Bernie was as oblivious to the situation now as he was then! And yet here they were….

"Not in pretty parcels like these. My fault, I guess. I wasn't the best correspondent. I only found one or two I'd written in her things after she passed." Bernard chuckled. "I wrote to her after her cat died. And Monty? Did you save his letters?"

"Oh, no. We never wrote. Since I met him here in Wilmington, there was no need to write…. You know, those dresses Mother saved in her steamer trunk should be in a museum somewhere! They are much too delicate to give to any movie studio." AB laid her hand on Bernard's arm as she eyed the infamous blue flapper dress that was draped carefully across the back of her favorite wing chair. "I'm dying for Elle to see the blue-sequined dress we found from the manuscript about Lumina we read. That dress was special. I want to keep that one," AB said wistfully.

"Yes, you should. Since those dresses debuted at Lumina, maybe you should offer the others to the Wrightsville Beach Museum of History if you don't want to be bothered with them. Do you think your children would want them?"

"Huh! They don't want any of my things. No, I think they'd love for the museums to take the stuff off their hands. None of it would be of any importance to my kids. Besides, they weren't that interested in the story about Lumina anyway."

"That's a shame. It was a great story. The museum would love to have your collection."

AB's nose dripped from the dusty boxes, so she wiped it discreetly on a tissue she'd pulled from the cuff of her sweater sleeve.

"That's a wonderful idea, Bernie. Those dresses sure aren't doing any good up in my attic, are they? And how on earth would I preserve such a collection? And at my age, well, what would be the point?"

"Mm, I suppose," he agreed. "What dates are you finding in the diaries?"

"Let's see. Here's one from 1929…oh, I'll bet she talks about the stock market crash. And here's 1928. Oh, look, Bernie! This must be the one Mother started in college after the summer we just read about. Let's put them in order."

Bernard looked through the diaries and then started checking the postmarks on the envelopes in his piles of letters. He helped AB arrange them along with the diaries. "The packages of letters are arranged by year, at least. We can thank her for being organized."

They worked across the table from each other until both boxes were emptied and a train of letters and books spread across the table. From the open window they both heard the distant roar of tires from an SUV coming down the street, getting louder as it turned into the driveway. It was unusual for her to be there, but still Bernard smiled. Their mountain girl no longer needed her four-wheel-drive here at the coast.

"Huh. Speaking of Elle. Sounds like she just drove up."

ELLE

After shopping, Elle pulled into the familiar spot under the crape myrtle tree, taking a sweet moment to calm herself and to reminisce about the cozy guest house she'd rented from AB when she'd first arrived in Wilmington last May. She'd enjoyed living in this little nest until Thanksgiving when she moved in with her fiancé Nate just two doors down. First, she'd opened a bakery, and a month later, she'd met the love of her life. Her previously stagnant life had changed quickly. And now there was a worldwide pandemic! How rapidly things had changed with the arrival of the coronavirus! Costco had been mobbed after the announcement about the pandemic. Panicked shoppers were tossing not one but two cases of toilet paper into their carts. In contagious alarm, Elle did the same thing, thinking she'd keep one for herself and Nate, and give the other to AB and Mr. May. Maybe the other shoppers had the same idea of sharing their loot, but the atmosphere had been one of urgency. *Who knew when there would be more?*

Elle's world had gone from normal to uncertain in a matter of just days. Worries about what would happen to her bakery if she had to close had kept her up at night for the last week. No one was talking about stores closing yet, but her business had been slower than usual the last few days, and two brides had canceled their wedding cake orders just today. That did not bode well for the seasonal wedding business Elle was anticipating. Even her own wedding might be put on hold. How long could the pandemic last? She had overheard people predicting that the coronavirus would blow over in a couple of months, but Elle had a bad feeling about it. If things got worse, and they were likely to, having to lay off her employees would be devastating to all of them. Her part-time staff didn't make a lot of money to begin with, and she could not afford to provide health insurance yet for Allyson, her almost full-time assistant manager, much less for herself. She was barely getting by. Thankfully, Nate didn't charge her rent to live in his uncle Phil's beach house, and his job should be secure. *Shouldn't it?*

Added to that, Elle worried that Anne Borden and Mr. May would be susceptible to the virus due to their advanced age and Mr. May's recent battle with cancer. What would happen here at home? Before the press was ousted from China, NPR had reported that people were dying alone in their homes in the Wuhan province, without any hope of getting help, because they had been ordered to stay inside. That thought alone had terrified Elle. Hearing that the disease had landed in America was frightening. She and Nate had been skiing in Italy just weeks ago, and now look what was happening there! What if she'd carried the coronavirus home with her? Maybe she was one of those people who remained asymptomatic but infected others in her path? She'd had a sore throat last week but didn't think anything of it. It went away…. Wouldn't she know by now, though, if she had infected her friends and coworkers? Anyone with a compromised immune system was likely to have a rough time fighting the coronavirus, so naturally she worried about Mr. May and AB, her older cousin Judy and her friend Marcus, both from her home in the mountains, and Nate's grandparents who lived two hours away in Cary.

And then there was her eighteen-year-old son Joey. Tucked away in special forces training at Fort Bragg, he should be safe enough, but the way military personnel traveled back and forth from all over the world, there was no telling what disease might have stowed away with them. The Spanish flu was believed to have spread from American soldiers to Europe during World War I. The flu had been responsible for ending the war, and then it spread to the United States following the peace treaty. At least Joey hadn't been in Asia where the virus originated.

Elle raked back her long blond hair and sighed deeply before getting out of her car, popping the tailgate to retrieve the large package of toilet paper. Distractedly, she patted her pockets. *Do I even have my car keys? Who can think under these circumstances?*

"Elle!" Nate's crisp voice startled her, making her almost drop her package. Looking up in surprise, she saw him sauntering down the driveway with Harley, their neighbor's black dog, on her leash. "Hey, babe, whatcha doing? I saw you pull in." He gestured to the dog. "Patsy had to leave, so I'm taking care of Harley."

"Hey! Where's Patsy?"

"She went to Kinston for a couple of days to check on her mother."

"Oh, well I just went to Costco to stock up, and I brought AB and Mr. May a pack of toilet paper, so I thought I'd drop it off...."

"Oh, that's nice of you," he said, reaching her and circling his free arm around her neck to pull her in for a hug. She reached up and held him tightly around the shoulders. "You okay?" he asked when she held on a bit longer than usual.

"Yeah, I think so. You know, this pandemic thing is freaking me out a little bit." Elle stroked Harley's head, which was nuzzled against her knee. Dogs always knew when people were anxious.

"Yeah, it's pretty scary, huh? With everybody stocking up, I'll bet the store was crowded."

"It was like the week before Christmas—except nobody was smiling. And it was weirdly quiet too. I don't think I've ever seen anything like it. I might have gotten the last two cases of toilet paper in the whole warehouse!"

"Damn!"

"Right? Forget about the milk and bread; everybody's hoarding toilet paper and hand sanitizer. I guess I have enough of that to last us a while."

"I heard masks and gloves are getting scarce too."

"Not good news for the hospitals. Hopefully, they'll have what they need. I had two brides call in today and cancel their wedding cakes. Weddings are getting canceled right and left."

"Man. That sucks."

"I know." Elle had another fleeting thought about the possibility of having to postpone their wedding plans, but she thought it better not to share it with Nate. Besides, it was best not to get too far ahead of herself. But for her, it was par for the course. Her old insecurities never failed to pop up at inopportune times. It was still hard for her to believe she was actually getting married. And to this fine man standing in front of her.

Nate shook his head. "You going up to see AB?"

"Yeah. You wanna go with me to take this to her? I haven't seen her or Mr. May in a couple of days. I really want to check on them; see how they're doing."

"Sure."

They walked along the driveway to the walkway leading up to AB's lovely white board-and-batten home. Tall forsythia bushes bloomed near the front porch as Elle and Nate passed. Climbing the stairs to the porch, they could hear the familiar voices of their friends through the open window. Nate called out, "Hello in there!"

"Oh, hello!" came AB's voice back. "Hold on just a minute."

Elle and Nate waited with Harley by the door until AB and Mr. May appeared together. AB laid her hand on the door handle, pushing the storm door open a few inches. Then she paused and glanced at Mr. May.

"Hi, there." Her other hand raised in caution.

"Hi," Elle and Nate said in unison.

"I was going to let you right in out of habit, but I think it might be best if we just talk through the door…for now at least. I'm sorry," AB said, a strange expression on her face. Mr. May's eyebrows rose; then he nodded slowly.

"Oh, right," said Nate, glancing knowingly at Elle.

"Oh. Oh, yes, of course. We need to give you your space."

"Social distancing," Mr. May said with a nod, pressing his lips together ruefully. "That's not to say we can't sit on the porch together and visit—as long as we're six feet apart."

They were momentarily silent, letting the new circumstances and all the implications sink in. Looking from one to the other, they each came to the simultaneous realization that life as they knew it had suddenly changed. No more hugs or handshakes. They had never been a touchy-feely kind of group in the first place, but even for them, the distancing seemed odd. It seemed rude to be so standoffish. Elle remembered the package she held and extended it to the older couple on the other side of the storm door.

"I went to the store to stock up, and I brought you some toilet paper," said Elle. Then to AB's questioning look, she added, "Apparently, it's quite the trendy thing now. Life is uncertain; eat dessert first and buy plenty of TP."

"Oh, thank you, Elle; that's kind of you. This should last a long time! I hadn't thought to stock up…" she said, opening the door so Mr. May could take the package.

"Would you like us to go to the store for you?" Nate was quick to ask. "You could give me a list and I can go. I'm working from home this week. And maybe for a while now."

"Oh, I'm sure we can manage," said Mr. May. "I like to shop early in the morning anyway before so many people get out. I'll take care of it. Not to worry."

"Well, let us know…anything you need; we'll be happy to leave it on your porch," said Elle.

"Thank you," AB said. "Well, enough doom and gloom! You know, we were just thinking about you both! After being glued to the TV news all morning, Bernie and I were up in the attic today trying to cheer ourselves up, and we found more of my mother's diaries and letters—just tons of them—and a steamer trunk full of her dresses. Elle, you won't believe it—we found Mother's blue-sequined dress!"

Elle gasped and looked at Nate. "Oh my God! From the story? The one she wore to Lumina in 1928?"

"Yes, the very same. Catherine's cast-off with the torn sequins," said AB.

"Oh! I can't wait to see it!" said Elle. She and Nate grinned and looked back at Mr. May and AB.

AB's eyes gleamed with delight. "What are y'all doing tonight?"

Elle gasped and her eyes lit up when AB brought out the blue-sequined flapper dress. AB laid it carefully across the reading chair on the porch for Elle and Nate to see. Sylvie had worn it to the first dance at the famous Lumina pavilion on Wrightsville Beach for the opening night of the season. Thrilled with her thrift-store find, Sylvie hadn't realized someone else at the dance could have donated it. Unfortunately, that person had been Catherine Carmichael, a seemingly snooty aristocrat from town who quickly became Sylvie's brother Kip's love interest. Reaching out to touch the dress, Elle was filled with a rush of mixed emotions: excitement over seeing the actual dress and admiration at the quality of the bright blue sequins with the fringe on the hem. A wave of distress washed over her as well. It was the very dress Catherine had worn in Havana the night her adopted brother Clifton raped her, impregnating her with a child Catherine would later give up for adoption, ironically at the same place her parents had found Clifton. Elle was angry that Catherine had been treated so poorly by society and even by her own family. It was a feeling she could relate to quite easily. Still, Elle held a few strands of the fringe delicately in her fingers. *If objects could talk*, she thought, realizing the value of such artifacts and what stories lay waiting in drawers, attics, and museums across the world. *If such history could exist in a mere dress, what more could she learn if she dug a bit deeper?*

Nate steadied Elle's arm as she let go of the fringe and took the diary he handed her. She smiled at his reassuring look and sat beside him on the porch swing. It was an honor to read the first night's offering from Sylvie's journal. Mr. May and AB took their seats as well, and the four of them tripped down the rabbit hole once again.

SYLVIE

September 9, 1928

Dear Diary,

I can already tell it's going to be hard to keep writing to you when I have so many people to write to and studies to attend here at Oberlin. Conservatory life, although more intense than regular Oberlin College life, is already so much fun and busy and distracting that I'm usually almost asleep as soon as I settle in for the night in my dormitory. Tonight, however, I'm wide awake and bursting with my experiences, so I will do my best to keep up. Where to start?

The train ride to Cleveland with Aunt Andrea and Father to visit their sister, my Aunt Nell, her family, and my grandmother was remarkable. I've only been there twice—once before when I was quite young, so I don't remember much, except it seemed to take an eternity to get there— and then back in the spring with Aunt Andrea for my audition. I was so nervous I hardly remember the trip. Now, it seems I do love a train ride!

This particular time around, it was like being in a storybook, gazing out the windows at the countryside, especially during the dewy West Virginia morning and sunbathed Ohio Valley evening. Taking meals with Aunt Andrea and Father in the dining car made me feel like a bona fide traveler. Even sleeping in the berths was an adventure with the rhythmic rocking of the train to lull me to sleep at night.

At the party Aunt Nell and Uncle Harry hosted in our honor, so many people commented that things were different here in Ohio than in the South, and I have realized that for myself. Oberlin, apart from having a prodigious music conservatory within the college, is quite progressive in its politics since it was a destination for escaped Southern slaves and the home of abolitionists around the time of the Civil War. The town is famous for its Oberlin-Wellington fugitive slave rescue that some say started the war. The way people have reacted to me as a Southern girl, you'd think I'd been a slave owner myself! Some have laughed in my face upon hearing my Southern accent. A rude boy here asked me if I wore hoop skirts! Can you imagine? I told him they were much too large to pack in my Pullman suitcase, so I left them at home on the plantation (which, of course, is not where I live) and his eyes got big as saucers. I find that humor is crucial in deflecting most unintended insults. Insults could be disturbing if I let them, but Andrea's advice to me is just to be myself and not worry about other people's prejudices or ignorance. Father says we all put our pants on the same way. I suppose he thinks this is helpful advice for me, so I will reserve judgment on those I meet in the same hope that they refrain from judging me.

The troubling thing is I have already heard from some of the more historically minded students in my midst who are aware of the uprising and coup d'état that occurred in Wilmington in 1898. It happened years after the Union victory when the city had a majority of black citizens. The white minority Democrats led a group of white supremacists and, aided by a group called the Red Shirts, overthrew the city's Republican government during the local election. Black citizens and some Republicans called Fusionists who supported them were running for office on the local ballot. Black citizens were threatened as they went to the polls. When the election results were in, the mob massacred countless Negroes, burned down their newspaper office, and ran many people out of town on the rails to "take their city back," so to speak. It was terrible, and it was reportedly the only successful coup d'état in United States history, so it was an important event and people here seem to know about it. Now that I live in a town that notoriously served as a stop on the Underground Railroad, I understand some of the dour looks I have received. Although I am not proud of what happened in my town, I must move on and hope for redemption through my own enlightened nature, if that is possible for those concerned with my heritage. I can't let this large and bloody stain on my hometown determine the course of the rest of my life. What else is one to do?

Mostly, I associate with music students rather than the historians, and we tend to live in our own fantasy worlds far apart from the realm of politics and such seriousness. In fact, I find my music colleagues to be rather fascinated with themselves, so I have not had to worry about my background, other than their interest in my accent and my use of terms like "ma'am" and "sir," which seem unnecessary to my new midwestern friends (not to mention my cursed red hair that makes me stand out like a sore thumb). My piano teacher, Mr. Finch, seems to like being called "sir," and he is of the mature age to be worthy of the title, so I will continue to address him as such. He is very dignified and grandfatherly, which is a relief since some of the professors are somewhat gruff and others seem to be rather wolfish. Perhaps the Oberlin faculty took pity on a mild-mannered Southern belle who is a fish out of water here in the Midwest when assigning my teacher! Anyway, I have heard Professor Finch is one of the best piano teachers and I will have him until I gradu- ate, so I am especially grateful to have him for my teacher. I have been assured the professors here will host students unable to travel home over the holidays. I will probably visit Aunt Nell and Uncle Harry over the shorter holidays so I won't have to burden Mr. Finch with my presence. Still, I think it is quite generous that they do that here.

As students, we are required to keep our dormitory rooms neat and clean our bathrooms, which are shared by several of us girls living on the same floor at Talcott Hall. My roommate is a large, pleasant girl named Dorothy from Cincinnati, who is a voice major. She wears her chestnut hair in the latest shingle cut bob with bangs, and she has large blue eyes and milk-white skin with a small spatter of freckles across her nose. Upon meeting new people, she always promises to sing for them, as if it will be a rare treat. I suppose it would be. She has quite a fine and loud soprano voice with a remarkable vibrato that is distinctive even in a chorus, which is generally cautioned against. The point of a chorus is to blend with other voices, but Dorothy seems determined to stand out wherever she goes. I should hope my piano performances speak for themselves without requiring my personal advocacy in advance. Dorothy and I do not talk as much as the Mercer twins—Margaret and Marjorie—and I used to do. I can't yet imagine baring my soul to Dorothy, revealing my hopes, dreams, and secrets, so I am hoping to find a kindred spirit soon enough who will fill the empty place that tugs at my heart at day's end.

And the men! There are so many! I still cannot believe I am attending a co-educational college. Oberlin is the oldest co-educational college in the country, and Marjorie is especially jealous since her every thought revolves around the masculine sex. There are many colored students here as well, as I had heard. Most of the Conservatory students appear to be equally narcissistic, but I've met a few gentle souls. Bartholomew (Bart) from Chicago is another piano student I've met and dined with at the Oberlin Inn where men and women are allowed to board together. Bart and I both have Mr. Finch as our teacher. Mr. Finch was a concert pianist who graduated from the Conservatory, so we are lucky to have him. Anyway, Bart is very agreeable, tall, and wholesome with rosy cheeks and a ready smile. He reminds me quite a bit of my modest friend Heckie, who is back home in Wilmington working in his father's shipyard. Bartholomew's friend Herschel is a violinist, and he is strikingly handsome, although short and wiry. He is Jewish and has lovely brown eyes and curly dark hair, and a wry sense of humor, I think. He is from New York City, so like me, he is also far from home and just as different from most of the students here. They both, at least, forgive me for being a Southerner. If I have just a few companions here, I shall be content. There is hardly any time to dally here or feel sorry for oneself, with classes, practices, convocation classes, and performances. I can't imagine how I will encounter any trouble at all!

What I really want to tell you about is what happened at home before I left for college. Most of it involves my brother Kip and his beloved "Catherine." I am forever to refer to her by that name when I write about her, and it is true that I called her Catherine, not her given name the last month before I left for college. We all began calling her that. With what happened to her, it seemed vital to Kip that she have an alias, at least whenever any of us writes about her. He has mentioned looking at my summer diary in case "Catherine" ever has any trouble over the car accident in which she accidentally killed her brother Clifton. It is hard for me even to write those shocking words, and I yet had no hand in it. I can only imagine how she feels. I think I understand why he wants to see it, but he should ask Catherine first.

The question on everyone's mind was whether Catherine remembered what happened after she woke from her unconscious state following the accident. She told me she recalled swerving away from Kip and toward the tree, where all along she planned to wreck herself to end her own life, but she found to her horror her brother standing there. She couldn't stop in time and pinned him against the tree, killing him instead of herself. I do believe her. Clifton was no one's favorite person, to put it mildly, but for her to have killed him is unimaginably tragic.

There is no fathoming how she can live with that knowledge and the memory of it. I have difficulty with the vision of Clifton's death, and it often haunts my dreams. She must have been so troubled to want to end her life, but she could not bring herself to tell me why when I asked. I knew Catherine had problems. My friends have speculated over the mystery of her absence during our senior year. I'm sure Kip knows why she left, but her secret is safe with him. The twins think she went away to have a baby, rather than study horticulture with her uncle in Long Island as she explained. Marjorie and Margaret say girls do it all the time. Also, if Catherine had had a baby, they thought she would have gotten over it by now, relieved at having escaped the expected scandal. Only her influential family could have orchestrated such a coverup. Catherine and I were friends, so why wouldn't she have confided in me? Perhaps giving up one's child is more painful than I can imagine. One never knows what crosses others bear. Anyway, I wish people would tell me what's going on, even though I know I should respect Catherine's right to privacy.

Catherine and I talked about the accident only once, in private, and she gripped my hand intensely at the telling. I won't be the one to bring it up again. My hope is that time will lessen the pain of her wounds and she can forgive herself for what happened. I know there must be much more to the story from the way she and Kip gaze at each other. He seems devoted to helping her regain her sanity since he has pledged to be with her for the rest of their lives; however, they are not engaged. The Carmichaels do not approve of their match, for reasons I cannot understand. Although my family is not in the same league as the Carmichaels, my brother is as good a man as there is, and he truly has Catherine's best interests at heart. Don't her parents want her to be happy? Perhaps they believe she is unstable, so it has nothing to do with Kip's social standing after all. I feel so helpless not knowing how to help my friend. I find myself curious and distracted by her tragedy and my brother's knowledge of what really happened.

It was surely for the best that we all left at summer's end, and the two of them are fortunately now in Raleigh for school, Kip to return to college at North Carolina State and Catherine to finish her term at St.

Mary's. She plans to strike out on her own and go to college in the North to pursue horticulture studies if all goes well. She is certainly bright and passionate enough to achieve her goals, but I hope she can heal and focus her mind on her studies without the distraction of her troubles—and the diversion of my charming brother! He must be delicate with her. What a love she is! I truly miss them both and look forward to getting the letters they've promised to write.

CHAPTER TWO

Mr. May

Bernard May set the sack of masks on Anne Borden's kitchen counter. He'd had them in his garden shed at home and had used them for lawn mowing and applying chemicals. *Chemicals*, he thought with regret. As an urban horticulture agent and master gardener for so many years, he'd used various brands of weed killers like everyone else until the warnings came out about their carcinogenic properties. Naturally, he'd stopped using the chemicals, but years later, he learned the damage had already been done. Non-Hodgkin's lymphoma had invaded his body—probably a year ago—but Bernard had discovered it in late summer after fatigue, concerns with his weight loss, and a lump in his groin had sent him to visit his doctor.

Never one to be cavalier about his health, and with AB's urging that he find out as much as possible about how to protect himself, Bernard had called his doctor after the pandemic had been announced to see what precautions he should take due to his compromised immune system. The doctor recommended all the things the president's coronavirus task force was telling the rest of America: stay six feet apart, wash your hands often, and avoid touching one's face. The doctor also advised Bernard to wear a mask. These old lawn-mowing masks were the best he could do for now.

Masks, like hand sanitizer and disinfectant wipes—and toilet paper—were in short supply everywhere.

The next problem to tackle was how to handle the visits from their young friends Elle and Nate who worked in high public contact jobs and were likely to be exposed to the virus at any time. Anne Borden had been emphatic that Elle and Nate should not enter the house until the pandemic blew over. Goodness knows when that would be. If it was like the Spanish flu back in 1918, it would last a long time and take a grave toll. Back then, 50 million people had died and 500 million were infected with the flu. Then the second wave came in 1920 when the ticker tape parade was held in New York City to honor the World War I veterans. With the large crowds and subsequent celebrations, the influenza started all over again. Bernard had a bad feeling about this one too. Those in charge seemed to know relatively little about how to keep this virus at bay, other than using the recommended mitigation strategies. Still, he and AB wanted to share the new findings of Sylvie's diaries and so many more letters with the young couple. Maybe they could wear masks and sit six feet apart on the open-air porch? There had to be a safe way to proceed without endangering everyone's health.

Nate had been kind enough to leave bags of groceries on the porch this morning. AB was adamant that Bernard not set foot into any grocery store. Nate had explained to her over the phone how to order groceries online. She could drive to the parking lot to pick them up and never get out of her car. They could also use Instacart and have the groceries delivered right to their doorstep. That would certainly be the ticket if one were to become infected and forced to self-quarantine. *It was good to have millennial neighbors!*

However they decided to proceed, this self-imposed lockdown was going to be tough! Maybe the hot summer weather would kill the virus as some had predicted. With the warm weather coming, he was looking forward to getting out of doors and taking walks as his strength allowed.

Exercise wasn't banned yet. Sitting on the dock across the street from AB's house would be so pleasant. As long as social distancing was maintained, exercise and outdoor activities were encouraged.

KIP

September 12, 1928

Dearest Sylvie,

I hope this missive finds you well—and behaving yourself! How are you enjoying college life? In Raleigh, the fall weather is fine—perfect for picnicking and football games. NC State has a good team this year and the games are a grand diversion from our studies. I understand that Oberlin has a good team too. Do you attend many games? I have just spent the most enjoyable weekend seeing Catherine. It's been my pleasure to squire her around to various activities, games, and campus parties. I have to say, I feel swell-headed at the envious reactions I've had from the other fellows! I believe Catherine has garnered quite a few new fans, the most enthusiastic being my roommate Perry. He is almost as enamored of her as I am.

You will be glad to know that the change of scenery seems to be good medicine for your dear friend. Catherine has returned to more of her old self at St. Mary's, without the constant memories of Clifton to haunt her and her parents fretting over her at home. Admittedly, I was worried about her stamina as she got back into the swing of academia and the social aspect of life. On the one hand, she has proven to be a determined and devoted student; although on the other, she admits to being somewhat reserved around the girls in her dormitory. I suppose that is understandable. Since some of them have read the newspapers about her family's tragedy, most of them have questions about what happened in Wilmington. She says they are kind but curious. I think it is natural that she would be guarded among her peers. In my opinion,

Catherine's tragedy seems to have made her more fascinating to others, but she is certainly under no obligation to share the details with these curiosity seekers. Still, our more intimate social situations don't seem to be too much for her to manage since she yearns to live a normal life again. I try to make my shoulder available for her at every opportunity, for whatever it's worth. It is surely a balancing act for us both.

You may not know, but at the last minute, our pal Heckie decided to enroll at the United States Naval Academy in Maryland. He is officially a midshipman! (Are you saluting?) His father wanted him to take the mechanical engineering course there to prepare him for changes in the shipbuilding industry. Heckie was eager to head off to college too, like the rest of us. I'm sure his course will not be as strenuous as the hard labor he is accustomed to in the shipyard! Anyhoo, he's asked me for your address, as he feels inclined to write to you. I hope you don't mind that I shared it. I can't imagine you will be inundated with ephemera from old Heckie!

I stay busy enough with my own coursework. I miss you, little sis, and I look forward to seeing you again at our Thanksgiving holiday and Aunt Andrea's wedding. You will make a lovely bridesmaid. I hope the fellows are treating you well there. Let me know if you have any trouble and I will hop a train and settle any scores with which you need assistance. I look forward to hearing news about your music, your studies, and your new friends.

Fondly,

Kip

SYLVIE

September 14, 1928

Dear Diary,

At Oberlin, it is required of all piano majors in the Conservatory of Music to accompany a voice student during their private lessons to enrich our musical experience and learn to provide a service we might offer professionally. In turn, we must also participate in a chorus to learn the art of singing. I have sung in church all my life and in our school glee club, so singing is nothing new to me, although I am certainly no diva. Anyway, I have dreaded this day when I shall meet the student I will accompany. Will it be a boy or a girl? No one has shared whether I shall be stuck with this person for the remainder of our college endeavors, or whether we are rotated through a variety of vocalists for the purpose of educating us on the different vocal registers of men and women, or what the case might be. I just hoped to avoid some groaning cow or screeching hawk of an amateur, but then again, I remind myself that I am at Oberlin Conservatory and the likelihood of finding such a dud would be miniscule. Still, one wonders. It would be just such luck to get stuck in an unfortunate circumstance.

So, on Tuesday, I arrived characteristically early to Miss Constance Devereaux's studio and took my seat at the baby grand piano, where a neat stack of three compositions awaited our student. One of the few women faculty members on campus, Miss Devereaux appeared to be a flamboyant soul who seemed to radiate energy and happiness as if she were the planet Mercury, as close to the sun as one should get. As soon as I entered her studio, she swept me in as a part of her world.

"Good morning! Come in; come in! I am so pleased to meet you, Sylvie!" she exclaimed. "I'm equally excited about meeting Willemina

Wadkins, the young lady you will accompany," she added. After gesturing to the piano bench, she allowed me a few minutes to look over the musical scores while she busied herself with a teapot and cups. Momentarily, a shadow filled the doorway where a slip of a young black woman hesitated at the threshold.

"Oh, hello! Willemina!" Miss Devereaux greeted her with glee.

"Hi," the girl whispered with some trepidation at her teacher's unrestrained greeting.

"Good morning! Please come in! Come in!" the teacher said, wrapping an arm around Willemina's thin shoulders and ushering her into the room. "I'm Miss Devereaux and this is Sylvie Meeks, your accompanist." I stood to greet my cohort.

"Hello," said Willemina softly, still awed by our new vivacious mentor. The contrast of Willemina's waif-like figure with Miss Devereaux's impressive, trim form was not so much a matter of size and shape, but a difference in the energy exuded from each. While Willemina was shy and reserved, Miss Devereaux was exuberant. It was as if God Himself had pulled a cord from the top of Miss Devereaux's brown bobbed head up toward heaven, the way her feet hardly touched the ground as she moved about the room and talked to us. She emitted quite a heady aura and was already teaching us without even meaning to. I felt my own shoulders lifting in response.

"I've prepared tea for us." At Miss Devereaux's gesture, I took my seat again at the piano bench while Willemina was offered a small velvet chair. Miss Devereaux poured us each a cup of tea and checked her wristwatch as she set her saucer on the piano. After a quick sip of her tea, she began the conversation.

"Let's get acquainted, shall we?" Miss Devereaux smiled radiantly, making me smile back. Willemina's lips curved up slightly, but her inability to lift her teacup betrayed her calm exterior. Three women in a room at Oberlin and one of them colored must have been rare, even for this place. I believed Miss Devereaux was certainly aware of this historic moment and was giving it the due it deserved.

"As you may know, I hail from Indiana, and I sang opera in Chicago before I decided to teach here at Oberlin. I felt called to teach, as most of us in the Conservatory have at some point in our professional careers. As a successful woman myself, I can offer you both the perspective you need to grow and succeed not only as musicians and performers but as people. You may decide to devote your lives to music, or you may marry and raise families. I believe you must choose one or the other. That decision for you will come farther down the road, so you will have to see where your road takes you. It all depends on the choices you make and how hard you work," she said, raising her hands in a weighing motion, lifting her teacup in one and the saucer in the other. "I expect you to take my correction with grace, to practice diligently, and to be early for *every* appointment. You must attend every convocation and recital. There is no time to waste here. I will help you navigate your courses, although I hope you both will choose the path of performance. A life of performance is quite exhilarating and rewarding, and you must seize the opportunity when you are given it. You never know how long your window will remain open. I am the very person you need to help you achieve your goals, so welcome to my studio!" She finished with a dramatic flourish and a grin.

Willemina and I sat dumbstruck at this speech. Miss Devereaux certainly did not waste time, nor did she mince words! Of course, I would be at every Friday convocation class to see the other students perform, and I relished the chance to hear the instructors and more advanced students perform in their recitals. Still, her urgent advice made me gulp despite myself.

"Now, tell me about yourselves," she commanded, gesturing to Willemina first.

Willemina studied her teacup and glanced nervously around the small studio. I could see her swallow as her eyelids closed for an instant before she spoke. She raised her head and began in a small voice.

"I am from Cleveland. My father is the headmaster of the colored high school there, and my mother is the music teacher. They are both musicians. They told me I sang before I talked." Her doe eyes peered up through long lashes at Miss Devereaux, waiting for her response.

"Then you have a gift, my dear," said Miss Devereaux, setting her teacup back in the saucer with hardly a sound. "You will find everyone at Oberlin is gifted."

Willemina swallowed solemnly. This girl was nothing like my confident roommate Dorothy. I wonder whether Miss Devereaux will be teaching Dorothy as well. Thankfully, I will not be accompanying her!

"And you, Sylvie; tell us about yourself."

"My mother taught me the piano. She was originally from Ohio—Cleveland where my aunt and uncle live—but I was born in North Carolina."

"Oh, yes. I wondered about your accent," said Miss Devereaux. "Where, precisely, in North Carolina?"

"Wilmington," I replied as Willemina's eyes darkened and flickered toward mine. "It's at the coast," I added for Miss Devereaux, while registering Willemina's reaction.

"Oh, I know it well. My family and I spent many marvelous vacations at Wrightsville Beach there when I was a girl. The dances at the Lumina are quite spectacular!"

"I *love* Lumina!" I exclaimed. I had spent the better part of my summer enjoying the dances there myself. A smile burst onto my face while Willemina's clouded over. Was she jealous that I was getting the attention while this was her voice lesson? On cue, Miss Devereaux checked her watch and decided that we were well enough acquainted.

"Then let's begin our warmup with vocalizations. Sylvie, I want you to play chords first and then ascending and descending arpeggios for Willemina, starting with middle C and then moving up by half-notes. One octave each." She moved over to the piano and demonstrated quickly. "Do you understand?"

I tried my hand at what she described, and Miss Devereaux nodded impatiently, directing me with the arc of her hand to play louder and faster. Willemina sang along with "Aah," for each note I played, and I soon got the hang of it. As we moved up the register, Willemina's voice became more confident and rang out like a bell. It was a lovely sound, unforced and free, quite unlike the freight train horn of my roommate! Miss Devereaux's face beamed the higher Willemina went, and the two of them seemed to lift off the floor in pleasure.

Finally, when Willemina could do no more, Miss Devereaux clapped her hands and gasped. "That was a high C, young lady! You, my dear, are a true coloratura!"

I had no idea what a *coloratura* was, but I was sure it was not a term related to Willemina's race. The girl's smile confirmed it. Miss Devereaux must have recognized my bafflement and explained.

"A coloratura is a voice classification, like a mezzo or a lyric. It describes the high range and light quality of a soprano's register. A true coloratura is rare, and so we are privileged to work with such an entity! I knew you were special when I heard your audition," she said softly to Willemina. And I knew that a compliment like that coming from Miss Devereaux was indeed special as well.

Willemina continued to smile, and her face took on a radiance gleaned not just from her vocal exercises. Miss Devereaux checked her watch again and spoke eagerly to her student.

"You seem to be in excellent voice today. You must have warmed up before you came, yes?"

"Yes," said Willemina. It seemed odd to me that she didn't add "ma'am" after her reply, but I would have to get used to this form of etiquette in my new Midwest surroundings. Miss Devereaux was not offended and proceeded with a nod to me.

"Then let's not waste time and begin with something light." She handed Willemina a selection of sheet music. "'Someone to Watch Over Me.' George Gershwin is one of my favorite modern composers."

I was overjoyed! Gershwin is also one of my favorites, and I played this same piece at my concert over the summer at the Carmichael home, at Catherine's mother's invitation. It was a quite grand affair I lucked into because my mother (and then my aunt Andrea after Mother died) gave Catherine piano lessons. I looked beneath the top leaflet on the piano and found the Gershwin piece. I played the opening chords to familiarize Willemina with the key. Willemina seemed equally excited about the piece. Settling my fingers over the keys, I watched Miss Devereaux set the tempo with her hand. She looked to Willemina and then signaled me to begin the introduction. Willemina started to sing, and that was when the magic began. The bell-like quality of her voice immediately sent chills down my arms as she sang, and I played. It was as if we were one musician. As Willemina held the lingering notes, a subtle vibrato emerged organically. The longing of a girl on the brink of womanhood for a man who would love her deeply arose from this girl's lips. This girl who seemed to hardly know herself—much less the kind of man she would want and need in her life—this girl surprised me. Yet I identified with the longing in her song. Miss Devereaux swooned along with us as she directed the melody with her hands and her expressions. When it was over and the last tones faded from the air, the three of us burst into joyous laughter.

"That was lovely, Willemina! You sang from your soul. You were transformed! I loved it! And Sylvie, you hardly looked at the score! You are very accomplished. I assume you have played this one before?"

"Yes, ma'am. It's one of my favorites. I tend to play by heart. I hope I didn't miss the arrangement."

"Oh, no. It was perfect. Music should be intuitive as well as interpretive, and I believe we have just witnessed quite an intuitive performance from both of you."

Willemina glowed and shared a brief smile with me. I wondered how this young woman who possessed such talent could be so demure when she wasn't singing. Surely, she had only experienced a case of nerves earlier that rendered her a mere shadow of the person she had shown herself to be. Miss Devereaux busied herself with the next piece.

"My next choice for you is a French art song by Claude Debussy, 'Beau Soir,'" she said, handing the score to Willemina. "Do you know it?" Willemina shook her head. "It is quite poignant and controlled, as you will find with many of the French composers." Not having been privy to this girl's audition, I had no idea how she would handle the French language. I certainly could not pull off the pronunciation and wondered how accomplished Willemina would be. It was a first-day test.

"Have you been to your diction class yet, Willemina?"

"Yes, Miss Devereaux."

"And you have some command of French, *n'est ce pas?*"

Willemina grinned this time. "*Oui, Madame.* My mother taught me."

"*Bon! Alors, voyons!* Then let's see," said Miss Devereaux, winking at me.

I scanned the score briefly to see if it was as I remembered, while Miss Devereaux allowed me a moment of study. I nodded and she raised her hands, glanced at Willemina, and then signaled for me to begin.

The melody was pitched perfectly for Willemina's voice, making me realize Miss Devereaux was not the least bit surprised by her student's range or ability, and was, in fact, delighted with this prodigy she had been given to instruct. This time, however, Willemina tended to struggle with the French, which diminished the gentle power of the song. After a few lines into the song, Miss Devereaux cut it short with her hand motions and placed a forefinger to her lower lip. After a pensive pause, she spoke.

"Let's talk about the poem. Do you know the translation?"

"*Non. Pardon, Madame,*" Willemina murmured, retreating back into her shell.

"It's a French poem by Paul Bourget that Debussy put to music, quite perfectly, I think." She closed her eyes. "Just imagine the beautiful evening, *s'il vous plaît.*" Miss Devereaux began to recite:

> "When at sunset the rivers are pink,
> And a warm breeze ripples the fields of wheat,
> All things seem to advise content—
> And rise toward the troubled heart;
> Advise us to savor the gift of life,
> While we are young and the evening fair,
> For our life slips by, as that river does:
> It to the sea—we to the tomb."

Willemina nodded slowly, as if returning from that riverbank on a warm summer evening. She brought her eyes to Miss Devereaux's and asked, "It's just like what you were talking about earlier, isn't it, Miss Devereaux? Don't let life pass you by. Take hold of whatever beauty and wonder you can before it's too late."

"*Exactement, ma cherie!*" her teacher said intently. "Live each moment as if it may be your last! Embrace the passion. Just like you sang about that man a moment ago, dear. Life is too short to waste it on brooding, or convention, or other people's opinions of you."

They nodded together, as though some deeper understanding passed between them. I took note of her words myself.

"Now, let's try it again. Don't worry so much about the pronunciation. We will deal with it later. Sing your passion."

She signaled for me to begin again, and this time the song, the sunset, the river, and the joy all came alive in the room, shimmering in on the magic of Willemina's voice. I realized why all of us were brought together in this moment and that I had landed in the right place at just the right time in my life. Everything for me was falling into place. I felt my own window just beginning to open!

CHAPTER THREE

Nate

Warm weather has come early to the coast this year, Nate thought thankfully, as he and Elle took their usual seats on AB's front porch for the third time in as many days. The two of them sat a safe six feet away from AB and Bernie for their socially distanced reading of Sylvie's diary and the accompanying letters. Bernie and AB wore their allergy masks, and Bernie even wore his hearing aids for the occasion. It was good that their houses were at the end of a quiet street, where the faint hum of bridge traffic coming and going over the Intracoastal Waterway was hardly noticeable.

Nate glanced at Elle, giving her hand a squeeze. He hated seeing his beautiful fiancée so stressed out lately. She needed this break from reality. Indeed, they all needed an escape these days with COVID-19 in the forefront of everyone's minds. Even though they reveled in quarantining together, worries about the sustainability of Elle's new bakery during the inevitable shutdown weighed heavily on her. She and her staff had worked overtime to troubleshoot and make plans for various scenarios just as he had been doing with his colleagues for their TV fishing show. Traveling to potential filming sites had screeched to a halt. He had plenty of editing work for now to produce the shows already in progress, but what would happen when he finished those? How long would this pandemic last? The uncertainty of his job's future made Nate sigh deeply. Elle was still waiting for the governor and mayor's orders to see whether bakeries were considered essential businesses. They certainly were essential in Nate's mind!

Seeing Elle's delighted reaction to the actual blue-sequined dress that AB's mother Sylvie had worn to the Saturday night dances at the Lumina beach pavilion made Nate realize how important this diversion was to Elle. Together on this same porch last summer, they had all read the story of Catherine's damaged cast-off dress in Sylvie's diary about Lumina. These newfound letters and diaries would be their tonic for the worries that ailed them. Too many questions had remained unanswered from the manuscript about what had happened to Sylvie, Kip, and Catherine. AB didn't have the answers. She, too, was learning about her mother Sylvie and her coming-of-age adventures just as they were. Reading the diaries would be like binge-watching their favorite Netflix series!

Nate smiled gratefully at AB, and although he couldn't see her mouth for her mask, she smiled back at him with her eyes. Then AB walked over, handing Nate a letter from her nitrile-gloved hand. It was his turn to read.

HECKIE

September 17, 1928

Dearest Sylvie,

You must be so surprised to be getting a letter from the Naval Academy in Maryland! Admittedly, I am still a bit surprised myself to find that I've enrolled here. I am studying marine mechanical engineering to ready myself for the developments we believe are coming to our country's shipbuilding in-

dustry. Dad tells me the US Navy has big plans with respect to the battleships and submersibles that may be needed if the rumblings we hear from the Nazi party in Germany have sway with the world. It never hurts to be prepared, so I am doing my part for the cause. Hi ho!

Annapolis is a beautiful town with its busy harbor situated right on Chesapeake Bay. It is constantly windy here, although the air has more of a chill than at home. There is no sight more exhilarating to me than a harbor filled with sailing ships and smaller vessels with the autumn blue sky as the backdrop. You would enjoy it here, especially since the seafood offerings are surely better than where you are! The oysters are like none I've tasted before, and I can have she-crab soup every day if I want it. Do you miss the coast? I can't imagine being land-locked the way you are, but I'm sure Oberlin has its charms as well.

I am so curious as to how you are enjoying college life. You must be the talk of the conservatory by now! I hope you are happy there. I find that I like being someplace new and meeting new people. I'm sure you are making many new friends. Do you have a special beau yet? I do not have a particular girl yet. As you can imagine, there are no ladies on our campus, but there are plenty out in the town in search of midshipmen. There are dances and parties for us to attend on the weekends for a nice diversion. I enjoy my studies and the physical conditioning that is required of us. My roommate Steve is a chatty fellow from Charlottesville, Virginia. He seems very smart, so we have started studying together. I find it helpful to try to explain what I've learned to someone else. Science and mathematics have always fascinated me. Two heads are better than one, so they say.

I would enjoy hearing from you if you have the time and inclination to drop me a line. Thanksgiving will be here before we know it, and I look forward to seeing you at home then. I am sure you will have a full dance card with your aunt's wedding, but perhaps we can steal an evening to go out on the town and catch up with one another. Kip and Catherine can come along too if you'd prefer.

Best wishes for a successful semester.

Yours truly,

Heckie

ANNE BORDEN

Anne Borden sat at the piano, fingering through musical scores she'd pulled from the bench seat. Vivaldi, Mozart, Beethoven, Bach, Stravinsky…the list went on. Memories of sitting beside her mother, watching her play with such grace and feeling, wishing she could do half as well someday, came flooding back. She heard the melodies in her mind as if her mother were actually playing them. Sitting this close and turning pages for her mother, she could faintly hear her mother's fingertips striking the keys. With nails always trimmed and filed short, there was never the distracting click during a piece. AB ran the pad of her thumb absently across her own fingernails; they were habitually short, a continual effort after all these years to please her mother.

AB had not played since her mother had passed away almost twenty years ago. Neither had she combed through the attic until recently. It was enough to deal with settling the estate and disposing of Sylvie's possessions at the nursing home where she'd spent the last years of her life. The remaining possessions throughout the house that AB had sorted through and disposed of had left her emotionally depleted. She had thrown herself into her work at the movie studio supervising costume design for the last television series the studio had shot in Wilmington. And then her husband Monty, the manager of the studio, had gotten sick and died. The piano had waited patiently. Until today.

Placing her fingers in an arc above the keys, Beethoven's "Moonlight Sonata" emerged as her foray back into the world of music. Glancing at the score, AB realized playing was almost effortless. And comforting. Why had she not sought out this form of solace before? The instrument could use a good tuning, but overall, the sound was pleasing. Wouldn't Bernie enjoy listening to her music as well?

Recently, he seemed troubled by staying on at her home. Just days before he'd commented on how well he felt and that grateful to her as he was, he ought to be moving back into his own house, dusting off the place, and preparing his vegetable garden. But the pandemic had been declared and here they were, still together under her roof. Although they dropped the discussion on their living situation, it seemed they'd been reluctant to separate for whatever reasons. Moral support? Fear of living alone in the unknown? Convenience? Bernie was certainly a good companion, helpful even. A wonderful quarantine partner, actually. Now that he was better, he'd pitched in with the cooking. When he was up to it, he did odd jobs around the house. He relished being outdoors and working in her garden again, pruning things and spreading fertilizer around her azaleas. They played gin rummy, watched movies in the evenings, or read books in the afternoons. She had given Bernie her master suite on the first floor and taken over one of the guest rooms upstairs—her room as a child growing up in this house. She quite preferred the feminine coziness of it, the wall-to-wall carpet, her private bathroom, and the way she could watch the sunrise from the window overlooking the Intracoastal Waterway. Ospreys nested on top of a channel marker near her dock where she enjoyed seeing them dive for their breakfasts.

Finishing the sonata, AB rested her hands in her lap. Why was Bernie still here? Were they in love? What *was* love at age eighty? Love was supposed to be new possibilities and awakenings of the heart. Weren't they too old for that, especially cooped up in this house during the worst epidemic in a century? But what *was* new was Bernie's health returning. His sense of humor was back. Spring, her favorite season, was right around the corner. She was playing the piano again and enjoying it. Finding the blue-sequined dress and the diaries and letters was exhilarating and unexpectedly…fun! They were enjoying sharing all these treasures with their young friends Elle and Nate. They were having fun. Despite the coronavirus pandemic and all the fear and chaos that went with it, AB and Bernie May were having fun.

SYLVIE

Thursday, September 27, 1928

Dear Diary,

Professor Finch has started me on Rachmaninoff's "Etudes-Tableaux, Op. 39, No. 1 in C-Minor," which I have never heard. It is quite dramatic and invigorating. He told me that Rachmaninoff was known to play by heart like I do—without missing a note—which I don't! Making that connection between the composer and myself seemed like such a gracious compliment, but I did not feel bold enough to thank him. I hope my performance of the pieces will express my gratitude more appropriately. Mr. Finch has such a gentle way of teaching. He often sits beside me on the bench to demonstrate, which I enjoy. He is rather tall and lanky, and his fingers are long and graceful, so his presence is very different from that of the female teachers who have sat next to me in the past. He smells of pipe tobacco for one thing. Tobacco—and alcohol of course—is banned on campus for students, so perhaps he takes his pipe at home. As expected, he is quite gifted at the keys, although his style is very different than mine, stronger and, of course, more confident. I thrive on hearing others' interpretation of the music, which is obviously part of my learning experience here. The temptation is to mimic exactly how they have played, but the challenge is to create my own version of the composer's themes and callings. I believe this is what Professor Finch wishes me to do, to transcend the usual and to move the listener.

I see Miss Devereaux steering Willemina along this same course as she demonstrates and Willemina attempts to copy her, singing through each note by using the vowels and resonance cavities. The voice is such a complex instrument in ways that the piano is not. It is one thing to manipulate keys and to put feeling into one's melodies, but to have to rely on the power and control of one's vocal cords, air control, sinuses, and diaphragm to produce sound and convey emotion on top of learning and pronouncing different languages is something quite different. Willemina astounds me in the tones and interpretations of the music she brings forth every time she opens her mouth! It is an honor to accompany her. I feel an intimacy with her and her teacher as we all explore and participate in this collaboration of musical magic we make. It is interesting watching her personality transform as soon as she enters Miss Devereaux's studio each Tuesday. Each time I play for Willemina, I try to linger for conversation with her and become her friend, but she clams up and rushes off at the end of every lesson, leaving me to wonder what I have done to offend her. She must be painfully shy!

I asked Dorothy if she has met Willemina since they are both voice majors, but she has not made the effort. She seems to have no curiosity about the girl at all. On Wednesdays, all of us freshmen girls are in the Women's Glee Club together. Dorothy sits two seats down from Willemina in the first soprano section, so I can observe them easily from my seat in the alto section. They never interact, even while passing out musical scores, but I have chuckled more than once over Willemina's irritated expressions at Dorothy's foghorn voice! She is not the only one who objects. Our director, Mr. Peck, has made several subtle corrections to Dorothy to tone it down, but she merely nods contritely and continues singing her way. I understand the frustrations of being a teacher after having lived with two—my mother and Aunt Andrea—so I feel sorry for Mr. Peck.

I have even looked for Willemina in the dining hall during our meals to invite her to join me. Dorothy and I usually sit together. Willemina tends to sit with another Negro girl I assume to be her roommate, and they ignore us completely. They live in my dormitory, although on the floor above me, where the other colored students in Talcott live.

We have a convocation class on Fridays where all the Conservatory students assemble in Warner Hall to listen to the upper-class students perform. We are allowed to dine with the men in the Oberlin Inn on weekends. Sometimes there are a few of us, Dorothy, Bartholomew, and Herschel, who all sit together. After last Friday's convocation when the four of us were sitting down to dinner at the Oberlin Inn—I remember Fish on Friday well because the fish they serve taste nothing like the delicacies we have pulled out of the ocean at home—I finally saw her alone. Anyway, we were all greeting each other. It's gotten to be funny because sometimes we are so tired all we can do is utter a single syllable. It sounds like this as we nod to one another, "Bart... Hersch... Syl... Dot..." so now each of us goes through the roster each time we greet each other. Then Willemina walked by without her friend, and I had a chance to call out to her to ask her to join us. Reluctantly, she set her tray on the available corner of the table across from me and sat. I introduced her to everyone and, of course, they jumped into the routine, taking turns giving their monosyllabic names. This time, she smiled a little bit despite herself.

Then my curious friend Herschel asked her, "So what shall we call you...Wil?"

She took a breath and cut her eyes toward me. "Mina," she said in her soft voice. "My mother calls me Mina."

Herschel and I grinned at each other. Then I said, "But really, she's Willemina Wadkins. Remember her whole name because one day she will be very famous, and we will all say we knew her when...."

Willemina's eyes grew large in embarrassment, and she looked down, pressing her lips together.

Then, in typical fashion, Dot said, "We're all going to be famous, Syl. You all can say, 'I knew Dorothy Randall when she was just…'" she waved her hand for effect, "'Dot.'"

Bart and Hersch almost fell off their chairs laughing. Even Willemina giggled a little. I felt so grateful to my friends for making her feel comfortable. During dinner, Mina didn't say much, not that she could get a word in, but she listened to our ridiculous banter and critique of all things Oberlin, especially that awful fish. I felt like something opened up inside her so that maybe we could someday be friends, or at least have conversations that wouldn't be awkward.

I think Herschel wants to ask me out.

Saturday, September 29, 1928

Dear Diary,

I was right! Herschel did ask me out, but it was a double date with him and Bartholomew, who asked Dorothy out. I have never been to a speakeasy in my life, but last night I went! It was a covert little place called Dot Dot Dot. Of course, Dorothy loved that it was her nickname—thrice—and so she kept laughing about it all night. And, of course, we all had to go under the pretense of seeing a movie in town as we checked out with our dorm matron. It seems the entire student body at Oberlin is fascinated with the talkies these days! (Wink-wink!)

Dot Dot Dot is downtown off a back alley. Anyone could easily miss it since the doorway looks like just another back door of an establishment. There was a password to get in that only Herschel knew. He paid for us all to get in as his guests. We were led down a hall by the bouncer and then admitted to the actual bar by another man in a suit. Not expecting glamour, we were all surprised at the decor—lots of brass art deco on the walls, low lighting, and red velvet banquettes at small tables complete with white tablecloths. We crowded around a small table near the stage. I ordered the only mixed drink I know—a Sidecar—and then we all settled back to listen to the music. A jazz trio played under the spotlights. They were hardly visible for the smoke, but it was real jazz, played by Negroes who really knew how to play it. I understand now that as good as the Bob Weidemeyer orchestra was at Lumina last summer, this is the way jazz is supposed to be played. It was all very sophisticated and thrilling to be in such a clandestine atmosphere. Even Dorothy was quiet for a while. We loosened up after our second drink and chatted about everything over the week. Herschel and Bart smoked, but Dorothy and I did not. I can't stand cigarettes, and she has sworn them off wisely to preserve her voice. Bart is her accompanist, and he joked more than once about how loudly she sings. According to Bart, Dorothy's voice teacher has no patience for her perception of volume. I am anxious to see how successful he is with her! She is a good sport about Bart's teasing anyway.

Hersch seemed quite handsome in the smoky limelight of Dot Dot Dot. Something about him, his attention to me or his looks, causes a tug inside me somewhere that I cannot explain, but it makes me want to be near him. He has lovely dark eyes that sit just a bit close together, and his curly hair is radically longish. His smile is genuine, although impish, which I find infectious.

"However did you learn about this place?" I asked when the trio took a break.

"One of the saxophone players in my orchestra class brought me here the first week of school. He's a jazz lover too, and a junior who knows his way about town, you might say."

"How many times have you been here?" I asked, wondering how safe we were.

"Oh, only a few. My father would kill me if he knew I was here," Herschel said, grinning mischievously at me.

"Why? Well…I think I know, but killing you seems a bit drastic, doesn't it?"

He laughed. "My dad is a tailor in New York—"

"My father is a tailor too!" I said, interrupting him. "He owns a menswear shop in Wilmington."

"He sounds very successful. But…my father wants all his sons to become something better than he is. My three older brothers are working on it in colleges back east. My father wants us all to become bankers or doctors or lawyers, better ourselves and be respectable. Not musicians, necessarily," he said with a wry grin and taking a drag of his cigarette. "I couldn't get into Julliard. He made a deal with me when he allowed me to come to Oberlin. He said if I ever clashed with the law, or got a girl in trouble, he would cut off my musical study and send me a train ticket home. And as you know, alcohol consumption is banned at the Conservatory."

"As are cigarettes," I said with a nod toward Bart and their cigarettes. "Then you must thrive on courting danger?" I asked, immediately unsure of my safety, our safety, and the intelligence of being in a speakeasy with these boys, not to mention our brilliance in lying to our dorm matron about going to the movies. What would my own father and Aunt Andrea think? I glanced at Dot, but Hersch continued.

"Or maybe I thrive on secrecy. Ah? Is it just me, or do you enjoy courting danger as well, young lady?"

Do I? Again, that charming smile. I gulped. My sudden social discomfort reminded me of the summer dances with a college boy named David, for whom I fell, and who didn't quite fall for me. Bart was obviously listening to our conversation and awaiting my response.

"Well then, it was probably a bad idea to come here. I was hoping to be able to trust you. I hardly know you, Hersch. And the same goes for you, Bart," I said, hardly amused at the sparkle in his eye as he smiled at me. Dot, our single Dot, seemed oblivious to the discussion, sipping her drink while gazing openly at the interesting clientele and the waiters.

"Relax, dear," said Hersch, reaching over to lay his hand across mine on the table. "Nothing bad is going to happen. If it makes you feel better, we can leave after the next set and walk back to campus, treat ourselves to an ice cream cone, whatever you'd like. I'll always look out for you. I just thought you'd like the music and a new experience. Do you truly think I want to get kicked out of Oberlin and go home?"

"No," I said, feeling my face burn. By now, we had both Bart and Dot's attention. I had to bite my tongue to offer any encouraging words of gratitude for bringing me here and letting me feel like an adult, for goading me to take a simple risk. It was fun, exhilarating even, but then I started thinking of Clifton, Catherine's dead brother, and how he had manipulated people to get his way. I won't allow that to happen to me again. I had a feeling in the pit of my stomach that Herschel Bloom could be one to watch.

"In that case, may I have one more drink if we're staying?" Dot asked, batting her big blue eyes at Bart. He grinned lopsidedly and signaled the waiter for another Bee's Knees.

Of course, there was no ice cream cone on the way back to campus. Bart had to steer Dot all the way to our dormitory, where it was my job to manage her from there. Somehow, we made it up two flights of stairs and to the bathroom undetected by the matron. I was finally able to maneuver Dot to a toilet where she sat on the cold floor and spent the remainder of the evening intermittently vomiting her Bee's Knees into the bowl and wailing her apologies and regrets about her ailing stomach and her actions that had caused such. Two of our hall mates passed through to brush their teeth and looked on in horror at her predicament. I glared at them and handed Dot a wet cloth. They promised not to tell on us.

The whole time I kept thinking about Kip and Heckie's missives in which they valiantly promised to come up here and settle any scores I might encounter with any untoward young men. Little good their promises did me last night. I know I am on my own here. Were Bart and Hersch really the bad influences I believe them to be? They didn't try to take advantage of us, other than letting us drink more than we should have. I know I was complicit enough on my own, thrilled as I was to get away with our adventure. I was swaying a bit myself, but at least I was able to shepherd Dot between the bathroom and her bedcovers, the cleaning bucket responsibly placed on the floor near her head in case she upchucked again during the night. My own inebriated condition was probably for the best; otherwise, I might have been more perturbed with our situation than I was at the time. It certainly could have been me on the cold tile floor with my head in a toilet. I hoped Dot would take care of me, were I the ill-fated one.

It wasn't until this morning that I felt truly irritated with myself for allowing my mild infatuation with Herschel to get the best of my senses. Still, I won't mention this incident to Kip or Heckie, or even the twins who would probably just laugh at naïve little me for being drunk for the first time. Maybe I can tell Catherine. Surely, she would lend a sympathetic ear.

And maybe she will share her secret with me.

CHAPTER FOUR

Elle

As she pulled into the driveway at four-thirty, Elle saw her handsome fiancé waiting for her at his uncle's private dock across from the house Nate rented from him. Squinting at her from the afternoon sun, he waved her over when she got out of her car. *This is a nice surprise*, she thought, pocketing her keys and strolling across the street to meet him. Spanish moss fluttered from the live oaks in the breeze, beckoning her to the water. Water. It had such a soothing effect on the soul. As did Nate. And she could use some soothing.

The sound of her footsteps on the weathered wood was comforting as well. Not the hurried frantic pace of her steps at work, racing in and out of the walk-in refrigerator and back and forth from the kitchen to the café, but a leisurely pat-pat-pat-pat down the dock to meet the man of her dreams. *Yes, pinch yourself, you lucky bitch! The man of your dreams! He swept you off your feet by proposing and then took you to Italy for the vacation of your life.*

"Hello, my quaran-king!"

"Hey, quaran-queen!" Nate greeted her, the grin and the sound of his voice giving her that little tug in her gut that drew her to him like a wave to the shore. He'd raised a beer can and a wine bottle, looking to each.

"Your preference, milady?" he asked with a slight bow, his brilliant blue eyes never leaving hers. And that randy smile…*oh my!*

Elle giggled. They'd been watching far too many British series on Netflix these days.

"Which is colder?" she asked with a throaty laugh and her best English accent.

"Hah, need you ask?" he scoffed, extending the beer can toward her.

"And it's a Corona! You have such a sense of humor!"

"We have about an hour before dinner and then our front porch reading with AB and Bernie. Your gondola awaits," Nate said, gesturing to his Carolina Skiff moored at the floating dock.

"Aw, this is so sweet! What's the occasion?"

"It's Thursday," he said, giving her a little wink as he returned the wine bottle to his cooler and closed it.

"Okay…and what makes Thursday special?"

Nate grinned. "Because you're here and it's a beautiful spring afternoon, and because I felt like we needed a little cruise for a change of scenery. I'm bored to death sitting in the house all day trying to do something productive. So, here's to Thursday afternoons," he said, popping the top of his beer and stretching it toward hers.

"Well then, Captain, take me away!" she laughed, opening her own can and clinking it against his.

She'd been waiting for his kiss, and he did not disappoint. Slipping his free hand under her hair, he gently pulled her head in to kiss her, wrapping his other arm firmly around her waist, being careful not to spill his beer. She allowed herself to melt into his arms, returning his passionate kiss. "Mmm!" he said, releasing her and kissing the bridge of her nose. "Best part of my day. So far."

After stowing the cooler onboard, he helped her aboard the skiff and started the motor. As it purred to life, he released the dock lines and tossed them to the floor of the boat. They met at the bench seat of the center console, and he turned the craft away from the dock, pointing the bow south toward the bridge that would take them down the Intracoastal Waterway.

"So, how was your day?" she asked, holding her hair in the wind as they picked up a little more speed in the channel.

"Oh, same as usual. Lots of editing. Trying to think of something we can put together after these shows are all done. And how are things at Bake My Day?"

"Actually, things are really good. We're in the process of setting up a curbside marketplace on our patio."

"I'd kill for some excitement like that."

"I can imagine. Monai and Allyson are all over it. It's going to be very safe and user-friendly for people who want to place orders and pick up. We have Roxy answering the phone all day. Everyone is calling to see if we're still open and wanting to help us out. The public support is so nice! But they want to talk *forever*, and we have less time than before to spend on the phone! Jordan and Scooter are doing most of the baking. I do all the decorating and supervise the rest. Sarah is working on updating the website and adding new photographs. She's our social media specialist. Honestly, I never expected them to have so many skills or to pitch in like this!"

"You have an awesome staff."

"They are the best! I never thought we'd be this busy during the pandemic."

"It's good that you guys are thinking outside the box."

"Yes, well, we all want the bakery to stay in business, now that we know we are an essential business. God knows we sell comfort food.

Everybody needs cake at a time like this. Something to brighten these depressing days."

"Absolutely! Birthdays haven't been canceled."

"Or anniversaries or St. Patrick's Day…or breakfast."

"Or Thursdays," he said, chuckling and slipping his arm around her waist.

"Or Thursdays!" she grinned and took the wheel at his gesture. He pointed to a place under the drawbridge where she was to aim the bow. They watched as a lone man and his dog roamed Palm Tree Island just to the east, the little sand bar now exposed at low tide. A giant fake palm tree and an American flag staked claim on that spit of sand, thus the name. It was usually crowded with beachgoers in the summer. Golden sun sparkled on the water that slapped at the boat's hull as they cruised by without leaving a wake. Next, the public docks, where a variety of motorized crafts were moored, came into view.

"Any more wedding cancelations?"

"Not today. I don't have any big cakes in the works, but we've had orders for smaller ones. I have a few brides who are trying to work through the madness. Cupcakes are the perfect thing for self-service at a small COVID wedding."

They were quiet a moment. Then Nate cleared his throat and spoke.

"I know you must be worried about our wedding. We can postpone it if you want." Their spontaneous Valentine's Day getaway to Turin had been way too much fun. They'd skied, drank hot chocolate, eaten delicious food, hung out in the many palatial bars, and gone sightseeing until their feet fell off. They'd joked that it was like a honeymoon before the wedding.

She scoffed. "Yeah, life is uncertain. Have your honeymoon first."

"I thought it was especially brilliant."

"It was wonderfully brilliant, actually. Has your family asked you about our plans?"

"Nope. No pressure at all from them. This is just me talking. We can do something when this all blows over. I know a really good bakery," he said, raising an eyebrow.

She smiled. "Right. A *big do*. And everybody wants to see me in a white dress," Elle said and blew a raspberry.

"That's true, me included. After you've made cakes and baked everyone else's day, you kinda deserve your own special day. I think most people would agree. You *do* deserve this." At her hesitation he added, "It doesn't have to be huge. It could be sooner rather than later. Completely up to you."

Elle was quiet for a moment, feeling the wind blow back her hair and the sun warm her face. She had dragged her feet with the plans after they first became engaged. Her new friends didn't understand why, but *really?* Who would ever have thought she deserved anything like this? She was still that bad girl who had drugged a boy in high school to take sexual advantage of him, which made her the local pariah to her peers. But by age nineteen, she'd paid her debt to society after serving a year in the state's women's prison. Orange jumpsuit and the whole nine yards. And during her time served, she'd had a baby out of wedlock. A son by a boy—a different boy—named Aiden, who stood by her, knowing that to love her would be his undoing. Aiden had grown to be a man and still stood by her and their son. And then last year in a sad twist of fate, he had died. So yes, that was the girl she was. Nate knew all of this, and yet he interpreted her transgressions as a mere conduct mark on her report card. God bless him, Nate had done everything in his power to help her move on. At his urging, she had forgiven herself. Over and over again, she had forgiven herself, but somehow, she couldn't allow herself to let it go completely, no matter how many times she sang to herself the hit song from *Frozen*. She was that girl. Girls like that didn't deserve big dos in white dresses.

"You're hesitating again," Nate said, taking note of the commercial docks as he covered her hand on the wheel and watched her steer past the waterfront restaurants. They were passing the Bridge Tender's impressive dockside. Because of COVID, there were no people milling about on the deck as usual for a nice afternoon. It was sadly strange, driving home the point that life was changed. The Dockside was coming up. It was where she'd eaten her first meal at Wrightsville Beach, and where she'd made her first friend, Randy, who was one of the managers there.

Nate continued. "I think I know what this is all about. Let me name some folks who would love to attend your wedding: your son Joey, for one, AB, Mr. May, Patsy, your cousin Judy, your friend Marcus who's responsible for getting you here in the first place, everybody at the bakery, Randy from the Dockside here," he said, gesturing to the right as they passed the deserted dockside bar. "Jimmy Burns your handyman, my entire family and my friends you've met who all say they love you. Oh, and Jewel, who used to work at the winery next to your bakery. And Brandon her ex, who still does."

"Well…okay, that's about twenty people. I think that's the max for allowable gatherings these days. Hardly seems worth doing, don't you think?"

"What I think…is that you would make them all really happy allowing them to help you celebrate with me and dance at our wedding. Raise a glass with us. I want to marry you because I love you enough to shout it from the mountaintops—or across the ICW—or whatever, so I wish you'd give me the opportunity to do it. See, I think this is a big deal, Elle." He turned to her. "You're *my* big deal. I've been waiting a long time for you to show up. I can't let you sell yourself short. I don't want to sneak away and elope like I'm ashamed of us. I want you to have your special day. And maybe we can't have the dancing, but—"

"Okay! Stop it, please! You were so wonderful to take me away like you did. I mean, a mountain girl like me who's never left the state living it up with you in *Italy*? And honestly…. It's so weird to me. After I spent so much of my life dying for attention, it suddenly seems so inappropriate and embarrassing to want all this." She saw the compassion in his handsome face and immediately felt selfish. "But for you, I'll do it." She laughed. "And only because you want it so much. You should have your special day, too." *You are way more than I deserve*, she was unable to say.

He grinned in response.

"That's my girl. Thank you." He kissed her again. "You will *not* regret this."

When the four of them were seated on the porch, the older adults masked, and appropriately socially distanced, Anne Borden handed Elle the letter she had chosen to begin the evening's reading. Each couple had brought a blanket to snuggle under since the air had cooled down after sunset. A bottle of wine was always part of their tradition, as well as dessert—white chocolate and macadamia nut cookies Elle had brought tonight from Bake My Day.

"I thought this particular letter from my mother's Aunt Andrea might best be read by our bride-to-be," AB said, and Elle thought she detected a slight wink.

September 30, 1928

Dearest Sylvie,

I'm so happy that you have written to me and described your new collegiate experiences! Your roommate and new friends sound so interesting. Your classes sound fascinating. I know you are learning a lot and I am certain you are an asset to the Conservatory. Do you still like your teacher, Mr. Finch? It's important to have a mentor you like and respect. What are you playing? And how is the accompanying going? Has the girl warmed up to you yet? When will you perform? I know, so many questions. I am living vicariously through you. This is the time of your life! I hope you are duly soaking it all in.

Your father and I miss you so much! I am teaching piano lessons up until the wedding at your house, and then I will begin seeing all my students in my new home after Christmas. You may recall that Benton has a very nice upright Baldwin at his house. It will be quite a comedown from your magnificent Baldwin baby grand, but it will be sufficient for my needs.

You will be glad to know that your father is ready to hire another housekeeper beginning in November. Nellie, Pearl's daughter, is capable and friendly, but there will never be another like our dear friend Pearl. It was kind of your father to understand that I need some time to prepare for the wedding, as small as it is going to be, and to move my things and furniture into Benton's house, so Nellie's help will be quite welcome. There is so much to do by Thanksgiving!

I know you wanted to hear the details about the wedding. We are planning to have the ceremony at your house. It seems silly to have it at church since we plan to keep it small. Since both of us have been married before, it isn't proper to have a big to-do anyway. I plan to wear an ivory tea-length dress with lace on the bodice. You may wear whatever you would like. Your copper-beaded dress that you wore to the summer dances at Lumina is so pretty on you, and it would be just right for Thanksgiving. But if you want to have something new, please buy yourself something up there and I will send you the money for it. You should splurge and find something lovely that you might wear again. You always look so pretty in green, or blue to match your eyes! Just let me know. We'll each carry a nosegay of flowers. Your dad is going to give me away. I envision you and then me walking down the stairs where he will meet me in the foyer where the ceremony will take place. Benton's father will, of course, be his best man. Guests will be seated in the parlor where they can see and hear easily. Father Williams from St. Paul's has agreed to officiate. One of my students will play the piano. We'll have punch and wed-

ding cake in the dining room afterward, so it will be an intimate affair. If it's nice weather, we hope to spill out onto the porch. Please bring an escort if you like. Kip says Heckie will be home for the holiday, so maybe you might think about inviting him. Can you believe he is a midshipman at the U.S. Naval Academy? I have always liked that one! (Wink-wink!)

That's all for now. Please write again soon!

Fondly,

Aunt Andrea

Elle could barely contain herself. After they had all read the original manuscript about Lumina, they'd learned from Anne Borden that Sylvie had married Heckie and he was Anne Borden's father, so Elle was interested to find out when their courtship began. "AB, do you think Andrea's wedding is where Sylvie and Heckie started their romance?"

AB shook her head. "Your guess is as good as mine, Elle. My memory is so vague. I always thought Mama said they started dating after she left the Conservatory. I could be wrong, of course."

"Well, we know Heckie was a way better catch than Herschel seems to be."

Nate stuck up for the fellow immediately. "Oh, I don't think Herschel seems all that bad. He just likes to walk on the wild side."

"Sylvie was probably overreacting to being in danger at the speakeasy," said Bernard. "She was a bit naïve. He sounds like he would have protected her if anything had happened."

"Oh, I think all the Oberlin students were so worried about making a wrong move and getting themselves into trouble," said AB.

"Sylvie was smart, looking for proof before she could trust the guy," said Elle.

"I think it's sad the way Andrea feels as if she's not worthy of the wedding she deserves," said Nate. Elle glanced warily at him.

"Yes, I can see why you would feel that way, Nate," AB replied, "but back then, second marriages weren't celebrated like they are today."

"But I would think they would have been more and more common, considering all the men who died during World War I."

"Common perhaps, but not celebrated. In those days, weddings were assumed to be for virgins. Yes," added AB, smiling at Nate's surprised face. "These days, weddings are completely over the top and ridiculously expensive. I think young people getting married during the pandemic might realize how little a couple needs to have a lovely day. After all, it is just *one day*. Why should any bride want to spend so much money on one day? I have heard the average wedding these days costs upwards of $30,000. I think that's obscene!" AB stroked her neck as if reaching for pearls.

Elle felt the heat creeping up from her neck to her face. The price she'd been hearing from brides was almost double that. She felt Nate's hand give her shoulder a light squeeze from the porch swing where they sat. Elle looked quickly to him, a warning not to reveal their plans just yet. He smiled and raised his chin in subtle acknowledgment.

"You know, AB, Elle and I kind of agree with you," Nate began as Elle tensed. "I think smaller is way better. How can any bride and groom expect to talk to hundreds of people in just a few hours? Now, with the small, outdoor ceremonies people are forced to have, they can have fewer people. That way, the pressure is off to invite people they really don't want to have and just invite the ones who are the most special."

"That makes so much sense to me," agreed Bernard. "I remember at our wedding walking into the reception and not recognizing a soul!" He laughed and shook his head. "I knew I was at the right church, but I thought I was at the wrong party!"

Elle giggled.

"And that was even before weddings got so large!" said AB. "You and Daphne had the biggest one I'd ever been to at that point. Daphne was high society, though, so there was no choice. But, of course, she loved every minute of it! I believe you did too, Bernie." She glanced at Elle and Nate. "They were married at First Presbyterian Church in town in April when the azaleas and dogwoods were in bloom. It was just lovely, petals blowing everywhere," AB said, waving her hand to recreate the image for them.

"Yes, it was grand," Bernard said, smiling at AB. "And you were quite a lovely bridesmaid."

A heavy silence hung between the four of them.

"So, Elle and Nate," said AB, "I didn't mean to rain on any plans you're making. How are your plans coming?" Elle cringed inwardly at the question. "I mean, of course, once the virus blows over and we can all come out from under our rocks?" She laughed.

Elle and Nate glanced at each other and finally Elle spoke.

"Actually, we just discussed it today. Everything is up in the air right now, so we haven't made any plans yet. It will be something understated. Just family and a few friends," Elle said. "Of course, we expect you both to be there!"

Everyone smiled, and Bernard was the first to respond.

"I think that's a fine idea! The warm weather is on the way. It's already proving to be a beautiful spring! You deserve exactly the kind of celebration you want! We'll all be ready for a party by then. Whenever *then* is…" he said.

"Oh, how *fun*!" AB said, clapping her hands. "Please let me help you plan! I love to plan parties. I've never had a chance to plan a wedding!"

Elle did not expect this kind of positive reaction to their news. Without a mother—or even a best friend—to help, she had thought she would have to plan her celebration alone. Of course, her employees at the bakery would be dying to participate, she suddenly realized. Having AB on board surely would make her day special. Elle felt a slow smile bloom across her lips.

"I would be honored to have your help. Thank you, AB."

SYLVIE

October 2, 1928

Dear Diary,

I am so happy to write that I have had a breakthrough with Willemina! At least I think it is such. After her voice lesson today, we were packing up our music when I invited her to sit with me in the Arboretum. I frequently take a break there between my morning classes since there isn't sufficient time to secure a practice room in Rice Hall or even to study at the library. I find sitting amid the beauty of nature to be a balm to the frantic pace of the Conservatory. Admittedly, I was surprised when she agreed to join me.

This morning was as pure and crisp a fall day as I have come to expect and enjoy here. As we sat on one of the benches in our sweaters, I pulled two small apples from my bag and offered her one. She reacted as though I were the Evil Queen from Snow White!

"It's a honey crisp," I stated, hoping she really didn't think I'd poisoned it. "They're my favorite."

"Thank you," Willemina said quietly. She took the apple and bit into it gingerly. She is quite beautiful with her almond-shaped eyes and full lips. Her brown skin is flawless, and she keeps her hair in the neatest braid that wraps her head like a crown. She even holds her head like a queen, although she is still so soft-spoken and reserved. It is hard to tell if she likes me or not. I have never heard her speak unless she is asked a direct question.

Suddenly uncomfortable, I realized I was going to have to conduct an interview to encourage any conversation.

"Do you like it here, Mina?"

"Yes."

"I do too," I said. "It's so different here than at home, though. I like the weather so far. My hair doesn't curl here like it does in Wilmington where the air is so humid and sticky."

She peered at my hair and raised her eyebrows.

"It's not so different here for me," she said, taking another bite of her apple. "You won't like the winters here. After Thanksgiving, it's very gray and gloomy. And cold."

"Oh. Everyone keeps mentioning that. You're not too far from home. But still, do you miss it?"

"Yes, sometimes. I miss my family, but I like being away sometimes too."

"I miss my family too. Do you have a big family?"

"Yes. I have four brothers and a sister. I'm the youngest."

I smiled. "I have one brother…now. Now, I'm the youngest. We lost our mother and two of our younger siblings during the flu epidemic in '26."

"Oh. That's so sad, Sylvie. I can't imagine losing my mother. I have never lost a family member except for my grandparents."

"Did they live in Cleveland too?"

"Yes. They moved to Cleveland from Maryland after the War. The Civil War. My grandfather was from Wilmington."

She looked at me straight on and I swallowed audibly.

"My Wilmington?" I asked, wiping my mouth with my handkerchief.

"I suppose it is your Wilmington. I don't believe he ever thought it was *his* Wilmington," she said with an odd smile.

"What do you mean?"

She was quiet a moment, as if considering if she should continue.

"My grandfather was an escaped slave."

"Oh." I didn't know how else to respond.

"Do you live on a plantation, Sylvie?"

"Oh, no. We live in town. My father owns a gentlemen's clothing shop. My parents are from Ohio, actually."

"Of course. I have heard you say that."

"My parents' family did not own slaves, and we have never approved of the practice of slavery."

Mina regarded me curiously, making me a bit nervous. I asked her another question. "Do you know the story of your grandfather's escape?"

She hesitated again, so I said, "I'm sorry to be nosy. I'm just so curious since I've been here, learning about the history of Oberlin and how it has to do with former slaves migrating to the North. I know so little. Do you know his story?"

"Yes. It's passed down to us until we can tell it accurately ourselves. Our family is very proud of him and what he did. My mother reminds us to be proud of who we are and to tell his story whenever we can. Her father escaped during an outbreak of yellow fever in 1862. It was such a bad epidemic that everyone in Wilmington had either fled town or was staying inside to stay safe."

I nodded, knowing very well how contagious the mosquito-borne illness can be. She went on.

"My grandfather and some other men sneaked away from their slave quarters at Mr. Nixon's town house one night while the entire city was sheltering inside. They were able to rendezvous on the riverfront with some brave fellows who took them in boats down the Cape Fear River to the U.S. Navy's blockade. Then they boarded one of President Lincoln's Navy boats and they got away. My grandfather and some of the others joined the U.S. Navy so he wouldn't have to worry for his safety. Besides, they didn't have anywhere else to go, so the Navy took them in."

"You said Mr. Nixon? I've heard of him. Is he the one who owned the peanut plantation north of town?"

She seemed surprised that I knew of him.

"Yes. My grandfather worked the peanut farm at first, but then he was moved over to the house in town when Mr. Nixon realized he was a skilled stone mason. Mr. Nixon also had a house on Chestnut Street where my grandfather lived and worked. Nixon hired him out to work for other white people in town, who were building grand homes. Luckily for my grandfather, the house was close enough to the river for him and the others to manage the escape. They got away with it, thanks to the yellow fever epidemic, but they were mighty scared."

"I can only imagine," I said and nodded. I had heard stories about what happened to runaway slaves when their masters caught up with them. I had seen pictures, too, of Negroes lynched while white men stood in crowds to watch. Those pictures made me sick to my stomach. It also made me feel ashamed and I wished I didn't know. Those pictures always made me think about Pearl and her husband Gregory, who tuned our piano. I couldn't imagine something like that happening to them.

"I'm sorry for what he had to go through."

"You didn't do it, Sylvie." She looked at me evenly. "I can also understand your curiosity."

"But I can't imagine always living in fear of a whip, or a rope in a tree." I shook my head. "What a wonderful thing it is to be free."

"Yes." Willemina nodded, finishing her apple. "Yes, it surely is. He said he always had a good life. He learned how to read and write—in secret, of course. It was against the law in the South for slaves to be taught reading and writing. They weren't supposed to get rebellious ideas. They weren't trusted at all. The kitchen slaves even had to whistle while they carried food from the kitchen to the house so the white folks would know they weren't eating it along the way. So anyway, when he left the Navy, he moved to Ohio and got a job setting type for the town's black newspaper."

I realized then that Mina seemed as brave as her grandfather for speaking to me about these topics. Colored people back home rarely spoke so openly to whites. This was a new experience for me. Mina was a new experience for me.

"Your grandfather sounds very brave."

"He was. He had no other choice. And he was lucky too. Because of him, I've had a good life too…an even better life than he had. Better than some still do, especially in the South. And look at me now, just like you are, a student here at this wonderful, renowned conservatory where I feel safe and protected and where people value what I do. Telling *you* my grandfather's story makes me appreciate him and the people like him who did those brave things. Look at me…."

"Yes, look at you. I know your family must be proud of you. You're going to be famous someday; I'm sure of it. You sing with such little effort, and your voice is like none I've ever heard. You keep getting better and better every time you work with Miss Devereaux."

Willemina's lips pushed out slowly to a smile. "She makes me believe I can do anything. Not everyone gets a chance like this. To be here and to have this experience, I feel blessed and grateful. I don't mind working hard to get what I want. It scares me, though. I hope I can do well enough to stay on."

"Of course, you will!"

She glanced at me as if she wanted to tell a secret.

"And you…you'll do all right here too, Sylvie. You play so beautifully. There's nothing for you to be afraid of. And you're kind. I'm glad you're my accompanist. You're very good."

"It's certainly my pleasure. I so hoped I wouldn't have to play for Dot."

Willemina grinned and then she giggled. She laughed. She looked at me and we both laughed loudly.

CHAPTER FIVE

Nate

Nate disconnected the call from his Uncle Phil. Staring at the phone in his hand, he could hardly believe what he had just heard. It had been a brief conversation. Phil didn't know when he would get to visit at his own house to see Nate, or to see anyone else for that matter anytime soon. He was a pulmonologist at a busy hospital in Arlington, Virginia, and the pandemic was already requiring the staff to convert wards to COVID care isolation floors. He was working over eighty hours a week already, coming home to his usually empty townhouse, disinfecting himself and washing his clothes, sleeping a couple of hours, and returning to the hospital to put on the hazard gear and start all over again. Patients were dying more often than recovering from the new virus. Ventilators were in short supply as well as masks, face shields, and other personal protective equipment that had dry-rotted in storage and was now unavailable for purchase. Overall, the hospital felt confident they could handle the influx of patients, provided the numbers remained steady and people abided by the CDC's advice. His advice to Nate: stay at home, wear a mask, and check on the people you love. Also, and more chilling, he would prepare an email to instruct Nate what to do with his home and his boat if anything happened to him. He would copy the email to his brother, who was Nate's father and next of kin.

Nate sighed deeply and leaned forward, resting his elbows on his knees, and ran his hands through his hair. Phil had divorced Aunt Carla years ago. They had no children. Carla had remarried, this time to a business mogul, and now lived in Portugal. Phil was Nate's favorite relative and had graciously offered his summer home on Wrightsville Beach for Nate to live in while he worked in Virginia. Nate, admittedly spoiled by the opportunity, took care of the home across the street from the Intracoastal Waterway, maintained Phil's boat—a sweet Grady White center console—in addition to his own Carolina Skiff, and paid a modest rent mostly to cover utilities, a win-win for them both. Phil visited in the spring and fall, his favorite times for fishing with Nate and being on the beach with fewer tourists and less traffic. They were having the time of their lives together during those visits. Phil had met Elle on one of those visits and loved her immediately. He believed Nate had hit a homerun finding her. Even Nate's sister in Chattanooga was envious of his situation, if only for a free place to stay at the beach. It was unlikely that she or anyone else—even Phil—would be visiting. Travel was strongly discouraged. The beaches and public docks were closed anyway. Nate was lucky to have a boat for some sort of escape on the waterway.

Staying at home was the mandate until the end of April unless one had an essential job like Elle did. What if she got sick? What would he do? Was the Wilmington hospital any better equipped than hospitals anywhere else in the country? Surely, it was all relative. What if he got sick? How would Elle cope? Would she stay here or move back into the guest house at AB's? And what about AB and Bernie May? His own parents? People their age were dying from this thing. So many questions, so few answers. This was the most uncertainty he had ever faced. It was the end of March, and this virus wasn't going away anytime soon, he feared. He didn't even know whether his job security could last a long haul.

Every day, the president and his COVID response team gave a briefing, as did the governor of North Carolina. National borders were closed, and 2000 people in the United States had already died, three in North Carolina. New York was a disaster and completely shut down. FEMA was to set up makeshift hospitals in places like the Jacob Javits Center. No one knew anything except that numbers of infections and hospitalizations were going up and no one could get anything they needed. COVID testing was in short supply. Only those with symptoms were able to get tested, so what was the point? American companies were stepping up to develop tests, make personal protective equipment and hand sanitizer. More than two million people had filed for unemployment, and the government had passed a stimulus relief bill. Checks would be going out in the mail in just days. The stock market had crashed in February but was starting to take a turn upward. Gas prices were down to $1.50 a gallon since no one was driving anywhere. It was a lot to take in over such a short time, especially hearing the hospital statistics directly from Uncle Phil.

At least there was Sylvie's diary reading to look forward to tonight on AB's front porch with Bernie and Elle. Nate was already longing to see Elle's pretty face and hold her body close afterward. Maybe the four of them could have a couple of hours' worth of normalcy to take the edge off the situation. He clapped his hands on his knees and cleared his throat. He would call his parents later. For now, he needed to take a walk.

A long walk.

ANNE BORDEN

"Welcome, y'all!" AB said, eyes crinkling above her mask as her young guests walked up the porch steps, that comforting sound of old wood beneath feet, the sound of friendship. Nate and Elle looked a bit worse for the wear, AB thought. Bernie also smiled at them with his eyes as he opened the wine at the wicker table.

"Hey," Elle said, putting on her mask as she crossed the porch to accept Bernie's offer of a glass of white wine.

"Good evening!" he greeted them. "Wine, Nate?"

"Oh, hell yeah!" Nate said. "Thanks, Bernie; it's been a day."

They stood safely apart while Nate updated them on his uncle's phone call.

"We called all our family members today just to check in," said Elle. "Thankfully, all are well. And then, to top it off, we found out that Patsy's mother has COVID at the retirement center where she lives."

"Oh no! Our neighbor Patsy?" asked AB.

"Yes," said Nate. "And of course, they can't allow her to visit, so Patsy's stuck here worrying about her."

"What kind of a place does she live in?" asked Bernie.

"She has an apartment in a building there. They provide some assistance, but for now, everyone is locked down. Her breathing is normal right now, so they check on her a couple of times a day to make sure she's okay. They leave her meals outside the door. Patsy talks to her on the phone twice a day too. It's all she can do right now."

"I'm sure she feels so helpless," said AB, and the others nodded in agreement.

"Well, I know it's not much, but I've been sewing masks," AB said, handing Elle a brown paper shopping bag. "There are a few in here that I thought you two could wear and several more for the girls at the bakery. They can wear them to work, wash them out in the sink at night, and hang them to dry overnight for the next day."

"Oh, AB, this is great! Thank you so much!" Elle exclaimed. "It seems so wasteful to throw away the paper masks each day. And I don't know if I'll be able to get more by the time we need them. Where did you find these nice fabrics?" she asked, looking inside the bag at the assortment of masks.

"You know, I was a costume designer in the film industry before I retired. I have scads of fabric scraps and elastic and everything I needed. I found a pattern online and went from there."

"She Googled it!" said Bernie proudly. "There were several YouTube videos, so she watched one and took off with her sewing machine. I'll bet she made twenty masks just today!"

"Wow! That's wonderful, AB!"

"I've been reading in the news about how the essential workers need these. I know a little girl who works at the drive-thru at Chick-fil-A, and she was using a bandana folded around hair ties. She said she could hardly breathe in it! So, I made a few for the kids that work there. If you know of anyone else who needs them, just let me know."

"You have quite the cottage industry going on!" said Nate.

"Bernie has been watching videos on how to make face shields out of those plastic transparency sheets, weather stripping, and elastic. He has all that stuff at his house. You just staple it all together and voilà! We can supply whoever needs what. It sure beats sitting at home with nothing to do…well, after the gardening and cooking and cleaning are all done."

"We look forward to our reading get-togethers with you both," said Bernie. "They are definitely the highlight of the day. I'm ready to find out what happens with Sylvie and Willemina. Shall we?"

CATHERINE

October 1, 1928

Dearest Sylvie,

I think of you so often here at St. Mary's. I truly miss our enchanting evenings at the Lumina dances and the friendship we kindled over the summer. I hope you are doing well, and that conservatory life agrees with you. I cannot imagine how you would not like it, and I am certain you are well-received at Oberlin. I can't wait to hear all about it at Thanksgiving when we are all together again!

*For me, being back at St. Mary's is often very difficult with so many curious about Clifton's death and my possible role in it. I had hoped being back here would take my mind off the whole thing, but it seems I will never be able to let go of it. I find myself quite distracted from my studies, which I hope will come to an end in December, so I can move on to college far away where no one will know of my circumstances. Kip does his best to keep me sane, and I do love him for it. He takes me to football games and dances. We have been on scads of picnics and to some movies, but our best times are just when we sit and talk. I feel as though I can tell your brother anything and the world will be all right. What's troubling me lately is that *you* don't know what happened to me. Since I treasure our friendship as though you are my sister, I do so want to share with you what happened last summer, and well before then. It is important to me that you understand everything. Then, I think I will finally feel free.*

Let's plan some time to talk after your aunt's wedding. Kip has invited me to be his date and I understand that you are planning to invite Heckie. Hopefully, we can pair the boys off and have some time to ourselves so I can share my story with you and hear about your exciting studies!

Until then…

Yours truly,

Cat

SYLVIE

October 5, 1928

Dear Diary,

I have just returned from dinner following our Friday convocation and found that Catherine has finally written me a letter! I knew something happened with her last summer! I knew there was more to the story about Clifton's accident than I have been told, so I am dying to hear from her at Thanksgiving. I will be on pins and needles until then, and I have written to tell her so. I kept forgetting to write to Heckie and invite him to Aunt Andrea's wedding, although I am sure she will send him a proper invitation, so I dashed off a brief note to him at the Naval Academy to ask him to be my escort. I am looking forward to seeing him. I'm sure each of us will have changed for the better when we reunite at Thanksgiving. I surely do miss my family and friends!

As for my friends here, music has taken over our lives completely, as it should. There have been no more visits to the speakeasy for the four of us—or at least for Dot and me. That little escapade, daring as it was, may well have been the last bit of fun I will have at Oberlin! Boo! Bart and Herschel always seem to be together, naturally since they are roommates, walking to classes, studying, waiting for practice rooms, and eating in their boarding house, except when we all dine together at the Oberlin Inn following our Friday convocations. I don't know what those boys do when they are not with us girls. If they have gone to the speakeasy, Dot and I know nothing of it. Our lives involve little more than attending classes and practicing, eating, and sleeping, and then more practicing to memorize our pieces. After a solid month of Conservatory life here, I am beginning to understand the competitiveness among the music performance students.

What I initially thought was self-absorption with some of the music students may well be a disguise for anxiety over the constant worry that comes from not knowing whether one is good enough to succeed as a performer. I may be in the minority, but I believe success is possible with hard work. Each of us must believe that. For me, performance has always been exhilarating. I feel comfortable under the tutelage of Mr. Finch, and even of Miss Devereaux, although vicariously through her teaching of Mina, but some students don't have the same assurance from their teachers, as I surmised from Bart, Herschel, and Dot's commiserations at dinner this evening. Mina said nothing, nor did I. I believe we are deep in the weeding out process for the freshmen students. Although the weeding is not surprising, I often wonder which of us may not return after the Christmas break. On Sundays when all the music students line up outside Rice Hall for the practice rooms after chapel services, I can almost feel their fervent prayers!

Conservatory life is different for us as opposed to the other students in the general college who seem to have endless time on their hands for football games and dances, while we toil away at our talents. The only time I have found for respite is the short break I take in the arboretum on Tuesdays after Mina's voice lesson. I love to bathe in the autumnal beauty of the scarlet and golden trees around the duck pond. I try to walk by there as often as I can, just to drink in the calming scenery.

The dreary weather that has set in here as well as the grueling schedule has taken a toll on my spirits. Our campus sits close to the shores of Lake Erie, which I am told accounts for so many gray days. I envy Kip and Catherine's social life of dances and football games, picnics, and parties. Maybe when we are upper classmen here, we, too, will be able to enjoy those same social rewards. We simply plunge ahead each day and do our best to encourage each other—Mina and I, especially.

On Tuesday, there will be a special treat for Mina and me. Miss Devereaux's upper-class students will perform for us during the convocation hour in her studio. I am invited since I am Mina's accompanist. Each student will explain what they will sing, what they know about the piece and the composer, and how they prepare for performing. Miss Devereaux's voice students are the best at Oberlin. These performances should be very educational. I will have a similar experience next Thursday with all of Mr. Finch's students, except that he hosts his recitals at his home on Professor Street and his wife serves dinner to all the students. I can't wait to have a home-cooked meal! I hear he has a finely tuned Steinway, so I am eagerly looking forward to hearing it played. Maybe he will delight us with his own performance. Of course, on Friday again, convocation will be required, which I always enjoy. Freshmen will be invited to perform in the second year if we are up to par. It has happened on rare occasions that some freshmen are allowed to perform in the first year, but I am certainly not holding my breath that I will be asked! Still, I cannot wait for my turn to play one of those fine instruments in the majestic Warner Hall.

Tuesday, October 9, 1928

Dear Diary,

What a day in the Conservatory! It was a day to fully realize the power of practice and preparation. Mina and I were enraptured listening to the upper-class students perform their pieces in Miss Devereaux's studio. All her students who ordinarily look like regular nineteen and twenty-year-old girls in their plaid dresses and plain faces transformed into operatic stars as they took their places in the curve of Miss Devereaux's baby grand. Professional polish is truly something Miss Devereaux has taught and taught them well. Italian arias and French art songs flowed beautifully from their lips as if no exertion or concentration were required. Each of the women had her own special tonal quality to the voice, whether alto or mezzo soprano, but the professional quality of the performances was outstanding with each girl.

I was floating, but Willemina was shaking as we left the studio.

"Mina, what's wrong?" I asked, placing a steadying hand on her arm.

"I'll never be able to do this," she murmured in my ear as we headed down the stairwell and burst onto an equally disheartening fall day.

"Do what?"

Willemina glanced around quickly before she answered me. "I can't perform like that. Ever. I might as well quit and go home. Oh, lordy Lord! Oh Lord, help me."

"What?" I laughed. "You are being truly ridiculous. You are one of the best voice students in the Conservatory. Why would you say a thing like that?"

"Because I know myself. That's why. I don't have the courage to get up there and do what they all just did, much less get up and perform in front of the whole student body at convocation!"

"But that's precisely why we are all here!" I said, trying to reassure her. Her fear finally dawned on me. "Mina, do you have stage fright?"

"Yes. I have since I got here. I've never felt like this before. I don't know why, but I do."

"It's just jitters from listening to the others. I know they sounded exceptionally good today, but you are just as good. You will be as polished as they are by the time your turn comes. It shouldn't scare you to hear good students sing. It should inspire you to be as good as they are. And you are just as good or even better. You're especially better than the coloratura who sang the Mozart aria. Miss Devereaux should have had you sing 'Beau Soir' for them," I said, hoping to cheer Mina's spirits.

Instead, she shook with the image. "Hah! No, no. Oh, I'm so glad she didn't. I would have died of embarrassment. Thankfully, she didn't trick me into singing unprepared."

"She wouldn't do that! And I saw her watching you while the others were singing. I think she just can't wait to show you off! In due time, of course," I added as her face blanched.

We need a diversion, even if I must make one up myself.

After dinner this evening, we went with the boys over to the recreation center so they, Mina, Dot, and I could listen to records on the Victrola. We looked through the record collection and found some upbeat jazz to dance to. As always, Herschel was game to do something different, so I tried to teach them the Shag. I explained it was the dance our friend Lewis Hall invented and debuted at Lumina over the summer. Hersch was a quick study, and in a few minutes, we had the basics going reasonably well. Bartholomew partnered with me next, and he was more awkward, but I was sure he would get it eventually. Mina and Dot were genuinely happy to be dancing again, especially Dot since she has taken such a shine to Bart and the dance required holding hands. Our laughter was contagious, attracting some of the other girls, who came in to watch us. The center's director came in to chaperone our decadence, and even she had a smile on her face! She watched the new dance steps as we continued our dance party on the hardwood floor, which almost had the feel of summer nights at Lumina.

I tried my best to explain the place, our Palace of Light on Wrightsville Beach—how it is lit with thousands of bulbs, torching up the night sky, how the dance floor opened to the ocean breezes on three sides, and the beach cars we rode in over the waterways from various stops through town. I suddenly had everyone's attention, so I described the orchestra and the intermissions, even our walks over the trolley trestle to the sound side where we watched sailboats moored in the moonlight. Because the director was enthralled as well, I left out the parts about the men's buried flasks and the jetty-jumping that got poor Kip in trouble with Catherine's father. My friends were fascinated by my description of the fifty-foot surf screen on the beach that played the silent films where patrons could sit in Lumina's stadium seats on the ocean side to watch, with the breakers providing the background music. As familiar as I was with the place, it was still magic to me, and I think my friends were swept in as well from my descriptions.

At evening's end, we walked back to Talcott Hall where we bade Hersch and Bart a goodnight. Mina had a glow about her face and a leftover smile that enhanced her loveliness even more. Dot went upstairs to bathe before bed, but Mina and I wandered out onto the porch to see the waning moon, wrapping our sweaters around us in the evening chill.

"Dancing tonight brought back such nice memories for me," I confided to Mina.

"You must have had so much fun at Lumina," she said, smiling.

"It was wonderful. Such a special place. I wish you could have seen it."

"Me too." She was quiet for a moment. Then she said, "I did see Shell Island, though."

"What? You were there?"

"Yes. The summer I was fifteen, my family took the train south and we stayed at Shell Island resort for a week's vacation. My family wanted to see where my grandfather came from, so we went. It was wonderful! It wasn't Lumina, but I know just what you mean about the ocean breezes coming in from the beach. And so many people just like us in the South!"

"Yes," I said, realizing for the first time what it must have been like for well-to-do black people who had the freedom to walk that part of the beach any time of day or night without fear of recrimination unlike on the south end of the beach where they were banned. "Why didn't you say something about being there before?"

Mina's eyes flashed almost imperceptibly. "Do you mean when you and Miss Devereaux were discussing how lovely Lumina was?"

"Yes, I suppose you could have mentioned it then."

"Well, yes, I suppose I could have said, 'I wasn't allowed inside that wonderful place, but I did spend a week at Shell Island, the National Negro Playground.'"

Her words stung a little, making me remember our first meetings when her eyes had flashed at me, and she'd refused to speak to me. I didn't understand then, but I was beginning to understand now.

"When we took the ferry over to town and then rode the trolley downtown to see Nixon's house on Chestnut Street, we had an unfriendly interaction with one of the neighbors there. He said something ugly to my father, and we decided never to come back."

"Oh. He was white?"

"Yes. You can probably imagine the things he said."

I could imagine exactly what was said. It made me swallow hard.

"Anyway, we spent the rest of the time at Shell Island and had a lovely time."

"Our friend Gregory played at Shell Island in the orchestra before it burned down."

"You know a black man?"

I giggled before I could catch myself. Did Mina also imagine me at home swishing around in hoop skirts?

"Oh, Mina, of course! Not all Southerners are awful people! Gregory is Pearl's husband. Pearl was our housekeeper until she retired last summer. Gregory plays trumpet and piano. He has always tuned our piano, and he does very well all over town doing that when he isn't working in the snack bar at Lumina."

"Oh. They're your servants?"

"Well, Pearl is more like family. I've known her all my life. She taught me everything I know about housekeeping and gardening. Now she takes care of her newborn granddaughter. Nellie, her daughter, just started working for my father and my aunt Andrea. Aunt Andrea will be getting married at Thanksgiving and moving a street over, so Father will be alone. He will need Nellie's help more than ever then. But I sure do miss Pearl."

Mina was quiet a moment, gazing at the moon.

"My father told me that Shell Island burned down."

"Yes, it happened a couple of years ago. Lots of buildings burn down at the beach without a proper fire department to handle the job, and the ocean breezes make it worse. I heard there were a few kitchen fires there and that the last one really caught on with the winds that night."

"What a shame. It was quite a grand place. I don't imagine my family will ever go back to Wilmington. No relatives are left there; nothing for us there anymore."

"Well, you are right where you need to be, Mina. You will be great one day and people will flock to see you, the same way they flocked to Shell Island to hear the music and dance the night away. I can just imagine you starring in an opera in Chicago or New York. Your name will appear on marquees, and your rave reviews will be in all the newspapers."

She scoffed. "Now *that* would be something."

"You need to believe it. It could happen if it's what you truly want."

"Is that what your family tells you?"

"Yes. I believe it, too. What does your family tell you?"

"That it will be hard, but I must never give up."

I nodded. "Miss Devereaux believes in you, too. That's why we're here and that's why you have Miss Devereaux to teach you."

"Well, if I'm in the opera, you can be in the orchestra playing the piano along with the singers."

I didn't know how to respond. Although I enjoyed playing for Mina, I had never thought about being someone's accompanist as my life's work, spending my career in the orchestra pit wearing the same black dress every night. I wanted to be as big an attraction on my own, as I was sure Mina would be. I had dreams of touring the world in gorgeous costumes and playing the finest Steinways ever made. Then I realized her shoulders were shaking with laughter.

"I'm just fooling with you, Sylvie! You're going to be a star yourself. Don't settle for playing behind someone else. Even me!" she hooted.

I laughed and then looked at her with all seriousness.

"Aim high," I said, pointing at the moon.

"Aim high," she repeated with a grin.

CHAPTER SIX

Mr. May

Bernard couldn't wait for Nate and Elle to arrive. They would be here any minute. Earlier in the day, he had been listening to the news on National Public Radio as he finished wiping the groceries with sanitizing wipes and placing them on the other side of the taped line across the table for AB to take inside. They'd been cleaning everything that came inside the house this way, and now they were finding out it was all unnecessary, just like the nitrile gloves they had been wearing. Dr. Anthony Fauci, the chief medical advisor to the president, was explaining that the COVID-19 virus was spread through air particles, so wearing masks was the best way to protect oneself from the spread. Washing hands frequently or using hand sanitizer was sufficient to keep down infection rather than wearing gloves. Healthcare workers needed gloves in the hospitals, so he and AB didn't need to bother with them anymore. He would save his gloves for spraying chemicals in the garden, painting projects, and cleaning jalapeño peppers for his favorite recipes.

Despite AB's protests, Bernard kept going to the grocery store for whatever they needed. He couldn't stand being cooped up in the house and had to get out and about. If he maintained six-foot distances and wore his masks, he should be fine, according to Dr. Fauci. Bernard had given up on the senior shopping hours. It was like being a lamb driven to the slaughter! Arriving at Harris Teeter before sunrise at 7 a.m. reminded him of being in the crowded parking lot at Kenan Stadium after a Carolina vs. Duke football game! He would take his chances with the younger folks later in the mornings on Thursdays and still get his senior discount without the large crowds. He might have compromised health, but he was still a man, and one determined to keep his dignity intact.

At least once a week, he and AB took a drive around town for a change of scenery and the comfort that only green spaces and waterfront views can provide. Walking in the neighborhood allowed them a breath of fresh air. The parks and beaches were closed, so they often had cocktails on AB's dock, waving to Nate and Elle two docks over, who had the same idea, and the need for company at a safe distance. Hopefully by the end of April, the governor would rescind the Stay-At-Home order.

Now, as he plated baked tortilla chips topped with melted pimento cheese and jalapeno pepper slices, he listened to AB greeting their young neighbors who had just arrived on the front porch for their reading. Without seeing them from his place in the kitchen, he could almost imagine them without their masks from the happy sounds of their voices. He missed seeing Elle's pretty smile and Nate's bright grin, but everything could be said with their eyes if you looked for it.

"Hello, hello!" he called merrily, emerging from the kitchen with his appetizer.

SYLVIE

Tuesday, October 16, 1928

Dear Diary,

I could have sworn Herschel was jealous, watching Bartholomew offer me his arm before we took to the sidewalk on our walk to Mr. Finch's house this afternoon for the upper-classmen's recitals and dinner. There would be twelve of us in all, three in each class, so Bart and I would hear nine pieces, and hopefully a piece from Mr. Finch himself.

"Are you nervous?" Bart asked, showing his wide, mischievous grin to me.

"Only about being at Mr. Finch's house. Not about the music since I don't have to play. Why, are you nervous?" I asked, looking up impossibly high to meet his gaze.

"Maybe just a little. I get nervous listening to the others, knowing that one day it will be me at the piano. I'm thrilled to be here and can't wait for my turn, but it's a bit daunting to listen to the other students, don't you think?"

"I suppose so. I'm just so amazed by everything at Oberlin and all the people from everywhere. I know they do these more intimate gatherings to prepare us for what's ahead for each of us. I think Mr. Finch does it at his home to make us feel comfortable, so really, you shouldn't worry."

"You're my rock, Sylvie. You should have seen Dot at her teacher's convocation. She all but raised her hand to offer a song!"

"Now, that doesn't surprise me."

"The girl has nerves of steel. And a voice that shatters glass, but don't tell her I said so!"

"That's shameful, Bart. As her accompanist, you should be encouraging her."

"That one needs no encouragement!" He laughed as we turned onto Mr. Finch's sidewalk. His home was a lovely two-story Pennsylvania Dutch style with mature gardens in the front yard and a small porch at the entryway. How I missed sitting on our large front porches from home! What did people here do in the hot summertime?

Mr. Finch greeted us at the door, ushering us inside through the ante-room to meet the others. I only knew Anita, the other freshman student. We were introduced to the others while a tall pretty girl named Teresa, one of the seniors, poured cider into small tumblers for each of us. The recital would be first and then the dinner, which smelled heavenly from the kitchen. Sausages would be my first guess, since that is what we eat here in abundance.

Some of the older boys were already seated in the upholstered furniture, a high back sofa and wing chairs, so that left the spindle-back dining chairs for the rest of us. Southern boys would have offered Anita and me their seats. They snickered to themselves at my accent whenever I spoke, making the blush rise from my chest to my cheeks in one quick hot movement. Bart pressed my arm reassuringly and gave the boys a dis-approving glance. I could have kicked myself for letting those boys make me feel inferior just because of the way I talk, but I began to understand the insecurity my friends felt. Being different in whatever way was un-nerving. My palms began to sweat, and the glass of cider trembled a bit as I raised it to my dry lips. It took so little to rattle one's self-confidence. Mr. Finch gave me a brief wink and a smile as he called the group to attention.

I eyed his lovely Steinway baby grand and a bookcase behind it, filled with stacks of musical scores and records for the Victrola in the corner of the large drawing room. Mr. Finch and his wife smiled from a framed photograph on their wedding day displayed on one side of the mantle, while another photograph of their five children balanced it on the opposite side. A low fire crackled in the fireplace; instantly I felt at home.

"Welcome everyone!" he said, clasping his hands as Mrs. Finch emerged from the kitchen in her apron to join the group. He quickly pulled a kitchen chair through the kitchen door for his wife and gestured to her graciously as she took her seat. "I'd like to introduce you new students to my wife, Elsie Finch." He then gestured to us. "Anita, Sylvie, and Bartholomew, we are happy for you to join our group. I know you will enjoy the meal she's been preparing. It is our wish that you will enjoy this brief respite from dormitory drudgery and—hopefully—a pleasant little concert this evening." The older boys snickered again. "I'm sure you are all curious to see what your fellow students have been working on. Also, I believe the best teacher is an audience, which is why you are here, so without further ado, we will start with Teresa Burton," he said with a gesture from her to the Steinway.

Teresa, the girl who had served the cider, played first—Rimsky-Korsakov's "Flight of the Bumblebee"—from memory. Her fingers flew over the fine-tuned keys, making me glance at Bart, who swallowed audibly. The precision of her playing and her energy penetrated me, making my heart flutter and my eyes sting momentarily with tears. My time would come. How I had missed performing! This was what I was working toward. I felt my face flush and my soul come alive the way Teresa threw herself into her piece. When she finished with a reverent flourish, the group of us burst into applause and the older boys shouted, "Brava! Brava!" I realized then that they couldn't be as bad as I had thought. Even Bart seemed to relax and enjoy himself. Grins were shared all around, especially from Mrs. Finch, who applauded more loudly than anyone.

The rest of the students were equally as impressive, although I felt Teresa's heartfelt performance exceeded the brash boys' offerings. My stomach was making unflattering noises as the last of the students took his bow at the piano's side. Mr. Finch stood and thanked everyone for the pleasant concert and announced that dinner was served. Mrs. Finch invited us to take our places at the table, while Teresa and Wallace, one of the snickering boys, assisted her in the kitchen by bringing out heaping bowls of vegetables, potatoes, and gravy. Mr. Finch poured more cider and then brought out the platter of mouth-watering sausages I had hoped for. Mrs. Finch patted her gray hair in place and took her seat at the opposite end of the table with a basket of bread swaddled in a crisp white napkin.

Wallace rubbed his hands together. "Boy, this feels like Christmas!" he said with the glee we all felt as dishes were passed, and food was piled on plates. I had given up my dislike for him after he had helped seat Mrs. Finch. His friend Daniel chatted with Anita, making her feel comfortable with all the older students. Teresa sat to my left and Bart to my right. Wallace sat to his left.

"You play so brilliantly!" I gushed to Teresa as we exchanged the breadbasket for the butter.

"So do you!" she said, making me blush instantly. "I've heard you in the practice rooms. You know, we all listen. We need to know what the competition is like when you freshmen arrive on campus!"

Bart blew a raspberry—softly—out of respect for our hosts but just so Teresa could hear. "Competition? Huh!" He grinned. I wondered whether he was flirting with her! (Poor Dot would be crushed.) "Surely you mean the fledglings."

"That attitude will sink you faster than concrete, Mullins," Wallace muttered to him, while buttering his bread. "Mr. Finch always says we have neither the luxury nor the time here for self-loathing." Indeed, Mr. Finch had told me that himself; although, I think he said, "self-pity," but Wallace made the point so that Bart's face went scarlet.

Teresa came to his rescue. "I've heard you too, Mr. Mullins. You're also quite good, but it's Miss Meeks here who has scared the bejeebers out of all the senior boys!" she said with a chuckle and an admonishing gaze directed at Wallace. Were they an item or was the good-natured ribbing her way of keeping him in line? Serving myself a sausage, I watched carefully, not wanting to misinterpret anything and appear a fool.

Mr. Finch cleared his throat. "Thank you all! Each of you performed masterfully this evening," he said, summarizing the group's conversation.

"Hear, hear! It was a delightful display of virtuosity," said Mrs. Finch, boldly raising her glass of cider. There were giggles from the girls.

"If any of you freshmen would consider playing for the dessert course, we would all give you our grateful attention," my teacher said with a smile my way.

"Oh, what an excellent idea! Music with my bread pudding always improves the taste," said Mrs. Finch, and a round of applause ensued from the guests. Bart's face broke out in a sweat while Anita's went white. I grinned, fanning myself at the thought. I had not performed in months, and it was beginning to weigh on me.

"It's merely a thought, but there is no pressure implied at all," Mr. Finch continued, this time giving Anita the encouraging smile. "If you feel so inclined, I believe we will have time to listen before your curfews are imposed," he said. "We're all family here. As you said, Wallace, this is Christmas." He raised his own glass of cider. We all responded in kind.

I understood then how the camaraderie created by a simple meal shared at a table of friends can inspire fellowship, making me so grateful to the Finches to be included. It would be rude not to play if asked, wouldn't it? And I felt an invitation had been conveyed.

Or a gauntlet dropped.

"You played Christmas carols? In October?" Dot exclaimed in her nightgown at the foot of her bed when I returned. I hung my coat in the wardrobe and toed out of my shoes on the edge of my bed across from hers.

"Yes! I figured it was the best way to take the pressure off, and besides, they loved it! After the fall concerts, we are all going to be immersed in Christmas music, and anyway, Wallace said it felt like Christmas being around the Finches' table. Oh, and by the way, the food was delicious! Mrs. Finch is an excellent cook. I didn't see anyone there to cook the food but her, so I was duly impressed with the meal. Oh, her sausages! I ate two! Imagine, cooking for fourteen!"

"You're making me so hungry!" Dot complained, rubbing her stomach. "I can't wait to go home for fall break and have my mother's pot roast and potatoes! And I can't believe you just jumped up on the piano bench and played Christmas carols!"

"Well, Bart and Anita really didn't want to play, so I had to think of something fast. It was Wallace who inspired me, and they all sang along to 'Deck the Halls' and had a grand time. I don't think Mr. Finch minded. I did end with 'Carol of the Bells,' which was my most impressive contribution. I saw his eyebrow pop up at least once."

"Oh, that sounds like so much fun! I am *green* with envy that you have Professor Finch for your teacher. He's an actual human being!" she moaned, rolling over and stuffing her pillow under her chin. "What's it like, being liked?"

"I know your teacher likes you too, Dot. You're being melodramatic," I said firmly, scraping an emery board over my fingernails. "All you need to do is tone it down a bit. You have a lovely voice."

"Well, I for one can't wait until the fall concerts are over and we have some time to breathe. You should come home with me for the long weekend. I'll show you around Cincinnati! I can take you downtown where we can eat brats and metts, and you can get drunk off wonderful German beer, and I'll take care of you like you did me that night the boys took us to the speakeasy."

I placed my emery board on my desk and shook my head at Dot's sudden enthusiasm. I didn't care a lick for beer, I'd had my fill of brats, and I had no idea what metts were. But finally, we were talking like friends.

"I'd love to go!"

Friday, October 19, 1928

Dear Diary,

There was a dance last night, the last night before fall break. Fall festival activities have been going on all week, which included a myriad of concerts of all the music groups in the Conservatory, as well as the general college music groups. Drama students participated in wonderful plays. I have never enjoyed myself as much as I have with all these cultural events to attend! One can hardly wander anywhere on campus without hearing music, especially this time of year. I suppose it will be truly magical at Christmastime!

Dot and I were escorted to the dance by Bart and Hersch. It was a nice change to be out for such a gay time together! I watched to see whether Mina had a date, but she did not, and came with her roommate Cornelia. Sadly, despite their lovely dresses, they were wallflowers all evening until Hersch asked Mina to dance. I was shocked by the disapproving looks they got. Bart had to explain to me that it is because Hersch is Jewish, and Mina is colored, and that kind of mixing is frowned upon. I thought I was in the land of freedom and enlightenment in Ohio, but apparently, I have been under quite a delusion. Here I am a Southerner who does not care who dances with whom, but I am obviously in the minority even here. My blood was boiling. All they did was have a fun go at the Charleston, and they never even touched hands, but the sour faces and murmuring behind hands ruined it all. How I do love my friends, and I cannot see the logic in keeping people separated because of their religion or their skin color for an innocent dance! Especially here at Oberlin, where we are constantly reminded of temperance and tolerance. What hypocrites some people can be!

During the final dance, when Hersch held me deftly in his arms for the waltz, I asked him if it bothered him the way people behaved when he danced with Mina. He gave me a curious smile and said, "This is why I love you, Sylvie darling. Your acceptance of me—and of Mina—is what makes you so special!"

"Why wouldn't I accept you?" I asked, still puzzled.

I watched the ballroom's low lights playing on his dark curls before he responded. Then he said, "I'll tell you what. Ask your father what he thinks about you associating with a Jew and see what he says. Then you can decide if I may still hold a place on your dance card."

My face flushed once again that evening. My father's opinion has always been important to me, but I believed he would agree with how I felt. "I don't think he would mind in the least if I danced with a Jewish boy."

"Well, dancing may be one thing, but I'm sure he wouldn't approve of you becoming serious about a Jew." He studied my reaction as we swayed to the music.

Feeling bold from my anger, I asked, "Is that why you haven't kissed me yet?"

His eyes twinkled and he shook his head, smiling ruefully. "Honey, I'm a New Yorker; you're a Southern belle. You're an Episcopalian; I'm a Jew. It just doesn't work in our circles."

"Oh. I see. What you're saying is you don't think your parents would approve of me either."

"Actually…" he cast his eyes uncomfortably about and shrugged as we turned slowly around the dance floor. "No, they wouldn't. You're a *shiksa*." At my confused look, he continued. "It's Yiddish. It's what Jews refer to as a forbidden girl. A Gentile. My father would say a girl like you is okay for practice, but not for marriage."

"Marriage!" I gasped, letting that idea sink in. "Well, I never meant—"

"I am so sorry, Sylvie. I don't mean to be so presumptuous, but you did ask. You were just talking about a kiss. But, you see, that's the way our families think. Kisses lead to love and love leads to marriage and babies, hopefully in that order! I'm supposed to be looking for a nice Jewish girl to make my wife…after I become a respectable banker, of course." He smiled sadly at me. "But we're both a long way from home. We can do what we want. That's what college is for. Figuring out who we are. For me, being Jewish here has been a real challenge in many ways. I've given up trying to keep kosher. It's a task trying to follow our rules here…and now I've met you. But it's probably for the best if we just stay friends. And *you* are the *best*," he said, hugging me. I felt his lips press hard against my hair. As the song ended, he released me. The lights came up, signaling the dance was over. And so was my naivete.

On the train this morning to Cincinnati, Dot and I discussed the dance and my conversation with Herschel.

"I don't think you should be angry with him, Sylvie. He was very honest with you. I've never had a boy talk to me as frankly as Hersch did with you."

"That doesn't mean it didn't hurt—a bit. Because of his traditions, I do understand. I'm not angry with him. I just don't think it's fair the way we are supposed to act when we like people who are different from us. People are all people. My father says, 'We all put our pants on the same way.' And I'm so tired of people protecting me from getting hurt."

"I know. I'm sorry your feelings are hurt. I know *my* parents wouldn't let me date a Jewish boy. I think you're brave to ask all those questions, though. I think with Bart, I'm better off not knowing how he feels. I've certainly never asked him!" She scoffed. "It's much easier to just roll along with whatever happens."

The train car rocked, comforting me somewhat, as we bumped gently against each other in our compartment. I stared out at the verdant farms dotted with haystacks and red barns. Occasionally, a tractor plodded across a field. Houses nestled into the valley, wisps of smoke from their chimneys disappearing into thin air. I was lulled into a state of complacency, wishing the ride would not end.

"Has Bart made his feelings known otherwise?" I asked, gazing at Dot, her bobbed hair in need of a cut, but for the most part looking as untroubled as ever. Maybe she didn't wear her heart on her sleeve for a reason. I have never been one to hold my feelings in.

"Oh? Do you mean, has Bart kissed me?" she asked.

"I don't mean to be nosy. But since we've opened up this can of worms…."

"Well, no, he hasn't exactly kissed me."

"Exactly?"

"He's been the perfect gentleman."

"As Hersch has been."

"Bart has kissed me on the cheek once. And oddly, he did it in public, which was shocking, but no. There has been no wild romance. Sorry to disappoint you."

I groaned. "I'm sorry; I really don't mean to pry. Curiosity has ruined my manners. It's just that I have only dated a few fellows, and none of it has gone so well."

"I haven't dated anyone. Tell me everything!" Dot said, grinning with delight, the dimple in her pale right cheek appearing.

"Well, first, when I was sixteen, there was this terribly forward boy named Tommy. He was my first kiss, and it was dreadful. It was like being licked by a dog! Ugh!" Dot cackled at the comparison. "Oh, but it was true. Now he dates my friend Marjorie—she's one of the twins I told you about—and I must say, I really don't think she likes him, but she puts up with him anyway."

"Well, that sounds foolish."

"Oh, I wholeheartedly agree. Then last summer, there was a college boy at the beach named David, for whom I fell head over heels, but he only kissed me twice. He wanted me to enjoy my own college experience and not pine for him, so that was that." I was quiet for a moment, thinking about kisses, which led me to think about Catherine's older brother, Clifton Carmichael, who had kissed me and more. He had tried to molest me. The experience had been so unpleasant I couldn't bring myself to tell Dot about him. Some things are better left unsaid. She was waiting for me to continue.

"At least I got a nice charm bracelet from David," I said, raising my wrist for her to admire it.

"And a broken heart?"

"Only slightly bruised. And then there's Herschel Bloom. Really, I was hoping for more romance at this point."

Dot sighed. "I know what you mean. I've never had a beau. I believe I'll be waiting the rest of my life for romance. I'm happy just to have dates with Bart, even without the kisses."

Following her gaze out our window, I pondered Dot's lack of beaus. She was chubbier than most of the sought-after girls, and attractive but plain. Her talent will be most admirable once she learns how to harness her volume. Since I have gotten to know her, I find Dot pleasant enough, but I am not surprised at her inexperience with boys. Not that I am experienced by any stretch of the imagination. I don't care to count Clifton as one of my favorable experiences. And now, regrettably he is dead, so I shall not share those ugly details with anyone.

There must be a reason we are having trouble enticing men. Maybe Miss Devereaux is right. It is best to reserve one's personal life for the stage.

CHAPTER SEVEN

Elle

Elle turned down her street, comforted by the sight of the live oak canopy above the lane that welcomed her home every day. It was such a beautiful place to live, she thought, turning her head automatically from the awful, abandoned house between AB and Nate, refusing to let her mind return to the ugly events that went on there last year.

She felt a little guilty, arriving home each evening, both exhilarated and exhausted from Bake My Day's success at navigating the pandemic's challenges. Nate was bored working from home, wishing he had half as much activity. For Elle, though, each day brought something new at the bakery to figure out. Business had never let up when the world otherwise screeched to a halt. Other businesses that required inhouse services were taking a hit, and some would soon be forced to close. But with their new curbside setup, wearing masks, and social distancing in the kitchen, she and her staff were almost busier than they'd ever been. Initially, she had hoped to be this busy since the shop had only been open nine months. It was certainly the upward trajectory she'd hoped for, but not at all the way she thought she'd get there. There were silver linings in this mess for sure. And she had been very lucky.

Nate, on the other hand, didn't know what to do with himself. He was used to running with his hair on fire. Now, desperate for fishing events to produce, he missed the travel he craved and the camaraderie of his colleagues, instead of sitting in front of his computer screen for hours on end finding ways to edit TV show segments from previously recorded fishing trips. He had few options for reconfiguring his work. At least he was the show's editor and producer instead of the videographer, who was out of a job temporarily at best.

Elle had noticed Nate wearing the same stale clothes for days at a time. She made a point of tossing his shirts in the washer so he would be forced to wear something different each day. Feeling fresh could only help his mood. His hair, like everyone else's, was getting long and unruly, making him look more and more like Kyle Davis, the boy from high school she wished to forget. Nate worried more about the pandemic than she did, after hearing his uncle Phil's experiences at his hospital in DC. Maybe being so isolated worsened Nate's anxiety. At home, he was watching the grim news reports and updates on TV, seeing reality at its worst, whereas she was out in public seeing people going about their business, enjoying each other's company, and interacting safely.

And then there was the wedding. They'd stopped talking about it recently, wondering whether it could really happen with so much uncertainty around them. Nate had been so excited to get her on board with the idea of having a wedding. But with her bakery to run and new uncertainties cropping up every day, wedding planning always seemed to get pushed to the back burner.

Still, Nate was trying hard to make everything seem normal. Probably out of boredom, he cooked, did laundry, and prepared the coffee pot to be ready each morning. All she had to do was push the button and it would be waiting as soon as she stepped out of the shower. Other women she knew didn't have it this good at home during the lockdown.

Especially since she got to look at him every day. *And nights were even more fun!* She was still pinching herself.

Pulling her SUV into the driveway, Elle spotted Nate stretched out peacefully on the dock across the street, hands beneath his head, feet crossed at the ankles, probably gazing at the cloud formations over the Intracoastal Waterway. She smiled. The drink cooler was parked beside him with two metal wine cups set on top and food in Styrofoam containers. Dinner awaited! The man never ceased to impress her.

She crossed the street, waving to two women walking briskly along, each with a lively terrier on a leash. "How're y'all doing?" she asked, and the ladies responded with smiles and waves. Everyone was soaking up the fresh air as safely as they could. For many, getting out of the house for a walk was the highlight of the day. Seeing a friendly face was a bonus. Dogs were certainly getting the best the COVID quarantine had to offer, she thought with a chuckle as she watched them trot happily along with their people.

As Elle approached the dock, she saw Nate had showered and put on her favorite plaid shirt that hugged his physique. He wore a clean pair of jeans and the prerequisite leather flip-flops for coastal residents.

"Hey, babe," he said, grinning and tenting a hand over his eyes as he turned to watch her walk toward him. She never tired of his reaction to seeing her. Reaching down, she took his extended hand and helped him up. Nate kissed her eagerly.

"Hey, you," she murmured against his mouth, her eyes meeting his, and letting the best part of her day wash over her in the warmth of his arms. She breathed in his scent and sighed contentedly.

"I'm so glad to see you! You look nice. How was your day?" she asked.

"Same old same old. Yours?" he asked, rubbing her shoulders.

"Crazy busy, but good. How's Patsy's mother? Have you heard anything?"

"Yeah, I talked to Patsy earlier when she and Aubrey were out walking Harley. She says her mom is finally out of the woods. No more symptoms, and her doctor has cleared her to resume all of her activities, which just means walking around the grounds basically."

"That's good news. I'm sure Patsy and Aubrey are relieved." Elle worried about Patsy's thirteen-year-old grandson who lived with her. It was just the two of them quarantining in the house two doors down. The arrangement was a puzzle to Elle. Aubrey was of mixed race, so she assumed his father was black. She had never seen his mother. She didn't know them well enough to be privy to all the circumstances, but she understood first-hand how scary things can seem more magnified when you are flying solo with your granny. Especially when you act tougher than you are.

"Mm-hmm, you know Aubrey; seems okay on the surface."

"Yeah…. So, what did you go and do here?" she asked, smiling, and gesturing to the packages of food on the cooler.

"Shrimp and grits. I just picked it up at Bluewater. Timed it just right." It was one of Elle's favorite waterfront grills. "Trying to support our local businesses. Oh, and AB told me they'd be great to cater the wedding if we're looking at that kind of thing yet."

Elle nodded, smiling again. "How thoughtful of you both!" she said. "I've heard that too about their weddings. Too bad we can't tie the knot there. They have quite the view over the waterway."

"We can see. Maybe when the stay-at-home orders are lifted at the end of this month things will open up again. Shouldn't be much longer. A small outdoor affair could be possible on that huge porch they have."

Elle cringed inwardly, imagining AB and Mr. May in a crowd of people, anyone in a crowd of people, for that matter. Even a small crowd outside would be concerning. None of them could afford to get sick. It was too early to congregate for her comfort level. And here she thought Nate was the over-protective one.

"It does sound lovely," she knew to say so he wouldn't be disappointed. He twisted open the bottle of Sauvignon blanc and offered her a cup.

"I know what you're thinking," he said as he poured her wine. "It's still too soon to plan. I get it; I do."

"You do?"

"I do," he said, winking and raising his glass to hers. "There has to be something on the spectrum between what we'd really like to have and just eloping."

She clinked her metal cup against his. "We could have a teeny tiny wedding right here," she said, gesturing in front of them.

"On the dock?"

"Sure. It's outside and safe. Wouldn't it be pretty out here? It's kind of like an aisle, going out over the water. And I know how you love the water. It's catching," she said, grinning at him, watching his blue eyes flash. "The jasmine will be blooming on the gate arbor soon."

"Yeah. It's kind of perfect, right? It's where I brought you the first night we met, where I realized I wanted you in my life."

"It is perfect. I wanted you too, although I fought it."

"I'm glad you lost that fight."

"Mm." Elle smiled, thinking back to the night. After they'd met at the bar downtown and realized they were neighbors, Nate had invited her for a moonlit cruise; instead, they'd found Aubrey fishing on the dock past his bedtime, and unbeknownst to Patsy. And then later, they'd gotten to know each other even better in his bedroom. It had been a fast courtship. He interrupted her thoughts.

"I can see this as the perfect wedding venue," he said, looking from one end of the dock to the other.

"I think so, too. So, AB can be my matron of honor."

"Maybe we could get Mr. May to officiate."

"Then who will be your best man?"

Nate smiled and gazed out at the water as the breeze stirred his hair. "Well, I was thinking about Joey. If he could get some leave, he could give you away and then come and stand up for me. He's just the man to do double duty."

Elle's voice caught as she tried to speak. That Nate would include her son in such an honorable way touched her deeply.

"That's so sweet, Nate. You've really put some thought into this."

"I have."

"Your family has to be here too."

"If it's possible for them to travel, yes. And your cousin Judy and your buddy Marcus."

Elle smiled at the thought of them all together. "We could space them all out on AB's dock, and they could watch the ceremony from there."

Nate went on with his ideas. "If we get married right here, we could have a drive-by reception. Our local friends could drive down the street right afterward, and we could meet and greet them safely in their cars. Maybe Allyson and Monai could hand out cupcakes. Then you and I could have a Door Dash dinner like this—a surf and turf—and some champagne, cruise over in the Skiff to watch the sunset on the south end of the beach, and you know, start our life as Mr. and Mrs."

Elle stared at him, placing her hand on his chest. "You…amaze me. It's perfect. I love it!"

"Then let's do it."

"Oh, I just love your ideas!" AB exclaimed clapping her hands on the other end of the porch at that evening's reading. "Bernie, you could become a certified officiant! I've heard it's done all the time nowadays."

Bernard cocked his head. "Well, I'm certainly willing to look into it."

"Thank you, sir! I'll be glad to research it and see if I can help you in the process," Nate said. He was glad Bernie and AB were so adept at using the computer. It was good to be tech savvy at any age, but they constantly surprised him with their vitality and knowledge at eighty! "We want it to be as safe as possible for the two of you to be involved." The men gave each other the thumbs-up to seal the deal. It seemed to Elle even better than a handshake. A slap on the back was implied by their eyes.

"Have you thought of a date?" AB asked Elle.

"Well, there's not really much to plan. I guess I need to find a dress, but I could shop online like lots of brides are doing now. Why not June?" she shrugged.

"Oh, June will be so lovely! Let me host your dinner together in the garden. Bernie and I can hang up the string lanterns and it will be just beautiful!"

"I'd be honored to make your bouquet," said Bernard. "AB's cabbage roses will be in full bloom by then."

"I'd love it! Thank you," Elle said, glowing. She'd never had this much positive attention. It did feel good. Nate smiled at her.

"But...what if it rains?" she asked.

"It's not gonna rain," Nate said without missing a beat. "But if it does, we'll just do it the next day."

"There you go!" said AB with a smile for Nate. She picked up the diary and began to read.

SYLVIE

Tuesday, October 23, 1928

Dear Diary,

Life is certainly full of surprises. First, I feel different being back at the Conservatory. Being away in Cincinnati with Dot at her family's home has made me gain a perspective on my experiences here. Returning to our campus, I felt a sense of belonging for once, which will serve me well since we are ending our first semester as freshmen! I feel grown up in so many ways. You will soon see why.

Mina shared her mother's delicious homemade shortbreads with Dot and me in the parlor at Talcott Hall tonight. It was nice catching up. We discussed our trips home, most of which involved our love affairs with home-cooked food! Mrs. Randall did indeed make her pot roast and potatoes, as well as pancakes and homemade breads. It was obvious that we have eaten well. Dot could no longer fit into her concert dress and had to buy a new one when we went to town with her mother. I shouldn't criticize her since my dresses also fit tighter than usual after my newfound sausage consumption. Mina is still as slim and regal as ever, fitting nicely into her clothing, despite the fried chicken, greens, and cornbread she described eating over the break. Her family's Southern roots must be responsible for their cooking traditions, making me homesick for my own. I still dream about Pearl's biscuits!

"Did you actually drink beer and eat brats in Cincinnati, Sylvie?" asked Mina.

I was embarrassed to have her allude to my trepidation about beer and brats I had mentioned in confidence to her before Dot and I left.

"Yes, I tried it all. Cincinnati beer is not like the other beer I have had, and I must admit, I rather liked it. Brats and sauerkraut are good too. But none of it is advisable for our figures."

Mina raised her eyebrows as if scolding me for my sin, but I continued.

"The food was all wonderful, but the highlight of the trip for me was the shopping! With Dot and Mrs. Randall's help, I found a wonderful woolen winter coat in a pleasing shade of mossy green with a fur collar that is all the rage. I'm afraid Aunt Andrea won't like it, though. She says the best way to enjoy fur is to snuggle a kitten in one's neck."

The girls giggled. My aunt is very progressive in her thinking, like my father, and I believe their opinions guide me more often than I am probably aware.

"I also bought a lovely dress for Aunt Andrea's wedding. It's gold charmeuse with pretty beadwork around the collar, and it has a flowy skirt. I think it will be perfectly appropriate for the Thanksgiving wedding, and hopefully, for the last dance at Lumina for the season."

"Well speaking of dances, you girls were so lucky to have Bart and Herschel to dance with at our fall mixer," Mina said.

"You and Hersch danced a spectacular Charleston at the end!" I exclaimed.

"I'm glad *someone* finally asked me to dance! I'm not used to being a wallflower," Mina said forlornly.

"Hersch is special," Dot said with a grin.

"Oh, is he? How special?" Mina asked, batting her eyes at me. "Tell us, Sylvie."

I glanced at Dot. "He's a very good friend and a perfect gentleman."

"So is Bart," said Dot before Mina could pry.

"Of course, they are," Mina said. "So handsome and well dressed. Groomed to perfection, both of them." She winked.

"No kisses or untoward behavior from either of them," I said to squash the direction of Mina's questions.

"Oh, I think they'd rather kiss each other than either of you!" Mina said with a giggle, wiping a cookie crumb from her mouth.

An awkward silence fell like a grenade about to explode.

Dot was speechless.

"Mina, what in the world do you mean?" I asked in a hushed voice, looking around to see whether any other girls were about.

"Oh, girls! Haven't you noticed?"

"Noticed what?" asked Dot, finding her voice.

"They are constantly together."

"What of it? They're friends and roommates."

"Which makes it very convenient for them."

"What are you talking about?" I demanded.

"Ladies, those two are *fairies!*" Mina said, raising her palm as if we were fools. Dot and I gaped at each other. Mina went on. "I've seen them in the practice rooms."

"Of course. They rehearse together. They have a piece together," I reminded Mina.

"One night when I was leaving the music building, I looked back to wait for Cornelia, and I saw them through the window. I thought they were wrestling up against the piano, so I kept watching, but that wasn't what they were doing."

"How could you tell?" Dot asked with skepticism.

"Their expressions were so...torrid," Mina explained, clearing her throat.

Another grave silence fell. I could feel the color draining from my face and my throat went dry. *Bart and Hersch were lovers?* Dot's eyes grew wide, and her lips pressed together while my mouth fell open like a codfish's.

"No! Mina, you can't go around telling tales about them," I scolded.

"It's true, Sylvie. I've seen them with my own two eyes. They were *kissing.*"

"But…that's perverse," breathed Dot, wiping her hands on her skirt.

Mina shrugged. "Haven't you ever heard of boys liking boys before? You can just tell once you've seen it. I think the Conservatory is full of fairies. I will admit, I didn't think Bart and Hersch were like that at first. Sometimes they surprise you."

"I don't believe it," said Dot. "It's not…natural."

"Well, for them it seems to be!" Mina said.

"But they are so kind to us," I said, trying to understand what she was talking about.

"Of course, they are. They need your protection so they take you out, hold your arm, and peck you on the cheek so they can appear to be virile young men."

Dot and I considered this as though we were inwardly watching silent films of ourselves with the boys.

I sighed deeply. "But they do care about us. And we care about them."

"I know you do. And they do care about you both. They are good friends. But that's all they will ever be to you…friends."

"We could change them," I insisted, and Dot nodded.

"No, sweetie, you can't," Mina said, shaking her head sadly.

I turned to Dot. "Then we need to protect them!"

"We do?"

"Yes! They could be expelled from the Conservatory for this kind of conduct. Isn't that true, Mina?"

"Yes, Sylvie. They could. I've also heard of people being arrested for engaging in perverse acts."

"How do you know all this?" Dot asked her suspiciously.

"I come from a whole family of musicians. I've seen it a time or two. I've heard my relatives discussing it. People like that get picked on real bad. Get called sissies and faggots. Whites are no different when it comes to…that kind of thing."

"Oh!" Dot said, her eyes wide again. She shuddered.

"Does it turn your stomach, Dot?" Mina asked her.

Dot thought a moment. "I'm having a hard time imagining what they do…. I don't want to, and I don't understand it. But Bart is my friend."

"And Herschel is mine."

"Does it bother you, Sylvie?" Dot asked.

"Well, it's none of my business, truly. I'm a live and let live kind of person." Again, my father's influence spoke through me. "I can't let Hersch get into trouble. His father was worried that he'd get a *girl* in trouble! Golly, if he only knew!" I said, raking a hand through my hair. "He'd surely make Hersch withdraw from the Conservatory."

"And a lot worse than that, I would think," agreed Mina.

"The boys don't deserve that," said Dot after a beat.

"Then we must make a pact. We won't tell anyone. We won't even tell *them* we know. And we will do whatever we can to play along as the boys' dates and keep them safe."

Dot put out her hand. "Count me in."

Mina put her hand on Dot's. "Me too."

I placed my hand on top. "Me three," I said, more seriously than it sounded. I meant it from the bottom of my heart. No one must ever find out their secret.

Wednesday, October 24, 1928

Dear Diary,

I was up half the night thinking about Herschel and Bart. Now everything I was feeling makes sense, especially Hersch's romantic rejection of me and his plea to be only friends during our waltz. He was letting me down easily because he cannot give me what I want, not only because we are of different religions but because we prefer different sexes. I imagine he thought it would be much easier to dodge me because I am a Gentile than because I am a girl. If that is the case, he will have an easier time of brushing off the girls than Bart, who has no excuse since he is not a Jew. Surely, Bart will cling to Dot for the haven she can offer without minding a bit or challenging him. At least Dot and I know the boys aren't put off by our personalities, as trite as it would seem. Our looks, and our shapes, however, have considerably nothing to do with their attraction, sadly.

This morning in our music theory class, I kept stealing glances at Hersch sitting next to me. Twirling his pencil to a melody in his head, he was as sweet and friendly to me as ever, after receiving my assurances that there were no hard feelings between us.

"Nothing has changed," I told him as we left class together, implying more than he could know. Visibly relieved, he smiled and hugged me. As I took in his handsome appearance, I thought about yesterday's conversation. Was what Mina said true about his appearance? Of course, he is well dressed; his father is a tailor, so one would expect him to be turned out accordingly. As far as being groomed to perfection, his messy curls may have thrown me off. I, for one, understand the unruliness of curly hair, but that aside, even in his speech, I can find no sign that Hersch is a sissy in the way Kip would say it. He is neat and clean, which is most pleasing to me, but not by any means to the point of it being a giveaway!

In the middle of my sleepless night, I recounted the many ways Hersch laughs at my jokes, as if I am one of the boys. Hah! I suppose I *am* one of the boys! Or perhaps he feels like one of the girls. He always regards me with such earnest interest, if not lust, and always takes my arm, or inquires how I am if I look sad or angry. He is truly my friend if nothing else. If I can have his friendship, I have a far greater treasure than a casual date or two, a stolen meaningless kiss, or worse yet, being loved and left behind. Herschel Bloom is a gentleman in all respects to me. His affairs are private, and I will not invade his privacy by asking about his business. He has respected me, so I will honor him with the same. I do wish I could change him, but I realize that is out of my control.

In our friendship, I may have stumbled onto something strange but quite wonderful at the same time. Life is strange. There is much more to it than I ever thought. How I used to wish that people would tell me what I am to know in these situations, but who could ever cover this much ground? I suppose growing up is about discovering and embracing the good while discerning and avoiding the bad. Learning to tell the difference is what makes it so hard.

CHAPTER EIGHT

Anne Borden

"Oh, my poor mother!" AB said after listening to Sylvie's lament about Herschel. "It's amazing to hear my mom going through these tough life lessons just like I did. I remember heartbreak well." She shook her head. Bernie nodded. She forgot for a moment that he was the one who had broken her heart, but he seemed not to notice. *Life is strange!* she thought.

"I think it's admirable the way Sylvie embraced Herschel's homosexuality. Even though he might have hurt her initially, she certainly had an open mind about the situation," Bernie replied.

"Well, her heart might be smarting, but I think she'll be okay," said Nate.

"Of course, she will," Elle said with a smile. "Heckie is going to sweep her off her feet! I can't wait to hear that part of the story!"

"It must happen at Thanksgiving at Aunt Andrea's wedding," said Bernie.

"She hardly mentions Heckie," AB said with a frown. "I hope she treats him well when they reconnect then."

"This is your mother and father we're discussing," said Elle with a laugh.

"I know. They seemed so devoted to one another when I was growing up. I guess he did something to win her over. They never told me the details of their love story."

Nate smiled at Elle and gave her shoulders a rub as they sat together in the porch swing. *Those two certainly have fallen in love quickly*, thought AB. It was nice seeing young people find each other and begin to build a life. "Sylvie might think she won't find happiness, but it always seems to sneak up on you when you least expect it," she said.

"That's true," said Nate. "Good things come to those who wait…and suffer."

Everyone laughed. Elle reach up and squeezed his hand. She took the diary and began to read.

SYLVIE

Thursday, October 25, 1928

Dear Diary,

What a week this has been! Conservatory life seems to change by the minute now! It was all I could do to make it through the day to report all that has happened, starting with my piano lesson.

In addition to the new pieces Mr. Finch has piled on to add to my repertoire, he had me play through my Rachmaninoff piece, "Etudes-Tableaux." I have been perfecting the fingering in places it took me almost a month to master. It gave me just the technique I needed to express the piece as it should be played. Today, it flowed effortlessly from my fingers onto the keys from memory. I was pleased with my performance at last. As I mentioned, I believe the fall break gave me a sense of confidence when I returned from Cincinnati that I didn't have before. I feel worthy of being at the Conservatory, and Mr. Finch confirmed it.

"Well done, Sylvie; very, very well done," he said, steepling his fingers under his chin when I finished. "You know, I think you are performance-ready with that piece. Were it up to me, I would put you on the stage in a heartbeat."

My heart leapt at the thought of performing again. "Oh, my!" I cried before I could catch myself, making Mr. Finch chuckle.

"Well, you were so delightful at the recital the other evening, playing your Christmas carols by heart. If you can charm everyone with simple holiday songs, I can imagine how you will come across with your accomplished pieces like this one. You have what it takes. I saw it at my house last week. You charmed even the most critical students, as well as Mrs. Finch and me. You play with such feeling for your audience that I believe you would be an asset at the convocation. A real performer has a unique relationship with the audience. I think you yearn to perform. You crave the audience, and they crave you."

I nodded, swallowing hard, wondering what he would say next.

Mr. Finch thought a moment, then gave a rueful shake of his head. "Regretfully, as I said, it is not up to me. There are strict rules in the Conservatory and the director would not yield, I'm afraid. It would set a precedent to allow other freshmen to play when the goal is to reserve them until the second year of study, at least."

I swallowed again. It was disappointing to hear I was not eligible to play, but I was not surprised to hear it. Still, just to have Mr. Finch's endorsement was encouraging.

"I understand, of course. Thank you, sir, for the vote of confidence. I'll be ready when the time comes."

"Just keep working, dear. Your time will be here before you know it. I look forward to showing you to the world."

I tried to imagine what it would be like to get an invitation to play. There would be over three hundred students in the audience in Warner Hall and several dozen professors in attendance. Goodness, I have a year to prepare. I will indeed be ready!

Upon my return to Talcott Hall late this chilly afternoon, I took the side stairwell to my room on the second floor. The stairwell is often the venue for spontaneous entertainment by those musicians moved to take advantage of the marvelous acoustics the high ceilings and stone walls provide. Today was no exception. Shrill soprano notes rang out, the hallmark tones of my roommate Miss Dorothy Randall. The sound reverberated off each plane, causing several students to freeze in their tracks and listen, or tolerate, as the song caused every hair on my arms to stand on end. Mina waved and grinned down at me from the landing several feet up from where I stood, wrapped snugly in my new coat.

It was indeed my friend Dot, singing a Wagner aria she'd been practicing for the last month. I bit my lower lip to keep a laugh from bursting forth.

"At least the windows are still intact!" a girl muttered to her friend between Mina and me when Dot finished. They both giggled.

"My turn!" Mina said in a stage whisper to me from behind her hand. I nodded in agreement, then shrugged as if to say, "Good luck!"

Mina threw back her shoulders and advanced up the stairs. "Oh, Dot, it's you! I wondered where that Wagner was coming from. Your German is excellent, by the way."

"Thank you," said Dot.

"May I have a turn?"

Dot grinned and took a bow, I saw as I reached the landing for the show. At least the air had settled, and our ringing ears adjusted.

"Of course! What is your pleasure this evening, Mina?" Dot asked, gesturing to her.

"'Beau Soir,'" Mina replied. Of course, the song is one of many repertoire requirements for sopranos, so the other curious girls settled in on the steps, some taking seats for the lesson about to unfold. Mina rested her hand on the stairway railing, raised herself into her performance posture, bowed her head, and closed her eyes. When she looked up, she had transformed into the star I knew her to be. I caught her eye and pointed up, meaning, "Aim high." She smiled, refocused, and began. I wished I was able to play the introduction for her, but it was a moot point as soon as she opened her mouth.

Mina's controlled and pensive voice began to paint the evening picture of the meadow by the river, the pink clouds soothing her troubled heart. Each vowel she sang through soothed without need of English translation. Her voice did all the lovely work, her body still and serene as each note summoned the solace she needed. Her song recalled my conflicted thoughts about Herschel and the ache of my own troubled heart. The day's emotions filled my throat with tears that rose to my eyes, brimming over instantly. I wasn't the only one. When Mina's last note faded into the stairwell, there was silence followed by the collective sigh of the four of us who had fallen into the melancholy where she took us and then healed us. Others wiped tears. Applause began and swelled, making me realize that more had gathered in the stairwell to listen.

Miss Shelton, our dorm matron, was at the foot of the stairs, applauding and blowing a kiss to Mina. "That was wonderful, Mina!"

Mina glowed and smiled, bowing slightly to the girls in the stairwell. I grinned at her, nodding and holding my hands high in the air to show her my full appreciation of her performance. Dot gave her a hug, saying something to her only Mina could hear. The other girls stepped by us, praising Mina's singing as they passed. When we were alone in the stairwell, I hugged Mina and said, "You were a bright star! As I knew you would be! Oh, Mina, you moved everyone to tears! And not a smidgen of stage fright inside of you, was there?"

"No," she laughed. "Just think how good it would have been if we'd had a piano up here!" We laughed and squeezed each other's hands.

Then I asked, "What did Dot say to you?"

"She said, 'Thank you for showing me how it's done. Now I understand what people have been trying to tell me.'"

"Oh, good for Dot. As Mr. Finch says, the audience is the best teacher. You exceeded everyone's expectations here. You have just gotten a boost from your listeners, and Dot has learned from you. I do wish the teachers would let us perform."

Mina nodded, her eyes bright with excitement, as mine were. "It would be such a thrill. Do you have something else to tell me?"

"Well, not really. I just had a very encouraging lesson with Mr. Finch."

Mina smiled. "We could all use some encouragement now. With everything they are throwing at us, only the strong shall survive. I'm happy for you that he is so supportive."

"As Miss Devereaux is supportive of you, too, Mina. You're a gem. These girls were spellbound by you just now, and this is just a stairwell. Imagine how you will sound in Warner Hall!"

We held hands and grinned.

"Thank you, Sylvie! We need each other as much as we need our teachers at this stage of our training. It's wonderful to have you in my corner." We started upstairs as Mina turned to look at me.

"It's just like the song, Sylvie! We're making the most of life! Do you feel it?"

"Yes! Our time is coming! And when it does, look out, world!"

Saturday, November 17, 1928

Dear Diary,

I have been so remiss in entering my thoughts and feelings lately, but honestly, with all the rehearsals for the upcoming concerts and the pressure of keeping up with my repertoire, there has been so little time. I fall into bed exhausted each night. The weather here has turned cold, gray, and dreary—everything I have been warned about, and now I know why. It is deathly depressing! Homesickness overtakes me; I miss my family, the bright blue skies of Wilmington, and being able to see the ocean whenever I want to. Here, with all the leaves gone from the trees, there is little beauty even in the arboretum; still, I walk there every day, watching the ducks on the pond, looking for that "Beau Soir" kind of solace. I imagine Mina singing it to me as I walk. Sometimes she goes with me, quickly, for it is quite cold and windy even in my nice new coat! Aunt Andrea sent me a pair of gloves and a cloche hat she knitted in a green shade that almost matches. As busy as she must be, she is so thoughtful and kind to attend to my letters, and she appears to take in each detail I write to her of Conservatory life.

As the days grow shorter, I find the most beauty in our campus is found at sunset, when the dark trees etch their shapes against the pink and orange sky. Sometimes as the sun sets, there is no color at all, as if it is too sad to make a show for us. I understand it must get tired of all that effort every day to make some work of art, just like we are, which makes me appreciate it even more when the sun sets with glee.

A mood has settled over the Conservatory that even my glass-half-full outlook cannot ignore. Even I find the atmosphere oppressive. Once ambitious students seem to move about quietly, ignoring others, fervently practicing, trying to keep up with the repertory demands. As accomplished musicians, we are often given difficult pieces that we don't like or enjoy playing. I find it hard to play with feeling when I don't like the sound of a piece that requires such rigor. My motivation suffers as I approach such pieces. Without the praise of one's instructor, I imagine life here in this isolated place could be quite discouraging and lonely if one has not the luxury of friends.

I am one lucky person to have found my four friends. There are dozens of students here from New York, Philadelphia, and Chicago who think Southerners are stupid and refuse to give me the time of day. They constantly ridicule the way I speak, as if I am putting on a show. "What did she say? I can't understand a word that comes out of her mouth; can you?" they ask each other in their clipped, quick speech, and then they move on their way as if I can't hear them. They brush past me as if I am in the way and they have no use for me. It's maddening.

Last night, our gang went to see a drama workshop production of *Pygmalion*, a play by George Bernard Shaw. I found so much in common with poor Eliza Doolittle. In fact, I was embarrassed as we left the theater because I felt everyone—not my friends, but others—were looking at me and snickering behind their hands, as if I were Eliza. I have always been confident in my ability to speak well with people, but I am increasingly exasperated with some of these people's disdain of my speech. When I complained to Mina about the damn Yankees making fun of me, she took no offense and sat with me, explaining diction to me and that all I had to do was change my vowels and everything would fall into place. Just five letters in the alphabet. It should be so easy!

Then, like Professor Higgins, she had me work on ear training and had me imitate words with long o sounds like "home" and "coat" and "no." Long i sounds in the words "like" and "nice" and "right" were next. I realized how different my pronunciation was from hers and watched my mouth in the mirror as I tried imitating her. She was quite patient until we got to short e sounds, and she laughed when I said the word "red."

"It's one syllable, Sylvie, not two!"

When she said that, I thought it was indeed funny and I laughed too. We discussed the difference between "pin" and "pen" and not to drop the g on words like "frying pan" and "sewing machine." Apparently, I stretch out my vowels and I need to clip them shorter. She had me practice sentences to speed up my words, the opposite of what she does in songs, when she sings through the vowels. I told her she sang like a Southerner, and I spoke like a singer. We had a good laugh about that one!

All in all, Mina is a good teacher. As a voice student, she is naturally better at teaching diction than Bart—he just tells me not to drawl—and much more patient than Hersch, who shakes his head and gives up on me much too easily. Dot is mostly uninterested. Mina cares. She suggested that I practice by mimicking the movie stars and the radio broadcasters. I am overly conscious of my speech now. I practice all the time, whenever I open my mouth (although I am careful not to talk to myself in public). I realized today that I have not uttered the word "y'all" in months! I would get laughed all the way back to Wilmington for saying that. With Mina's help, there may be hope for me in the Midwest, yet!

On another note, I have realized today that I have been misspelling Herschel's last name all this time. I saw him write it on his paper. It's Blum, not Bloom, like I thought. I rather liked imagining that he blooms like a flower, but I am learning that not everything is like I imagine. I have so much to learn indeed!

FATHER

November 16, 1928

Dearest Sylvie,

I hope this missive finds you well, although Andrea tells me you are home-sick. This is certainly to be expected, as long as you have been gone from us. Rest assured, the feeling is mutual. We miss you terribly! Our best consolation is that you will be home with us soon for her wedding, which I believe will be a heart-warming affair.

If it helps, I felt homesick myself during the war. I trust you are having more fun than I was, but missing those you love is never easy. Andrea tells me also that you have made several nice friends, which eases my mind. It is good to have the company of friends, and if they are true friends, you are very lucky indeed. Since you have always followed the Golden Rule as you were taught, I am sure you have found good ones by your example.

You may already know that your uncle Harry is planning to collect you for the train on Saturday before Thanksgiving and he and Aunt Nell will ac-company you on the train as well. They are bringing your grandmother too, so there will be a party of you in your compartment for company. We look forward to seeing you, the relatives, and Kip for the holidays. It will be a joy to have a full house again. Andrea is especially thrilled that you all will be in attendance for the wedding, and it will do her heart good to see all of you!

Wishing you fair weather and safe travels,

Fondly,

Your Father

Wednesday, November 21, 1928

Dear Diary,

It has snowed here! I have only seen snow once in my life, when spending Christmas with my grandmother in Cleveland years ago. The ground is already covered in a neat white blanket that reflects the light so beautifully. The flakes are small and fall furiously, but in the lights from the buildings this evening, it is magical, turning this cheerless place into a fairyland! God must have heard my sad prayers! I'm sure I was not alone in my plea for something lovely to regard. He has healed my soul!

Seeing how delighted I am by such magic, Hersch invited me to a special event this evening. It wasn't a date really, but he knew I would enjoy the outing—and walking in the snow—so much that he asked me over all his other friends. I gladly took his arm so we could be seen walking to the music building together. He even put his arm around me to keep me warm in the flurry of snowflakes. I can't say I minded it a bit, even though he is just being kind. I know it means nothing more. But still, it was as romantic an evening as I have had here.

Knocking snow from our boots at the rehearsal hall door, we slipped inside, where the Conservatory's jazz band holds their practice sessions. Hersch pointed out his friend Jeffery, the sax player who had introduced him to the speakeasy. Jeffery was one of two white musicians in the band of eight students. Besides Jeffery on the saxophone, there was a piano player, a colored bass player Hersch knew called Ronald, plus a drummer, a guitarist, a clarinetist, a trombonist, and a trumpet player. Hersch found a few empty seats in the back of the hall, and discreetly, we took two of them, brushing snow from our hair and coats. Jeffery waved as soon as his passage was over.

"You're going to love these guys, Syl. They're as cool as can be!" he said grinning with dark eyes sparkling, patting my arm.

"You sound just like a jazz cat, yourself!" I said with a giggle. We listened for a while to "Sweet Georgia Brown" and then I asked, "Have you been back to Dot Dot Dot?"

He shook his head. "Actually, no. I haven't, thanks to you. You talked sense into my thick skull that night, Sylvie. You were right; we all could have been expelled for that kind of behavior—the drinking and smoking and being somewhere we weren't supposed to be. It's risky to take such chances around here. I didn't realize at the time how strict they are. And it's a real privilege being at Oberlin."

"Well, then we were all lucky. I knew I should have been mad at you that night."

"You had every right to be. It's a shame, though, that they don't allow us to take gigs outside of the Conservatory, you know? Can you imagine these fellows playing in town somewhere? They would knock the socks off everybody in the place and make some cash doing it!"

I nodded. "You're right about that. The musicians here are a well-kept secret. They sure know how to play jazz!" I said, tapping my toes to their arrangement of "Bye Bye Blackbird."

"They're swell, aren't they?"

"Yes! We don't even need alcohol to appreciate them," I said with a laugh.

Hersch chuckled. "You're right! That's the true test of Oberlin musicians. No vices allowed to create, and none needed to appreciate! If you can't abide by their rules and be successful, you're tossed out on your tochus!"

"Your *what?*" I asked, eyes wide.

"That's another Yiddish word. It means buttocks."

"Oh!" I said, going back to listening to the music. For once, I didn't blush!

"My brother Kip would love this! He plays the clarinet and goes to speakeasies all the time down in Raleigh."

"They have them there?" he asked, surprised.

"Yes, the South is not as backward as you may think. We even wear shoes!" I winked at him.

"Must be nice to be a regular college student and have a life!" Hersch laughed and shook his head.

"I know! Conservatory life has been tough. But Thanksgiving is coming. You'll get to be a real person again soon! Are you going home to New York?"

Hersch smiled and shook his head. "No, not until the end of the semester. I'm going home with Bart again. I enjoyed being in Chicago with his family for the fall break. His family is quite well off, and I admit I enjoyed the luxurious long weekend. I had never been to Chicago, and there's some great jazz there. We spent the whole time in the cabarets and speakeasys there—don't tell though—just soaking it all up. I'm looking forward to going back again."

"That's nice that he invited you to go home with him again! Is it that far to New York City?"

"No. There are other reasons I'm avoiding New York," he said. "But you're going to Wilmington, which is a hell of a long way. Didn't Dot invite you back?"

"It's not that. My aunt's wedding is the Saturday after Thanksgiving, so I have to go."

"Isn't your aunt a little old to be getting married?"

"Oh, she was married before, but her husband died in the war. Still, I don't mind the distance. I can't wait to go home. I miss my family and friends so much! And I'll get to stick my toes in the ocean again!"

"Won't it be too cold for that?"

I laughed. "No. It might be a bit chilly there, but not cold like it is here. I now know the difference!"

Hersch smiled and rested his chin in his hand. "Sounds wonderful. Do you have someone back home? A boy pining for you?"

"Hardly!" I scoffed.

"I can't believe it! A girl as pretty and special as you should have a whole line of suitors."

I wanted to say, "Well, you could be one," but secretly knowing Hersch's unusual circumstances, I thought it unkind to goad him.

Instead, I squeezed his arm and said, "Thank you for the compliment. I just like being with whoever is kind. Friends are more important than suitors anyway."

He smiled at me and nodded. "That's very smart, Sylvie. Another reason you should have a line of men at your door."

Friday, November 23, 1928

We had one more treat in the Conservatory before our Thanksgiving break began. At convocation this evening, Miss Devereaux gave a recital! It was doubly delightful because Mr. Finch was her accompanist. Mina and I sat with Bart, Herschel, and Dot in the center of the audience, so we had the best view of our mentors. Miss Devereaux wore a satin dress in a gorgeous shade of cerise, like a maraschino cherry, and it hung so tastefully on her frame. Still, I think many of the students and some faculty alike were a little scandalized! However, I loved it! Something about Miss Devereaux reminds me of my dear friend Catherine. They both tend to take the world by the tail, and I believe that lesson has been the theme for my first semester at Oberlin.

Miss Devereaux's huge smile and her exuberant stage presence were so infectious that Mina and I were almost giddy before she even opened her mouth. I am sure others in the audience felt the same way. This anticipation is what a seasoned virtuoso performer creates. Then she began with a French art song, "Après un Rêve" by Gabriel Fauré, followed by arias by Puccini and Handel, which were all exquisitely performed. She ended her program with Mozart's "Queen of the Night" aria from *The Magic Flute*. I had never heard this aria, or many of the vocal selections before, but this aria was astonishing! The range of notes, the pitch intervals, and the vocal calisthenics it took her to sing the runs so easily made a performance like I have never witnessed in all the convocations and recitals I have attended thus far. Her mouth movements during the many quick and controlled pitches of "ahhs" she sang were as fascinating to watch as to hear. I was enthralled by the song and Miss Devereaux's talent. At the end, all of us leaped to our feet as if one and applauded our hearts out. So moved were we that Mina was crying; I was speechless; Dot was crying, speechless, and openmouthed in amazement at what we had heard. The boys, now ardent fans, applauded and shouted "Brava!" as Miss Devereaux graciously took her bows. One of her students presented her with a spray of roses. Miss Devereaux gestured to Mr. Finch, who stood and bowed, then gestured back to her and applauded with the rest of us, who were still clapping and shouting.

Leaving the auditorium that evening, I felt proud to know Miss Devereaux and Mr. Finch. The five of us students went directly to the Oberlin Inn for dinner, where we discussed her thrilling performance and how honored we all are to be in the presence of such an inspiration as Miss Devereaux. Mina couldn't stop smiling, her eyes alight with all the possibilities before her. I think for the first time since she arrived at Oberlin, Mina believes she could be something like her teacher. I know she will be for a fact, and I told her so. For me, the best part is I will be able to witness Mina's rise firsthand from the bench of a Steinway!

CHAPTER NINE

Anne Borden

AB gave Elle a break from reading by pouring her a glass of wine. She passed wine glasses to the men next.

"Time for the seventh inning stretch!" said Nate, reaching his arms high over his head.

"I feel like we should toast Miss Devereaux!" AB said, raising her glass. The others responded in kind, standing, and stretching after Elle's reading.

"I want to hear about Sylvie's trip home and Aunt Andrea's wedding," Elle said after sipping her Sauvignon blanc.

"I want to hear about Mother's encounter with Heckie!" said AB. "Enough of this Herschel character."

Bernard laughed and handed around the plate of lemon bars, his favorites, from Elle's bakery. He seemed to be eating all his favorite things lately, to comfort himself during the lockdown. *That's why it's called comfort food*, he thought, aware that his pants fit more snugly than last month.

When they took their seats again, AB sipped the last of her wine, picked up the diary, and began to read.

SYLVIE

Sunday, December 2, 1928

Dear Diary,

As the train takes us back to Ohio, I have finally found the time to write. Between being amid so many family members, the Thanksgiving dinner, the celebration of Aunt Andrea and Benton's wedding, and seeing Kip, Catherine, and Heckie, I hardly know where to start. Everyone else is napping in our compartment. This trip has been wonderful, if taxing, and I am so wound up trying to sort through the details in my mind that there is no possibility of sleep for me. We have a long ride, so I will try to cover one event at a time so it will make sense to me one day when I am old and gray, looking back on these important events.

Uncle Harry, Aunt Nell, and my grandmother all exclaimed how grown-up I have become. They just saw me in August, so my burgeoning adulthood must be as obvious to them as it is to me. Surely the noticeable change in my speech has called the most attention to my progress. Leaving the piano behind for the train ride was a welcome respite, replaced by answering many questions and giving my impressions of life in the Conservatory. Talking about Oberlin was good practice for when I arrived at home and had to recite it over again and again, deciding what to leave in and what to leave out, depending on the company.

Kip picked us up at the train depot. His grin has gotten even bigger if that can even be possible! When he picked me up and spun me around, I could feel how he has filled out. He seems manlier in his manner too; we are all still growing, I suppose.

"Where is Catherine?" I demanded after he greeted everyone and had Grandmother's luggage in hand.

"And hello to you, too!" he chided me. "She is at home with her family, as she should be," he said, losing the smile for a moment as we moved down the concourse amid the new arrivals. "She sends her love. You'll see her on Friday and, of course, on Saturday at the wedding. Besides, with all of you to collect, I couldn't fit anyone else in Pop's car!" he said, laughing.

"Is there a dance at Lumina on Saturday night?"

"You bet there is! We're all looking forward to it. Especially Heckie!"

"You've talked to Heckie?" I'd almost forgotten he was coming.

"Yes! I stopped by his house on the way here to say hello. We made plans to take you girls out on Friday to catch up."

"Oh, that will be the bee's knees!" I said, shoving my knitted gloves in my handbag and fanning my coat. It was much warmer here, and the sunshine felt glorious on my face.

When we arrived at home, Pearl greeted us at the door, while Kip and Uncle Harry wrestled with the suitcases. Grandmother allowed Pearl to take her hat, gloves, and coat, and then Aunt Nell piled hers on. I hugged Pearl and offered to help.

"Hello, Miss Sylvie! Oh, you look fine! Jes' fine!" Pearl said, beaming at me as I peeled off my coat and removed my cloche.

"Pearl, it's so good to see you! I've missed you so much. I didn't expect to see you here, though. Isn't Nellie working here now?"

"Yes, 'um. She in the kitchen. Gregory at home keepin' little Birdie. He sho' do love that lil young'un!"

"Oh! How is Gregory?"

"Fine and fit as a fiddle. He was jes' here day before yesterday tunin' your piano for you. We figured you'd be playin' for the whole family. Do you like it at that school up there?"

"I do, Pearl. Please thank Gregory for me. I know the tuning will be perfect as always. School is wonderful, but there are so many damn Yankees there who think I talk so funny!"

Pearl laughed. "Miss Sylvie, I b'lieve they done changed you. You sound jes' like one o' them now."

"Oh, no, Pearl! I'll just have to go back to my 'native tongue' as they call it while I'm here!" I said, reverting to my Southern accent, and we shared a laugh as we hung coats and hats on the coat tree in the foyer.

Pearl nodded. "Ain't nothin' wrong with your talkin', Miss Sylvie. I've missed it, I have."

"There you are at last!" Aunt Andrea cried, coming through the kitchen and the dining room with arms open for me. "Oh, you look wonderful, Sylvie! You hardly have time to write, but it is so good to see your face!"

We hugged and my smile continued to grow upon seeing my aunt. "I'm sorry I don't write more letters! I just love my hat and gloves! See?" I said, pulling them from my handbag to show her. "They match my coat almost as if they were made together. And they're so warm! Thank you for making them and sending them to me."

"You are quite welcome. It was my pleasure to help warm you from here."

"You're cooking Thanksgiving dinner one day, getting married two days later," I said. "How on earth do you have time for such things as knitting hats and gloves?"

"Oh, I love to knit in the evenings when we sit and listen to the radio. It's quite relaxing. I like to feel productive too."

After settling Grandmother and Aunt Nell into their rooms upstairs to freshen up, Aunt Andrea and I went to work in my room unpacking my suitcase so we could visit in private. I showed her my new dress for the wedding, and she approved.

"So, tell me all about the Conservatory! Is it wonderful?" she asked, sitting beside me on the bed. I know she'd have given her eye teeth to attend a place like Oberlin.

"It is wonderful but depressing at times and hard too."

"Oh? How is it depressing?"

"The campus is very isolated, and they don't let you do anything except practice—no drinking or smoking, and hardly any dancing. The sky is always gray now. Everyone there is so ambitious; it's like crabs in a barrel, everyone trying to outdo the next fellow. Being a Southerner hasn't helped. I was just telling Pearl about it. I should be proud of my home and the way I talk. When I'm at the Conservatory, I feel such a need to please and fit in, but I really don't want to be like them. Some of them aren't all that nice. They think I'm ignorant because of the way I talk. They think it's an act. Mina has given me diction lessons."

"Oh, Sylvie, I'm so sorry!"

"I just want to be me, really."

"As of course you should. I know it takes courage to be among others who seem so different. I did notice you seem to have lost your accent. I wouldn't worry too much about your speech. Your fingers will do all the talking for those who count. And anyway, it's what you say that make us love you, not the way you say it."

I felt tears sting my throat for a moment when she said that.

"It sure is good to be home, Aunt Andrea. I need to hear things like that."

"I'm sure we're not the only ones who love you, dear. How about the boys? You've mentioned a few. Has anyone tugged at your heartstrings?"

"Well, I did take a shine to a boy named Herschel Blum. He's from New York City! He plays the violin, and I thought he liked me too."

"But?"

"Don't tell Father yet; I want to be the one to do it. Herschel is Jewish."

"Oh, how unusual. Are there many Jews at Oberlin?"

"No. He's about as rare as I am, being a 'Southern belle' as they call me. He thinks it would be best if we were just friends."

"Oh! Well, he is probably right. I would imagine you make an odd couple. You would both have problems if you became serious about him."

"That's what he said, too. I don't understand it, though. What harm is there in liking someone who believes differently than you do?"

"There are lots of rules that get in the way being with someone of a different religion or culture. Not everyone looks at the world the way we do, Sylvie. Your father and I think differently than most folks in Wilmington, and so do you and Kip. I believe we are ahead of our time. But even we share the same culture and traditions as most of the white people here. Birds of a feather tend to flock together. Even in New York City, I understand that groups live in neighborhoods together and they don't mix with others." She shrugged. "Italians don't associate with Germans; Jews don't mix with Christians. That's just the way it is."

I nodded glumly. If Andrea knew what Hersch's real problem was, I don't think she would have been so confident in her classification system.

I sighed. "I guess it really doesn't matter. He's a very nice friend, so I won't allow my heart to be broken. Miss Devereaux says as performers, we should choose family life or performance life. She doesn't believe one can have both."

"How sad, Sylvie!" Aunt Andrea looked concerned. "I suppose I have the best of both worlds, then. I can be married to Benton, and I can still teach piano to my students. Maybe that can happen for you, too."

I didn't want to show her any disrespect for how she has chosen her own life's path, but I believe I do crave the stage, as Mr. Finch says. "Professor Finch believes I have a bright future as a performer. He looks forward to when I can perform at the convocation. There are so many music students in the Conservatory that freshmen aren't even allowed to perform until the second year. By then, Willemina and I will both be a big surprise." I grinned, aware that my confidence had grown up too.

"You have mentioned Mina in your letters and how good she is. What is she like?"

"She's going to be a star," I said with conviction. "Oh, and she told me her family is originally from Wilmington."

"Oh! What a small world it is!"

"Yes. She and her family are very proud of their history. Her grandfather was an escaped slave. He worked for Mr. Nixon who owned the peanut plantation up on Porters Neck. Her grandfather worked at Nixon's house in town and stole away during the yellow fever outbreak in 1862 when everyone fled town. He joined the U.S. Navy and eventually made his way to Cleveland." I had omitted this story when telling my grandmother about the Conservatory. Not all my relatives are as broad-minded about colored people as my father and his sister. There was no sense in ruffling anyone's feathers.

"Mina is colored?" Aunt Andrea asked.

"Yes. There are lots of colored students there. She is quite talented. And Miss Devereaux, her teacher, is wonderful. She used to sing opera in Chicago. Her recital was Friday night, and I have never heard anyone sing like she did."

Aunt Andrea was pensive for a moment. "Sylvie, you are full of surprises! You have such a diverse group of friends." She looked sad. Hearing my report must not have been what she had expected. I didn't understand her feeling sorry for me.

"But I'm so glad to be there. I appreciate the sacrifice Father has made to send me to Oberlin. It's a privilege, really—all the concerts and plays I get to attend. I have such an opportunity ahead of me."

"You're very brave, Sylvie. I admire the courage you have to pursue your dreams."

I smiled. "I'm lucky. Please don't be concerned. My friends really are wonderful. We all support each other. Oberlin can be such a dreary and lonely place this time of year. It's nice to have good people in my corner."

I could hardly wait to see Catherine! Aunt Andrea encouraged me to invite her over on Friday to help with the wedding flowers. Catherine's dark bobbed hair was neatly trimmed and brushed until it was sleek and shiny. School had not changed her; she was as tall, slim, and beautiful as ever. She came bearing a basketful of beautiful roses from her rose garden! I had forgotten her passion for gardening.

"Oh, Catherine, thank you! These are heavenly!" exclaimed Aunt Andrea.

"There is not a single rose to be found in Ohio this time of year," I added.

"Where did you learn to grow roses like these, Catherine?" my aunt asked, in awe.

"My mother's cousin taught me everything! He and his wife live on Long Island, and I have spent a lot of time there, learning from Richard," Catherine said, her eyes demurring, as I saw my aunt catch her breath and nod quickly. "My mother allowed me to plant a rose garden."

"You should see it, Aunt Andrea. It's quite spectacular!"

"Well, they are all just gorgeous. I have never seen some of these varieties."

"Yes, they are hybrids," Catherine explained absently. "I hope to start a landscape business someday."

"Oh!" Aunt Andrea said, eyes wide at Catherine's precociousness. "I recall Kip saying something about your plans to study horticulture when you leave St. Mary's at Christmas."

"Yes. That is what I hope to do. I've already been accepted at a college in Massachusetts."

My heart fluttered when she said Massachusetts. It was so far away…like I was. "Oh, Catherine, that's wonderful news!" I said. "Congratulations!" I kept "but you'll be so far away" to myself.

After the bouquets were made and several arrangements placed in the house, we were dismissed to go on our merry way, so Catherine and I decided to ride the trolley over to the beach to stick our feet in the ocean. It was a gloriously warm and sunny day. Kip and Heckie were playing golf with a couple of their friends who were also home for the holiday. Catherine and I had all day to catch up before the boys took us to dinner at the Oceanic Hotel later.

We walked on the beach near the yacht club and sat in the sun. I took off my hat, letting it warm my face. It was heaven, sitting there with my friend, basking under the vast blue sky painted with cottony puffs of white, and watching the waves spill and roll over the sand. How I have missed the ocean and that shade of aquamarine! Gulls soared overhead and sandpipers skittered in perfect synchrony along the quicksilver sand in front of us. A father and his two young sons fished for blues in the surf. I breathed deeply of the pungent salt air; at last, I was home!

I had told Catherine about my experiences at the Conservatory, playing for Mina, and how I seemed to be catching onto what they want us to do there. Then she asked me about my love life.

"There's not much to tell," I said woefully.

"I don't believe that for a minute!" she scoffed.

"Well, there is a boy. A Jewish boy that I like…liked."

"Oh, I suppose *that's* a problem."

"I don't care whether he is Jewish or Buddhist, but that really isn't the problem."

"What is it, then?

"Herschel prefers other boys."

"Oh, dear! Well, that does pose a new problem for you."

"The thing is, he doesn't know that I know. He and Bart present themselves as models of decorum, so I would never have guessed, but Mina pointed it out to Dot and me. I really liked him. Anyway, Hersch's roommate Bart is Dot's accompanist, and he and Bart are a couple, apparently. We girls are trying to protect them by pretending the four of us are dating. Neither of the boys has any idea we know about them, but they seem glad to squire us all around campus. They don't realize that we know we are keeping them safe, which may be their goal. You know, they could get kicked out on their *tochuses* for perverted behavior!"

"Oh, golly! You're learning *Yiddish*…and so much more! Sylvie, you are a changed woman!"

"Life is quite different at Oberlin, that's for sure."

"It's shocking how different it is. That a colored singer and a sissy Jewish boyfriend are two of your four friends is certainly different from what you are used to here. However, you seem well-adjusted enough."

"They are all my friends, Catherine. And they are all wonderful. I have always resented when people have tried to cover things up to protect me, but now I think I understand why they do it. Now I'm the one covering things up for the good of others."

"Yes, there usually are very good reasons when people keep secrets from one another," she said, gazing out to sea. She placed my hat back on my head and smiled at me, letting her hand rest on my shoulder, and smoothing an escaped curl behind my ear. "Don't worry about this Herschel fellow, Sylvie. Heckie is dying to see you!" she said, digging an elbow into my side and making me giggle.

"Heckie is the best. I almost forgot he was coming!"

"Don't tell him that, Sylvie. He'll be crushed!"

"Yeah, I would be too if someone said that about me. He's going to be at the wedding tomorrow."

"And don't forget you're seeing him tonight for our dinner date. I think he's arranging an evening sail for the four of us, so bring a coat. It will be chilly in the wind."

"How gallant!"

Catherine snugged her skirt down over her knees and rocked them back and forth contentedly. Then she pulled a pack of Lucky Strikes out of her pocket and lit one, offering the pack to me.

"No thanks," I said. "They don't allow smoking at Oberlin. Not as if I have ever smoked anyway. When did you start smoking again?" I asked.

She smiled ruefully at the sand. "Soon after I returned to St. Mary's," she said, staring at the ember on the cigarette's tip. "It calms me."

"Being away from home is hard," I said.

"I actually love being away from home. Not this part of home, though," she said, gesturing to the beach and the ocean in front of us. "That's what I need to talk to you about, Sylvie. My disdain for home and why that is," she said, turning to me and smiling sadly. She blinked back tears and balled her fist at her mouth.

"Oh, Catherine, what is it?" I asked, laying a comforting hand on her shoulder.

She shook her head. "I have so much to be thankful for, Sylvie. This holiday has reminded me of it especially. My friends, you and Kip. You're both wonderful. I love your brother so deeply, Sylvie. He means the world to me for so many reasons. He has been the Rock of Gibraltar for me when I needed his shoulder. And I have needed it. I thought when I returned to school in Raleigh again that all my troubles would be gone, but little did I know it was not to be the case." She sighed, studying the cigarette again. She inhaled it and let out a stream of smoke before she could continue.

"This is about Clifton, isn't it?" I asked, stroking her back.

She nodded. "I can't erase what happened. I can't forgive myself for killing him."

"Oh, I know it was horrible, but Catherine, you didn't mean to do it! You said it was an accident!"

"Yes, it was. I was trying to kill myself, and then Kip was there, standing in the road before me, so I swerved to the Rosy Tree, which was my intention all along and…there was Clifton…standing there. And…I plowed right into him."

"But you couldn't stop. That's what you said before."

"No, I couldn't. I *couldn't*. And worse, I didn't want to. I recalled that thought later, after I had regained consciousness. I didn't want to stop. Kip is the only other person I have told."

I was speechless for a moment.

"That's why I need to talk to you, Sylvie. There is so much you don't know. I can't expect you to understand much of it. I can't expect you to forgive me for the lies…for everything I will tell you now."

"What lies?"

"I haven't told you everything, so there are many lies, or sins of omission, if you will. When I'm finished, I wouldn't blame you if you walked away from me and never wanted to see me again. Kip found out parts of my past in the worst way. I have shared the rest of the story with him, and it was difficult for him to hear, as it will be for you, but he has resolved to stand by me because he loves me so much. Even though you are my friend and I love you as I would love a sister, I can't expect the same from you, Sylvie. The truth is just too much to bear, even for me. Thus, the cigarette," she said, waving what was left of it in the air, then stubbing it out in the sand and returning it to its pack. Catherine was never one to make a mess.

I placed my hands in my lap and looked her in the eye.

"Try me."

A wisp of a smile crossed her lips and she stared down the beach toward Lumina.

"Did you know that Clifton was adopted?"

CHAPTER TEN

Mr. May

Sylvie had written such a long passage that AB's voice had started to give out. Bernard had thought everyone needed to stay to hear what was about to unfold; they already knew from the book they had read over the summer, but it would be interesting to hear the story from Catherine herself. Sylvie was certainly learning more about the world at the Conservatory than she thought she would, and now being back at home was about to catapult her smack into adulthood. Secrets and lies were an inevitable part of life, and no matter how hard one tried, it was difficult to maintain an innocent perspective on life.

Bernie had lived with a secret too. He knew AB had liked him all those years ago when he had courted Daphne and then married her. He had never mentioned it because what was the point? AB had married Monty. Revealing that he knew would have been hurtful to both women who had been friends until Daphne died years ago. And look at the two of them now, living together at the ripe old age of eighty, almost like a married couple, taking care of each other. Maybe their situation had turned out for the best, but it was still odd that he and AB never discussed it. They just went on about their business. Quarantining together had created an interesting situation. He was well enough to return to his own house, yet here they were. Still the secrets were there beneath the surface, beneath the unspoken words.

He took the diary from AB, cleared his throat, and began to read:

SYLVIE

I was indeed surprised. "No!"

"Yes, he was. Early in her marriage to my father, my mother thought she would never have children. My parents were on Long Island visiting her cousin Richard and his wife Penelope. There was a girl who had been staying with them. She had had a baby out of wedlock under their care. The baby was to be put up for adoption, but the couple changed their minds. As you can imagine, it was a difficult situation for Richard and Penelope. Knowing how much my parents wanted children, Penelope asked if they would consider taking the child. It was a boy. They took him home and named him Clifton."

She glanced at me to see the appropriate surprise register on my face.

"But your mother did go on to have children."

"Yes. To her surprise, she had Warren, then me, and then Willard. As you know, Warren died from scarlet fever and Willard had polio, which kept Mother quite busy. But Clifton was not my brother. It's important that you know *that*, Sylvie."

"Okay," I said, expecting her to continue.

"We found out one night when we were stargazing on the roof and overheard our parents by the pool talking about the girl who gave Clifton up. Neither of us knew he was adopted until then. I was ten at the time and Clifton was fifteen. We were shocked, of course. We didn't let on that we knew, but Clifton was so angry that they'd kept it from him. I felt sorry for him. He soon became my best friend, not my brother after all, but that was what everyone else thought. We were young; we didn't even consider how the world might view us."

I nodded, starting to understand what she meant, and feeling a bit light-headed. I waited for her to gather her wits to tell me the rest.

"Our mother retreated into herself when Warren died. She was still taking Willard up to the Boston Clinic for his polio treatments. Clifton and I had to take care of each other a lot during those times, and we got even closer. I depended on him, and I loved him so much for being there for me. By then, we were a bit older, and we both wondered about the feelings that were developing between us."

I breathed in. "What kinds of feelings?"

She hesitated, running fingers through her hair. "Sexual feelings. We slept together during scary thunderstorms, and one night, we…we went too far."

I gasped.

"I know. You don't understand. I'm so sorry to shock you like this."

"Why are you telling me this?" I asked, jumping to my feet and walking a few feet from Catherine. She stood and followed me.

"I have to tell you this because he kept on doing it. I wanted him to stop, but he kept on for years. He forced himself on me, Sylvie. For years. He raped me, and I didn't know what to do about it. I couldn't tell my mother."

"Why not? Surely she would have helped you!"

"No. I was so ashamed I couldn't. I knew loving him was wrong, but I did have a part in it. When I was thirteen, my mother told me having a period meant I could have babies. I was too ashamed to tell her what we were doing. When I realized what could happen to me, I thought I could stop the encounters, but he didn't want to. He was eighteen and undeterred. Your aunt was always so kind to me, so I tried to tell Andrea one day at my piano lesson, but she wouldn't talk about it. She said it was a family matter that didn't concern her. She refused to teach me anymore. That was why our lessons ended."

I shook my head, wanting to cover my ears, but I knew there was more.

"Then when our family was in Cuba, Clifton forced himself on me again. It was the night I wore the blue-sequined dress that you bought at the thrift shop."

I looked at her aghast. I had no response except to stare. My head was spinning.

"I had a baby, Sylvie. My parents didn't know it was Clifton's. I couldn't tell them what we'd done. They sent me to live with Richard and Penelope, and they found adoptive parents. I had a girl, Rose, and I gave her away. I felt so awful abandoning the child I'd borne, but I was a child myself! No one knew I was pregnant, except Dr. Sidbury and his nurse, Betsy Pile. I was so afraid she would tell everyone when I started dating Kip."

Many things were starting to fall into place. My father had decided not to marry Betsy Pile after a disagreement he said they'd had. It must have been about Catherine. Clifton had almost had his way with *me*. I could only imagine the fear and shame Catherine had been through. I remember how Aunt Andrea was so distraught after the accident when Kip came home from the hospital and talked to her in private.

"I thought you might have gone away to have a baby. That's what Marjorie thought. Did you tell Kip?"

"Yes. But I refused to tell him who the father was. I was so ashamed and afraid he would be repulsed by me and let me go. I admitted being misguided and he forgave me."

"Did my father know about the baby?"

"Yes. Kip told him. Your father said he and Betsy talked about it since they were newly engaged. Because I was a disgrace, she advised him to tell

Kip to drop me like a hot rock. It would have been an epic scandal for my family if the knowledge were made public. Kip convinced your father to guard my secret because he loved me so much, despite my circumstances. My parents were horrified that I'd gotten with child, and they kept me under their thumb when I returned. Of course, they didn't know the baby was Clifton's. The ironic thing was, once I returned from having Rose, they made Clifton chaperone me all summer to protect me, when *he* was the very one who had gotten me in trouble."

"That's why Kip and Clifton were always at odds over the summer?" I couldn't imagine my brother being so tolerant of Clifton.

"No, not at first. Kip didn't know until the night of the accident. But all summer Clifton was quite manipulative and overprotective of me, and it irritated Kip. I couldn't tell Kip that Clifton had fathered my child. I hated keeping the truth from him, but I knew I could never tell him. Kip was shocked enough about the baby, of course, but he was surprisingly forgiving and sympathetic. I didn't deserve it. That's when I knew he truly loved me. Not many men these days would support a ruined girl like me. It was so much worse, though, because Clifton was the father. Do you see why I kept it from everyone?"

Despite the ugliness of what she'd told me, I couldn't imagine going through what Catherine had experienced. And after my own experience with her "brother," I understood how horrible it must have been for her.

"Why couldn't you have told your parents, though? If Clifton took advantage of you, why didn't you just tell them?"

"Because he would have denied it. He told me they would never believe me. And he was right. I was reckless and rebellious, and very hard to handle. Plenty of boys liked me and wanted to court me." She scoffed. "My parents would never have taken my word for it, thinking I was covering for another boy. Knowing he was adopted, Clifton played the model son because he was desperate to inherit his part of my father's fortune. He did everything he could to ingratiate himself to my father. He was learning the shipping business, doing my father's bidding for whatever whim or deed he thought needed doing to prove his fealty to the family."

"That's terrible, Catherine. But I saw that side of Clifton, too. He tried to manipulate me to keep Kip away from you. Now I understand why he did it."

"Yes. He was out of his mind with jealousy. Being controlled by him was terrifying! All I wanted to do was run away from him, this place, and all of them. That's why I am so determined to go away to college and learn how to make my own way in the world."

I thought back over the summer's events and how all the clues had been right under my nose, but I had seen none of it. Kip was surely good at keeping all this a secret. That's why at the end of the summer he was so distant.

"How did Kip find out about Clifton?"

"I didn't tell him. On the night of the accident, Clifton was drunk, so Kip saw him home after the dance at Lumina when all of you did the Shag and I was sick at home. You see, I thought I was pregnant again."

"With Kip's baby?" I gasped, my hand going to my mouth.

"No! I was never with Kip that way. But Clifton tried to blame it on Kip and told my parents to make him leave me for good. He thought Kip and I had actually…been together. Do you remember the night in the rose garden when you and Clifton found me with Kip?"

I nodded.

"Clifton realized I was in love with Kip, so he raped me again that night in anger. The night of the Shag debut, I had missed my period and was sure I was in trouble again, so I stayed home from Lumina and begged my parents for an abortion."

"No!"

"Sylvie, I couldn't go through having another child to have it taken from me again. I just couldn't. Having an abortion seemed the only answer for everyone's sake."

I shuddered, stunned and sickened. Catherine was right; what she was telling me was too much to comprehend.

"That's the conversation Kip and Clifton walked in on by our pool that night, and then everything unraveled. When Kip heard I was pregnant again and my father accused him of taking advantage of me, he couldn't believe it. Kip had treated me like the perfect gentleman he is. He asked me if it were true, and I said it was. My father started to attack Kip, believing he was the father. I shouted for him to stop and blurted out the truth to them about Clifton. They were all stunned with disbelief. When Kip heard that Clifton was the father of my first baby, he looked at me with such an expression of disgust that I knew it was over between us. I told them all that Clifton had been the one who had taken advantage of me, forcing himself on me again and again.

"Then Clifton told them all that he and I knew he was adopted and that he wasn't my brother, and that we'd been in love for years. Kip said our love didn't matter, that Clifton had still raped me. He got so angry, and Clifton was just laughing about it. My father threw his glass on the ground, and everyone was yelling, and it was just chaos! My mother was crying. I was so…devastated. Here, I thought I was pregnant again. Knowing I had lost Kip forever was too much to bear. My life was over anyway, and my family was going to be scandalized, so I decided to wreck myself on the Rosy Tree. If I couldn't have Kip, I wanted to die."

She swallowed and shook her head, rubbing her arms to calm herself. "They were still arguing. Kip said Clifton had been seen at Shell Island, pouring gasoline on the place, and lighting it on fire with his cigarette. Then they started fighting and my father was trying to break them apart. My mother was screaming for them to stop. I couldn't take any more, so

I just…ran off. Kip had taught me how to drive, so I knew just what I needed to do to end my life."

"No! Catherine!" I cried, knowing that was exactly what she had done.

"I had nothing to live for. I couldn't live with myself, knowing what Kip must have thought about me. The look on his face…. I was a total disgrace; I had no future, so what was the point of going on? I'd just lost the love of my life."

We were silent a moment. I recalled that night when Kip didn't come home. Our household was distraught until he arrived the next morning and explained about the accident and spending the night in the hospital with Catherine. So much was left unsaid. He wouldn't tell me anything except he needed to be with Catherine. After brief talks with Father and Aunt Andrea, my father left him alone. Aunt Andrea withdrew to her bedroom, weeping.

"So, when you left the hospital, you came home and got better. I don't understand. What happened to the baby? Your pregnancy?"

"There was never a second baby. While I was unconscious, the doctor examined me and saw my monthly flow had started. I was never pregnant after all."

"Oh, Catherine!"

"Ironic, wasn't it? All that worry and chaos for nothing. I would have killed myself for nothing. Well…almost nothing. Kip still knew about Clifton and me." She shook her head and continued.

"My parents were beside themselves that Clifton was dead. My father kept saying it was an accident. They were relieved that at least I wasn't going to have another baby and ruin their reputation," she said bitterly.

"But thank God, you were alive!" I looked at her, incredulous at what she implied.

"That's what Kip said. He was wonderful, staying by my bedside, swearing to my father that he loved me and that he would take care of me if the whole story got out and a scandal caused my father to disown me."

"Oh, but your father wouldn't do a thing like that, would he? You're his only daughter! Surely your mother had some say in the matter!"

Catherine scoffed. "I'm on probation, so to speak. If I can get through college without ruining them, I can have my trust when I turn twenty-five. If not, I'll be on my own. I want to be on my own anyway, so I don't even want the money. I can't get far enough away from them, Sylvie. And your darling brother says he will follow me to the ends of the earth to be with me."

I stared at the ocean, taking in everything she'd said. It was a horrible story. Horrible things had happened to Catherine when she was just a child. She'd had no one to turn to. Even my aunt had shunned her. Her own parents had thought she had disgraced them. Everyone had turned on her, except my brother. He, like me, realized that Catherine was a victim…and a prisoner in the jail of that terrible secret.

How she was able to hide her pain and live a seemingly normal life was beyond me. I admired Catherine's courage and her determination to move on and make something of herself on her own terms. I was happy that my brother was a strong and sensible man and sought justice for her, his beloved. It stirred my heart, making tears run down my cheeks.

Catherine turned to face me.

"I'm sorry, Sylvie. It's too much to take in. I didn't mean to ruin your holiday and your aunt's wedding. It was selfish of me to unload my burdens on you."

I took her hand. "I'm glad you told me. You aren't the least bit selfish. It took great courage to confess your story to me. I hope it helped."

Catherine bit her lip as if unsure.

"You didn't deserve what happened to you. It wasn't your fault. I'm sorry about what Clifton did to you and how confused you must have been about your feelings for him. I'm sorry you lost Clifton without being able to work through your problems. I'm sorry your parents are punishing you. They don't see what a wonderful person and friend you are. I hope you'll be able to share all this freely with them one day. They have to understand."

She shook her head. "One step at a time, I think."

"I understand. But you haven't been selfish in keeping your secrets; you were just trying to survive. Kip knows that. And you haven't ruined anything. I hope by telling me everything, you're able to let go of the past and live in peace. I want that for you. I want you and Kip to be happy and to do whatever you want. You must embrace whatever makes you happy in this life and not dwell in sorrow and regret. I'm your friend, Catherine, and I'll try to help you find your happiness."

The worry on her face melted into relief, and a smile pushed slowly across her lips.

"Thank you, Sylvie. Yes, I think telling you has helped me. I've asked you and Kip for help because you are the only people who seem to care enough to help me. Thank you for being my friend. I do love you as if you were my sister."

"I feel the same way about you, Catherine!" I smiled at her and hugged her. Beaming to the sky, she raised her hands into the air as if a heavy burden had been lifted.

ELLE

The four on the porch sat in stunned silence for a moment, letting Catherine's story set in. Her details explained so much and answered questions they'd all had after they had finished the manuscript from last summer.

"My God! It must have been such a relief for Catherine to unload all that on Sylvie," Elle said. "And Sylvie needed to hear the whole story. She really seems to have grown up enough to handle what Catherine went through with Clifton and her parents."

"Now I see what good friends they became after Catherine told her everything," AB agreed. "I always wondered whether she intended to kill Clifton, but it really was an accident."

Mr. May nodded. "Yes, it was. But he brought his own fate upon himself, I suppose."

"Karma's a bitch," Nate added with a nod as the others chuckled in agreement.

"I don't think I understood before what a scandal they all were trying to cover up, you know?" Elle wondered aloud. "First there was a baby, then a sort of incestual relationship, and then a sociopathic adopted son who died at Catherine's hands."

"How much worse could it get?" AB added.

"If I were Catherine's father, I'd be glad Kip was in the picture to give Catherine an honorable out," said Nate.

"But still, Kip wasn't of the same social standing as the Carmichaels. In those days, it was always advisable to 'marry up,' even if the girl were wealthy. Kip would need to have been a prince to win Catherine's hand back then," AB explained.

Elle shook her hand in the air. "That seems like such—*baloney!*" she said passionately, refraining from what she really wanted to say. "Thank God we've moved on!"

"I think in some families, class distinctions are still very important, especially in places where family lineages mean something. Old Wilmington families, for example, are much like Old Charleston families in how they view social status. The grandparents and parents still have quite a say in who marries who," said Mr. May.

"That's right," AB agreed. "And it's not just in the South. Wealthy people from old money have always believed in bettering the next generations to keep their families in high esteem. And then there are the social climbers…."

Elle shook her head. "I think it's crazy. It all boils down to money and inheritances. People should just marry for love."

"I agree," said Nate, taking her hand.

"What could be worse than getting stuck in a loveless marriage just because it looks good on a family tree?"

"Well said, my dear. That is certainly true," said Mr. May.

"Chalk one up for Kip and Catherine," said Nate. "At least we know they married, but we don't know whether Catherine ever got her inheritance."

"Well, like her, I wouldn't care about the money. I've never had money and I don't expect I'll ever have much. I'm just so happy to have found the love of my life," Elle said, surprising herself, and apparently, her fiancé beside her.

As Nate seemed to be speechless at her sudden candor, Mr. May filled in the obvious. "Being rich in love is the best kind of wealth," he said with a wink for Elle.

SYLVIE

After Catherine's disturbing revelations to me this afternoon, I worried how we would appear that evening with Kip and Heckie. Kip and I were to drive down to Catherine's house and take the trolley across the waterway to meet Heckie at the Oceanic Hotel for dinner. Seeing her parents again was the last thing I wanted, knowing what I now knew. All that worry dissolved as the butler greeted us at the door and Catherine breezed past him, gorgeous in an indigo blue chemise and long gloves, her coat folded over her arm, as if she had not a care in the world. Kip kissed her squarely on the mouth and we were off, as though nothing ugly had transpired in anyone's life. Living above the fray is how they cope, I thought.

It was such fun riding the trolley again! Several people we knew were also aboard for the evening out on Wrightsville Beach, so we chatted until the beach car stopped at Station One and we hopped off. A good-looking, blond-haired man greeted us with an infectious smile and a hand down. It was Heckie!

My hand went to my mouth as he greeted me. "Sylvie Meeks, you are a sight for sore eyes!"

He swept me up in a bear hug and swung me around, much to Catherine and Kip's amusement, not to mention the others stepping off the beach car behind us.

"Oh, Heckie, it's so good to see you!" I exclaimed, looking him over and over. Not only had he transformed his physique with all the calisthenics he mentioned, but a new sense of confidence had taken control of his face. He had grown up too! And quite admirably, I thought, gazing up at him, rather speechless. Catching myself feeling his muscled arms as we held each other, I dropped my hands quickly. "You've changed!" was all I could muster, a ridiculous grin on my face, I'm sure.

"Well, so have you. You have gotten even prettier than I remember. Oberlin has done you well, it seems," he said with a wink and offering his arm. His voice was still as gentle as I remembered, but I thought, *Is this my shy, awkward friend?*

He greeted Kip and Catherine for the second time since they had all been home, so they seemed used to his new appearance. Still, Catherine gave me a special smile which acknowledged my reaction to the new man in our midst.

"Life as a midshipman agrees with you, as well, Heckie. You look fine yourself," I finally said. "You must enjoy what you're doing there," I added after a swallow, trying desperately to appear nonchalant.

"Yes, life in the Naval Academy is good. It's very exciting—hard—but exciting once I got into the routine."

"I find I crave the same novelty and excitement at the Conservatory. It was a bit of a shock at first, learning the expectations and getting to know different folks from other parts of the country. I rather like getting to know new people and learning about how others live. Of course, I stick out like a sore thumb! And the *music*, oh, there is so much to learn and experience! I have a satchel *full* of new pieces that will become my repertoire. It's all just wonderful!"

Heckie looked down and grinned at me. I'd forgotten how tall he was, or maybe he was still growing! Now I couldn't stop talking, but I think he liked it. Catherine and Kip smiled, listening to us go on about our new experiences. They were used to being away from home and doing new things. Plus, they had each other. Suddenly, my brother seemed so worldly and wise, and Catherine was equally impressive with everything she had overcome. Although we were the same age, in some ways she was eons older than me. As my eyes took in each of them as we walked along, it dawned on me how precious these times together would come to be, as we each grew up and went our separate ways. After Christmas, who knew when we would all be together again? I felt a tug at my heart as Heckie held the door for me, ushering me into the Oceanic's lobby, then held it for my brother to admit Catherine.

It was such a treat to go out for dinner in the hotel's elegant dining room. We swapped school stories over the delicious meal of fried chicken, mashed potatoes with gravy, collard greens, and baskets of cornbread. It was divine being back home and having a good Southern meal for a change. We toasted each other enthusiastically with tall glasses of sweet tea. I had missed food as much as I had missed family and friends.

The four of us laughed and reminisced about the dances at Lumina. When Heckie mentioned the night that the Shag was introduced and how much fun we all had dancing until the wee hours of the morning, the mood fizzled. He must have forgotten Catherine's mysterious absence that night and that Kip left early to see about her, following a drunken Clifton home to ensure he got there safely. Apparently, Heckie had forgotten the accident, having no idea about the events that had led up to it, a multitude of events I had just learned that afternoon.

To rescue him from the awkward silence about to ensue, I said, "I look forward to going back tomorrow night and showing them a thing or two on the dance floor."

Kip took up my mission, saying, "Yeah, it's the last dance of the season. It will be good to kick up our heels again and make some new memories there tomorrow night after Aunt Andrea's wedding."

His reference to the wedding segued neatly into a new conversation about what to expect about the ceremony at our house. After the men paid our bill, Catherine and I stopped at the coat check, and they helped us on with our coats. The air had turned crisp but not too chilly—a perfect evening to stroll the short distance from the hotel to the Carolina Yacht Club. It was already dark, the harvest moon just rising over the ocean, a huge golden orb sitting right on the water, making us catch our breath in wonder.

"I knew something special was in store for us tonight," Heckie murmured to me as we took our time walking down the sidewalk by the trolley line. He rubbed my hand, which hooked comfortably around his arm. I felt safe and content for the first time in ages. Glancing discreetly at Heckie's tanned face in the moonlight, I realized how handsome he had grown. His hair was precisely trimmed, and his chiseled features were no longer beefy and ruddy against his collar. He carried himself efficiently and competently, the perfect gentleman and protector. Would I have such a man by my side were I to choose a life of performance over family, as Miss Devereaux advocated? More than likely not.

Heckie had known me most of my life. It occurred to me that for most of the strange events of last summer involving first Clifton and then David, Heckie had always been there in the background, looking out for me. I had thought he did it as a favor to Kip, who was distracted with wooing Catherine, but possibly Heckie protected me for *me*. *How did I miss it?* All his quiet vigilance was deliberate and important without ever calling attention to himself. He caught me looking at him and smiled.

"Thank you for a lovely evening," I said.

"It's not over yet," he replied, his eyes meeting mine and making me blush.

"I know; it's just that I appreciate your bringing me here tonight, and I'm having a wonderful time already."

"Well, the best is yet to come," he said, grinning as we reached the gates for the yacht club. We turned toward the sound, and after passing several large boats moored at the club's docks, Heckie led us aboard a sleek wooden sailboat with a single mast, its sails wrapped in canvas covers.

"Here we are, mates!" he said, gesturing to Catherine and me to take seats. Then he reached inside a seat compartment and pulled out two woolen blankets to cover our laps. "I brought these for you. You'll get chilled in the wind once we set sail," he explained.

"Thank you, Heckie. How thoughtful of you," Catherine said, spreading her blanket over her lap. I took mine and started to sit on the seat beside her, but Kip laid his hand on my arm.

"Why don't you sit with Captain Heckie?" he asked with a sly grin.

"Oh, of course, you want to sit next to your sweetheart!" I said, winking at them, a little flutter of excitement inside me, knowing I'd be expected to sit near Heckie. I wrapped my blanket around my waist and stepped over to the steerage where Heckie gestured for me to sit on the wooden bench while he started the motor.

"Sit here, Sylvie. As soon as Kip and I cast off we'll be underway."

I nodded my thanks as the men darted around the boat, untying lines, loosening sails, and pushing off. We puttered down the channel for a bit, the men preparing the boat for sailing. I saw clearly that Kip knew his way around a sailboat and particularly Heckie's, as I watched their nimble performance of duties. Heckie hardly had to tell him what to do. After unfurling the headsail, Kip saluted Heckie and took his place beside Catherine, tucking her blanket around her legs.

Heckie chuckled at my brother's antics and scooted in beside me, cutting the engine.

"You warm enough?" he asked as the wind took the sails, increasing our speed—a most exhilarating sensation. I took my cloche from my coat pocket and pulled it on over my hair that was whipping in the breeze.

"Yes! This is so much fun!"

He chuckled again, his flecked green eyes warmly taking me in. "We're just getting started."

"You keep saying that!" I said, and we shared a comfortable laugh.

"Well, I kind of mean it," he said thoughtfully, glancing sideways at me while he steered the boat toward the channel markers. I wondered what he meant, but I decided not to ask. Kip and Catherine were caught up in their own murmurings, so I knew this was to be my special time with Heckie.

"Your boat is so beautiful!" I said, admiring the fine craftsmanship and the beautiful wood everywhere, especially on the steering wheel. "Tell me all about it." I wanted to hear him talk to see who this man I thought I knew really was. We were sitting close enough for me to catch his scent, aftershave, hair tonic, and line-dried clothes; the rest, apparently and pleasantly, was him.

"This here is a twenty-eight-foot sloop," he began, a hint of pride in his reserved voice. "She's called the *Hannah May*, after my mother, of course. Her hull is built of solid oak, and her mast is the sturdiest long leaf pine. She's planked out in local cypress and trimmed with imported teak. My dad and I built her in the shipyard on weekends. Well, he designed and built her, and I helped. Aside from watching him measure, and being instructed in the sawing and hammering, I did a lot of the heavy lifting, sanding, staining, and varnishing. That's the way you learn, though. I am his apprentice in many ways."

"Oh? How?"

"I'm learning all the ins and outs of the shipbuilding industry. One day, Dad will be too old to run it anymore, so I hope to take it on. That's why I'm studying at the Naval Academy. I need to get a degree in marine mechanical engineering. The newest trends in ship design are beyond Dad's expertise. We need to be ready for the demand for wartime vessels in case our country is ever at war again." He sounded so serious.

"Oh, Heckie! We just got out of the worst war ever. Do you think a war of the world will really happen again?" I had never thought of that before.

"Yes, I do. It's inevitable, I'm afraid. If you pay attention to what's going on in the world, the way people in Europe are flocking here for a better life—Russians, Italians, Germans, Jews—you can bet there will be large conflicts down the road. We're all enjoying ourselves for now, but our good fortune can't last forever, you know."

"Oh, Heckie! That sounds very grim."

He covered my hand with his. "Don't fret about it, Sylvie. Much of the world's business is out of our hands, so there's no point in worrying. I just want to be ready to do my part when I'm needed."

When I sighed, Heckie seemed to realize the conversation was not going his way.

"Here, would you like to steer?" he asked. When I nodded, he guided my hand to the wheel and held it there. The teak felt as smooth as glass, with no threat of sending a splinter into one's hand. We steered together, heading south into the channel toward the ocean. The moon had risen to the size of a large beacon and led the way, leaving a path ahead of hammered silver on the dark water. The lights of Lumina up ahead were dazzling. We locals called it our "Palace of Light," and it was living up to its name. The boat seemed to be one with the water as we glided along.

"You and your father did well!" I exclaimed.

"Thank you, ma'am." I found his reserved Southern manners endearing. We listened to the creaking of the mast straining against the wind in the sails. Buoys dinged softly as we passed and water lapped at our sides. The sounds of sailing lulled me into a peacefulness. Heckie's arm went around my shoulders and I felt myself relax into his chest. I sighed happily.

"Are you dating anyone at the Conservatory?" he asked, lips brushing the top of my head as he spoke.

"No," I said quickly. How would I explain Herschel Blum? We certainly *dated*, but it was not the kind of thing Heckie meant, so I felt confident that my answer was truthful. Heckie's hand wrapped me securely against him at my response.

"I'm not either, Sylvie. No one serious. We have dances and parties, but I think of only you. And now that I've seen you again, I'm afraid I won't be able to forget you at all once I return to the Academy."

My heart skipped a beat when he said that. His candor surprised me. Imagine, me on the arm of this handsome midshipman! Heckie was a man, a real man, with a bright and serious future who knew me and wanted me. I wondered even as a successful concert pianist how I would manage my career, how to plan a tour, how to arrange my business affairs. Would they teach us any of that at the Conservatory? My future was all so daunting that it kept me awake nights with worry. *Could I do this?* What if Miss Devereaux was wrong about choosing performance over family life? What if Aunt Andrea was right? I could teach and have a family like she was content to do. And I could be home....

"A penny for your thoughts?" Heckie asked, bringing me back to the present. For such a large man, his voice was soothing and soft-spoken, like I recalled, but now, so close to my face, it sounded intimate, rather than shy as in the past. I took a moment to compose myself, letting him take the wheel. We were following the channel from the sound into the ocean, so the water churned a bit, though I knew it would calm as we hit the low swells. Soon we would turn and see Lumina's lights from the ocean side.

"I don't mean to hesitate, Heckie. I find your company delightful. I realize now that I always have. We don't have many dances or parties at the Conservatory. We're not allowed to drink, or carouse, but dating isn't forbidden. But with all the practicing and memorization that's required of us, I'm lucky to go to the movies occasionally. I have friends, dear friends, but no one special in the way you mean."

"That's a shame, Sylvie. I know you're ambitious, but a girl like you should be wooed appropriately. If I were there, I would take care of your social calendar and see that you were properly entertained. You need fun in your life."

I had heard the same sentiment from Herschel before I left Oberlin.

"You flatter me, Heckie."

"That's not my intention, Sylvie. You should accept my compliments, all politeness aside. I mean to declare my feelings for you. I hope you don't think I'm being too forward," he said guardedly.

When I didn't respond, he continued.

"I've had my eye on you for a while, and I've watched the other guys crash and burn. They had it coming."

The remark was morbidly ironic since Clifton had died; still, his comment made a giggle erupt from my lips. Heckie, of all people, knew how devastated I had been when Clifton, who was much older and far out of my league, had tried to seduce me at his family's home. Heckie knew Clifton and I weren't a good match from the beginning. He had also watched me nurse my wounds over David, who never intended to be mine before he left at summer's end.

Heckie thought a moment and rested his chin on my head.

"I've waited patiently for you, Sylvie. Sometimes, the time isn't right. Sometimes it is. I feel as if this could be our time, if you think I could be the man for you."

What he said stirred me. I turned my face to him. When he gazed tenderly at me, I smiled; then he dipped his face to kiss me. I didn't care whether Kip and Catherine might be watching since they were probably doing the same in the darkness. For such a large and impressive fellow, Heckie's kiss was sweet and tentative, as if waiting for my approval. I gave it and we continued, until a swift gust and a large swell lifted us, commanding Heckie's immediate attention.

He looked up and called out to Kip and Catherine. "Ho! Look alive, mates! Prepare to gybe!" Then he took my arm firmly and ordered, "Duck, Sylvie!"

CHAPTER ELEVEN

Nate

"Jeez! Sylvie wrote a book on the train back to Oberlin!" Nate exclaimed as the four of them assembled on the porch again and paged through the night's diary reading. Everyone agreed. It was a beautiful evening, early in May, and with people out and about again after the stay-at-home orders had been lifted, they continued to enjoy their time on the porch together while social distancing. The masks they all wore now were becoming second nature. AB passed around Elle's plate of fudge brownies. Elle poured more red wine. They'd allowed whoever was reading to remove the mask since it was hard to hear on the porch, especially for Bernie, who had hearing problems anyway. No masks were required during snacks either.

Nate could relate to Heckie, trying to win Sylvie, in much the same determined way he had campaigned for Elle. At thirty-three, Nate had come to realize what he had to offer much later than Heckie had known at twenty! But that was the way things were back then, he supposed. Rules and conventions had positive ways of shaping one's behavior, which wasn't trending these days. He'd wasted precious time with his own recent debauchery and promiscuity, he thought. A previous affair with a married woman had almost cost Nate his relationship with Elle, but she was also a woman of the world with her own baggage. They had plunged together into the uncharted waters of faithfulness and true love without looking back. He had been more successful than she at letting go since she had more issues to drag her down; nevertheless, here they were, planning a wedding and a life together when life was anything but certain during this pandemic! And here she was, professing her love for him in front of AB and Bernie May!

Elle must have been thinking the same thing, as often happened when two souls rest on the same wavelength. She looked inquisitively at him and smiled.

Then, to her companions, she said, "This was what I've been waiting for! Finally, this is where Sylvie and Heckie's romance all began, on a sailboat cruise with the lights of Lumina in the background!"

"Absolutely!" agreed Bernie. "With all that Lumina magic surrounding them, they were destined to be together."

"Yes!" AB chimed in. "It's so romantic! I think it's fascinating hearing Mother's story all these years later. I'm so glad that she was nice to Daddy. I worried that she wouldn't pay him any attention!"

"Who could ignore Heckie? He turned out to be *hot!*" exclaimed Elle. The others chuckled at her modern assessment. "He swept Sylvie off her feet!"

"Yes, he did. I have their wedding picture somewhere. I'll show it to you next time," said AB. "They made quite an attractive pair! Their start reminds me a little of you two," AB said wryly, wagging her finger between Nate and Elle. Nate wondered whether AB had seen them off on their evening cruises, with the two of them steering the boat together.

Elle looked at Nate and she was smiling again.

He winked at her.

SYLVIE

Wednesday, December 12, 1928

Dear Diary,

It is hard to believe that I have merely just returned from Wilmington, when I shall travel right back down there on the train in three more weeks for the Christmas break! Now I understand why some students elect to stay here over the holidays or visit with friends who live close by, such as Herschel has done with Bart. I haven't caught up with the boys at all. There has been no time to breathe with the usual practicing, memorizing music, and Christmas concerts for which to prepare. I have only seen my friends during classes and, of course, the girls in the evenings when we dine in Talcott Hall. We will have to wait to socialize with the boys until Friday after convocation.

I am frazzled from playing tonight. Mr. Finch has given me Chopin's opus in G flat, an interesting piece played with only the black keys. My brain and fingers had to shift gears to get the hang of it, but I find it intriguing. This evening I made it a point to settle myself at the desk again as I am wide awake. I should finish writing what transpired over my Thanksgiving weekend since my hand almost fell off from writing on the train! Dot arrived back at campus with the sniffles, achiness, and a fever, which has worsened over the last few days. She is spending the night in the infirmary, so I am free to burn the midnight oil without disturbing her.

There is so much more to tell from my visit home, even though it all flew by so quickly. Aunt Andrea's wedding was lovely. Aunt Nell took over directing the wedding on Saturday morning so Aunt Andrea could relax and enjoy being the bride. A friend of Benton's came to take pictures.

Pearl was there, setting out the refreshments for the reception in the dining room—deviled eggs, small ham biscuits, nuts, and butter mints. The punch bowl sat at one end of the table, and the wedding cake at the other end. The table had been left expanded to its full length to accommodate the whole family for Thanksgiving dinner as well as the wedding spread.

Father greeted everyone at the door as the guests arrived. Benton's parents were the first to arrive, his father dressed in wedding attire since he was the best man.

"Hello, Charles; you look quite dashing!" Benton's mother said to my father. He took her hand formally and made a small bow. Looking splendid, Heckie and Catherine arrived together from the trolley. Aunt Nell and Uncle Harry, Kip, and my grandmother chatted with them in the living room, while Aunt Andrea's student, Polly Prentiss, played love songs and hymns on the piano. I visited briefly with everyone, but once the priest and Benton arrived, Aunt Nell shooed me upstairs to help the bride prepare for her grand entrance.

Aunt Andrea looked radiant in her ivory dress with the lace bodice, a satin bow at the waist, and a lovely knife-pleated skirt. Her curly red hair was bobbed like mine, with small pearl earrings peeking out. Her makeup was perfectly and tastefully applied, which I noted for future use myself.

"Sylvie, you look lovely!" she said. "That is such a pretty dress. The gold suits you."

Reaching out, she smoothed my skirt and smiled happily at me.

"Are you nervous?" I asked, handing her the new gloves Aunt Nell had given her for the occasion.

"Just a little," she said, examining the gloves again. "More excited than nervous!"

"I'm so glad you are happy! Benton really is a fine man," I said. Getting to know him more at our Thanksgiving dinner had made me realize how devoted he was to my aunt.

"Thank you," she said, smiling.

"Oh, Aunt Andrea, I'm happy for you," I blurted, "but I can't believe you won't be here when I come home for Christmas."

"I won't be far away, just over on Princess Street," she teased.

"I know, but I'll miss our late-night talks. I used to wish you would tell me everything I needed to know about life, but I feel confident now that I can figure it out for myself. You have taught me how to think things through, to be fair to people, and to make good decisions. You've prepared me to live on my own. I know I'll be gone eventually and that you are marrying the man you love, but you've been like a mother to me, and I shall miss you. We all seem to be going our separate ways. It's a bit sad."

Aunt Andrea slipped one of my errant curls behind my ear and smiled at me.

"Sylvie, you darling girl! You're so grown up. It's been my honor to step in to help when we lost your mother. I'm so very proud of you. I can only imagine what the future holds for you. Don't let anyone or anything discourage you from your dreams!"

"I won't."

"Your mother would be so proud of you, too," she said softly.

We regarded each other quietly for a moment and then she drew me close. I wiped tears from my cheeks as she released me. We smiled and tried to correct our makeup.

"We have a few minutes. I want you to open my gift!" I said, retrieving the box I had wrapped late last night.

"Oh, Sylvie, you shouldn't have!" she said, her hand covering her mouth.

"Nonsense, Aunt Andrea. It's your wedding day. I wanted you to have something special."

Delicately, she slipped her finger under the tape, lifting a small section of the paper.

"We don't have *that* much time. Just rip it open!" I laughed.

She grinned, tearing the paper from the box, and gasped when she saw what was inside. Lifting the silk peignoir from its tissue paper wrapping, she looked at me in awe.

"Oh, Sylvie, it's lovely! And it's *pink!*" she cried, looking at me as if I had lost my mind.

"I know! We redheads aren't supposed to wear pink, but who cares? It was the prettiest one, and it will look beautiful on you! Only Benton will see it, and I doubt he will complain at all!" I laughed.

Aunt Andrea blushed and held the soft garment to her cheek. "Oh, I love it! Thank you, Sylvie! How sweet and kind—and very adult—of you!" We both giggled.

She stood, hastily slipping my gift inside her suitcase on the bed, which was packed with her trousseau bound for New Orleans, just as Aunt Nell appeared in the doorway.

"It's time!" she said, leading us to the top of the stairs and handing us each a bouquet—Catherine's cream-colored roses for Aunt Andrea and yellow ones for me. "Everyone is seated, and the music will start when I give Charles the cue. He's waiting for you at the foot of the stairs, Andrea," she said with a smile. "Sylvie, you go first."

I swallowed and gave Aunt Andrea a quick hug and a kiss before I began descending the stairs, being extra-careful not to trip. The music began, a familiar hymn, "All Things Bright and Beautiful" drifted up from the piano. Father beamed up at me and I smiled, eager to see Heckie's face as I appeared at the foot of the stairs. I saw Kip and Catherine first, and their encouraging smiles. Then Kip elbowed Heckie beside him and Heckie's face burst into a grin, his cheeks burning the way I remembered seeing him each time we met at dances or at the beach, or wherever I happened to run into him. After our kisses the night before, it made me giddy to see his reaction. Looking away, I concentrated on taking my place at the left side of the priest, smiling at Benton and his father.

The Wedding March commenced, and everyone stood to honor lovely Andrea as she descended the stairs and took my father's arm. He passed her to Benton, who was visibly perspiring, and escorted her three more steps to face the priest. The ceremony began. I hardly remember any of it, other than taking Aunt Andrea's flowers and holding my breath while they repeated their vows, and then again when Benton fumbled for the ring. Anyway, the ceremony was over before I knew it, and my aunt was married again.

When Aunt Andrea tossed her bouquet, it came directly to me and I caught it, but immediately passed it to Catherine, which drew a laugh from all the guests. Heckie chuckled and shook his head, reserving any more comment; after all, Catherine and I were the only two single girls there, except for the pianist, and she and Kip were a lot farther along than Heckie and I were. Still, he held my elbow as we approached the refreshment table after hugging and congratulating the newlyweds. I took over piano duty so Polly could enjoy a piece of wedding cake and a cup of punch. The reception was joyous and over in an hour. After farewell hugs were shared all around, Pearl joined us on the porch with a silver bowl filled with rice for us to throw as we said goodbye to Aunt Andrea and Benton. She handed the bride a basket filled with ham biscuits and cake slices for their trip. Aunt Andrea embraced Pearl, and I saw tears in both their eyes. Then the newlyweds were showered with rice as they dashed down the sidewalk. Father had already taken Aunt Andrea's suitcase to Benton's Chevrolet, which was parked in front of the house. While I'd been at the piano, it seemed Kip and Heckie had been outside, tying empty tin cans to the rear bumper and writing "Just married" with shaving cream on the back window. Everyone laughed at the racket they made, driving off down Market Street, waving and honking their horn while we cheered and shouted best wishes.

ELLE

What a sad little wedding, Elle thought. Saying it out loud would be a buzz kill for AB and Mr. May, who seemed to be basking in the warmth of the narrative. There was nothing of Andrea in the ceremony, other than her nice dress. It was her second marriage after losing her husband in World War I, but still! And who in the heck was Benton? No one ever talked about him; he was just the fiancé and then the husband. Andrea needed someone to watch over her so her brother wouldn't have to anymore. But they'd done the traditional thing and even had a priest conduct the ceremony at their house. The size of the wedding wasn't what bothered her; it was the absence of any personality!

As a cake baker, Elle was privy to multitudes of weddings, both large and small. Girls these days wrote their own vows rather than following a script, chose from a vast array of venues as opposed to the traditional church weddings, and personalized their ceremonies with décor and themes. Strapless ball gowns with cowboy boots underneath were no longer unusual. And men were marrying other men while two brides might be getting hitched. Wedding cakes were being replaced by pies and cupcakes to spare expense and suit the tastes of the couples. Ministers were being replaced by friends as officiants since many couples weren't church-goers and they wanted someone who knew them to oversee their ceremony. It was the way she would go. Nate was working with Mr. May to become their officiant. Their bespoke wedding would be small and intimate, but it was going to be their own creation, and it would be a blast!

She took Sylvie's diary from Nate and began to read:

SYLVIE

After the wedding cleanup, Pearl went home. Aunt Nell and Uncle Harry went on a trolley ride to the beach, and Grandmother was resting upstairs. Father and I then decided to play gin rummy in the parlor.

"What do you think about the Conservatory, Sylvie? Is it what you had in mind after all?"

"I think so.... Father, I appreciate the opportunity you have given me to study at Oberlin. I feel very privileged to be there. I'm working hard and enjoying meeting new people. In some ways, though, it's harder than I thought it would be."

"How so?" my father asked, peering at me over his glasses while he rearranged the cards in his hand.

"Well, there are a few things. I can handle the work and the music. Mr. Finch is a fine teacher, and he gives me new pieces to practice each week to build my repertoire. I am doing fine with all of that. He has confidence that I have what it takes to be a performer. I just wish they would teach us how that is all going to work, once we leave the Conservatory and go out on our own. Will I have a manager, or am I to arrange concert tours all by myself? It hasn't been addressed yet, and I feel anxious about it."

"Then talk to Mr. Finch. Surely they have a plan."

"Yes, surely, they do.... And there is something else I'm curious about. I have made friends with Mina, the colored girl I mentioned whom I accompany, and with a Jewish boy named Herschel."

My father nodded. "And?"

"I rather like Herschel. He—well—I wondered if you mind that I associate with him?"

Father regarded me again.

"Because he is Jewish?"

"Yes. He said he thought you wouldn't approve."

Father laid his hand of cards face down and sighed, then studied me. My fingers twitched in my lap.

"It isn't customary. How serious are you about this young man?"

I smiled. "Actually, I'm not serious about him at all. We're just friends, but what if it were different; what if I did really like him and he felt the same way? How would you feel?"

Father pursed his lips and thought before answering.

"Sylvie, you know we—your mother and I, and now Andrea and I— have taught you to be discerning and compassionate about the people you choose as friends. You must decide for yourself if you believe the match—or the friendship—to be a sound one. You need to consider the person's background and how he treats others. If he's above reproach, works hard, and is truly sincere, it's a benefit. If he can make a good living, it's even better. I think you need to have deep discussions about how important your religion is and whether you can accommodate each other's beliefs. If you are of one accord, then you should feel comfortable in continuing your association; however, that doesn't mean society will accept you. That can be difficult at best. I would like to meet the person to see whether I agree you have made a good match, and then…we shall see."

My eyes got wide as my father went on and on. I had never expected a sermon from him!

"Well, I was only talking about going on dates, not marrying the fellow!"

Father laughed out loud. "I know, dear, I know. But that is often how these things start."

I laughed. "That's what Herschel said his parents would say!"

Father nodded. "I'm sure. You need to be careful in the alliances you form. If it is not the right person, you mustn't lead him on. When you associated with Clifton Carmichael, Andrea and I worried, even though he was from a good family, and look how that turned out. Sometimes even the most polished people can surprise you."

I nodded in complete agreement. We had all been blindsided by Clifton, and I didn't know how much my father knew. They thought I knew none of it since they were all trying to protect me from the sordid truth, so I decided to play along.

He continued. "It's much easier to aspire to someone with whom you have much more in common. Someone like Heckie, for instance."

"I know, Father. I've known Heckie forever, and I like him very much. He and Kip have grown up together, and they are as close as brothers. There is no mystery there. I have more of a chance falling in love with Heckie than my friend Herschel." I sighed, Miss Devereaux's advice lurking in my mind.

Father nodded. "I like the man Heckie has become. Still, you seem troubled?"

"Even if I do fall in love with Heckie, some of the professors at the Conservatory believe we should choose a life of performance over a family life. We can't have both."

This time Father's eyes grew wide.

"That seems awfully radical. Mr. Finch has told you this?"

"No, actually Mr. Finch is married and has a family. Miss Devereaux, Mina's teacher, believes that. She is not married and has performed in the opera. I don't see how she could have done that with children to raise."

Father rubbed his chin. "I see the truth in that. Children need their mothers. But I believe you should give her philosophy a bit of thought. You are young in terms of your studies and your career—your whole life really. Although it is somewhat uncommon, I have never been of a mind that a woman's place will always be in the home. I believe you should do what you feel called to do. A person with your extraordinary talent should not be held to ordinary standards. It is for you to decide how you wish to live, not your teachers; although, they must certainly feel obliged to weigh in. They are investing their reputations in you. You have plenty of time to determine what is best for you. You should follow your heart as well as your head."

"I hope to make the best choices. I'm glad there is time to think about it all. I want to make you proud."

"Of course, I am proud of you, Sylvie. But your life is up to you. You may work hard, choose to live alone, and reap glorious benefits, or you may squander your training away if you haven't the grit to bear the responsibility of a piano career. If you choose family life, you need to be prepared to alter your goals. Then again, with the right man beside you, there is a possibility to have both. You have too much gumption to let opportunity pass you by. I trust you will do whatever you believe suits your life. I believe an education isn't meant to chart your life; it merely awakens you and shows you how to find your course."

My father's advice weighed on me all afternoon. He surprised me in speaking so openly about my predicament and his perspective. I was glad to hear he would support me in whatever rational decisions I might make, and that he would be available to help me work through my uncertainties. Being grown up is one thing, but a person should not have to go it alone, as Catherine is doing. It still mystifies me how her parents can disengage from her as they have. Thank goodness she has my brother for a sounding board. He has goals and dreams that include her, so she has a good chance of having a happy ending. Still, I am grateful for my supportive family.

Kip and I repeated our performance of driving over to Catherine's house to pick her up before we caught the beach car over to Wrightsville Beach.

"You okay, Sylvie?" he asked. "I know you and Catherine had a talk on the beach. I hope everything is all right between you two."

"Yes, she told me everything. I can't believe you all felt you couldn't tell me any of it."

Kip shook his head. "Well, you have to admit it's a pretty sordid tale."

"It's terrible. It's just terrible what Catherine went through—everything Clifton did to her. She told me that he might have been the one who set fire to Shell Island. He was crazy, wasn't he?"

"He was ruthless, Sylvie. He would have done anything to get his hands on the Carmichaels' fortune."

"I can't believe she wanted to kill herself over what happened. I hate the way her parents treat her, as if she's all washed up and will never amount to anything. Their whole life is simply a façade. She is the bravest person I have ever met."

"Yes, she is."

"And you are wonderful for standing by her. Not every man would be so magnanimous."

Kip looked at me and smiled. "Magnanimous? You're getting awfully big for your britches up there at that fancy school."

I laughed as Kip turned down the lane to the Carmichaels' expansive home. I was hoping the butler would greet us again so we could avoid an awkward encounter with Catherine's parents. I hadn't seen them since Clifton's funeral, and even then, it was only briefly. I could hardly bring myself to speak to them. This time, though, instead of the butler, the Carmichaels greeted us at the door. They were both formal, shaking Kip's hand and hugging me as if I were one of the family, as if Clifton's death had not occurred just three months ago.

"Mr. Meeks!" Mr. Carmichael said smoothly while clasping my brother's hand. "And Sylvie, what a delight to see you both! I trust you had a pleasant Thanksgiving celebration with your family."

"Yes, thank you," Kip replied, omitting the customary "sir," as if the two of them were equals. "I hope you did as well."

"Yes."

Mrs. Carmichael greeted us next. "Sylvie, so nice to see you! I trust your aunt's wedding went off without a hitch?" she asked, giving me a hug and a faux kiss on each of my cheeks. The façade continued, so I played along in disbelief.

"Oh, yes, Aunt Andrea's wedding was lovely. Catherine was so kind to bring her beautiful roses that made it extra special." I thought of Long Island and the adoption scenario, but Mrs. Carmichael made no expression of acknowledgment.

"I'm glad! She is very gifted at growing those."

"Yes, she is very talented. And a wonderful friend!" I added, hoping to show Mrs. Carmichael how special her daughter was. Kip smiled gratefully at me.

"Where are the newlyweds honeymooning?" she asked.

It made no sense—how nice they were to us while distrusting their own daughter. Catherine trotted down the staircase in a red wine-colored dress with long black gloves and a feather in her headband. I couldn't help but marvel at her bold sense of style and self-confidence.

"New Orleans," I replied as Catherine gathered her coat and met us in the foyer. She winked at me and grinned at Kip, who helped her into her coat.

"How lovely! Clayton and I have been there many times. Give her our best wishes when you see her. At Christmas, I hope?"

"Oh, yes! I will."

"And the Conservatory? How are you enjoying Oberlin, dear?"

"Very much, thank you. The time is certainly flying by. I have missed home, so it has been lovely to be back and to see Catherine and my family."

"Well, good," said Mr. Carmichael. "Y'all enjoy your evening. Don't be too late, darling," he said to Catherine as if nothing in the world were amiss.

"Thank you, Father. Don't wait up."

She gave her parents a peck on the cheek, and we were off.

We finally relaxed when we arrived at Lumina. We met Heckie there since he wasn't on our beach car. He seemed as glad to see me as I was to see him. Catherine and I warmed our hands at the fireplace, while Heckie and Kip checked our coats. I always looked forward to the fireplace that created an extra special ambience in the fall.

"My parents told me today that they are hosting a dance for me at our home at Christmas," said Catherine. "You'll be invited, Sylvie. It will be black tie. I hope you'll ask Heckie to escort you."

"Oh, how marvelous! I'd love to come," I said, thinking frantically what I should wear to a ball. "I'll have to find a dress!"

"Wear that emerald-green satin one!"

"But you gave it to me. Won't people know it's your dress?" I asked, recalling my mortification when I wore her thrift shop castoff, the infamous blue-sequined dress, to Lumina last summer. The same dress Clifton raped her in.

"No! I only wore it once, in Paris, so no one here will know it was mine. Besides, it looks so beautiful on you, and the color is perfect for Christmastime!"

"Oh, well, in that case, thank you once again for coming to my dressing dilemma rescue! What's the occasion for the dance?"

"It's my graduation present and also a way to introduce me to the remaining eligible bachelors in Wilmington," she said, unsmiling.

My face fell, too. "Oh! So, they haven't accepted Kip after all."

"No. He can't even be my escort. To add insult to injury for Kip, they are taking the family to Charleston for New Year's—for me to meet more aristocrats—and then I'll be back home, packing and getting ready to leave for college."

"No! Is there nothing you can say to your parents?"

"I've tried, darling Sylvie, but they are convinced they need to keep presenting me to the society families in the hopes I'll fall for someone who has standing. Old money is what they're after. Bless Kip's heart for helping them cover up our little scandal," she whispered bitterly in my ear as boys and girls swished around us, greeting one another after long absences.

"That's so wrong," I said, beginning to seethe. "Why don't they just leave the two of you alone? Let you have your happiness. After all, you're going away to study and then you'll go on to pursue your landscape business."

Catherine shook her head sadly. "It's because they think I'll fail. It's best if they can just marry me off as soon as possible, before I disgrace them again."

"Poor Kip!" I groused. "And they have surely underestimated you!" I added, making her hug me.

The Bob Weidemeyer orchestra, there for the grand finale to their summer season, was already playing lively dance tunes for the crowd. My previous good mood was dashed at Catherine's news. Looking around at many familiar faces in the jumble of people around us, I saw it was a good crowd for the last dance, locals mostly, although it was nothing like the Fourth of July mobs or the Feast of Pirates dances that went on until the wee hours of the morning on the beach after Lumina closed its doors. Those were the best days!

Catherine was in the thick of the crowd, greeting friends right and left, putting on her best debutante smile.

"Sylvie! I can't believe it's you!" cried a familiar voice behind me.

I turned to see my childhood friend, Marjorie Mercer, whom I hadn't seen since the summer. She was as pretty as ever, with wavy brown hair and a face like a Kewpie doll, with adorable dimples just like her twin sister Margaret. "Hello, Marjorie!" We hugged. "Oh, I was hoping you would be here! Is Margaret here, too?"

"Yes, she is powdering her nose. We saw your group getting off the beach car! Are you with Heckie tonight?"

"Yes!" Then I recalled how Heckie and Margaret had often dated over the summer, so I asked discreetly, "I hope I'm not in trouble. Do you think Margaret will mind?"

"Oh, no. Margaret's moved on! She is serious with a boy named Frank, and I came with Jimmy Spivey. I'll introduce you later."

"Oh? No more Tommy Willis?"

Marjorie threw back her head and laughed. "No, no, no! He's been long gone. I've learned my lesson about lecherous men!"

"Good for you, Marjorie."

At that point, Kip and Heckie returned, and my brother greeted Marjorie with his worn-out nickname for her. (They'd lit a bonfire together once and it had blown up, singeing off her eyebrows!)

"Hi, Browsie! You made it!" he said, giving her shoulder a friendly squeeze.

"Hi, Kip! It's good to see you! Hello, Catherine!" she said, her eyes darting to Heckie behind them.

She turned to me. "That's *Heckie?*" she asked.

When I nodded, she laughed. "Well, Margaret might mind now! He's turned into quite a catch!"

I giggled. Then she said, "I always thought Heckie had a crush on you. You never noticed, did you?"

"I guess not. I was rather a dolt, wasn't I?"

"Well, you were distracted by all the other men last summer!"

Our cheerful mood sobered as we both thought of Clifton, and Marjorie's eyes cast toward Catherine.

"How is Catherine?" she asked under her breath.

"Holding up pretty well. Kip is her rock."

"Yeah," Marjorie sighed. Kip had been her crush until Catherine won his heart. "Good old Kip…. Y'all are both lucky gals." She gave me a wink and a little wave when she spotted her date. He approached and, without an introduction to me or the others, whirled her out onto the large dance floor. Heckie took my hand and did the same. The orchestra played a waltz and Heckie held me in his arms. I loved looking up at a man while dancing. Heckie was as light on his feet as ever.

"You must forgive me," I apologized. "I'm a little rusty at dancing!"

He gave me his warm smile. "Nah, you're great. I always love dancing with you."

"Thank you. The feeling is mutual, but I can tell you've been practicing."

"That I have, but this is heaven!" he said, and spun me on the next three count.

"I tried teaching my friends at school the Shag." I laughed. "Somehow, it didn't have the same feel as it does when I'm here."

"Funny you mention it," Heckie said. "I've had the very same experience in Annapolis. There was nothing like the night we showed everyone here."

"You're right. There's so much I've missed about home."

He looked encouraged. "Same here. I hope I'll get to see you at Christmastime. Will you be home again then?"

"Oh, yes. I'd love to see you then too. The Carmichaels are hosting a ball for Catherine over Christmas to celebrate her graduation. I hope you'll go with me. It's black tie."

His eyebrows rose. "I'll stop by your pop's place and get myself properly situated. I'd love to escort you!"

I thought about how we were all going our separate ways and how precious the times we had together would be. Perhaps Heckie felt the same way.

We danced waltzes, two-steps, fox trots, the Charleston, and the Shag. All our friends got in on the fun and we mixed it up, changing partners until I ended up with Kip for a Shag number.

"Are you having fun, Sylvie?"

"Yes! It's great being back here and dancing again. I've missed dancing! I've missed my friends, too!"

"Heckie seems happy," he said with a grin.

"Well, I guess that makes two of us!" I said, grinning back. "I've invited him to escort me to Catherine's ball."

The light in Kip's eyes faded, although his smile was still in place.

"Catherine told me about it earlier," he said. "Seems a bit rushed for the Carmichaels, but I guess that's what you do to get rid of a fellow who's out of favor."

"I'm sorry, Kip. I know you were hoping to have time with her before she goes away to school. Massachusetts is so far away...."

"I'll find a way to make it work; that is, if no one sweeps her off her feet after the ball or on her trip to Charleston."

"Oh, Kip, you know that won't happen! Catherine loves you with all her heart!"

My brother smiled bravely, and the song ended.

When the orchestra called the first intermission, Heckie found me and took me to get a Coke. I was relieved he didn't smoke or make a production out of digging a flask out of the sand like some of the other boys did. I was done being daring. Being with Heckie was comfortable. We wandered out onto the Promenade deck, where the cool air was welcome after all that dancing.

"What will it be like when you graduate from the Conservatory, Sylvie? What are your plans then?" Heckie asked.

"That's still a long ways off," I said, hoping to postpone the conversation about plans. "I hope to be traveling and giving concerts. But I really don't know yet how it will all work. It's a bit unsettling."

Heckie nodded and looked out over the ocean. The waning moon was high in the sky, shining its silvery beam across the black water. The salty breeze swept my hair back from my face and pushed my skirt tight against my legs.

When he didn't respond, I asked, "What about you? What will happen after the Academy for you?"

"I'll serve the required amount of time in the Navy and then come back to work with Dad. By then, I should be an expert in my field."

"That could take a while."

"I know," he said, smiling tentatively.

I didn't know whether to be relieved or worried. If I needed time to figure myself out, so did Heckie. Maybe we would both have to wait and see if a future together was in the cards.

"I'd wait for you, Sylvie. Like I said, sometimes the time is right and sometimes it isn't. I know it's complicated for you. You're not like other girls," he said, turning to me, his eyes flashing. "But that's exactly why I'd wait for you."

As I gazed into Heckie's eyes, my heart fluttered, but I felt torn. He was so earnest and sweet that I didn't want to disappoint him. My father's words came rushing back. *If it is not the right person, you mustn't lead him on.* In that moment, I believed Heckie was the right person, but it certainly wasn't the right time. Yet, if I let him slip away, I knew I would regret it. *Who knew what the future held?*

Heckie saw my hesitation and saved me from my inner turmoil.

"You don't have to say anything, Sylvie. We have years ahead of us. Before you leave tomorrow, I just wanted you to know how I feel."

"It's early, Heckie, but I think I want you to wait."

Heckie smiled, then bent and kissed me sweetly.

I had just promised myself to a man.

What on earth had I done?

CHAPTER TWELVE

Nate

Aubrey was shifting around in his seat at the kitchen table, looking at the laptop computer screen and then scribbling in his notebook. In his over-sized T-shirt and jeans, he looked somewhat uncomfortable. Nate looked up from the chicken he was boiling and asked, "Everything okay, buddy?"

"Yeah," Aubrey said, his hand cradling his chin. "It's algebra. It's okay; I'm on mute," he said and sighed. School was being conducted online now, and Aubrey would be taking classes in Nate's kitchen and sleeping in the guestroom for at least two weeks. His grandmother and guardian Patsy had just tested positive for the coronavirus and was quarantining at home. Harley was curled up on the kitchen doormat, watching Nate's every move, probably hoping for a taste of chicken. Elle was about to find out all the details, Nate thought, hearing her car in the driveway. He'd left her a text message to tell her about Patsy, but he couldn't quite bring himself to drop the whole bomb on her in a text. She'd been too busy at work to talk.

"Hey!" Elle said as she entered the kitchen. Her eyes quickly took in the situation, glancing at Nate with a smile on her face for Aubrey. "*Two guys!* And a dog! How's it going?"

"Hey, babe! We're good," said Nate, giving her a kiss and taking a white box of baked goods from her so she could put down her purse and hang her keys on the row of hooks by the door. He spoke quietly, so as not to disturb Aubrey, who was easily distracted. "Aubrey's doing his schoolwork—don't worry; he's on mute—and I'm making a chicken pie for us and one for Patsy."

"Wow! You're having a fun day!" Elle said, eyes wide.

"Yeah, it's kinda nice to talk to someone other than myself!"

Elle laughed. "How's Patsy doing?"

Nate raised his eyebrows, steering Elle toward the stove. "Well, she's got a fever and congestion, headache, aches and pains, and is really tired. I uh…offered to take Aubrey over here for several days until she's over it. Hope that's okay with you." He shrugged slightly. The kid had nowhere else to go.

"Oh, of course! Absolutely," she said, nodding while Aubrey watched them discuss his future.

"He got tested earlier and he doesn't have it—for now at least."

"Oh, right. Good."

"I didn't go in the house. Patsy and I talked it all over on the phone."

"That was smart. We should wear masks, though. I mean, here I come every day from work where I could pick it up from our customers and give it to him. Well, I could give it to you, too, but I guess we've thrown caution to the wind…" she said, a delicious smile raising her lips at the corners. It was worth the risk of catching COVID to take Elle to bed with him every night, but Nate thought if Aubrey had COVID, they'd better protect themselves too. Elle didn't need to take it back to her employees and customers at the bakery. It was a public health emergency, after all, so they had to be smart about their actions.

"Yeah, you're probably right. Aubrey, you got a mask?"

"Yeah," Aubrey said, pulling a blue surgical mask from his pocket. Elle put her mask on and took one off the key hook for Nate. He put it on and then pulled the chicken from the boiling broth with tongs, looking at Elle with uncertainty.

"What about tonight's reading? Shouldn't we isolate?" she asked.

Nate had already thought about the risk of exposing Bernie and AB.

"Yeah, no, that's not gonna happen on the porch now. I have a Zoom meeting scheduled for us. We can read together over Zoom."

"Oh! Great idea. Does AB know how to do Zoom, though?" she asked, taking two cookies from the white box and putting them on a plate for Aubrey.

Nate chuckled. "I called her earlier and walked them through it on the phone. We did a practice meeting on AB's computer and they passed with flying colors! There's nothing to it. I think we'll be good to go around seven. I told Patsy I would bring the food down around six and leave it on her porch. I dropped off some other things earlier. I went to the store. There's no beef to be had—supply chain problems—so I got chicken," he said, gesturing to his project on the stove.

Elle nodded, appearing to take it all in—a teenager in the house for ten days at the least and a dog. And what if Patsy had to go to the hospital? Or worse. Nate didn't want to think about it. Poor Aubrey! And poor them! So much for the love nest they'd made during quarantine.

"So, Aubrey, do you have some clothes here?" Elle asked.

"Yeah, Nate had me pack a suitcase. He told me what to bring."

Elle nodded again. "Well, I guess you guys have it all under control." She set the plate of cookies on the kitchen table, watching Aubrey pull down his mask and grin at her, his mouth full of braces.

"Life is uncertain; eat dessert first!" she said, smiling back.

AB and Bernie's images popped onto the screen, their faces inquisitively peering at Nate and Elle as they tried to maneuver their way around the Zoom platform. AB shirked away from the screen, apparently shocked at the appearance of her own face on it. They appeared to be sitting at the kitchen table, Nate thought from the view he recognized. He and Elle were seated comfortably in the living room on the sofa with a lamp behind the screen to better illuminate their faces. After a couple of gestures and puzzled looks between the older couple, their voices became audible.

"I can hear you now, AB," said Nate, grinning at her surprised expression and subsequent smile.

"Wow! We did it, Bernie!"

"Yes! Oh, look at your wonderful smiling faces!" said Bernie.

"Yeah, it's nice to see yours too!" agreed Elle.

"How long do we have to read tonight?"

"Unlimited," said Nate. "I have the premium Zoom subscription, so it won't cut us off after forty minutes."

"Good!" said AB. "I'll bring you the diary so y'all can read to us next time."

"That works," said Nate.

"How's Patsy? How is it going with Aubrey?" asked AB.

"He's settling in. He and Harley are in the den watching TV so we can all have a bit of a break. Patsy is pretty sick, but she said on the phone that she ate some chicken pie. She can't taste it or smell it, but she tried her best."

"Oh, gosh, that's a shame. I hope she doesn't get any worse," said AB grimly, and they all shook their heads in agreement. "No symptoms at your house, then?"

"Nope, not yet," Nate said.

"Well, we hope you all stay well over there and keep safe," Bernie said.

AB picked up the diary and cleared her throat. "Ready? I have an invitation to Catherine's ball to read to you first."

Mr. and Mrs. Clayton Binghamton Carmichael

Request the honor of your presence at
A Ball to celebrate the graduation of their daughter

Catherine Elizabeth Carmichael

From St. Mary's School in Raleigh, North Carolina
At their home at 5 Live Oak Lane, Wilmington, North Carolina

On the evening of Thursday, the twenty-seventh of December

Receiving line starts at five in the evening
Cocktails start at five-thirty

R.S.V.P. by the 15th of December 1928
With the enclosed card

Attire: Black Tie

SYLVIE

Friday, December 7, 1928

Dear Diary,

I have good and bad news to report. The good news is I received the invitation to Catherine's ball. It's so exciting! I sent the R.S.V.P. immediately—and a note to Heckie to see if he received his. It's a relief to know Catherine approves of me wearing the beautiful emerald-green satin gown she gave me; it flows over me like melted butter, and it will be perfect for the Christmas season and the occasion. A fur stole to wear with it would be the perfect accessory. Being an adult is expensive!

The bad news is that Dot has got the flu! There is an overrun of students in the infirmary with it, and I am so concerned about her. The epidemic of '26 was a bad year for so many, for our family when we lost my mother and younger brother and sister. I'm still not over their losses. I miss my mother terribly. I hope it doesn't get bad here. I have written to Father to let him know what is happening. The health bulletins came out all over campus telling us to sleep with our windows open, drink orange juice, and eat our vegetables. Washing hands is also important. I have heard on the radio that people on trains are told to wear masks to keep from spreading the disease. I suppose I will have to get one for my trip home in a couple of weeks.

Mina and I have been practicing here in Talcott Hall at the piano in our parlor to keep from mingling with other students. Lots of girls in our dorm have the same idea, so Miss Shelton devised a schedule for us. Usually, there is an audience whenever anyone practices there, but I have noticed that Mina draws a larger crowd. Miss Shelton shoos them off, though, out of concern for everyone's health. Mina's latest song is Faure's "Après un Rêve," the song Miss Devereaux sang at her recital, and Mina sings it beautifully, even in the parlor! Convocation was canceled due to the flu, but we are still allowed to dine in the Oberlin Inn, for now, where we went this evening to meet Bart and Herschel as we usually do on Fridays.

The boys are still inseparable and seem to have grown closer after their Thanksgiving trip to Chicago. Bart talks constantly of jazz and wishes to play in a jazz band after college. One day he is convinced he will join a symphony orchestra, and the next it could be a jazz band or whatever idea strikes his fancy. He has been to the rehearsal hall with Herschel many times to hear the band Hersch and I saw before the holiday. Their trips to the speakeasies and music halls in Chicago seem to have lit a fire in Bart.

"I want to sign up for a jazz group so bad," he told me, "but they won't let me until I have chamber ensemble out of the way."

"I know," I said, putting my hand under my chin in commiserative fashion. "I have a chamber music quintet next semester, too," I groused. "I have never played the harpsichord, so I am sure it will be different. That music will be so different from the Rachmaninoff that Mr. Finch has me playing," I explained to Mina and Hersch.

"I'll be in one of those chamber music groups, too, so maybe one of you will be in my group," said Herschel.

I grinned, thinking it would be fun to be in a group with Herschel. I had heard him practicing and he is quite a virtuoso!

"So, what is your dream when you leave the conservatory, Hersch?" asked Mina, taking a bite of her chocolate pudding.

Hersch grinned and ran a hand through his curly mop of hair.

"I want to play in an orchestra on Broadway."

"Broadway? I've always wanted to go to New York and see a show!" Mina said, uncharacteristically revealing her feelings.

"It's as good as you can imagine. Probably better! I love Broadway, the excitement of the theaters, the incredible music, the actors, and their talent, just the whole feeling, being around all that energy. I could live in a theater."

"And you would," said Bart, nodding and taking a sip of his root beer. "That would be your life."

"You could do it, too, Bart," said Hersch, taking a bite of his usual dinner of corned beef on rye. "It would be a gas!" he said, making me look away from his full mouth. *Did no one teach him table manners?*

"Yeah!" Bart agreed. "I love Chicago, but it's time to go somewhere new. I wouldn't mind taking a bite of the Big Apple."

"Change is good," Hersch said, and they nodded together enthusiastically. I had to agree.

"What about you, Mina?" Bart asked. "What's your dream job after the Conservatory?"

"Opera," she said simply. "Anywhere, I don't really care. Just opera."

"You can do it! We could all end up in the Big Apple! Sylvie the concert pianist, kicking off her tour at Carnegie Hall!" Hersch said, giving me a wink.

Bart shook his head. "And Mr. Finch will make sure that happens."

"How can you possibly know that?" I asked, truly wondering.

"Mr. Finch thinks you hung the moon, Syl. He'll take you around the world himself if you don't find a manager."

"How *does* one find a manager?" I wondered aloud.

"If you're good enough, the faculty takes care of you and helps you set it all up," Bart said, wiping his mouth with his napkin. "I'm not that good, so I won't have that luxury. If I can't get on with a symphony orchestra, I'm hoping to play in a jazz band. I won't have fame and fortune, but I'll be a happy man."

"You could play in a Broadway orchestra, too," said Herschel. "Come to New York with me. We can do it together, share a place, save money on rent. It's a decent living, especially now that the musicians are unionizing."

"What does that mean?" I asked.

"They demand fair wages and decent hours," Herschel explained. "It's catching on, and Broadway is all the rage in New York. There are over forty theaters on Broadway as we speak and growing all the time! People are going to shows in droves these days. Imagine playing the music of George Gershwin and having him right there to conduct!"

"That sounds like a dream indeed," said Mina. "I love the Gershwins' music."

"I'm going to a show when I go home for Chanukah."

"What is *that?*" Mina asked as if she had misunderstood. "It sounds like you're coughing."

Hersch chortled, shaking his head indulgently. "It's our Jewish holiday. We celebrate it around the same time you have Christmas. I'll miss the first few days, since I'm expected to be here at school, but I'll get there eventually."

"What show?" asked Bart, folding his napkin.

"It's a show called *Paris* by a new composer named Cole Porter. It's gotten rave reviews on Broadway. My mother got us tickets—and backstage passes. She's the musical one in the family. My father doesn't give a rat's ass about the arts or seeing any shows, but she *loves* them. Our family friends are going, and it will be a big celebration for all of us."

ELLE

Standing at the counter opening a bottle of pinot grigio, Elle felt arms go around her waist and a head press against her shoulder blade. Hairs stood on her arms as she wondered what Aubrey, in his thirteen-year-old mind, must be thinking about her. None of it could be good. In her experience, boys usually felt perfectly welcome making themselves at home on one part of her body or another, seldom invited in for the sampling. But it was Aubrey, and he hardly seemed the type. Hearing a sniff and feeling him tremble, Elle realized this encounter was not at all what she thought. Unaccustomed to comforting young boys, even her son Joey, she felt compelled to tread carefully, so she swallowed and turned to him, circling her arm around his soft shoulders.

"Hey, Aubrey. What's the matter?"

He released her waist long enough to remove his mask and wipe his nose on his T-shirt sleeve.

"Is Grandma Patsy gonna die?" he asked, replacing his mask.

"Oh, Aubrey!" Elle said with a sigh. It was an obvious question given his grandmother had COVID, while he was exiled to a household of strangers, strangers who were unused to having children afoot. Still, his question deserved a careful answer.

"Honey, I think your Grandma Patsy is doing her best to rest and fight off her illness so she can get better as soon as possible. And then you can go back home with her." As soon as she said the words, she realized she and Nate needed to have a conversation with Patsy about her next of kin and Aubrey's. As neighbors, they knew alarmingly little about the family's details.

"Yeah," he said. "I FaceTimed with her earlier. She didn't look good."

Elle stroked the fuzz that was the top of his head. "Yeah, I can see why you would be worried. COVID makes people feel really bad. Her mother had it and got well and she's *really* old! But, you know, her doctor says she is doing well for the second day. She's tired and feels crummy, but she is breathing okay, and eating, so there is good reason to think she will pull through."

"It worries me that she's down there by herself."

"I know. Nate checks on her a couple of times a day. She knows he'll check in, but she needs her time alone to rest. COVID takes a while to get over, and nobody wants you to get sick, so I hope you don't mind staying here with Nate and me."

Aubrey said nothing, just sniffed and hugged Elle again. It was the frightened hug of a small boy, not a horny adolescent. It was a hug she understood.

"I know, honey," she said, rubbing his shoulder.

"It's scary when they're the ones who get sick. I used to live with my granny, too," she said, recalling the days she spent taking care of her grandmother before ovarian cancer claimed her last year. She chose not to share that part.

"You did?"

"Yeah, from the time I was five years old." Elle filled two glasses of water from the sink and motioned for Aubrey to follow her to the living room sofa. "Come on in here." They sat side by side, and Aubrey turned his chubby face up to Elle's.

"What happened to your mama?"

"Well…" Elle said, running fingers through her blond hair, thinking how best to word what had transpired so many years ago. "My mom was pretty young when she had me, really just a girl herself. I don't think she was ready to be a mom, so she took me over to Granny and Pa's one day so she could go shopping and she…just never came back." She shrugged and pulled her mask down to take a sip of her water and looked at Aubrey.

"*Never?*"

"Nope. I never saw her again."

"That is *weird!*" Aubrey said, shaking his head.

"Isn't it?"

They sat together, nodding, Elle wondering what happened with Aubrey's mother, and wondering whether it would be appropriate to ask. Then he told her.

"I never met my mama," he said. "She had me and she couldn't take care of me, so Grandma Patsy took me."

"Oh," Elle said, wondering about Aubrey's father but having the sense not to ask. Her own memories of explaining the absence of her father weren't pleasant. "Do you ever see her?"

"Sometimes. She has mental health problems, and she struggles with addiction, so the court won't let me live with her. She's nice and all, but I guess she was kinda like your mama. She just couldn't be a mom. My daddy's in jail, so they told Patsy she had to take me. I was three."

"Oh, I'm sorry."

"He shot a cop."

"Oh, no!" *Aubrey's daddy was in jail for a really long time!*

"Didn't kill 'im, though. My daddy got pulled over, and he thought they were harassing him because he's you know…black and all. But he had drugs on him." He shrugged, as if the rest would be common knowledge.

"I'm sorry to hear that," Elle said, thinking his story was much like hers, but he didn't need to know all that now. *Maybe when he turned twenty-five, they'd talk.* For now, however, she needed to lighten the mood. "Well, you really lucked out with your grandmother. Patsy's the best."

"Yeah. I try to be good so she don't have to worry about me too much."

"That's very good of you. I'm sure she appreciates it."

"Well, sometimes it ain't easy!" He giggled, exposing his mouthful of braces, then taking a sip of water.

"Well, don't try to pull any crap on Nate and me, okay? I remember being thirteen…. I was a handful."

"Okay. Grandma Patsy said I should behave myself and mind my manners."

"Which is great advice. Nate will report you if you don't. Just don't try to test us. It won't end well for you! We're doing you a favor letting you stay here. You're lucky we like you."

"Thanks. I like y'all too."

"If you're like I was at thirteen, I didn't give much consideration to either of my grandparents. I was just interested in having fun. It wasn't until I had a baby myself that I started to appreciate what good people they were and how much they helped me."

"You had a *baby*?"

"Yes, it was a long time ago when I was too young to know better. My son Joey is nineteen now and in the Army."

"Wow! You weren't married?"

"No, I wasn't." She chose to omit the part of her story where she'd served a year in the state women's prison. She and Aubrey had a lot in common, hanging by a thread. But she'd had her grandparents in her corner, and then Aiden, Joey's father, had surprisingly stuck around to help her raise him. They had been more like best friends than lovers anyway, which was better than being kinfolk. At least, what she knew of kinfolk.

"My daddy and mama weren't married either," said Aubrey.

Elle nodded, wondering how the child had coped. Joey's life had been hard enough, but at least his father had been around. "Even though we weren't married," she said, "Joey's father helped raise him. He was a good man."

"What happened to him?" Aubrey asked.

"He passed away just recently," she said, wishing to avoid talk of death and failing.

Aubrey sighed. Nate appeared masked at the door with his laptop for the evening's Zoom meeting with AB and Mr. May. Elle updated him with raised eyebrows since her mask hid most of her expression. He pulled his head back as if ready to nod.

"So, Aubrey, do you have some homework you need to start on while we have our meeting?" Nate asked.

"I finished most of it already. But I have to read for Language Arts."

"Oh? What are you reading?" Nate asked.

"*The Diary of a Young Girl* by Anne Frank," said Aubrey.

"We're reading a diary too. It's by AB's mother from 1928," Elle said, making her eyes smile at Aubrey while thinking Sylvie's story was a much more upbeat read. The poor kid was having a depressing day.

Nate nodded, perhaps thinking the same thing. "Well, after you finish, you can play your video games for a little while before you go to bed," he said, and before Aubrey could protest, he added, "Patsy's rules. Limited screen time before bed. You know that."

"Yeah, okay," Aubrey said.

"Did you thank Elle for dinner?"

Aubrey shook his head. "Thanks, Elle. Hotdogs are my favorite."

Elle scoffed. "You're welcome. It was nothing, really." Then she asked Nate, "Did you talk to Patsy after dinner?"

"Yeah," he said, understanding that Aubrey needed reassurance. "She's feeling okay." He extended his hand and angled it back and forth to indicate a balance. "Not great, but at least well enough to talk and thank you for the dinner and the lemon bars," he said to Elle. "Aubrey, if you'd like to call her later, she'd probably love that."

Aubrey nodded. "Yeah, I'll probably text her to see if she's awake."

"Good plan," Nate said, winking at him.

SYLVIE

Sunday, December 9, 1928

Dear Diary,

Dot is finally out of the infirmary! She has been sick for days and she still looks pale and weak. More students are getting sick and ending up in there. Most of the Christmas concerts have been canceled, to everyone's dismay, but it is for the best to keep us all healthy enough to travel home in two weeks.

I brought Dot chicken soup from the dining hall this evening and sat with her while she sipped it slowly.

"The good news is I'll bet I can fit into my old concert dress again!" she joked.

I laughed. "If your sense of humor is back, you must be feeling better!"

"I guess! I really missed talking to you while I was in the infirmary, Sylvie."

"I missed you too, Dot!" I said, organizing my music history notes for studying later. "Did you have a wonderful Thanksgiving?"

"Yes. Thanksgiving is my favorite holiday. I love the food! It was nothing out of the ordinary, but it was nice being home, of course, and seeing my grandparents and cousins. I want to hear everything about your aunt's wedding and everything you did. Did you go to dance at the Lumina?"

I smiled and blushed despite myself. "Yes, the wedding was love-ly, and my aunt and her new husband went to New Orleans for their honeymoon."

"That's so romantic!" Dot crooned between sips of her soup.

"It was wonderful seeing my friend Catherine and my brother Kip, too. We all went to Lumina for the last dance of the season. Our friend Heckie took us on a moonlit sail the night before. He's a midshipman at the Naval Academy in Annapolis," I said with a bit of pride, face ablaze.

"And who, pray tell, is Heckie?" she asked with an impish grin.

"Heckie is my brother's best friend. He's twenty," I said, unable to keep my feelings from my face.

"And, apparently, he is a special friend of yours, too!" Dot laughed. "You must tell me everything!" she said, handing me her empty soup bowl, which I returned to its tray.

"I've known Heckie most of my life, I guess. He is always around, pinch-hitting as my chaperone when Kip was wooing Catherine last summer. Heckie has always been my dance partner at the dances, and he was always nearby whenever I needed him, though I hardly realized it. This time, when I saw him, I hardly recognized him. He's more hand-some than ever. The Naval Academy has whipped him into quite a fine shape!" I laughed.

"Oh, dear, you are smitten, aren't you?"

I smiled, twirling a red curl around my index finger. "I think I might be. I think he is too. He said he would wait for me." Being back on Oberlin soil, the words sounded foreign and more grown up than I felt. I felt ridiculous, but Dot didn't chide me.

"Oh, Sylvie, that is very sincere of him. Are you quite bowled over at the prospect of a man who has pledged to wait for you?"

I looked unsure.

"What did you say when he told you that?" she asked, grinning as if I had won a cakewalk prize.

"He will have a long wait. We both will, but Heckie is lovely and I...I said I think I wanted him to wait."

"Oh, Sylvie! What will Miss Devereaux think? You have just promised yourself to a man!"

"Have I?" I asked, knowing I'd drawn the same conclusion, but she had just nailed my coffin.

"Yeah, I think you have!" We stared openmouthed at each other. "Some people might even say you're engaged!"

"What?" I felt the blood leave my face.

CHAPTER THIRTEEN

Sylvie

Wednesday, December 12, 1928

Dear Diary,

Today our music theory classes performed for each other in the choir room. It has tiered seating like an amphitheater, and the lowest level is where the director sits with the piano and other instruments if used. It can also serve as a performance area. Students in each class were divided into groups of three or four. Our task was to create an arrangement of a tune or song in a different genre than originally intended. Hersch and I were in a group with a clarinet player, and we did a dressed-up classical version of "Hava Nagila," a Jewish folk song that is a favorite of Hersch's. It was great fun for all of us, particularly for Hersch, who shone on his violin lead. As the song increased in tempo, the audience participated by clapping their hands and tapping—then stomping—their feet. Everyone applauded, and it was so exciting to be taking bows again! The professors seemed to like it as well.

Next, Mina and Bart played with a bass player and a guitarist from the jazz group that Hersch and I saw before Thanksgiving. Their piece was a jazzy rendition of "Greensleeves" with Mina getting into the beat, snapping her fingers, and crooning the words in a bluesy performance that seemed to suit the song perfectly. They got a standing ovation. It was interesting to watch the impressed looks people shared when they heard her sing. Mina smiled radiantly as she took her bows, then graciously gestured to the other musicians in her group. As she left the stage, the bass player took her hand and gave it a squeeze. I recognized him instantly. He was the handsome black bass player from the jazz band Hersch and I heard that first evening it snowed. I planned to ask her all about that later!

Something about the thrill of performing must make people uninhibited. Hersch took me in his arms and kissed me on the cheek after the class was finished. As we spilled out the doors of the choir room, everyone was talking excitedly and laughing, something not often seen among the freshmen here. It was wonderful to feel that joy of accomplishment and be able to share our talents. Now I understood what Mr. Finch meant by, "The audience is the best teacher." It is indeed nerve-wracking to get out in front of others, especially for those with true stage-fright, but the reward of a performance well-done is exhilarating! I always look forward to convocation because I love to identify with the musicians on stage, but there is nothing like being the performer oneself and having people love you. We all crave that and can't wait to feel it again. It is almost like what I imagine addiction must feel like.

Still, Hersch surprised me with his unexpected kiss in public. I will ask him about that later, too!

After dinner at Talcott, Mina and I took our scheduled spot at the parlor's piano for a practice session. As I arranged my skirt at the piano bench and waited for Mina to select her pieces from her satchel, I couldn't contain myself any longer.

"Who is that handsome bass player?" I asked, grinning.

I saw her blush immediately. "That's Ronald," she said with a dismissive wave of her hand.

"Okay. Tell me more."

"Ronald. That's all I know. I don't even know his last name or where he's from."

"Well, he sure is cute, and I think he might like you."

She made a face and pulled her head back as if I were out of my mind.

"Oh, Mina, come on. I saw him squeeze your hand. And you didn't seem so surprised either."

She set a piece of music on the piano and regarded me indulgently.

"He's cute. I guess I kind of like him too. Maybe he's a fairy, too, and trying to throw others off his scent!"

"Oh, Mina, I doubt it. I was convinced by his smile for you."

"Maybe so, but I'm not getting in over my head here. You know that, Sylvie. I'm just trying to work hard and make my way to the top of the pile. I can't let him bring me down by distracting me."

"Crabs in a barrel," I murmured.

"What?"

"It's an expression. When people push others down to get ahead, it's like crabs in a barrel."

"I beg your pardon. It's nothing like that. I'm not trying to do Ronald any harm."

"Then why not give him a chance, Mina? Have some fun. It's not like you're going to marry him any time soon…if ever!"

"I knew that's how you would feel. You have that boy back home who wants to wait for you."

I felt as if I had been slapped. "How do you know about that?"

"Dot told me. She thinks you might even be engaged."

"Ah! So, the two of you have been talking about me behind my back."

"Well, if you had told me yourself, I wouldn't have had to hear about it from Dot."

I felt bad when she put it that way. "I'm sorry, Mina. I wasn't keeping a secret from you; we just haven't been alone much so that I could tell you."

"Then tell me," Mina said, her face melting into a smile, resting her elbows on the piano.

I didn't want to waste our time since others were waiting for the piano, so I said, "Here's the short version—we can discuss it at length later if it's necessary—his name is Heckie, and I've known him for years. He's my older brother Kip's best friend, and now we like each other. He's a midshipman at the United States Naval Academy in Annapolis, Maryland, so we are both going to be busy with our own commitments for several years. Anyway, he told me he would wait for me, and I said I'd like him to. That's it. We certainly are not engaged."

Mina lifted one eyebrow and picked up her score. "If you say so."

Friday, December 14, 1928

Dear Diary,

It is snowing again! For the others who have lived in the Northeast or the Midwest, seeing snow must seem commonplace, but I am enraptured with the swirling feather-like flakes every time they appear! Bundling myself against the cold and wearing boots with woolen socks has become mundane now, but I don't think I will ever tire of seeing the beautiful snowfalls here. Oberlin is so gloomy in the fall and winter that we need the beauty of the snow to cheer us up.

Convocation is still closed due to the flu, but the jazz group continues to practice. This time, Hersch invited Mina and Bart to come along. Dot wasn't up to going out in the cold after being so sick, so she chose to stay in where it was warm and study for exams. Given the choice of studying for exams or walking in this winter wonderland with my friends to listen to a live jazz group, I decided to live it up just one more time.

As always, Hersch offered me his arm for the walk, as did Bart to Mina in Dot's absence. I wanted desperately to ask Hersch about the kiss, but I couldn't speak so frankly with the others around. Especially Bart. I didn't know what he would think, other than Herschel was being smart to kiss me in public to show he liked girls, not boys. By the time we reached the rehearsal hall, I had resigned myself to believe that's all it was—a cover—and that I was helping preserve their image. That is our mission, after all, as we girls have pledged to help keep our friends safe, yet I feel it isn't enough for me. I want more intimacy with Hersch, even though I have strong feelings for Heckie. Anyway, the kind of intimacy I want with Hersch is just honest, friendly conversation. I do like him deeply as a friend, and keeping his secret is starting to bother me. Admittedly, I am curious as well about his feelings for Bart. I watch them together all the time, looking for clues to show me they are anything more than friends, but they are masters of deceit, it seems.

"Almost there!" Hersch said, grinning at me and squeezing my shoulders as we walked closely together through the snow. His wool cap was pulled down over his ears, but a crown of dark curls peeked out around the edges. "Are you too cold?"

"No, thank you; I'm fine."

"Be careful; it's starting to get slippery."

When we reached Rice Hall, we stamped snow from our boots and entered the building, shaking off snow and pulling off our hats and gloves. Bart's hair stood on end and Herschel's was a wild mass of curls, as I am sure mine looked, but Mina's was neat and tidy when she removed the woolen scarf from her head, and she looked as regal as ever. We sniffed from the cold and carried our coats into the hall, looking for seats as our eyes adjusted to the dark recesses. While the musicians were discussing portions of the piece they were playing, Ronald and Jeffery looked up and waved at us. A large smile lit Ronald's face when he recognized Mina. She and I sat close together to keep warm between the boys.

We grinned at each other when the pianist began tickling the ivories because we all recognized the new hit song, "Sweet Lorraine." The trumpet player did a fine job using his mute to create the muffled sound so typical of jazz. Then we were surprised when Ronald began to sing. He had a nice baritone voice, but the best part of his performance was when he sang the words to Mina. Her face went scarlet, but her smile gave away how much she enjoyed being sung to in such a way. We clapped and cheered when the song was over. Then they moved to the next song.

The band leader counted them in, and I gasped when I heard the melody. It was Gershwin's "Someone to Watch Over Me." Mina and I shared a look and a smile, but then the music stopped, and Ronald began talking to the others.

"I don't want to sing it. No, I think there's somebody right here who can sing it the way George Gershwin intended. It's a girl's song, and she's sitting right over there!" he said, pointing to Mina.

Mina looked alarmed and whispered to herself, "Oh, no, you don't. Ronald. No, no, no…."

But her protests went unaddressed as Ronald set his bass in a stand and began walking toward Mina.

"Come on, doll," he said, reaching out to her. "Give us a song. I know you know it. Your friend Sylvie can vouch for you. Please," he said, placing a hand over his heart, that same big smile taking over his face. He was quite irresistible, and finally, Mina sighed and rolled her eyes before standing and letting Ronald escort her to the stage. I had no idea he knew who I was. In their music theory group, she must have told him quite a lot about herself to mention both her accompanist by name and what she was singing. And none of it had been lost on Ronald.

"Here, Miss Mina. Stand right here where we can hear you the best," he said, indicating the center of the stage. Mina stood in the spotlight he showed her, unnecessarily patting her perfect braid in place and then smoothing her blue plaid skirt. She looked around nervously and finally located us in the darkness. I waved to let her know I was rooting for her. She cleared her throat and nodded at the band. Bart, Hersch, and I looked at each other and giggled excitedly.

The leader set the easy tempo again and counted them in. From the first notes I liked the arrangement and wondered how Mina would follow along. Her eyes were locked onto Ronald's, and when she recognized her cue, he nodded and she began. Her voice filled the hall, sweet and clear as a bell. As she moved through the lyrics, her voice grew stronger and more confident. Her eyes closed and she turned toward the seats where the audience would be. The three of us on the back row held our breath, listening to her unfold the story of the man she wanted. She sang as effortlessly as ever, her fine practiced vibrato enhancing each note she held, her diction perfect, and her performance charming. When she ended the song gently with the last line, "Someone to watch over me," the room went silent and then the three of us burst into applause. We stood and shouted, "Brava!" while Mina laughed, and the band put down their instruments and clapped along with us. She took a humble bow, her second of the day, and started back to her seat.

"Thank you, Miss Mina!" Ronald called to her, making her turn around to see his large grin. "I knew it would be that good. I just knew it. You slayed it!"

When she returned to her seat, I grabbed her hands, which were trembling, and then hugged her. "You were great!"

"Thank you, Sylvie," she said demurely as ever.

Bart and Hersch congratulated her, and then we sat back in our seats to watch the rest of the band's rehearsal.

Wednesday, December 19, 1928

Dear Diary,

It's been a strange day. Hersch and I walked back to the dorms after our music history exam this afternoon, stepping carefully around the icy spots on the sidewalks that had been shoveled clear of snow. In an encouraging show of goodwill, the sun had come out, making me smile and squint. In three days, we will leave for the holidays, marking the end of our first semester at the Conservatory. Hersch grabbed my arm just in time to keep me from falling.

"Whoa!" we said in unison, laughing. His supportive arm went around my waist.

"I'll miss you, Sylvie," he said as we approached my turnoff to Talcott Hall.

"Yes, I'll miss you, too, Hersch. You'll have so much fun seeing your family and friends again. I know you've missed them."

His brown eyes warmed as he smiled at me. He was hardly taller than me, I thought, as we leaned into each other. Then to my surprise, he cradled my chin with his gloved hand and pulled my face close, kissing me softly on the lips. I let the kiss linger and then pulled back to look at him in surprise.

"That was unexpected," I said, looking around, seeing no one to witness what had just happened.

He chuckled. "I've been wanting to do that for a long time!" he said, giving me another kiss on the tip of my nose.

"Really?" I asked, realizing that I'd wanted it too.

"You seem surprised," he said, looking uncertain.

"I—I thought you weren't interested in me, after our conversation at the dance," I replied, honestly confused.

"Well, I didn't say I wasn't interested, just that it probably wasn't advisable. We did say that college is for trying new things," he said.

You have tried so many new things, I thought.

"So, you thought you'd just try out what it's like to kiss a *shiksa?*" I asked, hoping I pronounced the word correctly.

Hersch laughed. "I'm sorry, Sylvie; I guess I did rebuff you with all that stuff about my Jewish family expectations. I have to say, though, if I'm going to be away from my family as I hope to be one day, I can't worry too much about what they think about everything I do."

Knowing what Mina had seen with Hersch and Bart, I believed that had been his philosophy long before he kissed me.

"Well, I don't want to be a mere cultural experiment for you," I said, turning to walk to my dormitory.

I felt him reach for my arm. "Wait, Sylvie. I—I'm sorry. You're not a cultural experiment. You may be the best friend I have at Oberlin. Please don't be angry with me."

When I turned to look at Hersch, my irritation melted away at the vulnerable expression I saw on his face.

"I'm not angry with you, Hersch. I'm curious to know exactly what it is you want."

He breathed deeply and ran his gloved hand over his face.

"The truth is…I don't know what I want, Sylvie. I've let myself run the gamut of what could be possible outside of my family's expectations, and I'm more confused than ever right now." He glanced at me.

"What are you confused about, Hersch? You've kissed me twice. I haven't encouraged it, but you have kissed me twice. What is the problem?" I asked, believing I knew exactly what the problem was.

"It's you, Sylvie. I don't know…I thought one thing about what I am, who I am…and here I am with you and…you make me feel safe. It's as though everything in the world is right when I'm with you, but I know I shouldn't be with you."

I could see the turmoil in his face, even though he was looking at the ground, not at me. He continued.

"I don't know. This place has opened so many possibilities for me, musically, personally. I don't know who I am. I don't know what I am. I'm eighteen years old. I can't expect you to understand me when I don't understand myself." He looked up at me. "Do you know what I'm trying to say?"

I nodded. I did understand. I was wrestling with many of the same issues myself, aside from the glaring one that separated us more than Herschel wanted to admit.

"Yes, Hersch, I think I do understand." I wondered what I could say to him to assuage his conflicting emotions without revealing exactly what I knew. There was one thing I could tell him that might put one of his options to rest. "I think you should know I've promised myself to a boy from home. His name is Heckie. We decided it over Thanksgiving. We both have several years to wait until we can possibly be together, but he and I want to wait for each other."

Herschel gave a sigh of relief. "Oh, Sylvie, that's wonderful. I'm happy for you. I'm sorry if I overstepped my bounds. But your friendship means the world to me. I'd be honored if you felt the same way."

I reached for his hand and squeezed it. "Of course, I do, Hersch. You are very dear to me as well. Let's try not to spoil it, making more of it than it is."

He glanced up at me and nodded slowly. "Like we said before; back to square one."

"Yes," I said. "Square one is a good place to be." He started to withdraw, but I held fast to his hand. "You know that I have your best interests at heart, don't you?" I asked.

He chuckled again. "That's what a guy usually says to a girl, isn't it?"

"I don't know; is it? I guess in the Clara Bow pictures, it is. I just want you to know how important you are to me."

He looked uncertain, as if I were the boy talking to the girl, so I tried to clarify.

"We have so much to accomplish here, with our music and our careers, we have to stay focused on what we came to Oberlin for. I'm in your corner. I want you to get exactly what you want, whether it's the first chair violin in the New York Philharmonic or an orchestra gig on Broadway. Don't let anyone keep you from your dreams, okay?"

He smiled. "I won't, Sylvie. Thanks for being in my corner. I've got your back, too, you know?"

"I do know that. Thank you," I said, releasing his hand and turning to walk to my dorm.

"Hey, wait. Are you taking the morning train to Cleveland on Saturday?" he asked.

"Yes, and then I go home from there," I said. "Mina is going, too, so we can all ride together, at least until Cleveland."

"Good. That will be fun," he said, reaching for my arm one more time.

"Make sure you get a mask for the train from the infirmary."

"I will," he said. We hugged goodbye before I went inside Talcott Hall.

Who would have thought??

Saturday, December 22, 1928

Dear Diary,

I am on the train alone for my first solo ride since leaving my friends in Cleveland, and my heart is still pounding. Wearing a mask to protect myself and others from catching the dreaded flu that took my mother and two siblings two years ago is frightening enough, but I thought changing trains on my own would be the most challenging part of this trip. After what happened on the first leg of my journey, I feel unsettled and unwilling to strike up a conversation with just any other passenger, so I am choosing to immerse myself in my journal whenever I need to.

Mina, Hersch, and I said goodbye to Bart and Dot at the depot and boarded the morning train, finding seats in an empty compartment. We had it enjoyably to ourselves until three men boarded and sat with us. Hersch moved over beside me in our seat to accommodate the others. They were newly acquainted businessmen who had met on the train from Chicago. All three were heading home to Philadelphia for Christmas. Even though I was wearing a mask, I could still smell they reeked of cigarettes. Appearing to be in their late thirties, they talked among themselves at first, which I found mildly disruptive because I wanted to chat openly with my friends. It's hard enough to communicate while wearing the cone-shaped cloth mask the trains require to protect us from the influenza. Due to the holiday travel, the train was crowded, so we didn't have much choice in our company.

Mina closed her eyes for part of the trip as her way of withdrawing from the conversation in general. Hersch and I tried politely to ignore the men's conversation until they at last acknowledged us and asked where we were headed.

I replied that I was going home to North Carolina for Christmas and then Hersch chimed in that he was New York City bound—for Chanukah—which got a big chuckle from the men. I thought it was rude of them to laugh, even though Hersch seemed to be making a joke. Then they asked me about the sleeping girl, to which I replied that she was my friend and that we were all students in the Oberlin Conservatory of Music. They all went wide-eyed and professed their amazement at our virtuoso status. Immediately fascinated with us, they began asking questions about what we played and how it was going for us there. They wondered whether we would be famous musicians one day. Mina woke up and observed the conversation, although none of the questions was directed at her. Hersch did most of the talking, but whenever I said anything, the men elbowed each other and snickered, the way the other students treated me at Oberlin, confirming my belief that the whole world must ridicule Southerners. Finally, when the train pulled into the Cleveland station, the ordeal was over, and Hersch stood to help Mina and me retrieve our luggage so I could change trains and she could meet her family.

As we stood in the aisle while Hersch extracted our bags, we could hear the men talking inside the compartment. "Imagine that, a Jew, a country hick, and a nigger all at Oberlin together!"

"Yeah," said another, "Jeez-oh-Pete, what a menagerie that place is getting to be! I didn't understand a word that redhead said; did you?" They fell into raucous laughter and snorting.

"Hell no, I don't speak Southern! I'm from Philly!" More laughter followed.

The three of us looked at each other in shock, not knowing what to say. Mina's face transformed into the angry countenance I had seen when we first met. She closed her eyes and clenched her jaw as people bumped against us, trying to get off the train.

"Move along, please," said the conductor, reaching out to assist us with our bags. Hersch escorted us off the train so we could say our quick farewells.

"Oy, what morons!" Hersch muttered, adding an expletive under his breath he didn't intend for me to hear.

"Try to sit somewhere else," I advised him.

"I'm one step ahead of you," Hersch said, tapping his coat pocket where he had stashed his book for the ride to New York.

"I hope you have better company for the rest of your trip," said Mina, giving his hand a squeeze, which was noticed by other exiting passengers, casting disdainful glances their way. We ignored the looks and said our goodbyes.

"Oh, look! There is my family!" Mina cried, removing her mask, grinning, and waving to a group of people in the crowd waiting on the concourse. "Have a safe trip, Sylvie," she said, hugging my neck.

"I will; thank you, Mina. Have a Merry Christmas with your family," I said and then turned to Hersch. "Happy Chanukah, Hersch! Have a great time in New York. And give my regards to Broadway!"

We laughed and hugged.

"Take care, sweetheart! Tell Heckie to watch out for my girl," he said, giving me a wink.

"I'll do that. Be careful on the train. Nobody's worth fighting on this trip."

"Nah, don't worry about me! I got a pocketful of jokes to distract the idiots."

The three of us held hands, bid each other goodbye, and then went our separate ways.

I can't describe how hurt I am by what those men said about us. I hurt even more for Mina and for Hersch, who have had to endure much more offense than I. None of us deserved what those foolish men said. Their tone in lambasting each of us so freely was perhaps what bothered me the most. I realize that in the South, insults (and worse) are frequently spewed about colored people and Jews alike, but I suppose I didn't expect it here, in Ohio, in what I thought was the great land of enlightenment and tolerance. What I have come to understand is that prejudice is alive and well everywhere, and that birds of a feather do indeed flock together. If I plan to travel the world as a concert pianist, I must get used to ignorance, cherish the good people, and develop a thick skin in the process. As unpleasant and unfair as life can be sometimes, I will strive to look on the bright side. Still, it doesn't do to be batted around at will by those who know nothing of what they speak. At some point, I must think of an effective way to stand up for myself or others who are wronged for who or what they are. This will deserve a considerable amount of thought.

I can't wait to be home again!

CHAPTER FOURTEEN

Mr. May

Bernie shook his head. Sylvie and her friends were dealing with a lot, with the racial slurs and insults they'd endured on the train. Wearing masks on the train would indeed have made Sylvie anxious since her mother and siblings had been taken by the flu just two years previously. He could certainly understand the worry about spreading disease. Who would have thought almost one hundred years later, he and the rest of the world would be dealing with the same thing? Wearing masks was a necessity now, but he felt that seeing only half of people's faces limited social interaction. What a difference a smile could make! It was nice seeing his friends' faces for a change on the computer screen, courtesy of their Zoom meeting, even if for an hour or two.

"What a bunch of assholes!" Elle said to her friends on the screen, looking quickly behind her to see whether Aubrey was within earshot.

"Thank goodness, it seems like we are turning the corner on that kind of racism here," AB said.

Bernie felt skeptical. "Well, I guess in our little bubble here it can seem that way, but I think others feel differently."

"Our bubble…" AB mused.

"Our privileged neighborhood," Bernie said carefully, aware that AB didn't keep up with the local news as much as he did, although lately, with the pandemic, they watched enough to know infection rates, how other places were affected, and the CDC's guidelines. "There are still acts of racial reconciliation going on even now in Wilmington." He addressed Nate and Elle, who were newcomers to the city. "You may have seen the Confederate statues being covered with plans to permanently remove them. There's also talk of Hugh MacRae Park being renamed because he was complicit in the Massacre of 1898, when over one hundred blacks were murdered and many more run out of town on the rails following the election."

"That's horrible!" said Elle. AB nodded, probably recalling the story. "What was it all about?" asked Elle.

"At the time, the town's Republican government supported blacks holding public office, bearing arms, and voting—they were called Fusionists, believing in Abe Lincoln's ideas of freedom for all men—but there was a group of Democrats, white supremacists, who didn't agree and wanted their town back, as Sylvie explained when she first arrived at Oberlin. Hugh MacRae was one of them. The group threatened blacks to keep them away from the polls and a riot ensued. The killing was horrendous. It was an actual coup d'état—an overthrow of government—the only one on record in the United States."

"Wait, wasn't MacRae the guy who built Lumina?" asked Nate, after taking a swig of his beer.

"Yes, he was. He did wonderful things for the town and for Wrightsville Beach. Lumina wasn't his only great achievement. MacRae was head of the power and light company. He converted the town's train system to electric trolleys. It was his idea to carry the trolley system all the way across the train trestle over waterways and add the beach cars which could carry more people. He basically built Wrightsville Beach, but it was at the expense of black labor."

"But blacks were not allowed on the beach until after dark—unless they were working, right?" Nate asked.

"That's right. Friends of MacRae's built Shell Island as a place blacks could go to enjoy the beach for themselves. It was immensely popular with well-to-do blacks from all up and down the East Coast. At the time, Shell Island was an actual island across from the undeveloped north end of Wrightsville. Now it's all filled in from storms over the years, but back then, the only way to get there was by ferry or private boat."

"Ah, naturally segregated," Nate said, nodding. "Makes sense when you think back on the story Gregory referred to in the Lumina manuscript we read when he saw Clifton and his cohort setting fire to the place in the middle of the night."

Bernie nodded. "There were scant reports in the old newspapers about it. A series of fires was apparently the cause of the place burning down, as was common in those days, and the ocean winds would have made the fires whip out of control, but research shows those fires were 'mysterious' at the very least."

"I would imagine there is still resentment in the black community here about what happened back then," said Nate. "I've actually been researching it some myself since we read the manuscript last summer."

"I don't see how anyone could ever get over that kind of thing happening," said Elle. "Once you know about it…."

"The city has done many things recently to recognize what happened and to make amends in a grand attempt to move on, but as with everything else, not everyone is on the same page at the same time. The best thing our city can do is find all the facts and commemorate the whole story, not just what has been handed down by the old guard, so to speak," said Bernie. "History can be fiction if we let it. We learn more all the time, and the stories should be told as they occurred."

"I agree with you, but some of those families' descendants—the MacRaes in particular—are very fine people and don't deserve the bad names their families bear," said AB, fingering her non-existent pearls. "Hugh MacRae's grandson served our country valiantly in World War II and developed much of Wilmington and Wrightsville Beach quite admirably. It must have been so sad for him to have seen his grandfather's name being tarnished the way it is now. But…people move on. People *do* learn from the mistakes of the past. It's a complex issue. People in general are complex. At this stage in my life, I think it's best just to be genuinely kind to everyone and hope to set an example that way. We never know what others are going through. Others from all walks of life. All we can do is try to move forward. You can't change the past," she said wistfully.

"Spoken exactly like your dear mother," said Bernie with a smile. "She was certainly trying to do the same thing."

SYLVIE

Monday, December 24, 1928

Dear Diary,

After my long train trip—in many ways—I slept for ages, even missing breakfast, which is unusual for me! Nellie took pity on me and saved me a biscuit with a delicious slice of country ham inside it. That and a glass of fresh-squeezed orange juice made me feel almost human again. I had a bath, too, so I will be presentable for the Christmas Eve midnight church service. I always look forward to having Father's mulled cider while we wait and watch for the carolers who are bound to stop by in evening. I helped Father and Kip decorate the house and our front porch with pine garlands and berries. Aunt Andrea came over to help us decorate the Christmas tree since Benton was working. It was so good to see her that my heart almost burst when she walked through the door!

As we strung brand new electric lights around the fragrant cedar, I couldn't get over how radiant Aunt Andrea looked from her honeymoon, and she smiled at me, assuring me that she was happily married, and that Benton is a wonderful husband. We will see him at church tonight after he is finished working at the bank, and then of course, tomorrow for our family's Christmas celebration of opening presents and our traditional turkey dinner. We are missing some of the family. With the dangerous outbreak of flu in Ohio this time of year, my grandmother and Aunt Nell and Uncle Harry decided not to make the trip, since they had just been here at Thanksgiving.

There is so much to do! After we finish the tree, Father and Kip will set up Kip's electric train around the tree to complete the picture. The gifts will go inside the track. I had wrapping to do upstairs, so I invited Aunt Andrea to accompany me so we could catch up. When she kicked off her shoes and settled on my bed, I showed her the invitation to Catherine's ball, which she had already heard about.

"Oh, Sylvie, this is wonderful! Is Heckie escorting you? What are you going to wear?" she asked, unable to contain her excitement for me.

"Yes, Heckie is taking me," I said, feeling the blush creep up from my neck to my cheeks before I could turn away to conceal it. My aunt noticed and smiled even wider if that were possible. I went on as if I weren't overcome with the sudden passion I felt, remembering Heckie's kisses. How ridiculous it is that putting lips together can do such a thing to a person! Yet I can think of nothing else when his name is mentioned.

"I'm wearing the emerald-green satin that Catherine gave me."

"Oh, that will be glorious on you! You haven't worn it yet, have you?"

"No. I'm glad to have the proper occasion for it."

Andrea looked troubled. "Will others recognize it as her dress, though?"

"No. Catherine said she only wore it once—in Paris. I guess it will be the gown's Wilmington debut!"

"Wear your mother's emerald earrings with it," Aunt Andrea suggested.

"I will. And the diamond bracelet you gave me. I left all of that here, knowing I wouldn't need it at Oberlin. All we wear there are our traditional black dresses for performances, and there are no grand balls at all!" I laughed.

"Then I'm glad you have an opportunity to enjoy this one. And with that sweet young man, Heckie. Golly, isn't he the surprise of the season? He's changed ever so much, but still as respectful and kind as he always was."

"Yes, he is. As impressive as he looks, he is still our dear Heckie," I agreed, remembering the warmth of his voice as he murmured agreement with his pleasant "yes, ma'ams" when we spoke at Thanksgiving.

"Are you two an item?" Aunt Andrea asked.

I hesitated. "Maybe." When she waited for more, I felt obligated to tell her the rest.

"He told me he'd wait for me," I said, feeling the heat again.

"Oh my! I suppose since he's going to be in the service, he's trying to let you know just how serious he really is."

"I know! I was shocked. He knows I'll be involved with my music after I graduate. And then I'll be traveling with my tours, hopefully, if all goes according to plan, so our future is quite up in the air."

"Well, you have a lot to think about. How do you feel about him, Sylvie? Although, I think I know." She giggled.

"I've thought a lot about boys since last summer, as you well know. I feel so drawn to Heckie, and he's always been around in case I need him.

It's nice to have support and a little more than that, I think. I told him I'd like him to wait."

"Oh! That's wonderful! I think the two of you are a perfect match."

"Except for all the waiting.... What on earth does it mean, Aunt Andrea? Does it mean he won't kiss other girls the way he kisses me? Do I have to refrain from kissing other boys—not that there is another boy in my life at the moment—but what does it mean?"

Aunt Andrea pressed her lips together in thought. "I think only you and Heckie can figure out what it means. You're right; you have a long wait, so you'll have to decide what you both want and expect."

"But—I'm not engaged, am I?" I asked, setting my gifts aside and sinking down on the foot of the bed next to her.

"No." She chuckled. "If Heckie were ready to propose marriage to you, he would have gone to your father to ask permission. And hopefully, he would come to you on one knee with a ring in his pocket, so no, I don't believe you are engaged."

"That's what the girls at school are saying."

My aunt laughed outright. "Maybe that's how they do it in Ohio, but no, I think your friends may be misinformed. They are probably misinformed about a lot of things…" she said, scratching her head. "Sylvie…I think we need to have a talk."

My aunt began to tell me all the things I had questions about. The things about IT that I have wondered about over and over in my mind that no one ever discusses. She was frank and detailed in her description of how a man and a woman "make love," as she called it, rather than "having sex." I knew there were other vulgar words for it, so I spared her what I knew. She said it was special and that most women waited until they were married, but that she knew these days, girls were more promiscuous. I got the feeling she didn't approve of me having sex yet, but she wanted me to be armed with the proper knowledge, should the opportunity arise. My thoughts of Heckie and me in the throes of such passion flooded in and out of her explanation, making my head spin to the point of making me almost sick to my stomach. She also advised me not to do it if I wasn't ready, and to expect a man to take "no" for an answer; if he didn't, he wasn't worth my time. She told me about condoms, or rubbers, or French letters as they are sometimes called. Then she described what she used—a little rubber cup she called a diaphragm that women place inside themselves to ward off a pregnancy. I had no idea such a thing existed, but she explained that married ladies can get them from their doctors, discreetly, of course, but if a man is not prepared with a condom, I should get fitted for one to use when I get married. She said she convinced her doctor to give her an extra one in case hers broke! We laughed so hard about that, but I was over being embarrassed by then, and grateful that she thought enough about me to tell me all this important information. She even confided in me that at her age—thirty-nine—she was not expecting to have children, but one never knew what could happen. It was best to be prepared.

"I can't thank you enough, Aunt Andrea," I said, giving her a hug around her neck. "I didn't know who to ask about these things."

"Of course, you didn't. That's why I took it upon myself to tell you. Without your mother here to guide you, I felt I needed to be the one to step into her shoes."

I smiled. "I can't imagine Mother explaining this to me. I guess by now, we would both have grown into the task, though," I said, smiling at my aunt.

"I would hope so, Sylvie, but even mothers have a hard time sharing so much with their daughters. As much as I loved Anne, I think she would have shied away from being so open with you because of her own discomfort. And maybe by the time she realized she should have told you, it might have been too late."

We were both thinking of Catherine at that moment.

I broke the odd silence. "I thought of asking Catherine, but I thought it might be too painful for her to talk about."

Aunt Andrea looked grave and sighed. "I wondered how much you knew about what she went through."

"She told me everything at Thanksgiving. Everything."

"Then, you may know more than I do." We regarded each other solemnly.

"I know Catherine didn't mean to kill Clifton, if that's what you're wondering," I said, thinking I was answering her unasked question. "Kip stepped in her way to try to make her stop, to keep her from killing herself, but when she aimed the car at the Rosy Tree, Clifton was standing in front of it, and she hit him. It truly was an accident."

The words seemed to fill Aunt Andrea with relief. Obviously, she had wondered whether Catherine meant to kill Clifton, and whether they had covered up yet another sordid secret.

"She thought she was pregnant for the second time," I said, "because Clifton had raped her again when he realized how much Catherine loved Kip, but later after the accident, she had started her period, so all of it—her suicide attempt, her confession to her family about her bond with Clifton, and what he had been doing to her—was all for nothing. Did you know Clifton was adopted and that he wasn't even Catherine's brother?"

Andrea's face was pale, and she nodded. "Yes, I know. Kip told me that and how Clifton had abused her. He also mentioned that he knew Catherine had asked for my help when I was her teacher and that I refused to discuss her plight. I thought her mother should be the one to help her, but I didn't understand the family at all. I was wrong, so very wrong," she said, her voice breaking and tears spilling over her onto her cheeks. She wiped them away as I hugged her shoulders. "I'll never be able to forgive myself. I should have known how desperate she was to reach out to me," she said, sobbing into my shoulder.

"It's all right," I said, rubbing her back. She pulled away, fumbling in her skirt pocket for her handkerchief.

"No, it's not, Sylvie. I should have tried to help her. Catherine and I will never be the same, no matter how much we both try. I can tell she is trying to look past my betrayal, but how can she? She was just a child, a child in so much trouble that I couldn't even imagine! And then to know that Clifton really wasn't even her brother…. The whole thing is unfathomable! How confused she must have been!" Aunt Andrea wiped her eyes and blew her nose delicately into the hanky. "Just the idea of what a huge scandal the story could have been for her family and for *her!* Something like that could ruin her forever and her family would be in disgrace."

"I know," I said, helpless to provide the relief she needed. "It's unimaginable what she is still going through, having to keep it all a secret. And poor Kip. The Carmichaels are hosting the ball so that Catherine can find a suitable match because they want her to marry above her status."

"Of course, they do. If she marries well, she can receive her trust when she turns twenty-five. I've worried about Kip since he fell for her. He loves her so deeply and she loves him, too. If he were ever to change his mind about sticking with her and the truth about her baby came out, I know they would blame him for it publicly. Even though it isn't true, his reputation would be ruined as well."

"He's damned if he stands by her and damned if he doesn't," I said.

"That's true. But if what Kip says is true about what Clifton did at Shell Island, they're counting on him to keep quiet. So, they tolerate him seeing Catherine—for the time being."

"You knew about that too?"

"Yes, your father told me. Your brother is playing a dangerous game with Clayton Carmichael. I don't want to think of Kip in bad favor with that man. Kip has another year and a half of college left, and then he, too, will be free of that family."

"Well, I for one think they will be all right. Catherine is leaving for college in Massachusetts, and after she graduates, she will be on her own and won't have to see her family ever again."

Andrea shook her head. "I know they both dream of that happening and being together, but Sylvie, that's probably a pipe dream for them. Those wealthy families have so much hold over their children that they can make true love quite painful. I hope they can prevail, but it's not likely. If she were to marry Kip, she would be disinherited. That's important to remember."

"But Catherine is a *flapper*, Aunt Andrea! She's different. She doesn't care about their money."

Aunt Andrea laughed sadly. "She is certainly idealistic, Sylvie, and Catherine is young and starry-eyed over our sweet Kip. Why wouldn't she be? He's as good as a man can get. But he's not a prince. The Carmichaels' wealth is truly a fortune, and she will realize how important that is when she is older, especially if the family can keep her name clean in society. Protecting her financially is their idea of love, no matter what she or Kip has told you."

I shook my head, attempting to comprehend how manipulating Catherine could be love in any way, shape, or form.

"It's true, honey. Wealthy families do things very differently than we do. Believe me, the Carmichaels think they are doing what is best for the daughter they love. I think she knows it, too."

CHAPTER FIFTEEN

Elle

Elle took a break from her reading to rest her voice and take a sip of wine. The others decided to take a short break, so there was a moment to digest what had just been revealed. So, Elle thought, Sylvie finally had "the talk" from Andrea. It was about time! Thank God Andrea had the guts to tell the poor girl the facts of life, and even better, how to love a man. Elle wondered if AB felt uncomfortable hearing this conversation between Andrea and her young mother. Maybe it was best to keep her thoughts to herself out of respect for AB.

Elle quietly pondered Aunt Andrea's critique of Catherine's situation. It was so unfair back in those days to treat women who had been violated like trash. None of Catherine's situation was her fault. Previously, Elle had identified with Catherine's spunk and character, but Catherine was a victim and Elle wasn't. Elle had had her share of bad luck and had experienced derision from others who looked down on her, but she had always been able to rise above and move ahead on her own terms. That was the difference ninety years later. But then again, Elle wasn't from a wealthy family either. There was no one above her holding the purse strings and trying to control her with the family inheritance. Having never been from wealth, Elle had scrabbled her way out of her circumstances, working her way from the mountains where few people liked her to Wilmington where she was now a small business owner on the rise. Marcus Gilmer had helped her by introducing her to AB initially, but it had not been easy. Still, she had called her own shots and she was stronger for it. She wondered whether having money would have hindered or helped the course of her life. Could she have walked away from the Carmichael fortune the way Catherine was planning to do? Although walking away from money was not currently a dilemma for her, Elle hoped she would be strong like Catherine in that regard. With Kip by Catherine's side, anything was possible. Catherine must have known it! It was so romantic! With Nate by Elle's side, she was starting to realize endless possibilities. He *was* her fortune, just as Kip was Catherine's. Maybe she and Catherine were more alike than she thought. She looked at Nate and smiled.

SYLVIE

Kip and I had barely spoken to each other alone since I arrived at home. My conversation with Aunt Andrea still had me reeling and pondering so many things about my life and how we are all growing up and growing apart. I know after college my life will be so different, and my life at home here in Wilmington may only be a holiday glimpse from here on.

Kip and I hung back from the others as we strolled the block and a half to church. The new St. Paul's building was just beyond the next corner from our house on Market Street. I'd spent every important moment from baptism to confirmation in our church, along with most Sunday mornings in my life. Christmastime is my favorite season in the church, and tonight our family will welcome Christmas at midnight with lighted candles, singing "Silent Night" together in the sanctuary. It is a tradition I will miss sorely if I'm not able to be home.

I looked at Kip. "Are you concerned about the Carmichaels' ball?" I asked. "Since you weren't invited to be Catherine's escort? That would make me angry."

Kip turned to me and grinned that huge grin of his. Nothing ever seemed to faze him.

"The ball is just another Carmichael charade, designed to hedge bets on Catherine's marriage to a proper suitor just in case her tragedies are uncovered. But she and I have our life plan all worked out. I'm not worried. Don't you worry about us, either. The world is a lot bigger than Clayton Carmichael and Wilmington, North Carolina."

"Golly, you sound so grown-up. I wish I had your confidence in my own life plans," I said, a pang of insecurity running through me.

"I can understand that. Life comes at you hard and fast sometimes, and you're new at this," Kip said, taking my arm as I stepped off the new curb at the intersection onto the freshly paved street. "The world is changing. Not many girls your age are bound for such an adventurous life. It's exciting and scary. And so far, you're doing it all by yourself. I remember being a little afraid of committing to what I wanted to do. Rejecting Pop's offer of taking over his business to pursue making cars; it's daunting, leaving home and comfort behind. At least Heckie is trying to get a chance to be your partner in all this uncertainty."

"I know," I said, the now familiar heat flying up my neck. "Heckie is wonderful. It would be so easy to move back here and just teach piano lessons and marry him—if that's what he wants. But then, there are so many possibilities for me if I am brave enough to handle the pressure."

"You should do it while you can, Sylvie. Take the world by the tail. Heckie's rooting for you. Of course, he has his own commitments, but he's never stopped thinking about you."

"I don't imagine he thinks of me in the same way you think of Catherine."

We were standing at the steps of the church and the others were looking back to see if we were coming.

"I wouldn't be so sure about that. You'll soon see how he feels," Kip said, grinning, and suddenly, I did feel grown-up.

Friday, December 28, 1928

Dear Diary,

What a blur the last few days have been! Christmas in all its wonder has come and gone. The flurry of seeing friends and family have filled all my time, leaving me no time to write as my head hits the pillow in exhaustion each night. I think traveling and the possibility of what my life may hold wears me out even more than my hectic days in the Conservatory. At least there, I am used to the routine and how to spend my energy.

The ball was unlike any experience I have had. It was so elegant and exciting! The Carmichael home on Live Oak Lane is quite breathtaking most days, but all decked out for Christmas, it was a spectacular sight. Valets were on hand to park cars, so we entered the grand foyer like nobles attending court. Aunt Andrea gave me a lovely pair of long white gloves and a white feathery stole for Christmas to complete my ensemble for the evening. Heckie seemed taken aback with the whole look of me dressed for royalty. He was a pure dream in his tuxedo, which my father had perfectly tailored for him. He and Kip made quite the handsome pair as both escorted me into the Carmichael home, which got me lots of envious looks from all the girls who saw us making our entrance during the cocktail party.

But then Catherine came into view, rendering me a mere wisp of attraction in her presence. On her tall slender frame, her clothes always looked exquisite, and tonight was no exception. She wore a long white gown with a fitted surplice bodice and a flared skirt adorned with ostrich feathers at the bottom and the ends of the long, tight-fitting sleeves. Her glossy dark hair was waved and loose, caught over her left ear with a matching feather. She wore sparkling earrings and a delicate necklace of what I am sure were diamonds. Looking like a prince himself in his new black tuxedo, Kip greeted her in the receiving line with a formal bow and kiss of her hand. She laughed and pulled his hand in to give him the hug he wanted, murmuring she would save the last dance for him on her dance card, and I couldn't help swooning. Catherine Carmichael is class personified.

Heckie and I went through the line as well, where I introduced him to Mr. and Mrs. Carmichael. He had met them previously at my concert there in the summer before I left for Oberlin, but this time, it was obvious that we were together, so a more formal introduction seemed necessary. Mrs. Carmichael gave me a sincere hug and told me how marvelous we looked together, and she hoped I had a lovely Christmas with my sweet family. Mr. Carmichael also wished us a Merry Christmas and thanked us for attending Catherine's party.

When I got to Catherine, I gave her a heartfelt embrace, exclaiming how beautiful she looked.

"Merry Christmas, Catherine, and congratulations on your graduation!" I said, realizing I wouldn't see her again until the summer.

"Thank you, Sylvie! You are a *vision*," she said with a wink since I was wearing her dress. "And Heckie, Merry Christmas to you, too! You are so handsome!" she said, holding him back so she could take him in, making Heckie smile.

"Merry Christmas. Thank you for inviting me. Congratulations, Catherine. Where are you going to college?" he asked, something I didn't actually know myself.

"The Lowthorpe School of Landscape Architecture," she said. "It's in Groton, Massachusetts, far, far away from home." She gave another wink aimed at the three of us.

"That's quite impressive, Catherine, and indeed very far away," said Heckie, checking for my reaction. I gave a pout I was truly feeling, and eyed my brother, who was beside me, hanging on every word.

Turning to me, Catherine continued, "It's a two-year program, so I should be finished a semester after Kip. Then we can be together at last." She whispered the last part so her parents wouldn't hear as she glanced lovingly at Kip, which made me giggle and Heckie nod. "We'll talk more later. I hope y'all enjoy yourselves."

Heckie and I waited in the salon for the receiving line to end and the dancing to begin, while Kip passed us champagne from the waiters circulating around the room. Only the Carmichaels, the shipping magnates of the Cape Fear, could have access to so much free-flowing champagne during Prohibition. If Catherine had no interest in working in her father's company, who would take it over? Willard, Catherine's younger brother, the boy stricken with polio? He seemed bright, but it would be years before he would be ready to take the helm.

"So, Miss Meeks," Heckie began in his gentle voice before we were ready for a toast. "What happened to your Southern accent?"

I looked up at him and laughed, not expecting him to notice, and replied, "That's a long story, all about trying to fit in up in Ohio. I had a lapse, which caused a bad experience on the train coming home, so I'm practicing my Midwestern vowels while I'm away."

"Ah, well it suits you, especially since you're going places. It seems I'm getting to know a whole new girl. I'm more intrigued than ever," he said, kissing my hand as Kip arrived with his own coupe of champagne. Then Heckie raised his glass and said, "To vowels!"

Kip shrugged and drank anyway.

"To Catherine!" I said, and we drank again.

Kip grinned, raising his glass a third time. "To big changes, for all four of us!"

"Hear, hear!" said Heckie, and they drained their glasses.

They looked at my coupe, which still had a sip left. To alleviate my awkwardness for not keeping up, Heckie said, "The last toast is up to you, Sylvie."

I raised my glass as they lifted their empty ones.

"To National Prohibition; may it never end!"

The fellows roared at the irony as we clinked our coupes, and I drank.

I had not been to a dance with dance cards in ages. They were going out of fashion and hadn't been used at public dances like the ones at Lumina in years, though I thought the reason the Carmichaels had kept the tradition alive was one more way to ensure that Catherine danced with the other men in attendance. If she'd had her druthers, I know she would have spent every moment on the dance floor with my brother, but that was far from the point of this evening's entertainment. Not that it was an inconvenience for Kip to be unattached for the evening; every girl in the place had their eye on him and vied to be his dance partner, since it seemed obvious that after tonight, he could be a free man. I sighed, knowing the situation was all for show and that Catherine and Kip were playing their own game in an undercurrent of purpose and passion. Still, the Carmichaels were a formidable family and usually got what they wanted, so I couldn't help watching whenever I looked at Catherine and Kip dancing. Would this be their last ball? They made the perfect pair on the dance floor, as polished and matched in beauty as any guests in attendance. Kip made a point of steering Catherine to the center of the floor when he danced with her, causing all eyes to view their starry-eyed gazes as they turned in each other's arms in time with the music. Good for him!

I was rather distracted, though, by my own dance partner, who had boldly penciled his name in my card for almost half the dances, which was frowned upon, but apparently, Heckie didn't care, thinking we weren't the focus of decorum for the night anyway. I certainly didn't mind, and I noticed we'd gotten lucky with all the Shag numbers and several waltzes, in which we got to hold one another across the floor.

"Emerald green is your color," Heckie said, taking me in his arms and whisking his eyes over me, clearly appreciating the way the satin charmeuse slid perfectly over my curves, which I supposed was the objective with one you are crazy about. It was the opposite look my father had given me on my way out the door. Heckie pulled me close before the music started, breathing in my Soir de Paris, and giving me a discreet but alluring kiss on the side of my cheek. I felt the electricity pass between us as he gazed tenderly at me with his warm green eyes, as though telling me things he couldn't say aloud. Clearing his throat, he set me in my dance space, and we began a waltz under the dazzling crystal chandelier that lit the ballroom in the most romantic way.

After the waltz ended, the orchestra took an intermission, giving us a thankful reprieve from dancing with others we'd committed to, and a chance to wander out onto the veranda in the chill evening air. For December, it was unseasonably warm, but just cool enough for it to be proper for Heckie to wrap his arm around my shoulder. It was wonderful having him all to myself, but I couldn't help but wonder whether this was the place the ugly scene occurred after the Lumina dance in August when Catherine and Clifton's affair unfolded to her parents and Kip. The night....

"I'm glad I didn't scare you away at Thanksgiving," Heckie murmured into my ear, the sound of his voice stirring an intimacy I didn't expect.

"Why would you think that?" I asked, truly curious.

"When I said I'd wait for you, I was afraid I'd come on too strong. We hadn't really talked over the summer, and you were…preoccupied with other guys."

I reached up and touched his face, seeing his eyes search mine for further signs of alarm.

"No, you didn't scare me. I feel the same way about you, Heckie. It kind of hit me like a lightning bolt, and I don't know why I didn't see you before," I said with a laugh, "when all the other guys were distracting me with disinterest and insanity, but no. You have always been my man. I just didn't realize it."

He smiled and then sighed deeply. "That's a relief. There won't be a lot of times like this for us."

"Yes, there will. If I come home for the summers and the holidays and you do, too, there will be plenty of times for us."

"And then? When I go into the service, and you start traveling all over the world…."

"Really? Maybe my travel will be all over the *country!* I think we can handle that. It should be up to me, shouldn't it?"

"Absolutely!" he said with relieved enthusiasm at the possibility I wouldn't go too far away.

"Of course, I'm flattered that you think I'll be good enough for a tour around the world, but I'm not getting ahead of myself."

We smiled at each other, and then he leaned down to kiss me. His usual sweet kiss became one of longing in our corner of the veranda in the dark, where no one else seemed to be looking. I kissed him back, and a dam broke somewhere inside me that I didn't know existed before those kisses. He held my face carefully as if I might break.

"What does it mean, though, waiting?" I asked. "We will have a long time apart, even though we'll see each other as much as we can. What will you be doing while you're waiting for me?"

His eyebrows raised. "I'll be waiting for you. What do you think it means?"

"I'm sure you'll still go to all those dances and parties you've told me about. Will you have a special girl to take along?"

Heckie looked uncertain and I saw him swallow.

"I suppose I'll still go to the parties and the dances, just like I hope you will too, if you have the chance. I'll tell the girls I have someone special from home who has my heart. It's true, Sylvie. I wouldn't dishonor you by acting as though it weren't the case. But do you feel the same way?"

"Yes. Yes, I do. I've already decided I'll tell the fellows I have someone special. In fact, I already have," I added, coyly.

"Oh, yeah? Which fellow?" he asked, feigning jealousy.

I smiled. "A guy from the Conservatory. He's Jewish, so he says I'm not his type. And I think he prefers his roommate over me anyway," I confided, making Heckie laugh.

"Oh, I see. So, I really don't have much to worry about. At least, for the moment," he said.

"Right. Hersch is a good friend, probably one of my best, and he's a great date while my heart is set on someone else. While my heart is set on you." I said it seriously and Heckie kissed me again.

"Then I guess we're all worked out."

"I guess we are. I'm glad we had this talk," I said, grinning at him and working my fingers through his. He raised my hand to his lips and kissed it tenderly.

"Yes, ma'am, so am I."

The last dance of the evening came far too soon for my liking. I didn't want the night to end, and when the last dance began, the lights were lowered, and "I Can't Believe You're in Love With Me" began as couples found their special partners and began to sway to the music. Heckie and I took to the floor, which was another electrical moment, making me almost forget to watch Kip and Catherine in my pleasant distraction. Then I saw them, watching us! Still, Kip had done his part to steer Catherine to the center of the floor under the sparkling chandelier. When the song was over, he dipped her dramatically to a collective gasp from the guests. When he pulled her up, he brought her directly to his chest and kissed her fully on the mouth. She took his face in her hands and kissed him back with gusto, as if sealing their vows as husband and wife. The scene was not lost on anyone, with Catherine in her feather-festooned white gown and Kip in his formal tuxedo. It certainly looked like a wedding dance fit for a royal couple, and that is what everyone else saw too, judging by the applause they drew.

I believe my brother has just dropped a gauntlet!

Thursday, January 3, 1929

Dear Diary,

I am busily journaling away to repel the possibility of any conversation in my compartment for the train ride back to school. My heart is keeping pace with my frantic handwriting. Being a solo traveler, I am anxious about several things, such as contracting the flu on the train, encountering any chatterboxes or other unpleasant people like before, or missing my connection in Cleveland. It will be a long, lonely journey on my own until I reach Cleveland and change trains. Hopefully, I will relax then and maybe meet some fellow Oberlin students with whom to pass the time, but if I don't, I'm sure I will have more writing to do to tell of the events since the Carmichaels' ball.

Catherine's family left for Charleston on the 29th for their New Year's celebration with the Carmichaels' family friends, so Kip was left at home to be a third wheel for Heckie and me. Heckie was good about it, calling Kip the second wheel. We did a few things together, like going to the movies at the Royal, and strolling on Water Street to watch the boats. Other times, Heckie and I kept to ourselves for picnics on the beach and talks on the porch at his family's lovely home on Waters Edge.

I'd never been to Heckie's house until then, and his mother was so kind to give us tea and cookies while chaperoning from the parlor. Heckie has several brothers and sisters, all of whom are younger, so it was difficult to be out of earshot of the family while we were there. Mrs. Van Hecke—*Hannah May* as I already know her—invited me to dinner on New Year's Eve before the big party at the Carolina Yacht Club that Heckie had invited me to. She is kind and open, having the same blond hair and green eyes as her son. Her long hair is rolled and pinned at the nape of her neck and her dresses are simple but stylish and flatter her slim figure. There is a serenity about her manner, as if she is a part of the landscape, with her warm smile and sun-kissed cheeks, like all her children who play regularly outside. She calls Heckie "Eugene," which is his given name, but I find a different side of him at home than I knew previously. He seems mature and responsible, helping his mother out with the heavier chores while his father is working. I sat through a game of checkers on the porch with one of Heckie's younger brothers, Peter, whom Heckie said just wanted to get a look at me. It was kind of Heckie not to shun Peter, so I didn't mind. His fourteen-year-old sister Patricia showed me a watercolor painting she did of the beach, another act to get a glimpse of the new girlfriend, which I didn't mind either. Her painting was very good. The pale pink of the sky reflected in the water reminded me of the poem in "Beau Soir."

The Van Heckes have two homes, one I haven't seen on South Front Street in town, closer to the shipyard across the bridge, and the "summer house" on Waters Edge on the Intracoastal Waterway, where the family spends most of their time in the summer when school is out for the children. The Waters Edge house is one of only two homes on the road, with a dock across the road that sits directly on Wrightsville Sound. Although it is quite an elegant home, it's lovely and simple there, with views of the marsh grass teeming with birds—herons, egrets, crows, and osprey—along with the constant surveillance of gulls that call over us during the day. We even saw a lone bald eagle soaring high above the tall pines. In the quiet, we could hear woodpeckers hammering away on dead trees nearby, and owls that came to life at nightfall.

The house itself is lovely, with porches in front on both levels. It is built of white tongue and groove boards with a steep-pitched cedar shake roof. Without the usual gingerbread features on the homes seen in town, it is sturdy and peaceful to look at and comfortable inside, the perfect place to spend summers and even days during the winter, as they heat it with a coal furnace. It was a relief to see they have installed a cistern and indoor plumbing, which I must admit, I have fondly grown accustomed to. By New Year's Eve, I felt welcomed like one of the family. They even invited me to play for them on their piano, an upright which is quite a relic with rough action and in great need of tuning, but I felt grateful to have my talent appreciated. I sense I am perceived as extra-special because of whatever Heckie has told them. I also assume he has not brought girls home before from the curiosity evident since my arrival.

Mr. Van Hecke is like Heckie, quiet and gentle and massively built. He is there only in the evenings, so I have only met him twice. He and his wife sat with us and asked all about my studies at Oberlin, as well as about my family. Mrs. Van Hecke told me in private how sorry she was to hear that my mother and siblings had passed and that she had liked my mother very much. Of course, they knew each other since Kip and Heckie had been childhood chums. Kip tickles her, she said, and I knew exactly what she meant. He tickles me, too!

Kip was also invited to the New Year's Eve supper since he planned on attending the yacht club party with us. Mrs. Van Hecke had prepared a traditional meal of baked ham for prosperity, collards for wealth, Hoppin' John for good luck, and lace cornbread for gold. It was all so delicious, and I savored every bite, knowing I would return to sausages and potatoes for the next five months at the Conservatory.

The party was a fun affair, with the usual mixed drinks on hand, even though we are supposed to be in the midst of Prohibition. There was dancing and fellowship with friends I wouldn't see again until summertime. Everyone expressed their happiness that Heckie and I were a couple, and their condolences to Kip since Catherine was gone and would be packing off to the cold Northeast where he was bound to miss her sorely. He was good-natured about it, knowing they have a plan at least, and that they will both be working hard in school to make their dreams a reality.

At midnight, when the countdown ended, the crowd shouted, "Happy New Year!" and the band broke into "Auld Lang Syne," I gave Heckie the biggest kiss I could muster. He drew back and smiled at me. "I love you, Sylvie Meeks!" he said, stroking my cheek with his thumb. I said it back to him, too. It was wonderful! I can't believe I am in love!

Out of the corner of my eye, I saw Marjorie Mercer try to kiss Kip; he backed away quickly and put her off to the side. He said something to her to let her know he was still with Catherine, most likely. Some things will never change, I thought, wondering what Marjorie was thinking. And then the surprise of the evening came when her current boyfriend Jimmy found her, kissed her, got down on one knee, presented her with a ring, and popped the question, "Marjorie Mercer, will you marry me?"

Marjorie hesitated for less than a second, looking shocked, just long enough to pass a glance to Kip, and then she composed herself. She smiled at Jimmy and cried, "Yes!" The crowd gasped and then broke into applause. Kip was clapping his hands, grinning from ear to ear. Who would have thought Browsie would have beaten him to the altar?

Heckie watched along with me and murmured in my ear, "Well, I'll be a monkey's uncle!"

My thoughts exactly!

CHAPTER SIXTEEN

Nate

"What about that Browsie, huh?" Nate chuckled. "She's a piece of work."

Aubrey walked into the living room, a glass of water in one hand and a cookie in the other. Nate glanced at Elle as she looked up from the Zoom screen.

"Everything okay, buddy?" Nate asked Aubrey. It was Patsy's third day with COVID. They were all on edge.

Aubrey nodded. "Yeah. I finished my reading and I talked to Grandma Patsy. She's going to sleep now, so I wanted to know if I could come in and listen to your story?"

After a quick glance at Elle, Nate said, "Sure. Have a seat," as he and Elle put on their masks, Aubrey's cue to do the same. "It's getting really interesting. More fun than Anne Frank, I can assure you. So, Bernie and AB, Aubrey is going to join us."

"Oh, good," said AB. "Hi, Aubrey," she and Bernie said in unison.

"Hey," he said shyly, not being privy to the screen that Nate and Elle were viewing from the sofa.

"How's Patsy doing?" asked AB while Aubrey put down his snack and fumbled with his mask.

"She's feeling tired and achy, coughing a little more," said Aubrey. "I just talked to her, and she wanted to go to sleep so I came in here to listen." Elle patted the sofa next to her and he sat down beside her. He waved at the two faces on the computer screen.

There seemed to be a collective inhale from the Zoom participants upon hearing news of Patsy. Nate worried about what would happen to Aubrey if she succumbed to COVID. Elle had grilled him about Aubrey's next of kin and whether he and Patsy had talked about her affairs. It had been a tense few days, but they had made Patsy promise to call if she felt she was in distress.

After a knowing glance, Bernie broke the silence. "I hope a good night's sleep will make her feel better in the morning. Aubrey, you'll enjoy hearing what it was like to live back in 1928—well, now it's 1929. Sylvie, AB's mother, is just returning to college in Ohio after a fun New Year's Eve party over at the yacht club."

Nate chuckled. It was so like Bernie to launch into a history lesson for the younger folks.

"Oh, cool," Aubrey said, but seemed unimpressed so far.

"I'm dying to know," began Elle, "was Heckie's summer home your house, AB?"

"Yes," said AB, her eyes twinkling. "This house has been in my family for three generations. It's the oldest home on the street. The guest house in the back was added later as well. It was originally an artist's studio for Daddy's little sister Patricia. When Daddy grew up here, another family built the brick home down the road. It was just a dirt road for ages. You can imagine how isolated they were back then."

"You must have had work done on the place constantly. It's in beautiful condition," Nate said.

"Thank you, Nate. It's always challenging living in an old home. Mama and Daddy were always working on it. Then when I married Monty, he enjoyed the history of the place and took meticulous care of it," AB said. "You know how much he loved the gardens," she added, casting a fond glance at Bernie, who had maintained them for AB since Monty had passed.

"So, did Heckie and Sylvie live with his parents when they got married?" asked Elle.

"No, his parents stayed at the house in town when Daddy married Mama. Daddy loved this house, and he didn't mind going all that way to town to work. The trolley made it easy to commute. When I came along, I loved it too. I've never left it."

"Cool!" said Aubrey. "Do you know when Patsy's house was built?" he asked.

"I think that one was built back in the eighties."

"Uncle Phil's house was built in 1935," Nate added.

"And what about the one next door?" Elle asked, shooting Nate a glance. The house had been abandoned after the men who rented it had held a small boy hostage there for a few months the year before. It harbored terrible memories for everyone.

AB sighed. "It was built in the thirties, too. I just heard it's going to be torn down! Someone just bought the property, and they've decided to tear it down and rebuild there. Isn't that wonderful news?"

"Hallelujah!" said Nate, and Elle smiled with relief. It was time the creepy old place got erased from memory.

"That's where those perverts lived, right?" asked Aubrey.

"Yes, honey," said Elle. "This is *really* good news. You can tell Patsy that the house will be gone soon. That will make her feel a whole lot better. We're all going to feel better once it's gone." Elle put a protective arm around Aubrey. She was the one who had discovered the child there and called the police. The story had made the national news, and after that, she had been known around town as the Sunshine Girl. She'd had her fifteen minutes of fame, but also haunting memories ever since. Everyone on the street was relieved the ordeal was over. But the ramshackle old house was a terrible reminder of what had happened inside.

"So, did the Carmichaels live near here?" asked Nate, changing the painful subject.

"Yes, they lived across the road, near where Pembroke Jones lived at Airlie. He owned most of the land on this side of Wilmington, Airlie, and his hunting lodge called Pembroke Park, what's now known as Landfall," said AB.

Bernie added, "It was named that because it was where Verrazano first made landfall here in 1524."

"Oh!" said Elle. "I didn't realize what Landfall was. Pembroke Jones owned quite a lot of property!"

"Yes, he was quite wealthy. The Carmichaels couldn't hold a candle to him—no one could keep up with those Joneses—but the Carmichaels had their share of power back then, too," AB said, looking at Aubrey.

"What happened to them?" asked Elle.

Bernie took up the narrative from there. "I've been researching them a bit. I read that their home was sold to another family in the fifties. I don't know what happened to Willard, but I believe he did inherit the shipping company. His company may also have been sold. We call it *logistics* these days," he said for Aubrey's benefit, "but it was actually *shipping* back then. Goods were taken down the river in flat boats from the plantations and then sent out to sea on ships from the port. Then when the railroad came, goods were 'shipped' out by train. Heckie's daddy built the ships and Carmichael arranged the shipping of the goods."

"Shipping and handling," said Elle for Aubrey's benefit. "That's where those terms come from. You know, like when you order something from Amazon, they charge you shipping and handling fees."

"Oh, yeah," said Aubrey, nodding. "Unless you have Prime and then it's free shipping. Now they send it out in an Amazon van, and you get it on your porch the next day."

"Right," said AB. "We have come a long, long way from the way things used to be done."

"Imagine, having to wait that long for a package to arrive," said Elle, smiling her eyes at Aubrey over her mask.

"You have one on the porch," Aubrey said. "I heard a truck drive up while y'all were reading." He sucked his braces, turning his tawny face up to her.

"Oh! It might be a uh, a dress I ordered!" Elle said, sitting up, her face turning pink. Nate's eyebrows rose. Amazon was becoming Elle's addiction; his, too, if truth be told—fishing lures, rods, and reels.... Trolling for goods on the internet had become a dangerous way to kill time during the pandemic.

AB gasped. "Could it be a wedding dress? Your wedding is coming up in just a couple of weeks!"

Elle grinned. "It could be! A wedding dress or two...."

SYLVIE

Wednesday, January 9, 1929

Dear Diary,

Thankfully, I found Mina at the train station in Cleveland! By that time, my hand was tired from writing, and I was happy to have her company. We chattered away like magpies the entire ride. Our return to winter in Oberlin was met with several inches of snow on the ground. It is cold and windy every day now, and the sky always seems to be a dull metal gray. If ever there was an incentive to spend time wisely in the practice rooms, this weather is it!

Returning students have brought the influenza with them from our holiday visits home, and the infirmary is filling up fast with new cases. We continue to eat our fruits and vegetables and try to get as much sleep as possible, leaving windows cracked for the fresh air. It seems dreary to be here, but I find my new attitude buoys me along pleasantly. Being in love has much to do with my newfound lightheartedness, but also having a semester under my belt has removed much of my insecurity about being in the Conservatory. Possibly, knowing that I might have choices about my life's path makes the daily grind somewhat easier to bear as well. My time away from here and deep family talks have expanded my perspective about many things.

I have just returned from my chamber music ensemble class! We are a quintet: me on the harpsichord, Hersch on violin, a girl named Hazel on viola, one named Millie on cello, and the biggest surprise of all, Ronald on bass! I can't wait to tell Mina! I will keep my eye on him for her if that's what she wants. She told me on the train to Oberlin that she ran into Ronald at the Majestic Hotel on New Year's Eve with her parents and aunt and uncle, out for a grownup dinner and some jazz entertainment. Ronald was also there with his family. Who knew he was from Cleveland too? They even live in the same neighborhood! She calls it Little Harlem. It is such a small world! Mina was all smiles about it, since apparently Ronald made a good impression on her father. That can only mean one thing; Ronald likes Mina too!

Anyway, the chamber music group is somewhat tedious. Not the group so much as the music itself. At least I have good company to entertain me while I peck away at Bach on the harpsichord. Mr. Finch says it is a "dispassionate instrument" and that I must learn to play it with precision, not passion, the way I play the pianoforte. There are no pedals to modulate the sound; all you have is your fingers. Instead of hammers to produce the sound, it plucks the string like a harp, thus the name. And so many trills! The music seems so frivolous, but I suppose I will have to get used to playing it. No wonder all the old-fashioned people in books and movies seem so stodgy and boring! I think of the girls in Jane Austen's books who were moderately talented trying to entertain their chaps in the parlors on those harpsichords. If I were a fellow, I'd certainly do my best to run away to the gardens!

"Your face is all screwed up, Sylvie!" Hersch joked to me as we packed up our music at the end of class.

"So is yours!" I shot back, making him break into laughter. "This music is so stuffy. I much prefer Rachmaninoff or Debussy. Satie is simpler but much more beautiful than that tinny sound the harpsichord makes."

"I'm glad you like the challenge of those others, but Bach is amazing and chamber music has its place, so we must get the complete musical experience while we're here," he said patronizingly, though his twinkling eyes gave him away.

"That's for sure," Ronald added, walking with us out of Rice Hall. "Give me jazz improv any day!" The grin that makes Mina blush spread across his face.

"I guess. We're singing Gregorian chants in chorus. Those aren't so bad. I rather like them. We sang them in Warner Hall just to get the feel for how powerful and spiritual they could be. All the voices echoing in the hall…it kind of gives me the Willies, but I love it."

I felt the boys' indifference to my ramblings as we walked, and then Ronald turned off to the rehearsal hall for his orchestra class. I shouldn't be a musical snob, as Mr. Finch has cautioned.

"See ya," he said.

"Aren't you going too?" I asked Hersch.

"Yeah," he said, thumbing toward the orchestra room and lingering near the door. "I just wanted to catch up with you before I go in. Did you have a nice holiday?"

"I did," I replied, knowing instantly that my red face was telling all.

"Looks like it!" he smiled. "Did you and your guy hit it off?"

"Yes. His name is Heckie, by the way. And your holiday? Did you meet any nice Jewish girls? And how was the theater?"

"So many questions!" Hersch scolded with laughing eyes, swatting a hand at me. "My holiday was fantastic. The theater was wonderful! That Cole Porter—*Paris* was a great show! He has this wonderful song, 'Let's Do It, Let's Fall in Love!' It'll slay you when you hear the words! We went with family friends, so sure, my 'date' was a nice Jewish girl. We hung over the orchestra pit railing gabbing with the musicians. But sadly, not a glimpse of Cole Porter all night! Then, we went backstage and met the cast. It was the bee's knees! And, yeah, I guess you could say I met someone," Hersch said sweetly. He looked happy.

"That's nice," I said, though I felt a pang for Bart. I wondered what they felt for each other. Did Hersch still feel the same way? Would Bart understand? What would happen with the two of them if Hersch liked someone else? It would be hard to be involved with a roommate, I decided.

I got a letter from Catherine. She is settling in at college and already complaining about the cold winter weather and the piles of snow! "How is one to find a landscape under all that snow?" Oh, the girl makes me laugh out loud! She misses Kip like crazy. Her fellows from the ball and her Charleston trip are writing to her, but she has assured them she has her heart set on someone else, Kip, of course, but I don't suppose any of them needs to know the details. She was as bowled over as we all were that Marjorie is now engaged! Personally, I thought Marjorie was holding out for Kip, especially since rumor had it that he was free after the ball, but maybe I was wrong. I wrote back and advised Catherine to work hard and immerse herself in Lowthorpe, so the time will fly until the summer when she and Kip will be reunited. That is exactly what he is doing, so she should take heart. I told her I miss her too and that I will be happy to see her when summer comes. I miss Heckie fiercely already. It is a wonderful but painful thing to be in love! Absence does make the heart grow fonder!

In a stroke of serendipity, Heckie must have been feeling the same way I was! It is both a relief and a boon to know we have mutual feelings for each other. I've tucked away a letter he wrote that arrived in today's post to treasure it.

HECKIE

January 20, 1929

My dearest Sylvie,

Not a day goes by that I don't think of you. I'm grateful for the wonderful times we shared over Christmas, from the magnificent ball at the Carmichaels' home to the peaceful afternoon we spent on my family's front porch. You were so gracious to my brothers and sister, and you were a big hit with my parents as well. I hope there will be many more shared Christmases for us. As my father says, we are an "interesting pair," and in my own words, a complicated pair at that. Not many folks our age have such grand plans for their lives, but I have come to love you, Sylvie Meeks, and I want you to do whatever makes you happy. If it's your concert tour, traveling the globe, or whatever kindles your fire, I hope I can make the cut, adding to your happiness. Until then, I hope to hear from you. Please let me know what is happening in your world. I will hang on every word.

Your Heckie

KIP

January 27, 1929

Dear Sylvie,

I hope you are faring well in the winter up there in Ohio. Catherine has written to complain about all the snow and cold in Massachusetts. A Yankee she will never be!

It was wonderful to see you at home during Christmas. We all had such a good time, and it delights me to see you and Heckie getting on so well. He is truly over the moon for you. I'm afraid my friend Perry is quite disappointed that he will not get to court you next summer if you and Heckie continue to see each other. Perry is so interested in all the goings on at home and how Lumina has become the magical setting for our social scene on Wrightsville Beach.

Speaking of last summer, I was wondering if I could peek at your diary. I know I mentioned it before and that it's a very bold request. I realize how personal a document a diary is. The reason I'd like to see it is that Perry and

I think a story about Catherine's experiences should be recorded in case the Carmichaels or anyone else ever gets it in their mind to prosecute Catherine for Clifton's death. What you might have written about her character and your own experiences with Clifton could be valuable information for anyone looking to understand how the events of the whole summer unfolded. I confess that though I haven't kept a journal, I have written several letters to Perry over the summer about what happened from my point of view, but then, as you know, I am quite biased when it comes to Catherine. Perry loves her too and would be willing to give writing a memoir a shot if it could help set the record straight about her if it ever came to that. Now that you know everything that has happened to her, I know you would do everything you could to help her as well. I have run the idea by Catherine and she thinks it might be a good idea. She is rather fascinated that our love story could take form from this endeavor.

I understand this is an unusual request and it may leave you reeling, but I only ask you to take a few days to consider it. If you decide to do it, please send me the diary at my campus address. I will return it to you after Perry finishes writing his narrative. I believe I had mentioned before that he is an aspiring author, and a good one, from what I have read. If he does indeed write a good book, it will be nothing more than practice for him, as the manuscript will never go to publication. It will remain as truthful a record of events as we can hope to produce. If nothing else, it will make interesting reading for our descendants one day!

I wish you all the best as you continue to build your repertoire and expand your world at college. Whenever you are ready to give a concert, let me know. I will hop a train and make my way to Oberlin or wherever to hear you perform. I am so very proud of you! We all are!

Yours truly,

Kip

Tuesday, February 4, 1929

Dear Diary,

My darling brother Kip has written to me to request the use of my summer diary for the purpose of writing a memoir to exonerate Catherine if she is ever prosecuted for Clifton's death. How brilliant of him to think ahead for her sake! Knowing the Carmichaels, I can see why he might be concerned about how they might manipulate her for their own purposes. Having the summer's events documented by my handwritten account would protect my brother as well! Maybe he has thought of that too. I have certainly endorsed him as the perfect suitor for Catherine, however unsuspecting I was. As I read back over my entries, I find they are so naïve and somewhat embarrassing, but I am hardly the girl anymore who wrote all that rubbish last summer. There is nothing for me to be ashamed of, other than my naivete, so it took me only an hour to decide certainly that I would contribute my diary for the cause. I never thought about how documenting my days could be so important, but in hindsight, writing as much as possible may be indeed important in someone's history.

Which brings me to Herschel. I hope the fellow is not getting himself in trouble, but I have seen others watch his interactions with Bart with questioning looks. Herschel is so talented and has such a bright future that I fear he may sabotage himself if he is not more careful. The three of us were in the practice rooms this afternoon, and I was practicing my latest assignment, the piano score for Gershwin's "Rhapsody in Blue." Hersch and Bart wandered in, perching around the piano to listen as I finished up. They always practice at the same time and walk to dinner at their boarding house together to end the day, much the same as I do with my dorm friends.

"Mr. Finch gave me the same piece," Bart said, suspiciously.

"Don't we all play the same pieces for the most part?" I asked.

"This is for the freshman orchestra concert," Bart said. "I heard whoever plays it best gets to perform with the orchestra at the next concert in March."

"Oh. I hadn't heard that, but I wondered since it's not a standalone piece. That makes sense."

Bart's eyes shone as he spoke. "Then we might as well congratulate you now, Sylvie. You know you're going to get it."

"No, I don't. That's why he's giving it to all of us."

Bart smiled. "He's just following procedure."

"Don't think that way or I *will* get it," I said, placing the score in my satchel and reaching for my coat and hat.

"Spoken like Wallace," Bart said and scoffed, giving me a disdainful look. He and Wallace never have hit it off.

"I think Wallace just tries to give you good advice," I offered. "After all, he's a senior, so he's not competing with you…." I also thought Bart's attitude was defeatist at times. Herschel's eyes darted back and forth between the two of us. He had the best attitude of the three of us. He loved music, whatever kind it was, and the opportunity to play another day, and being at Oberlin Conservatory was his dream come true, at least until he would land his dream job in a Broadway orchestra.

"Don't let her take you down," Hersch scolded Bart with a laugh and a finger aimed at Bart's nose. Hersch handled most of his conflicts with humor, and this comment made Bart laugh and lightened the mood. Then Hersch regarded Bart with a look that I could only interpret as love, making me avert my eyes from their private moment. Bart was lucky to have Hersch rooting for him. We all needed our friends, no matter what shape, size, or form they came in.

We left the practice room at the same time Teresa and Wallace were coming down the hall, chatting about a piece they'd just played.

"Speaking of the devil," Bart muttered. "You can walk with them, okay, Syl? I don't feel like listening to his condescending—"

"Okay, now," Hersch said, nudging Bart's elbow to urge him along. "We'll see you later, all right, Sylvie?"

"Okay," I said, wrapping my scarf around my neck and patting my coat pockets for my gloves.

As soon as they hit the stairwell, Wallace and Teresa were even with me. I closed my door and greeted them.

"Hi, Sylvie!" said Teresa, her arm threaded through the crook of Wallace's arm. They certainly seemed to be dating, I thought, being aware these days of all the couples who had formed over the first few months of school. I wondered if they were truly in love, how they would handle the separation they might soon face after graduation and pursuing their own career goals. It was impressive to make it through all four years at the Conservatory, so I knew their future careers were poised to launch soon.

"Walk with us," said Wallace, gesturing politely for me to proceed with them down the hall.

As we exited the stairwell and headed for the door, Wallace said, "I heard you practicing the Rhapsody score. You sounded superb!"

"Thank you! I just love the Gershwins' music," I replied, grinning while thinking about my diction and wanting to impress these upper-classmen. Maybe they would know the answer to my question. "Is it true that Mr. Finch gave the piece to all his freshmen students to see who will play it with the orchestra?"

"Just you and Bart," said Wallace. Then, to my questioning look, he said, "Didn't you hear? Anita didn't come back from Christmas vacation. She quit."

I gasped as we stepped onto the sidewalk, carefully picking our way around mounds of snow piled beside the walkway. The icy air hit me in the face, making the hairs inside my nose crystallize instantly. "No! I didn't realize…. I thought she was just in the infirmary with the flu!" I said, putting on my gloves.

"No. Mr. Finch mentioned that several freshmen chose not to come back after the holiday," said Teresa.

"Oh, no! That's so sad!" I said, tears coming to my eyes at the thought.

"Well, it happens all the time at the end of semesters," said Teresa. "The professors call it weeding out."

"I've heard about it, but I suppose…I just didn't think it would happen to people I know."

"Well, just think of it this way, Sylvie; it narrows the playing field for you," Wallace said slyly. I felt a cold wave of dislike flow through me. Maybe I was right about him at Mr. Finch's recital. Holding the chair for Mrs. Finch and helping in the kitchen may have been his way of apple polishing for his teacher, his unsuspecting wife, and apparently his girlfriend. How quickly I was beginning to see people for who they were these days.

Crabs in a barrel, I wanted to say, but held the thought. We walked along, holding our breath against the cold wind. Several yards ahead of us, I could see Bart and Hersch walking together quickly, talking and laughing raucously. Then they bumped shoulders and turned to each other, sharing an endearing look, and laughing again.

"Well, isn't that *sweet?*" Wallace said, an effeminate tone to his voice. "The lovebirds are at it again!"

"Hush, Wallace! You don't know that for a fact," Teresa scolded him, her free hand holding her scarf over her face for warmth.

"Sweetheart," he said with a chortle. "I can smell a faggot a mile away."

"What makes you say that?" I asked, thinking fast about how I might throw him off, a sickening feeling beginning to take hold.

"Have you not seen the way they look at each other? I've seen them in our boarding house touching and gazing at each other when they think no one is looking. They're roommates, and so much more, my dear. You should know; you associate with them enough."

"I've never seen any of that," I said evenly, stating the truth, but wondering whether what I had just seen in front of me was innocent camaraderie or something else. I still didn't want to believe the truth, even though the truth might be what made Hersch and Bart happy. Not that I was trying to change them, but the boys were my friends, which made me want to lash out at Wallace, but I was afraid my defensiveness would only make their situation worse.

Teresa and Wallace stopped in front of Teresa's dormitory. It was too cold to discuss it further, which was probably for the best.

"Well, this is my stop. Goodnight, Sylvie," said Teresa, giving me a kind smile with her eyes, since her face was mostly covered by her scarf.

"Goodnight," I said to them both, watching as Wallace walked her down the sidewalk to her door.

I looked around, hoping to catch up with Hersch and Bart, but they were already gone.

CHAPTER SEVENTEEN

Elle

Pulling into the driveway at home, Elle noticed the Grady White boat that normally rested on its lift was gone. It was such a beautiful day; Nate must be out on the water—with Aubrey—she realized as an afterthought. It was hard to get used to having another person in their house, and some of their previous routines had been adjusted since Aubrey moved in four days ago. Lack of privacy was the number one change. How uncertain these COVID times were!

Elle checked her watch; 4:45, at least an hour before dinner, which would be followed at seven o'clock by their Zoom reading. She figured the guys would be out for at least the next hour, giving her just enough time to try on the bridal gowns she had ordered online. After all, it would be bad luck for Nate to see her in her wedding dress before the big day. The *little* big day, she thought with a chuckle. It was somewhat of a relief not to have a big do, she thought again, even though her friends and coworkers at the bakery were absolutely thrilled that she and Nate were getting married and finalizing plans for just two weeks from now. Her heart made a small thump.

Harley's absence also was apparent from the house's silence. The dog must have been invited on the boat outing as well, Elle thought with a smile. Putting away her purse and keys, she went into the bedroom she shared with Nate and pulled out the large box from underneath the bed. He had not asked about the dresses to afford her the sacred privacy of trying them on. A thrill went down her arms as she opened the box and took out the three gowns, laying them side by side on the bed. Maybe he knew she needed this time alone and had taken Aubrey out on purpose? That kind of thoughtfulness would be so like him.

The gowns were simple in design, though different in character. One was a vintage lace over tulle sheath with a plunging V neckline and jeweled straps; one was a classic ivory crepe with a folded portrait neckline and covered buttons spilling down the back; and the third was an ecru strapless fit and flared delight, covered with sparkling beads and embroidery. She knew they would fit by holding them up to her and checking each one in the full-length mirror in the corner of the bedroom. Surely one would suit her, and she could return the other two. Online services made dress shopping—even wedding dress shopping—so easy these days.

One after the other, the dresses fit perfectly, hugging her body the way she'd hoped. She wound her hair into a loose chignon at the nape of her neck, imagining that the breeze at the end of the dock would make a mess of her hair, imagining Nate's reaction to each dress. The strapless dress fit beautifully, but she felt it would be too risqué for Mr. May, who would be officiating. The crepe was elegant and mature, and she knew Joey would approve. She saved the vintage lace for last, slipping the straps over her shoulders and smoothing the bodice over her waist. It hung beautifully, leaving no visible or embarrassing bumps or bulges. Tiny soap bubble sequins made the dress shimmer in the light. The small train would be perfect for the dock, and the plunging neckline was tasteful, if not revealing enough to turn Nate to jelly. An image of herself waltzing with Nate under the Carmichaels' crystal chandelier flashed through her mind. A shiver of excitement ran through her, bringing tears to her eyes as she turned to view the deep V back of the gown in the mirror. Stunning.

This was the one!

SYLVIE

Wednesday, February 5, 1929

Dear Diary,

After a restless night of tossing and turning, I thought it best to bring Hersch's behavior to his attention, however tactfully I might manage it, to hide my knowledge of his liaison with Bart. I caught up with him as we walked to chamber ensemble this morning.

"May I tell you something, friend to friend?" I asked as we hurried along in the bitter wind.

"Of course, friend," he said, grinning at me.

"Last night when I was walking back to Talcott with Wallace and Teresa, we were behind you and Bart."

"Okay," he said, expecting me to continue.

"You and Bart were carrying on, you know, talking and laughing, and sort of bumping into each other." I hesitated and Hersch looked questioningly at me. "Wallace said some things about you and Bart that I didn't like. I just think you should know…." I shrugged.

"What things did he say, Sylvie?"

"I really don't want to repeat them, but it had to do with boys preferring boys," I said, shooting him a sideways glance. His face was all seriousness. "I think you should be careful."

Hersch nodded, taking in all the implications I'd delivered. I expected him to shoot down what Wallace had implied. I expected indignation, anger, the same defensiveness I'd felt at Wallace's insults; instead, he sighed deeply. "Okay. Thanks for telling me, Sylvie."

I smiled reassuringly. "I just think it's getting even more competitive around here now. Did you hear that several freshmen withdrew from the Conservatory after the semester?"

"Yes, I did hear that," he said, looking as though he were reading between the lines of what I meant. He veered off on another course. "I think the professors are stepping up the competition as well."

"I know. Bart is worried we were assigned the same piece for the orchestra audition as it were."

"Yes. He thinks Finch wants him out. They're starting a special freshman convocation once a month as well. We will play in front of each other to demonstrate our repertory skills."

"Oh, I didn't know."

"My violin teacher told me that today. They'll be looking for musical mastery as well as poise on stage. I'm sure Mr. Finch will tell you at your next lesson," he said as we entered the room where our quintet was assembling.

Hersch turned back to me before opening his violin case. He studied me carefully. Then he said, "Thank you, Sylvie."

Hersch's acceptance of the information I'd delivered made me think one thing—Mina was right about their preferences.

NATE

Elle was coming out of the bedroom, smiling brightly when Nate and Aubrey came inside. Harley's nails clicked on the kitchen's tile floor as she searched for her water bowl.

"Hey!" Elle greeted Nate, putting her arms around his neck and giving him a welcoming kiss.

"Hey," Nate said, regarding her seriously. "Hold on a minute." He raised a finger. "Hey, Aubrey, how about going outside and hosing off the fishing rods like I showed you, okay?"

"Aye-aye, Captain," Aubrey said comically, making Elle giggle.

When he was out of earshot, Nate said quietly, "They took Patsy to the hospital today."

Elle's face fell. "Oh, no! What happened?"

"She called me about two o'clock and said she was having trouble breathing. I told her I'd call 911 for her, but she said she'd already done it and unlocked the front door for them. The ambulance came for her about ten minutes later. AB and Bernie were standing at the mailbox when it came down the street."

"Sirens blaring?"

"No. They turned them off after they turned onto the street, but the whole thing pretty much freaked Aubrey out. I took him fishing for a diversion since there was nothing else we could do. And it took his mind off her for the most part." He let the blow settle while Elle raked fingers through her blond hair and sighed hard. "Patsy said she left a copy of her will on her desk for me to pick up if I needed to. Also, she made a list of all her accounts, the account numbers and passwords, insurance agents who manage her policies…. Anyway, I went down and locked the house after she left in the ambulance."

"What about Aubrey? Who do we need to contact if…?"

"Covered. Patsy's daughter's information is in my phone as we speak. Patsy texted it to me this morning. We'd talked this morning, and she was coughing more than I'd heard before. I was worried then. It all went south from there."

"Have you heard anything from the hospital?"

"Not yet. I'm going in my office to call in and check on her before Aubrey comes back inside. I'll put the boat away later."

"Okay. I'll go out there and supervise the cleanup while you call."

"Good idea. I'll call AB next with whatever update I can get. She and Bernie were pretty shaken."

"I'm sure," she said, turning to check on Aubrey. "Wait, are there any fish to clean?"

"Nope. No luck today."

"Good!" she said. "We can pull a frozen pizza out of the freezer for dinner."

ANNE BORDEN

AB peered at Aubrey on the computer screen, looking for signs of despair over Patsy's hospitalization. He seemed quieter than usual, but who wouldn't be, seeing as how his only functioning relative and primary guardian had just gone into the hospital with COVID? It would be normal to be quiet, processing what was happening and trying to manage one's emotions. At any moment, the poor child was likely to break down and cry. AB wondered how much of the news Aubrey was allowed to watch down at Nate's house. The news of COVID infection rates and images coming out of New York, of body bags going inside refrigerated trucks because the morgues were full, frightened her, and in her eighty years, she had seen her share of horrific things. What effect did the grim scenes and stories have on today's isolated youth? Having loved ones in the hospital and being unable to visit them was alarming and distressing. At least Nate's news of Patsy was somewhat hopeful. She was in the hospital on oxygen and *not* on a dreaded ventilator—yet.

Aubrey's participation in tonight's reading seemed preferable to the news for the time being. Nate was reading the last entry from Sylvie's diary to catch him up. The desired distraction appeared to be working.

"So, Herschel and his friend Bart are *gay?*" Aubrey said to clarify.

"Yes," said Elle.

"Okay," said Aubrey, shrugging slightly.

AB was amazed that Aubrey did not think anything of it now.

"Back then, being gay was a really big deal, Aubrey," said Nate. "It was against the law to be gay then."

"Really?" Aubrey looked surprised.

"Yes, but Sylvie loves Bart and Hersch, so it doesn't bother her," Elle explained, and Aubrey nodded.

"My algebra teacher is gay, I think," he said, shrugging. "It doesn't bother me, either."

SYLVIE

Thursday, February 7, 1929

Dear Diary,

I had a lot to discuss with Mr. Finch at this morning's piano lesson. After my quick warmup of scales and arpeggios, I was bursting with my questions.

"Is it true that Anita left the Conservatory, sir?"

From his chair beside the piano bench, he nodded matter-of-factly. "Yes, it is, Sylvie. She came to the realization on her own that Conservatory life is not for her." He pressed his lips together in a sad sort of smile.

"Did you agree with her choice?" I asked.

"Yes, I believe if any student has doubts at this point, it's best to move on and find what she or he really wants to do."

I nodded gravely, understanding the process, but feeling sad for Anita. It must be a relief to lose the pressure we all feel here, but I was sure she had more doubts moving forward trying to discern her next steps. Maybe there was a fellow back home she would marry.

"She is still at Oberlin, changing over to being a music major, just not in the Conservatory anymore. She hopes to teach piano in the future."

I was relieved she hadn't quit music altogether. I sighed, wondering about my next question.

"What was it like for you, if I may ask, Mr. Finch? I know you were a concert pianist before you came to Oberlin, but how did you manage to have a family and tour the way you did?"

Mr. Finch crossed his arms and raised his head in thought. "I was a lucky man," he said. "I met Elsie here at Oberlin. We were both studying piano in the Conservatory. After we married, she chose to stay home and teach lessons while I toured. She had two of our children and raised them while I was on the road. Even though she had her mother to help, teaching and childrearing wasn't easy for her, so I came home to Cleveland and put down roots. We shifted gears and I became the teacher, and she took care of our children. We had three more children, so my change, of course, was the best solution for everyone." I recalled seeing his family's picture on the mantle in his living room. "And then, of course, we came back here where I could teach in the Conservatory."

Feeling a little sorry for his wife, sacrificing her music for his career, I blurted, "Miss Devereaux tells us we need to choose family or a life of performance—that we can't have both."

"Yes, I know Miss Devereaux has been quite vocal about her opinion on that matter," he replied. "And as a woman who has had an illustrious opera career, she knows best. She's absolutely right that if a musician wants to dedicate her life to her work, there is no time for having babies and raising children."

"That seems so absolute," I said, apparently testing his patience since I saw him glance at the clock. "It just seems that with the right partner, all of that could be done."

"I'm afraid she and Mrs. Finch would tell you that idea is pie in the sky, young lady," he said, not unkindly. "Is there anything else?"

"Yes, please. I've heard about a freshman convocation."

"I was just getting to that. At the end of this month, we will start having monthly convocations for the freshman class. Since the larger convocation has been canceled due to the influenza, we feel the smaller groups will be safer and beneficial to you. Each professor will offer his students, and my piano students are going first. That means you and Bart will play on the twenty-second. Violin and viola students will also play, and Miss Devereaux's voice students will sing. It looks as though you will be busy that evening!" he said, smiling at me, his eyes lighting up. "I think you should play the 'Etudes,' don't you? It's by far your best, of course."

Rachmaninoff. For an audience. I swallowed. "Yes, of course."

"Wonderful. Let's hear the 'Rhapsody in Blue,' please."

I have two weeks.

This evening after dinner—one of sausages, potatoes, and cooked cabbage as predicted—Dot asked me to accompany her in the parlor. Since male student visitation had been banned during the flu outbreak, Dot worried that she and Bart wouldn't be able to practice as much as they needed to. Although Dot wasn't scheduled to perform in the freshman convocation yet, she wanted to be ready when her time came. She stood in the curve of the baby grand and, after her warmup, began her rendition of "Beau Soir." Mina's stairwell example had worked its magic on Dot. Her voice was warm and restrained, like I had never heard it, although she was unable to produce the light shimmer of Mina's voice. No one could sing like Mina. Still, for Dot, the performance was a milestone in her vocal journey. Even Miss Devereaux's accomplished voice has lost the luster of youth that Mina's possesses, reminding me that especially for voice students, the window of opportunity is limited, and one must strike while the iron is hot. Without doubt, my fingers will remain intact far longer than one's vocal cords.

When the last note of the song faded, I rested my hands in my lap and smiled at Dot.

"That was truly beautiful, Dot!" I said. She must have seen the sincerity in my face since a grateful smile lighted her own.

"Thank you, Sylvie. I owe it to Willemina Wadkins." We both grinned.

"Your teacher must be so pleased."

"Yes. He thinks there may be hope for me yet," Dot replied.

"I'm glad you had that stairwell epiphany," I said.

"Jealousy is a relentless teacher."

"I don't think you're jealous, Dot."

"It's as contagious as the flu around here," she replied.

"Maybe what you caught was motivation, not jealousy."

"Here, everyone wants to be the best, and being on the bottom rungs is a wretched place to be."

I sighed, realizing she had a point and well aware that I was not there.

"Mina is a prodigy. And so are you, Sylvie. You have it all—talent, poise, beauty, and charm—and now you're in love! I think I'm the only person in the Conservatory who's not paired off with someone. Bart has Herschel, Mina has Ronald, and you have that handsome midshipman back home."

I gave her an impatient look. Bitterness would not help her climb from the bottom rungs or find love.

"You can't allow yourself to think that way, Dot. You must imagine the brighter side if you want to be successful in music and in love."

"It's not that easy, Sylvie. I can imagine anything I want to about Bart, but I know he's never going to be my Valentine because he loves Hersch!"

Valentine's Day is next week, and I was hoping for a special missive from Heckie. Ridiculously, I had even allowed myself to dream about our future wedding at St. Paul's. Heckie's father would be his best man, and Catherine would be my maid of honor. Heckie and I had waited for love. So could Dot.

"Maybe Bart is not the one for you, but love will find you, too, Dot. In the meantime, don't let anyone or anything make you feel inferior. You can't have a defeatist attitude," I said, recalling what Wallace had said to Bart. "How did you get into the Conservatory in the first place? Because you were excellent! You are excellent! Don't forget that for an instant."

Tuesday, February 12, 1929

Dear Diary,

I sat at the piano bench in Miss Devereaux's studio for Mina's voice lesson. Mina was also being informed of her freshman convocation invitation, something she already knew about by the time her lesson came around. What followed was not at all what I expected.

"Mina," began Miss Devereaux calmly but firmly, "I must caution you regarding any affiliation that will interfere with your studies here and derail your future pursuits as a performer, as we have previously discussed."

Mina's face clouded in confusion. "I'm sorry, Miss Devereaux, but I don't understand what you mean," she said. I could almost hear her heart beating in her chest.

"It has been brought to my attention," said Miss Devereaux, "that you are seeing a boy in the Conservatory and that you seem quite serious. I don't want any frivolous affair of the heart to keep you from your dreams."

"Do you mean Ronald Galloway?" Mina asked, her face going scarlet.

"I suppose so."

"But how on earth do you know this?" Mina wondered aloud, her eyes cutting to me, making my head rock back in disbelief that she would suspect me. I shook my head at her. Of course, it wasn't me who had tipped off Miss Devereaux. Were there people watching us? Who would do such a thing?

Miss Devereaux did not answer her question, but said gently, "I only advise you to tread carefully. You are too talented to let one reckless act destroy your dreams."

Mina was speechless for a moment. I wanted to say something to clear my friend's reputation, which seemed to have been sullied by someone, but Mina spoke before I could.

"Miss Devereaux, I suppose you could say that Ronald and I are sweethearts, although certainly not the way you have been led to think. You don't need to worry about me. I have no plans to ruin my career over a *boy*." A hint of indignity was in her voice. I was proud of her for standing up for herself.

"He may be a very nice boy, and I hope he treats you respectfully as a gentleman should. Just be careful, Mina. You needn't be a cautionary tale to the other students here," Miss Devereaux replied.

She glanced at me then, which made me realize her lecture was not solely aimed at Mina. "It's a wonderful thing to have friends and support while you are here at Oberlin, ladies, but you must be careful not to cross the lines that can trip you up. I don't tell you this to invade your privacy or make you angry, but as your mentor, I believe I must guide you both as I see fit. You have probably noticed that several students in your freshman class have already dropped out for one reason or another. Some have to do with talent, with drive, stage fright, or inability to memorize the music, but there are others who have made missteps that have nothing to do with their abilities and must leave because of their own unwise choices. By the time students reach the senior year, only the strong and truly dedicated will survive. I hope both of you make it that far. Your futures are exceptionally bright."

Friday, February 15, 1929

Dear Diary,

I am positively swooning! Heckie sent me a store-bought Valentine card with a nice handwritten note! I made a card for him, too, and hope it arrived yesterday.

Our gang of five had our usual Friday dinner in the Oberlin Inn. The flu is starting to wane a bit, but the convocation is still canceled until the infirmary clears. Mina was tight-lipped about her date the previous night with Ronald, but she had no issue with regaling everyone about Miss Devereaux's lecture on Tuesday.

"She's a wet blanket! Who you love is completely none of her business," Hersch said, before biting into his hot pastrami on rye. Dot and Bart laughed, but I thought better of making fun of Miss Devereaux, especially if there were spies afoot! Hersch shook his head and swallowed before bursting into song. It was the first verse to "Let's Fall in Love," and I was surprised at the derogatory lyrics about Chinks and Japs—not only that but that Hersch found it appropriate enough to sing them.

Bart threw back his head and laughed. "Well, if Cole Porter says it's okay to fall in love, I think Miss Devereaux should get onboard."

Mina frowned. "That's not very funny, Hersch. What's the difference in those words and what those men on the train said to us at Christmas—or Chanukah?" she asked.

"You're right. I'm sorry, Mina. It's bawdy humor, meant to be harmless, and the New York audience ate it up, even the Jews I was with. Porter's lyrics are more like cabaret than Broadway if you ask me. But, yeah, you're right; it's insulting. My point was that I don't think Miss Devereaux should be nosing around in your business; that's all I'm saying."

"I'd like to know who told her about Ronald and Mina," I said.

"Who would talk to her about her students?" Dot mused.

"Who would see you two together?" Bart asked, concern etched on his face.

It hit me then. "Miss Shelton! Our dorm matron. She knows who comes to call from the sign-in book."

"But Ronald hasn't been allowed in the dorm since the flu outbreak," Mina said.

"Do you think they let the teachers see those books?" Hersch asked, hands in the air.

"Maybe," said Bart. "Or maybe Miss D just saw you two walking around on campus."

Mina shrugged. "I guess so. It also could have been another student trying to bring me down…or do me a favor in a strange way. I've never tried to hide being with Ronald. We even hold hands sometimes. I didn't think we were doing anything wrong. It gives me the Willies that she knows what I'm doing."

"I know," I agreed. "But Mina, she was just trying to be helpful. I understand why she is concerned. My father said the teachers are investing their reputations in us." I knew Miss Devereaux was banking on Mina being her next bright star and didn't want to lose her, but I didn't want to say it in front of the others. It would be rubbing salt in a wound.

"I doubt Mr. Finch would lecture me," Bart said and scoffed.

"That's because you're a boy," Mina said. "You can't get into the same kind of trouble a girl can."

From Catherine's story, I knew Mina was right.

"Well, anyway, Finch would probably be glad if I left."

"Bart!" I scolded, tossing my napkin at him and making him laugh. I gave Dot a warning look too about negative talk. This conversation wasn't helpful for anyone. "I think we should just drop it. It's a good thing you boys quit going to the speakeasy."

"You were lucky your visit there was early in the semester, when no one there would have recognized you," said Mina. "If we don't toe the line here, we could be on a train home in a flash."

Hersch held up his hands in defense and smiled mischievously at Bart. "I know, I know; guilty as charged. But we haven't been back to the speakeasy since the night Dot got blotto on us."

"Hersch!" Dot said and threw her napkin at him.

CHAPTER EIGHTEEN

Mr. May

Bernard and AB got back in the car after spending a productive morning at his house near Bradley Creek. He had mown the lawn, pulled weeds, planted tomatoes, and cut a bucketful of peonies from the flowerbed beside the house while AB had cleaned inside. His was a welcoming sort of home, not as grand as AB's, but comfortable and pleasing to the eye. It had good bones and three bedrooms with a master on the first floor—something everyone wanted these days. Since Bernard was a master gardener, abundant flower gardens with interest for each season filled the views in every direction, and a three-season vegetable garden was central to the sunny backyard. The house was especially pretty in May.

AB seemed thoughtful as they drove along Oleander Drive back to her house. She took a long drink of her water.

"What are you going to do with your place, Bernie?" she asked, gazing out the window at the boats moored at the creek's dock as they drove over the bridge.

"What do you mean?" he asked, knowing very well what she meant.

"You have such a beautiful home. Are you going to move back into it, or are you going to stay with me?" When he hesitated, she said, "You can, you know. You can stay with me."

She shook her head when he didn't respond. "We should partner up. I think about Patsy living without a husband and poor Aubrey left with no one if she doesn't make it. Because of COVID, it makes the most sense to live together, especially at our age," she said, fingering those imaginary pearls at her neck. "We do well taking care of each other, don't we?"

"We do," he said, smiling over at her. He thought about reaching for her hand, but he stopped short of it as she continued, a hint of anxiety in her voice.

"With my children and their families scattered across the country— Carolyn in Oregon and Derek in New Jersey—I know they don't want to come back here to take care of me, and I don't want them to. Your son isn't coming back for you either." AB had never been one to mince words.

"Yes, I've come to that same conclusion, and I don't blame Brandon," Bernard said, thinking of his son and his girlfriend of sixteen years who were doctors in Costa Rica. The surfing there wasn't bad either, which had been the initial draw for Brandon. "He and Lindsay have carved out their own special life. I don't expect them to come back to Wilmington. So, I'll hang onto the house until I have to sell it. I can move into a re-tirement center so Brandon doesn't have to worry about me." Until that time, though, keeping up the house and gardens was a lot of work. He went over at least once a week. But what else did he have to do? Now that the vegetables were planted, he would be there more often.

"I've had the same thoughts, but I really don't want to leave my home. Especially after we've all heard what Sylvie—Mother—had to say about it. I realize how important it is to keep it in the family."

"Have you discussed your house with Carolyn and Derek?"

"Yes, and they are exasperatingly noncommittal about it. I don't think they grasp the urgency of the COVID situation the way we have at our age. They're so busy with their work and their families' activities that they haven't been able to squeeze in a visit since Monty died. I haven't seen them or my grandchildren in two years. And now with my age and the COVID travel precautions, they *can't* come."

"I know you miss them. The phone calls are nice, but it's disheartening for sure not seeing them. I feel the same about Brandon. He's so far away. What do you think your kids will eventually do with your house?" *Once you're gone* was implied.

"I imagine they'll sell it," said AB. "It's always disappointed me that they aren't more attached to our family home or this area. They don't want my furniture. No one plays the piano, so they don't want it. They don't seem to want to come home. But I'm over worrying about it. The house is worth millions in this market. I've checked it on Zillow."

AB was one tough cookie. Her voice was devoid of the sadness he knew she felt. A sadness he'd felt as well about missing his own family.

"Then again, I'm not dead yet," she said.

"No, you certainly are not!" Bernard replied in commiseration. COVID was making everyone feel anxious about life's uncertainty. He had thought of Patsy's situation too, scrambling to get her affairs in order in case she didn't recover from the virus. They should start working on their affairs as well. He'd already made a list of his accounts and passwords in case AB needed to use them to pay his bills, but that was hardly a start. How the COVID situation had made the elderly come to terms with their mortality!

At the traffic light at Eastwood, Bernard coasted to a stop behind an old green Bronco headed for the beach with a surfboard sticking out of the back. Sunshine warmed his hands on the steering wheel, making him feel an odd mix of melancholy and hope.

It would be a shame to see AB's ancestral home go up for sale. But these days, kids tended to live farther and farther away from their parents. Even in the midst of the pandemic, people were beginning to move away. He'd read that the real estate market was starting to heat up. Interest rates were at an all-time low, and people were moving out of the crowded cities to the comfort and safety of the suburbs. Travel had reopened somewhat, though most were reluctant to fly, and a buyers' market had sprung up overnight. People had spent their time in isolation fixing up their homes, reassessing where they really wanted to live, and weighing new options for working from home. Wilmington had suddenly become a hotspot for relocation with its temperate climate, historic charm, excellent health-care, and nearby beaches to lure those with means, yet another example of the "haves vs. the have-nots." So many in the country were now strug-gling with job losses and paying rents. The "haves" were rebooting their lives and forging ahead as always, leaving the "have-nots" in the dust.

The light turned green, and Bernard turned the corner toward the Intracoastal Waterway.

"But selling my house wasn't what I was getting at, Bernie," AB con-tinued, training her blueberry eyes on his as he quickly glanced her way, while attempting to navigate his car in traffic. "Do you want to move in with me for good or not?"

I already have, he wanted to say, but that wasn't her intent.

"Well, seeing as I have already moved in with you…."

"Ninety-seven percent does not count," she said.

She had a point. His clothing was there as well as some gardening tools he'd brought to manage her gardens without going back and forth as he'd done before he got sick, and when COVID had locked them down, he'd never left. But that wasn't what she meant. The remaining three percent would put them over the tipping point in their relationship. He put his window down to take in the fresh spring air. And summon up his nerve. He had dragged his feet long enough.

"I have a comment about that, but I'd like to get home first," he said as they passed the impressive white walls of the neighboring Landfall community. *Home.* Bernard turned the car onto Waters Edge, and they drove down the street in silence. He pulled into AB's driveway, parked, and killed the engine in front of the guest house where Elle had lived when she first arrived in Wilmington, the very space that had been Heckie's sister's artist studio years ago. Cheerful pink petunias and lime-green potato vine spilled out of its flowerbox. There was so much history here.

"You deserve more than just ninety-seven percent from me, AB."

AB nodded, waiting for him to continue, her eyes fixed on the petunias.

"We fit together so well." He sighed and reached for her hand. "These are strange times to say the least, but living with you and reminiscing about our history after all these years makes me realize we should be together. Who knows how much time we have left?"

"Then we should get busy. We need to get our healthcare power of attorney settled, our wills updated, everything. We should get married," AB blurted. "Enough beating around the bush, Bernie. I want someone in my life who loves me. I don't want to live alone anymore."

"Me neither. Would you really marry me?"

"Yes. Yes, I would."

"I do love you, AB. I have for a long time. So, will you? Will you marry me, AB?"

"Yes, I will, Bernie. I'd love to marry you." She smiled and squeezed his hand.

SYLVIE

Friday, February 22, 1929

Dear Diary,

What a marvelous night it was! What a coup for the freshman class of the Oberlin College Conservatory of Music, indeed! If there was ever a silver lining in the influenza outbreak of 1929 in Ohio, this was it.

This was the moment my friends and I had dreamed of. Hersch, Bart, Mina, and I were honored to have performed for our fellow freshmen and teachers in Warner Hall. Granted, it was a much smaller audience than the full house would have been at convocation, but our performances were just as worthy of the full attendance. Mr. Finch, Miss Devereaux, and Hersch's violin teacher helped us get organized backstage, told us to break a leg, and then took their places in the audience. Dr. Maxwell, the Conservatory director, took over from there and introduced each musician along with the piece he or she would recite.

Bart played first, a lovely Chopin piece Mr. Finch had assigned him to prove he could play "less bombastically," as Bart joked. He succeeded and seemed pleased with himself as he should have been.

I played the Rachmaninoff "Etudes-Tableaux No.1." I thought it went well, but what I loved was sitting in the spotlight, enjoying the sounds of the music reverberating in the great hall, almost coming off the bench in my efforts to show off the piece as it should be played. Mr. Finch led my standing ovation, and I gestured my appreciation to him from the stage. I was thrilled to take my bows before I returned to the wings.

Mina sang last, as I had hoped she would. As she took the stage, a collective murmur could be heard from the crowd over her lovely, regal appearance in her simple black dress. It was as if she were royalty indeed the way she held her slim figure as Miss Devereaux had taught her, with her braid-crowned head held high. Mina placed her hand in the curve of the Steinway and bowed her head. Her meditation went on for several uncomfortable moments, making me fear she was petrified by a bout of stage-fright. Her knuckles were white where she grasped the piano. Focusing my eyes on her, I sent positive messages to my princess of the stage, willing her to raise her head and begin, aware that the audience was holding its breath too, rooting for Mina. Finally, she lifted her head and smiled upward, serenity radiating from her face, summoned by the song she was to impart. She placed her trembling fingertips together, my cue to begin. My own fingers called forth the beautiful dreamlike notes of Fauré as Mina began "Après un Rêve."

In perfect French, she told the story of a woman describing a dream of her true love appearing in an unusual light, only to wake to find him gone. The ethereal quality of her voice showed no fear, but shimmered in the dream, taking us with her, as I knew would happen. As the last note lingered, chills ran down my arms. I knew Mina had conquered her fear, giving the audience exactly what Fauré and Miss Devereaux expected. In the brief silence that followed, I felt a similar frisson of appreciation from the audience, before thunderous applause began, bravas were shouted, and students leaped to their feet for Mina, while she bit her lip and bowed humbly. She gestured to me, and I stood and bowed. When I smiled at her I saw her eyes fill with tears. She bowed once more to the continuing applause and then we exited the stage.

As wonderful as Mina was, I must admit that Herschel Blum was the surprise of the day. He strutted onto the stage and performed the violin solo from Rimsky-Korsakov's "Scheherazade." His small and wiry frame was commanding once he began the haunting melodious piece. The poignant, sweet tones filled with vibrato rang out through the hall. Hersch played passionately, his eyes often closed, completely given over to the story, making us visualize the allure of the woman who charmed the sultan into marrying her. Hersch's body ebbed and flowed with the melodious phrases as if he would float above the stage. He caressed the strings, playing the highest notes with concentration and care, giving each one the energy it needed to hover beautifully in the air. It was so erotic I felt my face burn! The way he carried the enraptured audience along until the end of the story made me realize how talented Hersch is. Again, the audience was on its feet, applauding and cheering as I watched my friend take his graceful bows with humility and a bit of amazement. I couldn't help but wonder whether playing in a Broadway orchestra wouldn't be selling himself short, as fine a musician as he is.

We ended up in the Oberlin Inn that evening to celebrate, with Ronald joining us to round out our group. Over sandwiches and root beers, we praised each other's performances. My friends said nice things about the Rachmaninoff.

"Bart, your piece was lovely!" Dot swooned, making Bart smile and blush. "I had no idea you could play so gently."

"Thanks, Dot. I'm sure you weren't the only one," he replied. "When it's your turn, you'll give them all a surprise as well." He grinned at her.

"I can't wait!" she said, her own face flushed at the thought. "I'm so jealous of you all!"

"And Mina, were you scared?" asked Bart. "You had us all holding our breath!"

Mina looked caught off guard. Then she smiled slowly. "At first, I was terrified! I prayed that I could work through my nerves and give that rotten somebody who told on me my best show. I could feel Sylvie's power radiating to me through the piano!" She laughed and shot me a sarcastic smile. "Miss Devereaux's coaching and positive words got me to lift my head, and I did the rest."

"You slayed it," Ronald told her proudly, reaching for her hand and giving it an encouraging squeeze.

"Yes, you did!" Hersch said, raising his root beer in a toast. "To Mina, for overcoming her stage fright tonight!" He grinned broadly at Mina, making me like him even more.

"You literally rose to the occasion, Mina!" I said. "I thought you were going to ascend to the ceiling once you started singing!" The others laughed. "And you, sir!" I raised my glass to Hersch. "You almost levitated yourself to the clouds!"

"To Hersch!" Mina joined in the toast and the others raised their glasses.

"I had no idea you could play like that!" I told him.

"Thanks," Hersch said humbly.

"And to think you would waste all that talent in a Broadway orchestra. You need to be a soloist in a grand philharmonic somewhere. Carnegie Hall is your destiny!" I proclaimed. Hersch looked uncomfortable under the weight of my praise, but the others were clapping to affirm my assessment.

"There's nothing wrong with Broadway," said Bart, "if that's where he wants to be."

We'd started to accept Bart's moodiness, but it seemed an unnecessary cut to Hersch. Hersch shrugged it off and grinned at Bart.

"Who knows where we will all end up?" said Hersch. "As long as my fingers and my brain still work, I hope to play another day."

"That's right," said Ronald. "The choice is ours if we put in the work."

Wednesday, February 27, 1929

Dear Diary,

Earlier in the week, I was invited to sit in on today's orchestra class to audition for the piano solo in "Rhapsody in Blue." Being referred by

Mr. Finch was a great honor, but it by no means secured my participation in the orchestra's spring concert in March. Others would sit in on the class as well for subsequent rehearsals, and I knew Professor Doyle, the orchestra conductor, would make the final judgment. I was glad I had memorized my parts, even though the score sat on the piano's music shelf. I played and turned the pages to see where the orchestra was in the score, but I knew my part by heart. Gershwin is so uplifting, and it was such a thrill to play with a full orchestra that I couldn't help smiling as we played. My heart pounded in my chest as I finished with a flourish. My hands immediately went to a prayer of thanks in front of my mouth. There was a round of applause by the orchestra members, and Professor Doyle gestured for me to stand and accept it. Graciously, he joined in the applause, and I left the session floating on a cloud. Wouldn't it be grand to have the opportunity to perform with them at their concert? I knew Bart and some others would join the rehearsals after me, so I had by no means sewn up the audition.

"My God, Sylvie, you did great!" Hersch said, squeezing my arm and grinning at me as we left the building together. "Doyle loved it!"

"Thank you! I won't get my hopes up until I see my name on the program, though," I said.

"Keep thinking those positive thoughts! Mina says it works, you know." He laughed.

"Oh, I was so happy to see her work through her stage fright!" I replied. "I know she'll continue to struggle with it, but now she has methods to control it. I imagine it makes a good performance all the more thrilling, though, wouldn't you think?"

"What I think, Sylvie Meeks, is that you're an inspiration. You've helped Mina and Dot, and now me."

"How do you mean?"

"The Scheherazade solo. I tried to imagine how you would play it. I think it added something to my own interpretation of it."

"It was quite…sensual," I said, feeling the heat in my face.

Hersch chuckled. "I know, wasn't it? That's why I love it, so I had to play it that way. Anyway, you inspire us to reach our potential. I've never met another student as giving as you are. I only wish the professors were as positive. All they want to do is set us up to see if we stand or fall. It's a rather gruesome way to train musicians, don't you agree?"

"Yes, I suppose it is. That's why we must stick together!" I said, giving his shoulder an encouraging pat.

In the practice room that evening, I played the Gershwin solo again. Closing my eyes, I imagined splendid dancers swathed in deep shades of blue shot through with silvery threads stepping and twirling to the music under a large moon over Lumina's promenade deck. Catherine and Kip appeared in royal blue for a pas de deux under the stars. When I'd finished, I sat quietly, letting the images settle, the song still playing in my head. From the rooms around me, I became aware of the other students practicing their own music. Another version of the "Rhapsody" solo echoed my own from down the hall. This version was loud and dramatic, angrily pounded out on the keys. The pianist played with such power! Who would torture the melody and the spirit of the piece that way?

My desire to play had soured, so I gathered my music to stow in my satchel. Thankfully, the other pianist was done murdering Gershwin. I put on my coat and wrapped my scarf around my neck, then found my gloves and put them on. As I opened the door to leave the room, a tall male student stormed down the hall carrying his own satchel of music.

It was Bart.

Thursday, February 28, 1929

Dear Diary,

Dot hums and sings more often than ever now. I've been accompanying her in the evenings in our parlor when Mina and I finish our practices. Mina stays to give Dot critiques, and Dot takes her constructive comments with aplomb. Other students watch and listen as they come and go, all of us duly impressed with Dot's progress. We have become an alliance of three, the Three Musketeers, as Dot has named us! Whatever we have learned here in the Conservatory, Herschel has pointed out the proven value in supporting each other. Quite possibly, we are teaching each other, which may be a goal the faculty has achieved by leaving us somewhat to our own devices. Survival of the fittest can often be achieved by banding together for the common good instead of sinking one's rivals. I think we are onto something positive at the very least.

As I brushed my hair before bedtime, Dot readied her clothing for the morning. I knew I would stay up for a few moments to write my journal entry, especially after she told me why she was so happy.

"I'm with Bart now, Sylvie," she said to my surprise. "He's more than my accompanist and friend. He kissed me today and asked me to be his girl."

A sickening feeling went through me after I'd heard him play last night in the practice rooms. I wanted to be pleased for Dot, who'd pined for a fellow since the rest of us had all paired up. "But I thought he and Hersch were together. Is this real?"

Her face clouded over. "I knew you'd react this way, Sylvie. Maybe Bart isn't queer like Mina says. Can't you just be happy for me? You're not the only one who deserves love and adoration…." Her voice broke off, having said too much.

I was stunned. "I'm sorry, Dot. I didn't mean to make you feel bad. I just thought—"

"I know what you thought," she said quietly, running a comb through her hair. "But you thought wrong." She picked up her toiletry kit and walked out of our room.

All the good conclusions I'd drawn from earlier in the evening went out the window as I absorbed her feelings pouring out, feelings of jealousy, directed at me. How could we make this right?

CHAPTER NINETEEN

Anne Borden

AB had thought it would be hard to keep her and Bernie's upcoming marriage a secret, but events unfolded so fast that she hardly had time to think about it. For one thing, Elle and Nate were so focused on their own wedding that they never would have assumed Bernie and she were planning their own! Patsy was still in the hospital, hanging on for the seventh day of her illness so far. The doctors said it takes time, AB remembered as she realized she was wringing her hands. While attempting to gather documents, she and Bernie had been glued to the television for the whole day, watching the horrific news account of George Floyd, an African American man, being restrained by the neck under the knee of a police officer in Minneapolis until he died. A day later, the world was outraged, as she and Bernie were, and protests were happening everywhere.

Their conversation with Nate earlier in the day had focused on Patsy's condition and how he was managing Aubrey. Nate said the news reports had made the boy angry and frightened, being black himself. Concerned about Aubrey's mental health, Nate had watched TV with him instead of making him attend his online classes, discussing what the repercussions of Floyd's death would be, and what was happening in many American cities. Fires had been set to businesses in Minneapolis where indiscriminate looting was taking place without police intervention. It was too much to comprehend amid the COVID pandemic. *How much worse could things get?* Protests over the murder of Floyd were happening in Wilmington too, which were peaceful so far.

As far as wedding talk went, Bernie assured Nate that he had obtained his credentials to officiate the ceremony and urged Nate to get his marriage license from the county office at least a day before the wedding. Nate mentioned that Elle had invited her son Joey and a few out-of-town friends. AB had offered the guest house for Joey's stay. Marcus, AB's friend who had introduced her to Elle, could stay at a hotel, as would Elle's cousin Judy and her family. Nate's family could also arrange hotel accommodations. If Nate's Uncle Phil could make it, he would, of course, stay at his own house with Nate and Elle. Hopefully, Aubrey would be back home with Patsy by then. Everyone could have takeout dinners from the local restaurants after the wedding. The food delivery folks would have a busy evening on Waters Edge! It was thought that no one would stay more than a day or two in town. She thought family members would prefer staying in the hotels on Wrightsville Beach for safe lodgings and to enjoy the beach for a few hours since there was no parking available there because of COVID unless they were hotel guests or property owners. Nate was responsible for the RSVPs and lodging arrangements since Elle was so busy with her bakery and because he had lots of time on his hands. With hope and prayers, they thought Patsy might be out of the hospital and well enough to sit on the dock with Aubrey for the ceremony.

AB and Bernie had promised each other to keep their own wedding a secret to respect Nate and Elle's nuptials. After the young people tied their knot, AB had arranged with a Presbyterian minister from the church she attended pre-COVID to perform their ceremony. Theirs would be a low-key and safe affair on the porch with only the unsuspecting Elle and Nate as witnesses. Of course, their families would be invited, although AB was almost sure they wouldn't attend. In the meantime, she and Bernie had been researching how to update their documents, wills, powers of attorney, deeds to their houses, and bank accounts. Bernie had contacted a real estate agent, and they had scheduled an appointment to show her his home. He had promised her some of the tomatoes from his garden to sweeten the deal! It was so like him to personalize the situation.

As if all that weren't enough to think about, demolition on the old house next door had begun! It was cathartic seeing the place come down bit by bit each day, and it would be a memory by the wedding. They felt sure the process would be completed by then. AB would hire Aubrey to scour the road for nails for the drive-by parade of friends they were planning, who would ride through to greet the couple after Nate kissed his bride. No one needed a flat tire to be part of the wedding memories!

They had ten days to be ready.

SYLVIE

Wednesday, March 6, 1929

Dear Diary,

What I have dreamed of and hoped for has come true! I have been chosen to play the "Rhapsody in Blue" solo with the orchestra! I was notified yesterday in a letter from Professor Doyle. I rehearsed with the orchestra this morning. Knowing the competition that I was up against was rigorous, I am absolutely thrilled! Mina and Hersch are also happy for me. The downside of it is that Dot has also heard about my assignment from her new beau Bart, and I am unsure how to tiptoe around the sour feelings she has toward me. She congratulated me, but I felt as if her heart was not in it. I do believe I deserve the solo, but I am so uncomfortable with the tension in the air that it has produced. I have not seen Bart yet, but I imagine our Friday evening gathering will be uncomfortable.

They have been practicing in Rice instead of in our dorm since the flu precautions have been lifted. At least Dot is performing in the freshman convocation on Friday, so we will be able to praise her for her performance, and Bart will be highlighted as her accompanist. Hopefully, I will not be the focus of attention.

For the next two weeks, I will be rehearsing with the orchestra until their concert on March 23rd. It will be the first concert open to the full Conservatory body as well as the public since the infirmary has cleared of the flu cases. Everyone seems to have breathed a large sigh of relief that the worst of the flu has passed. There has been no loss of life at Oberlin, which is another reason to celebrate. It will be wonderful to be back to normal. I shall write letters to my family and to Heckie and Catherine to announce my good news!

Friday, March 8, 1929

Dear Diary,

It appears I have worried for no reason about my friendships with Dot and Bart over my piano solo with the orchestra. All six of us had dinner together at the Oberlin Inn after the freshman convocation, and it was a lively and companionable celebration. Dot's performance of "Beau Soir" was as lovely as we had hoped, and Bart's accompaniment was equally as tranquil and captivating. All of us gushed about how good they were, but Hersch was particularly complimentary to them both and Bart seemed just as grateful to have Hersch's praise. There is still that intimate look between them at times, if I am not imagining it. If I am, I am as confused as ever about their association, wondering whether Hersch and Bart are actually lovers, or if we have all been misled. If anything, they still appear to be steadfast and devoted friends, even if Dot is the one on Bart's arm during our walks to and from the inn. Still, I recall my subtle warning for Hersch to be careful around campus with Bart and his earnest appreciation of my warning. Maybe they are being careful and are masquerading as real men! If that is the case, I'm afraid Dot is in for heartbreak surely. I have played that part and can see the red flags in the distance for her.

Then, in front of everyone, Bart congratulated me on getting the piano solo, and I felt such a relief since his words seemed sincere. However stung he was, he is my friend and I know him well by now. I believe I can tell when he is being genuine, as I believed him to be tonight. Dot followed his lead and told me she is happy for me to have such an opportunity, while reminding Bart that there will be other opportunities for him as well. He took her sentiment well in stride, even though his cheeks went a shade rosier than usual. The competition among us is indeed difficult, but I am relieved to see that we are all trying to be adult about it. There is no need for sour grapes, and I hope I would have conducted myself the same way had I lost the solo to Bart.

On the way back to campus, I hung back with Hersch to have a private conversation.

"I'm so relieved that Dot has come around! And that Bart isn't holding a grudge," I confided to Hersch.

"Bart is trying hard, Sylvie. He and I are…struggling." For him to admit even that much must have been difficult. "I can't get into it really, but he's trying to accept a lot of things."

"Then surely it helps that Dot is in his corner," I said, giving his arm a reassuring squeeze.

"Yeah, maybe so," he murmured as Bart turned to us.

"What are you two whispering about?" Bart asked, a humorous glint in his eye.

"None of your beeswax!" laughed Hersch. "But don't tell her boyfriend!" he added, giving Bart a wink that I thought should be intended for me.

"Oh, I'll never tell," Bart replied, winking back at Hersch and grinning at me.

Golly, I am so confused! I don't know this game!

ELLE

"Poor Sylvie, trying to navigate her own gaydar," said Elle when AB finished Sylvie's latest diary entry. "She might as well give up trying to figure out what those sweet boys were trying to figure out themselves! We all try hard to know what's what so we can label it and move on, but the truth is, things are much grayer than they are black and white. She needs to leave it alone and just enjoy the ride."

"That's for sure," Nate agreed. AB and Mr. May concurred on the audio feed.

"What's *gaydar?*" asked Aubrey, now a bona fide member of the Zoom reading group.

Seeing Nate's perplexed look about how to explain, Elle jumped in. "It's like radar, but it really means when you can tell if someone is gay or not."

"Oh, got it," said Aubrey.

His phone vibrated inside his pocket, and he pulled off his mask, grinning when he read the caller ID. "It's Patsy!" he said.

"Go ahead and take it, honey," AB said on the Zoom screen.

"Hey, Grandma Patsy!" Aubrey said and listened. His grin grew bigger. After several days in the hospital, she had never called him. This was a big deal.

He jumped up, looked at Elle and Nate, and laughed. "She's coming home!"

A cheer went up from Elle, and AB and Mr. May on the Zoom screen.

Then to Patsy, Aubrey said, "That's great, Grandma Patsy! When are you leaving? Tomorrow morning? That's awesome…. I think so. Let me put Nate on. Hold on." He handed the phone to Nate, asking, "Can we pick her up tomorrow?"

"Absolutely!" Nate said into the phone with an accompanying smile for Aubrey. "This is great news, Patsy." He grinned from ear to ear. "Did you hear the group cheer? Yeah, so how are you feeling?"

It struck Elle that Nate's affection for Patsy had grown from just neighborly friendliness to true fondness, as if she had become a family member in just the last couple of weeks. He had been so kind—shopped for her groceries, cooked her meals, taken in her grandson and her dog, watched over her house, collected her mail, and helped soothe her mind that all was taken care of. He was what her granny had called *a keeper*. And COVID could certainly bring people close; here they had practically adopted Aubrey—and the dog—and they had been contemplating doing it for real if Patsy had succumbed to the virus. It would be good to be married first, but they worried that time might not be on their side. The wedding was in six days. This was indeed very good news, she thought, sharing a smile with Nate and giving Aubrey a hug.

SYLVIE

Saturday, March 23, 1929

Dear Diary,

The concert was a smashing success! I would say this performance was so far the highlight of my musical experience. Hersch and I went to Warner Hall together before the concert to warm up and wait until we were to go on. The "Rhapsody" was not the only piece that the orchestra was playing, but it was the best and last, so I had to wait backstage after intermission until they were ready for me. Hersch seemed preoccupied compared to my giddiness, so I tried to boost him up so he would be on edge to play.

"Aren't you excited?" I asked, bouncing along beside him, carrying my score close to my coat in the cold.

He shoved his hands deep into his pockets and grinned at the ground, letting me slip my arm through his. "I am! I am! You're about to burst at the seams, aren't you?"

"Ha ha! You're making tailor jokes, are you? Very funny!" I couldn't help myself. My Aunt Nell and Uncle Harry and my grandmother would be in the audience since the concert was open to the public. All we were missing were our fathers—the tailors—and Hersch's mother. "I do wish your father could be here to witness your first concert!"

"Ha! That will never happen. Even though it's a long trip, my mother would have come, but the flu has made it to New York, so she's at home convalescing."

"Oh, what a shame! I hope she gets over it quickly!" I said sincerely, and Hersch took his hand out of its warm pocket to give my hand a squeeze.

"Oh, Syl, I'm sorry if I was insensitive. I know you must miss your mother at times like these. She would be so proud of you!"

I smiled, a bit caught off guard and feeling a lump in my throat.

"That's very sweet of you to remember her, Hersch."

"She must have been quite talented to have taught you," he mused.

"She was an excellent pianist. I wish she could have performed more than she did."

"She didn't play concerts?"

"Oh, no, she didn't go to college. Women didn't really go to college back then. She stayed home and taught lessons and took care of the four of us. I'm sure she and Father would have had more children, but she had plenty on her plate with us to raise and all her students."

"Will you marry Heckie and have oodles of children too?" Hersch asked.

"My goodness, I haven't gotten that far yet. Heckie hasn't proposed and Miss Devereaux has told us how important it is to perform while we are young and single."

"Then you should follow the lady's advice. I know it's wonderful to have a family, Sylvie, but you need to share your gift with the world. If I had half your talent, I'd be bound for Carnegie Hall for sure."

"But Hersch, you do! I'd expect nothing less from you. Broadway will get the deal of the century if you spend your talent there."

Hersch smiled. "Broadway has an allure all its own."

"I'd love to visit New York one day and take in a show."

"You should! You could stay with me. I'll show you the town and take you to the shows and the symphony, the opera, you name it."

"I don't know how happy Heckie would be with that," I said, chuckling.

"You tell Heckie he has nothing to worry about. I'm a gentleman after all, and your dear friend, I hope," he said, looking at me seriously.

"Of course," I said, as we entered the front doors of Warner Hall.

"Besides, my mother would be the chaperone from hell. Tell him *that*!"

Monday, March 25, 1929

Dear Diary,

The absolute worst thing has happened! It is past eleven at night and I am writing in the parlor because I must write this entry and I don't want to be near Dot. I am plenty vexed with her after the row we had earlier. My heart is pounding away with all that has happened and my being so angry.

Dot returned from this afternoon's voice lesson to tell me the news that Herschel Blum had been summoned to the director's office this morning and expelled from Oberlin College! Bart told her that Hersch had returned with a formal dismissal letter this morning and that he had twenty-four hours to arrange passage home. I was on my way to the music library to work on my new Bach piece for the chamber music ensemble on the harpsichord there when she came bursting in to tell me the news. I dropped everything and ran to Hersch's boarding house to find out what in the world was going on.

After he was sent for by the receptionist, we went outside to talk privately, wrapped in our coats against the wind. I'd never seen Hersch so shaken.

"What on earth, Hersch? Dot says you've been *expelled!*"

"It's true. I'm packing now." He swallowed. "I'll be on the morning train to New York. My parents are getting a telegram like the letter I received, so I'm trying to work up the guts to call them. I must tell my father…" he said, raking a hand through his dark curls, looking as pained as I have ever seen him. "He will kill me!" he whispered hoarsely.

"You didn't go back to the speakeasy!" I accused, rather than asking him.

"No. That would have been almost acceptable."

"Then what was it?"

Hersch looked at me and sighed raggedly. "I've been accused of 'perverted activity,'" he said harshly.

"*What?*" I cried, incredulously.

"Yes. Someone wrote a letter to the Conservatory Director saying I'd been seen repeatedly engaging in unsuitable behavior with another male student on campus. He said he had other proof." He swallowed. "I didn't deny it, so I never saw what else he had."

"Who? God, Hersch, who would do this to you?"

He thought a moment and scoffed. "That's what you want to know, Sylvie? Who would do this? Not, 'It can't be true, Hersch!'"

I regarded him suspiciously.

"You've known, Sylvie. I know you've known about me. How, I'm not sure, but you've known."

I digested his statement for a few seconds. "Surely…you don't think I've said anything!"

He shook his head. "How did you know, Sylvie? No, I don't think you did it—you'd be the last person I'd suspect—but how did you know?"

I shook my head, not wanting to think what I was thinking. "Mina saw you," I said absently. "She saw you and Bart one night through the window in one of the practice rooms. You were kissing."

Hersch's mouth fell open. "*Mina?*"

"No! Mina would never tell on you like that!" I said fervently, truly believing she wouldn't. But Dot…. My hand went to my mouth.

"What?" Hersch asked, desperate for any information I could give him.

"Dot knew, too. Mina told us both. We'd wondered why neither of you had kissed us, so Mina explained it. But we'd all three made a pact that night that we didn't care what you were or what you did and that we would do whatever we could to protect you both, taking your arm every time that it was appropriate…and such."

"To throw others off the scent," he murmured, studying the air in front of him.

"Dot would never…" I began, but lately I wondered. "If Dot would tell on you, then why wouldn't she include Bart? It makes no sense." But did it? She was Bart's girl now.

"Bart," he said, shaking his head.

I cocked my head, wondering what he meant. "Bart would never say a word. Wouldn't he have just as much to lose?" I asked.

"Unless he's already lost."

"What do you mean?"

Hersch sighed long and hard, turned away from me and then turned back, checking around to see whether anyone was in earshot of our conversation. He moved me farther away from the front stoop of the boarding house and checked again for privacy.

"There's a chance Bart is going to leave Oberlin too. Mr. Finch has told him he's barely keeping up with the music and that the Conservatory might not be the best fit for him."

"Oh, no!"

"He might be able to turn it around if he can memorize the music, but there's something else."

I waited for him to continue.

"It's true about me…and Bart. We've been…*together* since we started here. But remember I told you I'd met someone?"

"Yes, a nice Jewish girl."

He smiled wistfully. "Well, there was her, but I met an actor at the theater when we saw *Paris* on Broadway. He and I were taken with each other immediately. I can't stop thinking about him. Seems he feels the same way. We've been writing to each other ever since I got back from winter break."

I tried to keep up and stared at Hersch.

"The thing is, I can't find two of the letters. They're the ones with most of the 'romantic content' I guess you'd say."

"You think Bart found them and turned them over to Dr. Maxwell?"

"It's possible."

"That must be it! He's jealous of your actor and wants revenge on you for betraying him!" I cried, instantly realizing what had transpired.

"I don't want to believe it, but that's a possibility."

"Hersch, of course that's it." I was so sure, but then I remembered something else. "Wait—Wallace—he made derogatory comments about you and Bart the night I walked home with him and Teresa."

"I thought about that too, but how would he have gotten hold of those letters? It must be Bart."

"Have you spoken with him?"

"Of course; he brought the mail up this morning, so I opened my letter right in front of him. He seemed shocked and angry when I read it, telling him I was being summoned to the director's office. He wondered whether he might get a similar letter…."

"What are you going to do?"

"Besides die of humiliation? Oy vey! I have to go call my father. He will certainly disown me," he said, throwing up his hands in defeat. "I never had a chance at pleasing him."

"You can't be serious?"

"I'm absolutely serious. I'll be thrown out on my keister—that's another word for *tochus*," he added with a shrug. I grabbed his arm to find him shaking.

"Where will you go? What will you do?"

Hersch laughed tremulously and shook his head. "I know one person who says he wants me. Looks like I'm headed off to Broadway after all, Sylvie girl. I'll miss you," he said, tucking an escaped curl of my hair back inside my cloche.

"You're really going to go, aren't you?"

"Yes, ma'am, I am," he said with a slight bow. His Southern gesture of respect was something I'd never heard him utter before, but he'd taught me some proper Yiddish, so it touched me that he'd reciprocated our customs. "Parting is such sweet sorrow. I'll tell Broadway you said 'hello.'"

I swallowed hard and hugged him fiercely.

Tuesday, March 26, 1929

Dear Diary,

That was the last time I would lay eyes on Herschel Blum. After I wrote last night, I was still too agitated to sleep. I went to Mina's room and knocked on her door without worry of disturbing her roommate; Cornelia had left the Conservatory at Christmas, so Mina now lives alone.

"What is it, Sylvie?" Mina asked groggily.

"I'm sorry to bother you, Mina. May I come in?" I asked.

Wordlessly, she rubbed her face and opened the door to admit me, tying her wool bathrobe around her waist.

"What's wrong?" she asked, knowing I wouldn't disturb her unless there was a crisis. I explained the crisis and she sat perfectly still, hanging on every word I said.

"Herschel is leaving tomorrow on the early train," I said, ending my story.

"What does Dot say about all this?" asked Mina, wide awake now.

"I asked her what part she may have played in it all. And she told me, but I could swear she is withholding something important."

"As in, covering up for the boy she thinks she's in love with," Mina said, summing up my thoughts astutely. "What exactly did she say?"

"Dot told Bart weeks ago that we all knew he and Hersch were a couple. She told him to be careful and that she would help Bart pretend he wasn't a homosexual."

"She called him a homosexual?"

"I don't know—I think she said queer—but it's all the same thing, isn't it?"

Mina shrugged, rubbing her face again. "What else?"

"She said that was it, except that she told him it would help the cause if he kissed her from time to time and made it look like she was his girlfriend."

"How clever. Instant Prince Charming. She's been dying for him to be her boyfriend."

"I know. It just seems too easy. I asked her what she knew about Hersch, but she asked what I meant and didn't admit anything further. I think she was so desperate to get Bart to be her beau that she stooped to revealing our secret."

"Ah," Mina said, nodding. "She broke our pact."

"Actually," I started, threading my fingers inside each other and bending them backwards, "I kind of told Hersch I knew about them too, but in not so many words. I heard Wallace making disparaging remarks about Hersch and Bart one night when we walked behind them from the practice rooms, so I warned Hersch that he and Bart should be careful. I didn't say about what, just that they should be careful because people were talking about them liking each other. Hersch didn't question me, just thanked me for warning him. He knew that I knew…" I said, shrugging.

"Lord, I need coffee to keep up with this conversation," Mina said, placing her fingers on her temples and giving her head a quick shake. "So…who wrote the letter to the director?"

"I don't know. It could be the same person who told Miss Devereaux about you and Ronald. But I think in Herschel's case, the stolen letters his Broadway friend wrote might have been enclosed for evidence."

"I was thinking the same thing. I need to have a talk with Miss Devereaux. This has gone far enough."

Wednesday, March 27, 1929

Dear Diary,

I was up at dawn after having slept all of five minutes the whole night. While Mina planned on approaching Miss Devereaux first thing this morning, I went to see Hersch before he left and to find out from Bart what he had done. When I got to the boarding house, Hersch was already gone and Bart was in a state of shock, or so it seemed. He invited me into the parlor and handed me a letter that Hersch had written to me. No one else was about; still, we spoke in strident whispers.

"What did you do to Hersch?" I asked Bart, accusingly. His cheeks deepened in their usual rose as if someone had slapped him, which I had to restrain myself from doing. He remained silent, glaring at me as if I *had* slapped him.

"Exactly what do you know, Sylvie?" he asked, daring me to spill the beans first.

"Ugh! I know that you and Hersch have been together since the beginning of school. You were in love with him," I ventured, knowing I was correct as his cheeks deepened almost to crimson. He glared at me some more, and I could see his jaw clenching in determination not to speak. "I've known since Mina told us she saw you kissing in the practice rooms."

He almost nodded. I knew now that Mina's account was true, though it was not news since he and Dot had discussed it.

"You were angry and jealous when Hersch met that man in New York, the actor."

Bart's breathing became heavier, his hands clamped together.

I was tired of his stonewalling. "What did you do with those letters?"

He finally broke. "I was angry!" he whispered harshly. "I found the letters in our room and confronted Hersch. I took them when he was out. Knowing he'd found someone else was burning me up inside. I felt as if I would explode! It was so obvious how they felt about each other from reading those letters. I showed them to Dot in the practice room and told her how Hersch had betrayed me. I would never have shown them to Dr. Maxwell. I would have been incriminated as well. The guy described me, even used my name. They'd talked about me. Do you realize how humiliating that is?"

"Did you return the letters to Hersch?"

"No," he said glumly. "I told him I didn't have them."

"But you do."

"Yes," he admitted. "The letters are in my satchel."

"Let me see them," I said hotly.

His eyes bored into mine and his nostrils flared. After a moment, he rose and retrieved his satchel from the table where he'd set it when I interrupted his departure. Mechanically, he opened the latch and reached inside for his music, rifling through the scores until he found the "Rhapsody" solo. He opened it and carefully sorted through the pages. His eyes shot back to mine.

"They're gone!" he said and swallowed hard, the color draining from his face.

"Dot!" we said together.

Back at the dorm, Dot was nowhere to be found, so I ran to the duck pond at the arboretum to wait for Mina, as we had agreed. As I waited for her to return from her visit with Miss Devereaux, I had time to read Hersch's letter.

Dearest Sylvie,

A better friend than you one could never find. I am lucky to have met you. You have taught me so much and been so kind to me. I shall forever treasure our friendship. I know you will always be the professional you have grown to be and that you will keep to your standards of civility no matter what happens to you. Please don't allow anyone or anything to come between you and your dreams. You are far too talented a lady to be discouraged from your career. Oberlin is a gem, so don't let what happened to me prevent you from staying and reaping all the Conservatory has to offer. You're in the right place.

Do not worry about me. I am like a cat and will continue to land on my feet. My current misfortune has possibly led me to new avenues I was afraid to take, but I am excited to see where they lead. Love finds a way; I am sure of that. Don't be too hard on Bart. He thought the same thing about love.

When I get settled, I shall write to you again so we can stay in touch. Until then, keep playing by heart, Sylvie Meeks. It suits you.

Yours always,

Herschel

Mina was breathless from running when she arrived at our bench.

"What did you find out?" I asked, discreetly wiping tears from my face.

"Miss Devereaux was devastated to hear about Herschel," she said, breathing deeply to catch her breath. "She said someone wrote her a note about me. It was anonymous, short and to the point, but it was enough to make her start watching me. She happened to see me out of her studio window, walking with Ronald. She didn't know his name; I supplied that, but she saw enough to cause her concern for me. She said she only wanted to caution me, everything she said at my lesson that day. And I believe her. She's a smart woman and only has our best interests at heart."

I nodded, then smiled at Mina. She was right. Miss Devereaux was fighting for us.

"She wants us to keep on track. It's so easy to give up and do something less ambitious."

Mina nodded solemnly. She reached inside her coat pocket and withdrew a folded piece of note paper. "Here is the letter. I don't recognize the handwriting, but maybe you will."

I gasped. What a gesture of goodwill for Mina's teacher to give her the letter. I took it and opened it. Immediately, I knew the handwriting.

"Dot."

We sat with Dot in our room. Her tear-stained face represented the remorse she felt, but I could hardly feel sorry for her. Once she saw we had the letter she'd written Miss Devereaux, she confessed everything—her jealously of Mina's talent, her jealousy of Hersch whom Bart loved, and her love for Bart. Mina was too shocked and hurt to speak, so I conducted the interrogation.

"So, you took the letters from Hersch's actor—"

"His name is Paul," Dot sniffed.

"Paul," I continued, "and you sent them to the director, again anonymously, with a little note saying others had noticed Hersch's behavior on campus."

Dot nodded, the crying having distorted her face. Her mouth trembled, preventing a response.

"But didn't you realize that if Dr. Maxwell saw Bart's name, he would expel Bart too?"

"Yes, I was afraid of that. That's why I marked out Bart's name with a fountain pen."

"And Bart knows nothing of this plot you've cooked up to ruin Hersch?"

"No. I didn't tell him what I was doing. When the note I sent to Miss D went as I had hoped, I had no reason to doubt Dr. Maxwell would punish Hersch. But I never thought Hersch would be *expelled!*" she said, sobbing again.

"What did you think they would do to him, Dot?" Mina cried, coming to life.

"I don't know. I thought they would give him a stern talking to and maybe separate Bart and Hersch as roommates, but I never thought they would send him home!"

"Do you realize what will happen to Hersch?" I almost screamed at her. "Being expelled will put a black mark on him forever. He won't be able to enroll in another music program or any other college anywhere else for that matter. His father will throw him out on the street. He'll live like a pauper trying to earn a living in New York. Hopefully, someone will realize his musical genius and give him a chair in a Broadway orchestra if he's lucky." I stopped my rant, running angry fingers through my wild hair. "People are cruel, Dot," I muttered, my voice raw with emotion. "Homosexual men aren't looked upon with favor, and Hersch's well-being could be at risk since he is now exposed. At least in New York City, people won't know who he is…. I'm sure his parents won't advertise it," I said bitterly, thinking of Catherine.

"I'm so sorry. I don't know what to do," said Dot, wiping another flood of tears with her hanky.

"You need to think long and hard about what you've done," said Mina. "You need to make amends with everyone you've hurt. You need to think about how in the world you can stay here at this Conservatory and ever be a part of this community now, since you've so maliciously ratted out one of its finest musicians…and one of *your friends* at that. If I have something to say about all this to the director, you can be damned sure it won't be anonymous." Mina was seething. "I can't stand the sight of you, actually," she said and stormed out of our room.

I crossed my arms and stood quietly letting the dust settle, wishing I, too, could leave Dot here to brood alone, but it was my room too. After a tense moment, she sighed and wiped her face again.

"What should I do?" she asked softly, looking at me with her big blue eyes, which were tinged with red.

I sighed too and pursed my lips. "Well, I'm sure you'll think of something. After all, creativity seems to be your forte."

Her eyebrows rose as I turned to collect my coat and music satchel, deciding to get on with my day.

CHAPTER TWENTY

Nate

Nate and Elle had waited for Aubrey to arrive before they linked into their Zoom chat with AB and Bernie for the night's reading. Aubrey had asked to be included since the story had heated up and he didn't want to miss the ending. When Patsy had settled in at home, they'd taken a couple of days off from reading to make sure everyone had what they needed. Nate wanted time alone with Elle again, without COVID or riots or politics interfering in their lives. The wedding was in three more days, and they needed a bit of normalcy—whatever that was and however they could find it—before they got hitched.

As they sat together on the sofa, Nate took Elle's hand and stroked it gently, fingering the ring he'd given her, which had originally been disguised as a lightning bug prior to her discovering it in the palm of his hand.

"How are you feeling?" he asked, smiling at her, enjoying the quiet for a few more moments.

"I'm good. Very good," she said, returning his smile. "I'm glad Patsy's doing so well, and that Aubrey is happy and settled again."

"You were great with him while he stayed here."

"So were you," she said and paused. "You do know that if Patsy had died, I would have taken Aubrey in for as long as he needed us."

"That could have been years," Nate reminded her.

"I know. I was prepared for that. We mountain folk take care of people, you know?"

"Aye," he said with a chuckle. "I do know that. Your granny took care of you, and you took care of her, and Joey, and Aiden…and now me. I'd say you have the caring for others part of life down pat."

"And we get to make that commitment to each other permanent in just three more days!" she said with a giggle. "Who would have thought?"

"Yeah, who would have thought?" he asked, referring to himself. "But I'm glad that for the first round at least, it's just going to be us."

"If only everybody could be this happy," she said, reaching up and giving Nate a kiss.

The front door opened and closed, and Aubrey lumbered in from the foyer.

"Here I am," he mumbled.

"How was dinner?" Elle asked.

"Great! AB sent over some chicken and dumplings," he said, grinning before putting on his mask, as Elle and Nate did the same.

"I love those, but I can't eat anything like that until after the wedding!" Elle laughed, making Nate curious, wondering how she would look in her dress. He would know in three days.

"Are we on with them yet?" asked Aubrey, sitting beside Elle on the sofa. "I wanna see what happens to Dot."

"You and me both," said Nate, clicking on the Zoom link. "It's AB's turn to read."

SYLVIE

Thursday, April 25, 1929

Dear Diary,

After Herschel left the Conservatory, I haven't had the heart to write, other than letters home and to Kip and Catherine, and mostly to Heckie, about what happened here and the usual news. Since Dot left, I have had my room to myself, though next year, when Mina and I are sophomores, we will request a room together.

Dot left at Easter. She went home to Cincinnati and didn't return. I can't say I blame her; she was miserable her last few days here, no matter who forgave her for her deeds. She knew she no longer fit here, and it is for the best that she will pursue her music somewhere else. To her credit, she wrote several letters—to Hersch, his father, the Conservatory Director, Miss Devereaux, and Mina—confessing what she had done. The power of those letters reinforced the magnitude of the damage from her actions. Mina never forgave her. From Dr. Maxwell and Miss Devereaux, she received stern admonishments. Dr. Maxwell placed her on a probationary period for the remainder of the semester. Dot received nothing in our mailbox from Hersch's father, as I had predicted. Hersch sent her a cursory note included in a missive to me, saying that he forgave her but could never understand the malice behind her actions, and that he hoped she would change her ways. She was already gone when it arrived. As far as I know, Hersch is still looking for a job and living with Paul. He cleans the theater where *Paris* is playing. He has found a couple of students—actors' children—to teach violin lessons to during the afternoons. Mina threw her letter from Dot in the parlor fireplace after reading it. She never told me what it said.

As for Bart, he gave Dot the most painful prescription for her mistakes. He wanted nothing else to do with her, as hurt as he was, first for losing Hersch, and second because Dot caused Hersch's expulsion. As betrayed as Bart had felt, he said he would never have stooped so low as to incriminate Hersch the way she did. In the long run, Dot executed her own expulsion from the Conservatory, which I believe was for the best. Even though I forgave her in hopes that she could move on, it is certainly less awkward with her gone. Bart is still here, working hard to be the musician Hersch would have wanted him to be, and what he is capable of being without the distraction of the elusive-spirited Herschel Blum. I believe that for Bart, it is for the best.

The biggest surprise for me was Mr. Finch. Apparently, it was never Mr. Finch's intent to weed out Bart. He only wanted to spur him on to realize his potential. When Bart learned how his own jealousy was ruining all aspects of his life, he came around and got serious about his work as a musician, opening himself to constructive criticism and teaching. Bart and I have mended our friendship, and both of us are grateful to Mr. Finch for guiding us toward the correct path.

Today at my lesson, Mr. Finch asked me to take a break so we could talk.

"How are you getting on, my dear?" he asked in his kind, grandfatherly voice. "You haven't been yourself since your friend Herschel left."

"I know. I'm sorry, sir. I don't mean to be so distracted."

"Life can often throw unpleasant distractions our way," he said. "It's unavoidable, I'm afraid. If I may help, I would like to see you through whatever it is that troubles you. Sometimes teaching involves counseling as well as technique, so let's talk."

I sighed. "Hersch was a fine musician and supported all his friends here. Losing Hersch wasn't fair, Mr. Finch. For him, for his friends, or for the Conservatory, not that I always expect life to be fair. Since Hersch was expelled, I've wondered if it's worth it to live up to all the Oberlin expectations, but I know he would want me to be strong and see it through."

Mr. Finch nodded, as if he agreed with my assessment of Hersch's dismissal. Then he nodded again, as though agreeing with Hersch's encouragement.

"And then, I wonder if I stick it out, will I be smart enough to manage my career the way Miss Devereaux has done? She has set quite an example. Being a concert pianist would be thrilling, and I think I can handle the music, even though I'm somewhat perplexed about how I'm to go about creating a tour. But mostly, I worry about how I could go away on a tour if I were married and had a family the way most women do. You did it and were very successful, but you didn't have the babies. Mrs. Finch had to give up her dreams to stay home with your family."

Mr. Finch shook his head. "You're right, Sylvie. Your future deserves the most careful consideration. You are very talented, and I would hate to see you throw in the towel because of what happened to Herschel. I'll try to answer your questions. Mrs. Finch was quite talented, but she never really wanted to travel and perform, although she relishes a chance to hear our students play and develop. I was very, very lucky; she was quite supportive of my career. And by the way, I will help you figure out the tours. It's much harder for women these days to have a life of performance. Even if you excel at performing, there will be those who will disrespect and even despise you for it, for being selfish and for traveling on your own. If you decide to marry, you can only hope to find a person who will support you and love you no matter what. The rest will be up to you."

He walked to the window and took off his glasses, cleaning the lenses with his handkerchief, as I sat quietly, thinking of Heckie and how we both had desires and aspirations others our age did not. Heckie had promised to wait for me while I went after my dreams, the way Hersch had urged me to do. Surely, I would do the same for Heckie.

Mr. Finch continued, peering out of his polished lenses at the campus below. "There have only been a few other young ladies I have taught whom I felt truly compelled to urge toward a concert career, and who didn't go on to success. One such young lady reminds me very much of you. She had your same talent for memorizing music and playing it with passion the way you do. She was my private student when I taught in Cleveland about twenty-five years ago, before I came back to Oberlin. She would have made a tremendous concert pianist, but she chose instead to get married and have a family, which I am sure she did not regret. She actually looked a bit like you, although she was a blonde. Her name was Anne Borden."

He turned to regard me directly, clasping his hands behind his back.

"I believe she might be your mother."

I was so shocked by his revelation I could hardly speak! Tears sprang to my eyes, making me cover my face. I needed a moment to collect my emotions and take in what he said, and then I felt so proud to know my mother was indeed a prodigy. Of course, I knew it myself and people have told me for years how I play like she did. Still, it was wonderful to hear Mr. Finch sing her praises. Mr. Finch was deeply saddened when I told him my mother had died, along with my brother and sister in the flu outbreak of '26. He said he'd figured out she was my mother early on, but he didn't want to bias me or make me think he favored me because of his former association with her. He was overjoyed, though, to know she had created another pianist, one who had found her way to him at Oberlin, one who would embrace the stage, and one who plays by heart.

CHAPTER TWENTY-ONE

Elle

It's almost time, Elle thought with a flutter through her center. She had dressed herself in AB's downstairs bedroom while AB and Mr. May busied themselves on the back porch, putting the final touches on the sweethearts' dinner table there. New paper string lights dangled across the ceiling of the screened porch, but that was all Elle could see from a brief glance out the kitchen door. For such a teeny tiny little wedding, this was beginning to feel like a big do, just what Nate had in mind. Family, friends, flowers, cupcakes, a ceremony on the end of a boat dock, and a late dinner on the back porch followed by a sunset cruise. Every man's dream! And actually, she thought it was going to be the perfect wedding.

The plan was for Mr. May to walk over to the dock and wait for her with Nate, while Joey and AB walked her across the street. Joey was also getting ready in the guest house, and she was to come for him for his first look at six o'clock. Elle heard Mr. May share a gentle laugh with AB, and then he descended the back stairs. It was time to show herself to AB for the final touches. Taking a last look in the mirror, she checked her soft bun out of nervous habit. With all those pins, it wasn't going anywhere even in the sea breeze. Channeling Catherine Carmichael, she'd pinned a small white plume on the side for just the right look. Dress, earrings, sandals, a bracelet, and she was as put together as she cared to be. *Less is more.* Skipping the mask for once, she applied a final touch of lip color, picked up the folded paper containing her vows, and walked carefully through the kitchen to the porch.

"I'm ready," she said, meeting AB outside on the porch in the safety of the hot, salty air and six feet distancing.

AB's hands flew to the mask at her mouth. "Oh, my, Elle! How exquisite!" she said breathlessly, fingering the pearls at her neck. "Your dress is just divine! Turn for me," she said, twirling her finger in the direction she meant.

Elle struck a pose and turned slowly, showing off the vintage lace gown, the soap bubble sequins giving the dress a bit of sparkle in the afternoon sun. AB's eyes trained on the plunging neckline, and she chuckled. "Nate is just going to *die!*" she said. "And poor Bernie might have a heart attack when he sees you. I'll have my phone on me in case we have to call 911!" she said, laughing and patting her pocket. "Are you ready?"

"As ready as I'll ever be," said Elle. Her matron of honor was elegant in a tasteful blue taffeta dress with a fitted bodice and full skirt, setting off her blueberry eyes. For a woman of eighty, she pulled it off fabulously. "Aw, AB, you're beautiful!"

"Thank you. Wait, I have something for you," said AB. "You have something old, something new?"

"Something old, yes, these," Elle said, touching her grandmother's prized drop crystal earrings that had been a gift from her grandfather. AB scrutinized them and nodded. "And something new—my ring and my dress."

"Something borrowed, and something blue?"

"I have on the blue garter from Nate's sister. She gave it to us for the wedding."

"Oh, what a nice thing to do! Well, I have something you may borrow. It's my mother's hanky from her wedding." AB said, handing Elle a delicate white handkerchief, well-preserved for its age, edged in lace and embroidered with lily of the valley in pale green and white.

"This was from Sylvie and Heckie's wedding?" Elle gasped, marveling at the treasure in her hand.

"Yes. Lily of the valley was Mother's favorite flower. But I'll need it back," AB warned.

"Oh, of course! I'll be so careful with it. Thank you so much. This is so special."

"Well, be careful with it, and don't get mascara on it if you cry."

Elle blinked back sudden tears and giggled. *You always knew where you stood with AB.*

"Do you have your vows?"

"Right here," said Elle, holding up the folded paper. "Do you have Nate's ring?"

"Of course. I'm wearing it. I hope you don't mind," she said, holding up her thumb to show Elle the simple gold band.

Elle laughed.

"All right, your photographer is here, so let's go find that handsome son of yours to give you away!"

When Elle came to the top of the back stairs to look out, she saw the hole in the landscape next door, where the old house used to be. The empty space made her sigh with deep relief. Then, trying to catch a glimpse of Nate, the sight from the street took her breath. All up and down the street, cars were parked on both sides, leaving hardly enough room for traffic to proceed. *The reception*, Elle thought with a thrill. All their local friends and family members had turned out to witness the ceremony from the safety of their cars and to wish them well. It was the plan all along, but the reality of the kind gesture still caught her off guard.

"Look at that!" cried AB. "This certainly lends new meaning to the 'receiving line,' doesn't it?"

"Yes!" Elle nodded, taking a deep breath.

As they came down the back stairs, Sarah, Elle's employee from the bakery, was waiting near the guest house, photographing the pink petunias in the window box with an expensive-looking camera.

"Oh, my God!" she said when she looked up and saw Elle descending the stairs. "Elle! You look *gorgeous*!" Her mask concealed part of her expression, but the words said it all. "Hi, AB. Nice to see you again!" she added.

"You too, Sarah," AB said and nodded at her rather than giving the usual hugs women exchange; COVID was at the wedding too.

"Should I knock on the door for Joey?"

"I'm here," they heard him call as he opened the door. "Is it okay for me to come out?"

The women looked to Elle, and when she nodded, Sarah said, "Yes, come on out. Take off your masks, everyone. This beautiful bride is ready for you to give her away," she said with a smile, raising her camera to capture Joey's first look at her.

Joey appeared, dashing in his Army dress uniform, looking incredibly grown up, thought Elle, bursting into a proud smile upon seeing her handsome son. She recalled Sylvie's reaction to Heckie when she saw him at Thanksgiving.

"Wow!" the three women said in unison.

Joey regarded his mother for a moment, and his face broke into a happy smile, too. "Oh, my God, *Mama*! You look amazing!" He took her hands and held her out to look at her again. "Okay, do the turn thing."

She turned and when he hugged her, she heard him sniff back tears. Then she took his arm for the walk across the street. In vases on the bistro table were the two bouquets that Mr. May had made from AB's cabbage roses. AB took off her mask, took Elle's flowers, wiping them with a towel, and then handed the bride a bouquet of creamy roses mixed with green hydrangea.

"Thank you, AB." Elle wrapped the ribbon-bound stems in Sylvie's wedding hanky.

"Make sure to enjoy every moment. Drink it all in, dear. This is your day," AB said, winking, taking her own bouquet, and heading down the driveway, stepping carefully across the street. Sarah walked quickly ahead, keeping a safe distance while capturing more pictures. Elle and Joey held back until both women were across the street. Monai and Allyson from the bakery were waving excitedly, standing at the arbored gate beside two large coolers Elle knew contained the cupcake packages for later. She giggled with anticipation. Jordan and Scooter stood smiling on the other side of the gate where she could tell they were cueing up the music from Jordan's phone that would be played on Nate's Bluetooth speaker on the dock. Scooter gave her a thumbs-up and a big grin. Her staff never ceased to amaze her! It was nice to see the professionals she knew they were from the bride's viewpoint.

Elle could see Nate's family standing on AB's dock, except for Uncle Phil, sadly, who was still needed at his hospital. Her cousin Judy and her husband stood some distance away with Marcus Gilmer. Elle saw Patsy seated on the bench seat at the end of the dock with Aubrey standing beside her, dressed up and waving to her. She smiled and waved to them all. Knowing that the view of these docks extending out into the Intracoastal Waterway would be breathtaking to the newcomers, Elle thought it was still a spectacular sight, but for her, familiar, yet poignant. This was the perfect place to marry Nate. At the end of Phil's dock, he stood, gazing out over the shimmering water, with Mr. May, both handsomely dressed in black suits. Mr. May held the ceremonial book. Nate's hands were clasped in front of him as he turned to watch AB walk toward them under the arbor covered with blooming jasmine.

Joey turned to Elle and patted her hand on his arm. "I'm happy for you, Mama. Ready to take a little walk?"

"Yes, sir, I am," she said, giving him a kiss. "I love you, honey. It means the world to me that you're here." It had been so long since they'd been together, and here he was, offering his arm to give her away. *When did he become such a man?*

"I love you, too, Mama," he said.

When they started down the driveway, which was adorned on each side with AB's abundant flower gardens that flourished under Mr. May's care, Elle could hear the music, "Unchained Melody" by the Righteous Brothers, floating on the breeze, making her smile. She gazed across at the dock where Nate stood. Boats puttered by, leaving no wakes, and a pair of curious kayakers paddled close by. Streaked with mares' tails clouds, the sky was the clear blue of early summer, and the evening sun cast a golden glow over everything it touched. Elle held onto Joey's arm and clutched her bouquet as they reached the street. They passed the group from the bakery, sharing smiles with each one. Allyson wiped a tear and touched her heart as Elle walked by.

It was then that Nate looked purposefully their way. When he saw his bride, he did a double take, his face going from amazement to joy in an instant. He bit his lip and blinked, then closed his eyes to calm himself. "Oh, wow!" he said, giving Mr. May a chuckle. Nate smiled, shaking his head slightly in disbelief, and then the smile grew into his large appreciative grin as Joey escorted Elle under the fragrant jasmine-covered arbor and down the dock.

Nate's eyes were locked on Elle's as Joey kissed her cheek, then placed her hand in Nate's. Next, he moved to stand in the best man's spot to Nate's right. Handing her bouquet to AB, Elle clasped her vows and took both of Nate's hands, smiling at him. *He was so handsome! And they were doing the damn thing!* Mr. May cleared his throat and began the ceremony, welcoming the dearly beloved on both docks to get everyone's attention.

Elle's head swam with the weighty words of the ceremony. Mr. May's voice was calming and melodious, just the way she'd imagined it, lending both comfort and authority to the proceedings as he outlined their intentions and responsibilities in Christian Marriage. Following AB's advice to drink it all in, Elle glanced from dock to dock momentarily, to see family and friends looking on. The warm sea breeze blew Nate's hair, and she heard a gull call overhead as she gazed happily at his face. He seemed composed but well-aware of the solemnity of the moment in their beautiful waterfront setting.

Mr. May gestured for them to turn toward each other and addressed Nate first, asking him if he'd promise to take Elle for his lawfully wedded wife, to love, comfort, honor, and keep her, in sickness and in health, and forsaking all others, to be faithful to her as long as they both should live, to which Nate answered loudly enough for the people on both docks to hear, "I do!"

There was laughter at his bravado, making Elle giggle. It was so like him! She gazed adoringly into Nate's blue eyes as Mr. May asked her the same question, to which she also answered, "I do."

Next, Mr. May gave Nate the opportunity to recite his vows. He continued to hold Elle's hands and spoke slowly to let the words sink in as he pledged to her.

"Elle, you came into my life when I thought love would never come to me, but there you were. I haven't gotten you out of my mind from the first night we sat out here on this very dock, and now you are in my heart forever. I cherish every moment we've been given, knowing God's hand brought you to me, and I look forward to cherishing you and all the moments to come. I promise to love and respect you, appreciate your sassy, feisty, spunky nature, support you, help you, and lift you up to be the best person you can be. Our covenant with each other under God's guidance and care begins this moment, and I thank Him for bringing you to me. I will be by your side through thick and thin, in sickness and in health, in challenging times and prosperity, in doubt and in certainty. I promise to keep myself for you only and to be faithful to you as long as we live."

Mr. May turned to Elle. She closed her eyes and swallowed an unfamiliar lump, wishing she still had Sylvie's handkerchief that she had wrapped around her bouquet. When she sniffed, she felt AB touch her elbow, handing her the hanky.

"Oh! Thank you, AB." She smiled at AB and took it, carefully wiping her eyes, remembering AB's warning about not getting mascara on it while Nate, Mr. May, and Joey watched and chuckled gently.

Then she ran her thumb over the paper in her hand but had no need to unfold it. She looked up at Nate and began to speak to the man she loved. "Nate, when I met you, I also thought love had passed me by forever, and yet there you were. At first, I was awed by your presence, but I quickly learned that you are real. You showed me kindness. You accepted me for who I am when others shunned me, and you forgave me all my mistakes, the ones I couldn't forgive myself. You stuck by me and helped me when I needed help the most. You've supported me in my business and in the small, everyday things that make up a marriage. You've given me peace, patience, and understanding. I, too, believe that God brought us together. I've learned that from you as well. I'm grateful to you for teaching me what love truly is. So, Nate, before God and our family and friends, I promise to be faithful to you—always. I promise to love and cherish you, to care for you, to honor you, to listen to you and understand you, to hear your hopes and dreams, to lift you up to achieve your greatest potential, and to experience the joy of growing old with you as long as we live."

She blinked back her own tears when she saw Nate's glistening eyes. Mr. May smiled at them both, touched by their personal sentiments and commitments to each other. Joey and AB handed over the rings for Nate and Elle to exchange, and then they clasped hands. Mr. May placed his hand over theirs and said a blessing.

"Now you will feel no rain, for each of you will be shelter for the other. Now you will feel no cold, for each of you will be warmth for the other. Now there is no loneliness. May your days be good and long upon this earth," he said. Then he pronounced Nate and Elle man and wife. Nate kissed her slowly, not once, not twice, but three times.

"Third time's a charm," he murmured as he hugged her, sending a ripple of laughter through the wedding party. Then Mr. May raised his voice to the guests and presented them as Mr. and Mrs. Nate Aldridge. There was applause as Nate lifted their hands high in victory. AB returned Elle's bouquet and gave her a warm smile that sufficed for a hug before they went down the aisle. Another song, "Signed, Sealed, Delivered, I'm Yours" began to play over the speaker, and they laughed, dancing down the dock, waving happily to everyone in sight, on the docks and in the cars.

At a small table by the gate, the wedding party paused to sign the marriage license.

"We're really married!" Elle cried, setting down the pen, and Nate kissed her again.

The four bakery staff members waited at a separate table to serve the celebratory champagne toast. Jordan and Scooter popped champagne corks while Allyson and Monai poured the couple their first celebratory drink of the evening. When all were served, they raised their glasses while Sarah photographed the toast. After the staff put on their masks, congratulations and hugs went all around. Then, Monai and Allyson put on nitrile gloves and began organizing the cupcake packages into baskets to carry around to the guests in their cars, while Jordan and Scooter readied the champagne table covered in white linen for serving champagne to the families on the dock, who were making their way over to congratulate the newlyweds. It felt odd to stand apart from their family members and merely raise their glasses in love and gratitude, but it was the safest way to proceed. They chatted for a few minutes, and then Marcus reminded them that other people were waiting in their cars along the street. "Go see your friends! We'll be here when you get back."

AB whispered to Elle, "While you're greeting your guests, I'm going to order your dinner to be delivered. Everything is set up on the porch, so whenever you're ready, you can sit down and enjoy."

"Thank you, AB! We'll watch for the car and come in."

They thanked everyone for making the trip and then AB took over, introducing the families to Patsy and Aubrey and the men from Elle's bakery.

Holding their champagne flutes, Nate and Elle held hands. "Let's go see everyone!" he said.

"Yes, let's do it."

There must have been twenty cars lined up on the street with well-wishers honking and grinning from the open windows. Some wore masks, and some did not. Some handed them cards that Nate collected while Elle held a gift basket from her friend Randy, a manager at Dockside. It was wonderful to see everyone again, and they were touched that so many of their friends had come out to extend their best wishes to them. The cupcakes were a big hit, and the newlyweds thanked Monai and Allyson for doing such a beautiful job.

"This is the most fun wedding I've ever been to!" Monai exclaimed.

"Aw! Thank you, Monai!" said Elle.

"Well, everyone is so happy to be out!" said Nate. "And nobody was expecting cupcake fairies!"

The women laughed, and then Allyson pointed out that their wedding meal was arriving in AB's driveway. Nate and Elle walked back down the street, thanking everyone for coming and bidding them goodbye.

When they climbed the steps to the lovely back porch, Mr. May was already there, wearing a mask and pouring champagne into heavy crystal flutes. Romantic classical guitar music played quietly in the background. "Greetings, Mr. and Mrs. Aldridge. Your sommelier, at your service," he said with a flourish and a bow, inviting Nate to seat Elle at the table. Elle took in the sight. It was set with a crisp white linen tablecloth with matching napkins in crystal rings, and sparkling silver chargers awaited the dishes. More pink and white roses were arranged in a cut glass bowl in the center of the table between heavy crystal candlesticks that held lighted white tapers. Mr. May first offered a pump bottle of hand sanitizer to each of them, and they laughed at how even in this elegant setting, they automatically expected to use it. Then he set the champagne flutes at their places.

AB appeared next from the kitchen carrying plates of surf and turf served with roasted asparagus and creamy potatoes. "Voila!" she said, serving Elle first. "The Bluewater Grille has outdone themselves. And it's still piping hot!" she grinned. She set Nate's plate of steak and salmon in front of him. "Medium rare?"

"Yes, thank you!"

"My goodness!" said Elle. "This looks amazing!"

"Won't you join us?" Nate asked graciously.

"Oh, dear, no!" AB insisted. "We have our dinner set up inside, but we will check on you in a few moments." She set a basket of bread on the table. "Please, enjoy!"

"Cheers!" said Mr. May.

When they left, Elle noticed her bouquet sitting on a small corner table beside a little crumb-frosted wedding cake decorated with gold leaf accents and white feather plumes with golden letters saying Mr. & Mrs. perched on top. Elle recognized Monai's special touches.

"To my bride," Nate said, raising his glass to her.

"And to my husband!" Elle added, clinking her glass to his in the proper toast.

"It was the perfect day, wasn't it?" he asked, smiling at her and covering her hand on the table with his.

"It was. Perfect."

"You did a great job pulling it off!"

"Thank you. And thanks to you, AB, Mr. May, and the Bake My Day staff! It was a team effort for sure."

During the meal, they discussed everything about the day, who they saw, their feelings, and what they wanted to remember about their wedding.

"AB said to drink it all it, and I took her advice. It was wonderful seeing everyone so happy for us."

Nate smiled as he chewed.

"I know. You knew it would be this great," she said. "Thank you for urging me to go through with it. The day *was* perfect. AB has been on top of every detail, and Mr. May was awesome, wasn't he? And having Joey here, and your family, it just meant the world...even though we had to distance ourselves. It was odd but wonderful!"

AB and Mr. May appeared right on time to clear the dinner plates and facilitate the cutting of the cake. When they were finished, Elle looked at AB.

"I can't thank you enough for everything you did to make our day so special. You too, Mr. May. You were the perfect person to guide us through our vows."

They smiled. "You are very welcome," said Mr. May. "It was an honor to be a part of your ceremony."

"Besides not dancing, I guess the only thing we didn't get to do was throw the bouquet and the garter. I wish we could repay your kindness," said Elle.

Mr. May and AB looked at each other and shared a conspiratorial look.

"Well, there *is* one thing we'd like you to do for us, if you don't mind," Mr. May said, his eyes twinkling above his mask.

Nate and Elle walked, laughing, hand in hand down the street to the dock, as the blue sky lightened briefly, yielding to the orange sun that reflected off the water and slipped quickly below the horizon. They noticed that several cars were still parked on the street and that their family members milled around in small groups, chatting with new friends they'd met and delighting in the sunset. Aubrey walked from group to group, handing out something to each person as they began to line up on the dock in front of Nate's house, where the Carolina Skiff waited, ready for the sunset cruise Nate had promised his bride.

As they got closer, Nate wondered aloud, "What's all this?"

"I don't know," Elle murmured. She realized that AB and Mr. May were right behind them, catching up and getting something from Aubrey while Patsy and Judy grinned. Joey set a bucket of water by the arbor gate and clicked a lighter for Allyson and Scooter to light their sparklers.

"Sparklers!" Nate said and laughed out loud. "Cool!"

"Oh, my gosh! They all stayed to do a sparkler sendoff for us!" Elle said, grinning and watching Aubrey lighting Patsy, Judy, and Marcus's sparklers from his own. "Aubrey did this, didn't he? What a nice surprise!"

The three got back in line down the length of the dock as a dazzling display of miniature fireworks lit up the evening sky, now painted with rosy wisps of leftover clouds. A whoop went up from the crowd as Nate led Elle through the double line of friends and family, who were smiling and laughing and shouting, waving their sparkling lights, and wishing them farewell. Elle held her bouquet and turned to kiss Nate. He dipped her back and gave her a proper just-married kiss. Then she turned to the group as the last sparkler fizzled out. She raised her bouquet in the air and turned around, tossing it in the air, right toward her intended target. AB dropped her sparkler on the dock, catching the bouquet with both hands, and gave Elle a wry smile. The guests applauded while Nate discreetly lifted Elle's dress to her knee to the catcalls of the men. He slipped the blue garter from her leg and turned to the crowd, stretching the garter slingshot-style, and letting it fly into the crowd. Mr. May snatched it deftly from the air with one hand and gave a victorious shout.

A cheer went up from the crowd as Mr. May and AB stood together holding up their prophetic prizes, leaving all to wonder what was going on. Nate and Elle blew kisses and waved goodbye; then he helped her aboard his boat and started the engine. Aubrey and Joey stepped forward to untie the lines and cast them off.

"Bye! Have fun!" Aubrey shouted, standing with Joey, and grinning at the newlyweds as a round of applause went up from the guests, all shouting similar farewells.

"Thank you, Aubrey! Thank you, Joey!" Elle called. "Bye, everyone! Thank you! We love you!" She gave a special wave and a smile to AB and Mr. May.

Nate took Elle's hand and seated her next to him on the captain's bench. Then he kissed her as they cruised away from the dock and into the spectacular rose and orange sunset toward the south end of Wrightsville Beach.

EPILOGUE

Anne Borden

AB drank it all in, just as she had advised Elle to do in the afternoon before she went down the aisle. After AB and Bernard finished the wedding cleanup and the street became quiet again, she sat up later than usual. She pondered over all the happenings during Elle and Nate's wedding and looked forward to her own. Earlier in the evening, she had called her daughter and son to share her engagement news, and both were excited about her wedding plans. Carolyn and Derek had certainly surprised her, each saying they wanted to attend as soon as she and Bernie had set a date. *Maybe she had been wrong about her family's disinterest in her life.* There was too much to think about to sleep! As AB sat quietly in her room, she heard the owl hooting behind the house. Its call captivated her; she held her breath until it sang again. Or maybe it was another owl calling out—to its mate perhaps?

Barefooted, AB tied her bathrobe around her waist and tiptoed downstairs to the living room, careful not to wake Bernard. She found the diary—with the returned wedding hanky—and her glasses. She made herself comfortable, turning on the lamp beside her favorite reading chair. She smoothed the handkerchief across her knee; the lilies of the valley embroidery still perfectly preserved. It was beautifully intact without a stain from Elle's mascara. AB opened her mother's diary, finding what she was looking for. The last passage they had read together deserved a second look. After her young friends' wedding, and for her own upcoming nuptials, it seemed apropos to read her mother's reflections again.

SYLVIE

Friday, May 10, 1929

Dear Diary,

It's been a busy time since I began wrapping up my semester at the Conservatory and packing to go home for the summer. I am on the train headed south after saying goodbye to Mina and Ronald in Cleveland. This time alone will give me a chance to reflect on the last couple of weeks and record the final thoughts on my first year away from home and everything I have learned. Yet, as I put pencil to paper in my compartment, I find I have little to add that hasn't already been said. The best part about learning life's lessons is finding out how simple things are once we sit back to examine the journey—perspective, I believe it is called.

I was so relieved to hear from Herschel before I left. Thankfully, he is now a paid professional musician! He has found a job in a small theater on Broadway, playing in an orchestra for a show I've never heard of. He lives with Paul and seems as happy as a clam, so I am equally happy for him. He is where he needs to be for this season in his life. He has great potential, but nothing is written in stone.

Realizing we all have seasons in our lives seems to make the journey less daunting. Seasons give us options—hope when we fall short, and satisfaction when we move beyond our successes. This season in my life is for devouring music, learning to perform, and becoming a better friend. I look forward to my next act when I launch a career as a concert pianist and travel to reasonable places so I may continue to see my dear family and friends when I have breaks. Most of all, I look forward to building a life with Heckie whenever the time is right for us. For such a serious man, he writes faithfully—letters that are so tender and thoughtful they draw us closer despite the distance between us. I imagine us settling on the water somewhere—hopefully in Wilmington—to be near our families. If God gives us a sweet little boy or girl to love and call our own, I shall consider my life complete. Heckie will make a wonderful father someday. I want that happiness for him—for us both. I will chart the course in my own life, regardless of what others expect. I can have everything I want if I space my life out in seasons, accepting the changes as they come, and as Heckie and I plan for them. Like Mr. Finch has done, I too will shift gears. I look forward to a season in which I put my own family first, and I can share my gift teaching others. I have found such joy and purpose through music. In the best and the worst of times, music has always lifted me up and carried me onward. It is a wonderful thing to have found such a passion. No matter what happens in my life, I will always be one who plays by heart!

The End

Author's Note

In following Sylvie's journey from summer in Wilmington, North Carolina, to her first year at the Conservatory of Music at Oberlin College, I made every effort to represent life as it must have been in 1928 and 1929. From differences in campus life between the regular college and the Conservatory, curriculum, demographics, weather, vernacular, the yellow fever outbreak in 1862 in Wilmington, North Carolina, and the influenza outbreak in Ohio after Christmas in 1928, all aspects were researched and documented for history's sake. For a girl from southeastern North Carolina, Sylvie is enthralled by a few snowfalls during that winter.

In contrast, the timeline for the current-day Coronavirus pandemic of 2020 was also carefully constructed and documented from the author's personal perspective as well as from national and local news events. Recalling the spring of 2021 in North Carolina, I wrote about how refreshing and beautiful it was here, since all the other aspects of the year were understandably dismal with the COVID-19 backdrop for our modern-day front porch characters.

Writing this novel about so much music was an especially audible experience as well as a visual one for me as an author. Being a music lover, I found much pleasure in researching and listening to the various pieces of music for my characters to perform throughout *Playing by Heart*. If you are wondering about what these selections sound like, I urge you—as I did—to search the pieces mentioned online for video performances of such works as Debussy's "Beau Soir," Gershwin's "Rhapsody in Blue," Rimsky Korsakov's "Scheherazade," Rachmaninoff's "Etudes-Tableaux, Op. 39, No. 1," and the "Queen of the Night" aria from Mozart's *The Magic Flute*. I hope you find the magic in these performances as I did.

Happy reading!

References used in the creation of this fictional tale are as follows:

Cape Fear Unearthed: *A Most Daring Escape, the Tale of Former Slave, Union veteran William Benjamin Gould*, a podcast by Hunter Ingram, published January 30, 2021.

Cape Fear Rising by Philip Gerard, © 1994, reprint edition 2019, Blair/Carolina Wren Press, Durham, NC.

Oberlin History: Essays and Impressions by Geoffrey Blodgett, © 2006 by the Kent State University Press, Kent, Ohio.

Oberlin Architecture, College, and Town: A Guide to Its Social History by Geoffrey Blodgett, © 1985 by Oberlin College, Oberlin, Ohio.

Documents from Oberlin College Archives

Playing by Heart
Book Group Guide

1. During the 2020 coronavirus pandemic, the modern-day Wilmington characters must deal with significant concerns about protecting their health and the health of those they care about, while also being concerned about their sources of income. Were you able to relate to any of these situations? Did COVID leave a significant mark on you?

2. Sylvie Meeks leaves the security of her home and family to explore the possibility of becoming a concert pianist at the Conservatory of Music at Oberlin College. Being a Southerner, she stands out like a sore thumb in Ohio. Have you ever felt like an outsider? Do you think she handles her situation well?

3. When Sylvie begins accompanying Willemina Wadkins on the piano, they realize they share a Wilmington connection. Mina's grandfather escaped slavery in Wilmington and went on to serve in the US Army and gain his freedom, ending up in Cleveland, where Sylvie's parents are from. How does this connection hurt and help their ability to connect over time?

4. Herschel Blum seems to flirt with Sylvie but withdraws when she shows interest, in the same way that Dot's love interest Bart does. Once the girls figure out why the boys seem restrained in their affec-

tions, what do you think of how they respond? Are they wise to try to protect the boys? Do you think it was inevitable that the boys' secret would eventually be revealed?

5. Miss Devereaux counsels Sylvie and Mina, based on her experiences, to choose performance or family, cautioning that they can't have both. In 1928, do you think having to choose performing over family was realistic? How have times changed? Do the girls handle the advice wisely?

6. What did you think of Hersch's expulsion from the Conservatory for being a homosexual? Do you recall friends or family members coming out and the consequences? How is the situation different today from what it would have been in 1929?

7. Why did Catherine feel the need to confess to Sylvie about her relationship with her adopted brother Clifton? Do you think things have changed with women's experiences with sexual abuse? Was Kip wise to stay with her, despite the secret scandal?

8. Given the Carmichaels' insistence that Catherine marry an aristocrat, was Kip being realistic in his plans to marry her after they graduate from college? Is Kip playing a dangerous game with the Carmichaels as Aunt Andrea intimates, given that he knows what Clifton did at Shell Island?

9. Sylvie used to worry that no one ever told her anything, but she begins to realize she must learn things on her own, stating, "I suppose growing up is about discovering and embracing the good while discerning and avoiding the bad. Learning to tell the difference is what makes it so hard." How does this speak to her newfound maturity?

10. When discussing Sylvie's experiences at the Conservatory, her father tells her, "I believe an education isn't meant to chart your life; it merely awakens you and shows you how to find your course." Do you think this was wise advice? What does he mean? Have you found this to be true in your experience?

11. Does Sylvie's promise to Heckie seem sincere to you, or do you think she only likes him because he offers a degree of security in an uncertain world? Are they a good match?

12. Elle and Nate decide to have an intimate dockside wedding with only their closest friends and family in attendance. How have the COVID restrictions informed brides' wedding choices? Do you think more brides now prefer smaller weddings?

13. What does Anne Borden take away from Sylvie's experiences and Elle's as she comes to terms with her feelings for Bernard May? How does COVID play into her opinion on marrying him?

14. Why do you think the author chose the title Playing by Heart? What does it mean to you?

15. Is music important in your life? Do you have to play it to enjoy it the way Sylvie and her friends do? Did you have a music teacher, choir director, or another person who inspired you?

About the Author

A native of North Carolina, award-winning author Mary Flinn long ago fell in love with her state's mountains and its coast, creating the backdrops for her Kyle and Chelsea series of novels, *The One*, *Second Time's a Charm*, *Three Gifts*, and *A Forever Man*. With degrees from both the University of North Carolina at Greensboro and East Carolina University, Flinn retired in 2013 from her first career as a speech pathologist in the North Carolina public schools. Writing novels was always a dream for Flinn, who began crafting the pages of *The One* when her younger daughter left for college at Appalachian State University in 2009. The characters in that book continued to call to her, wanting more of their stories told, which bred the next three books in the series. *A Girl Like That*, a follow-up story and the grand finale to the Kyle and Chelsea series, featuring one of the series' characters, notorious mean girl, Elle McLarin, can also be read as a standalone. *LUMINA* is itself a sequel to *A Girl Like That* as well as also being a standalone. Other standalone titles include *The Nest*, *Breaking Out*, and *Allegiance*.

Playing by Heart, a sequel to *LUMINA*, is her tenth novel.

Mary Flinn lives in Wilmington, North Carolina, with her husband. They have two adult daughters.

For more information about her books, please visit www.TheOneNovel. com.

Other Books by Mary Flinn...

THE KYLE AND CHELSEA SERIES

THE ONE - BOOK ONE

"Is following your heart worth having it broken?"

"Powerful and timeless, *The One* is a heartwarming story illuminating a love that is, in this age, truly rare. Flinn's depiction of a young woman's ability to remain true to herself in the face of many trials is unrivaled as she powerfully proclaims the importance of faith, family, friendship, and above all, love."

— **Meredith Strandberg, Student,**
North Carolina State University

SECOND TIME'S A CHARM - BOOK TWO

"Forgiveness is easy. Trust is harder."

"Mary Flinn is the female equivalent of author Nicholas Sparks. Her characters are as real as sunburn after a long day at the beach. Hot days and hotter nights make *Second Time's a Charm* an excellent sultry romance that will stay with readers long after the sun goes down. The second book in a series, this story is a movie waiting to happen."

— **Laura Wharton, author of**
The Pirate's Bastard **and** *Leaving Lukens*

THREE GIFTS - BOOK THREE

"There is a Celtic saying that heaven and earth are only three feet apart, but in the thin places, the distance is even smaller."

"Throughout *Three Gifts*, you will be rooting for Chelsea and Kyle, young marrieds so appealing, yet real that you'll wish you could clone them. They settle in the mountains, near Boone, North Carolina, and when they are faced with tragedies, they handle them with courage and grace. Even those oh-so-human doubts and fears that threaten occasionally to swamp them are banished through humor and the abiding love that sustains them. This is a journey of hope, faith, and love that you'll want to share with them."

**— Nancy Gotter Gates, author of
the *Tommi Poag* and *Emma Daniel* mysteries,
and women's fiction *Sand Castles* and *Life Studies***

A FOREVER MAN - BOOK FOUR

"There are friends and there are lovers; sometimes the line between is thinly drawn."

"Just when I thought I would never see Kyle and Chelsea Davis again, Mary Flinn brings them back in *A Forever Man*; they returned like old friends you feel comfortable with no matter how much time has passed, only this time with eight-year-old twin boys, and a new set of life-complications to work through. In this novel, Flinn provides a deft look at marriage when potential infidelity threatens it. *A Forever Man* is Flinn's masterpiece to date, and no reader will be disappointed."

**— Tyler R. Tichelaar, Ph.D., and author of
*Spirit of the North: a paranormal romance***

And five stand-alone novels,
apart from the Kyle and Chelsea series,

Allegiance

"Mary Flinn's Allegiance is a beautiful glimpse into the lives of characters so rich and authentic you feel every heartache, triumph, loss, and gain. A story of fidelity, heroism, friendship, and family, Flinn leaves you in complete bliss but still wanting more long after you've turned the last page."

— Sabrina Stephens, author of
Banker's Trust* and *Canned Good

The Nest

"Mary Flinn realistically captures the ideals of an empty nest filled with rekindling passions of soon-to-retire Cherie and her rock-and-roll-loving husband Dave—then flips it all over when Hope, the jilted daughter, returns to the nest to heal her broken heart. Between her mother's comical hot flashes that only women of a certain age could appreciate, the loss of her laid-back father's sales job, and the good news-bad news of other family members' lives, can Hope find the courage to spread her wings and leave the nest again? Flinn's deft handling of story-telling through both Cherie and Hope's voices will send readers on a tremendously satisfying and wild flight back to *The Nest*."

— Laura S. Wharton, author of the award-winning novels
***Leaving Lukens, The Pirate's Bastard,* and others**

Breaking Out

"A harrowing incident involving her talented teenage son helps dermatologist Susannah realize she has kept herself from moving forward after the death of her beloved husband, Stan. At times humorous, at other times poignant, *Breaking Out* is an eloquent exploration of how difficult life can be following the unexpected death of a loved one. With a wealth of detail, including the complexities of family relationships, Mary Flinn creates a heartwarming story about the curious way two people can connect through grief and break out into a new life together. "

— Jane Tesh, author of the *Madeline Maclin Mysteries* and *The Grace Street Series*

A Girl Like That

"*A Girl Like That* is the story of the girl we love to hate—Elle is the bad girl hell-bent on making trouble. As Flinn's characters so often do, though, Elle surprises us with a complexity and humanness that make her sympathetic and even likable. She is good and bad, hard and soft, sweet and saucy—and we recognize Elle's battle very clearly because we all know girls like that, or truer still, because in some way, we are all girls like that."

— Sabrina Stephens, author of *Banker's Trust* and *Canned Good*

Lumina

"Hollywood is dying to tell stories like this one. The sparkling lights of Lumina, the music wafting out onto the beach, the dazzling dresses, the smell of bathtub gin, the Southern charm, and the family secrets that won't lay dying—they are all here, making *The Great Gatsby* look like child's play."

— **Tyler R. Tichelaar, author of**
When Teddy Came to Town** and **Narrow Lives

CPSIA information can be obtained
at www.ICGtesting.com
Printed in the USA
BVHW041722111022
649170BV00003B/37